The Hunchback's Gift Part 2, Superior Ones Risen

Book Eight of the Stillness Series

Richard Lee Ferguson

"As our own species is in the process of proving, one cannot have superior science and inferior morals. The combination is unstable and self-destroying."

— Arthur C. Clarke

"In pushing other species to extinction, humanity is busy sawing off the limb on which it perches."

— Paul R. Ehrlich

"If you want to see an endangered species, get up and look in the mirror."

—John Young

Also by Richard Lee Ferguson

The Stillness Series

Book 1: Stirring the Stillness, Part 1 Voices of Quest

Book 2: Stirring the Stillness, Part 2 Tortured Journey

Book 3: Stilling the Stillness, Part 1 Voices of War

Book 4: Stilling the Stillness, Part 2 Restless Spirits

Book 5: Becoming the Stillness, Part 1 Voices of Madness

Book 6: Becoming the Stillness, Part 2 Haunted Caves

Book 7: The Hunchback's Gift, Part 1 Voices of Defeat

Book 8: The Hunchback's Gift, Part 2 Superior Ones Risen

Book 9: Flames of Extinction, Part 1 The Last Voice

Book 10: Flames of Extinction, Part 2 Stillness is Stilled

For the full series, visit the Amazon series page: https://www.amazon.com/dp/B0F1WJ5J4N

Contents

Principal Characters

Voices – God and Goddess

Ming-huà Powers – First Superior One, daughter of Michael/Tamara Powers
   Michael Powers – Intermediate, father of Ming-huà
   Tamara Powers – Intermediate, mother of Ming-huà
   John Powers – Intermediate, grandfather of Ming-huà
   Bai Meiying Powers – Intermediate, grandmother of Ming-huà
   Child of Buddha – Intermediate, mother of Tamara Powers
   Zookeeper (aka Matthew Weston) – Intermediate, husband of Ming-huà
   Pythia Powers – A Superior One, daughter of Zookeeper and Ming-huà
   Jared Paine – First husband of Pythia Powers
   Siyabonga – Intermediate, second husband of Pythia Powers
   Kholwa – Intermediate, mother of Siyabonga
   Tara Powers – A Superior One, daughter of Pythia Powers and Siyabonga
   Abassi – A Superior One, son of Siyabonga and Tara Powers
   Anne Monroe – Intermediate, granddaughter of Walter Monroe
   Eleos – A Superior One, daughter of Abassi and Anne Monroe
   Zhang Yen – A Superior One
   Harihara – A Superior One, daughter of Eleos and Zhang Yen
   Lady Oracle – Mysterious Guide, granddaughter of Buandelgereen
   Scarecrow (aka Siren Rung) – Mysterious Guide
   Altan – Mysterious Guide
   Lance Romellion – FBI agent
   Queequeg – Mongol chief
   Temulun – Talking dog

Preface

Can Humans Be Replaced Peacefully?

Query: Are you one of the increasing numbers of people who think humans are irredeemably destructive and pose such a threat to the planet that their extinction would be a good thing? However, do you also abhor the massive destruction and suffering that would necessarily be the consequence of their demise? Bloody, violent dystopian novels often focus only on a few survivors of such devastation, not on the suffering that would extend to all other life forms on the planet. While there are many excellent dystopian novels, such a formulaic concentration on a small group of heroic protagonists can be narrow and unsatisfying.

So, how to unravel the ubiquitous human presence without simultaneously destroying the rest of the planetary ecosystem? Can a successor species evolve fast enough to replace humankind, or would it be extinguished before it has a chance to spread?

Such a successor species, by random chance or intentional design, must possess far greater cognitive and empathetic capacities to thwart the human proclivity for eliminating real or perceived threats. What would it be like for those first generations of advanced individuals surrounded by a sea of slow-witted but resourceful *Homo sapiens*? How would they survive the human penchant for fearing otherness and a relentless instinct to exterminate it? Whether the guiding force effectuating this change is Nature, Superior Alien, God or Gods, Goddess or Goddesses, here is an interesting way forward:

Replace *Homo sapiens* with a more advanced species, but not *drive* them to extinction through violent extermination, rather *dilute* their genes to insignificance over generations. There is precedent for such top-down genetic engineering. Human biologists eliminate dangerous pests by introducing mutant strains that breed with the targeted species to produce offspring harboring the desired genetic makeup. Generations later, the original species is superseded.

A new form of consciousness must necessarily arise—one in which strange Voices with immense cognitive power reverberate in advanced minds in the same way Voices once arose in the minds of early *Homo sapiens separating them from competitors such as Neanderthals*. Humans would initially diagnose those hearing such new Voices as schizophrenics, but they are, in fact, the incipient stirrings of a superior species. However, new Voices must be only the beginning, as this emerging species must also evolve powerful physical capabilities to overcome human weapons of destruction.

The doves must have sharper claws than the hawks . . .

The Stillness Series is the epic story of one such scenario.

Prologue

Previously. . . .

In *The Hunchback's Gift Part 1: Voices of Defeat*, the world reeled from collapse as fractured governments, cartels, and shadow agencies fought to control the rise of beings unlike any before. Humans, altered and broken, carried gifts that terrified as much as they inspired. Pythia, torn between survival and resistance, endured captivity until her powers awakened, exacting vengeance with surgical precision. Jared Paine, unsettled by his encounters with Pythia and Tara, drifted between skepticism and belief, while Agent Romellian pursued hidden truths with relentless conviction. From prisons to institutions, humanity's defeat unfolded, not by armies alone, but by the erosion of its soul.

Now the age of humans is ending. Not by fire, not by flood, but by replacement. They are not gods. They are not machines. They are not saviors. They are the Superior Ones—emerging not in cruelty or conquest, but in empathy, precision, and restraint. They walk the ruins of language, love, and blood. They do not seek to rule. They seek to remember. And then, to choose what comes next.

And so the final questions flicker:

If a species cannot change, does it deserve to remain?

Can love survive a shift in species?

And if humanity is not the end of evolution, might it still serve as the springboard to a new beginning?

~ Dear Reader ~

The answers are no longer ours to give. They belong to those who rise after us.

Chapter One

Time After Time

Devilry

To dispel any hint of aggression, Lance chooses to meet the professor on familiar ground. They sit in Jared Paine's office at Berkeley. Late morning light filters through the half-shut blinds. and dust hangs in the air, disconcertingly motionless.

"Have a seat, Agent Romellian," says Jared, gesturing toward the most comfortable chair. "What can I tell you that I haven't already said?"

"This time, Professor Paine, I'll be the one doing most of the talking."

"Suits me," Jared replies.

Despite the agent's clipped tone, Jared finds himself oddly drawn to him. That, of course, only heightens his wariness. The men who smile before they strike are the ones to fear. And though this man does not smile, Jared senses something worse: belief. Conviction wrapped in badge and bone.

Since parting from Pythia and Tara at the cave, Jared has moved through his academic life with a quiet detachment, unanchored from any clear sense of direction. His lectures have become hollow recitations. His research has languished, neglected and untouched. But now, seated across from him, this agent brings with him a sudden charge—an intrusion from the world he thought he had left behind. In her presence, he feels the sharp contrast between who he was and who he has allowed himself to become.

Lance, meanwhile, sees Jared as the last coherent node in a rapidly fracturing network of madness. He speaks plainly.

"My team recently visited the cave," he says. "And I'll be honest with you, I saw things. Disturbing things."

Jared stiffens. Not visibly. But internally, he stands on a cliff edge.

Lance notes the shift. His tone remains casual.

"Last time you were interviewed, you said you didn't know what happened to the others in that cave. Still your position?"

"That's right."

"Well," says Lance, "I think I know why you're reluctant to talk."

Jared opens his mouth to protest, but Lance holds up a hand. "Just hear me out."

He leans forward slightly.

"In my opinion, you saw what I saw. You encountered the same presence. The same . . . young woman."

"Young woman?" Jared repeats, feigning confusion. "Not sure what you mean."

"I think you do. But that's not the point. Let me finish. She has powers, maybe hypnosis, maybe not. But she's connected to your friends. And they're connected to these cases. These maimings. You seem like a decent man. Not the type to run with extremists. So I have to assume there's a good reason you're involved with people like this."

He pauses. Then, quieter: "Since I stepped into that cave, I've become open to things I never thought I'd entertain. So I'm giving you the same courtesy. Speak freely. I'm prepared to believe."

Jared lets the silence stretch.

"I doubt you would," he finally says.

"Oh, I would," replies Lance, voice edged. "I saw a multitude. Maimed. Without limbs. And I saw her—the young woman. She called them criminals. And then she said something worse: *They are us.*"

"Us?"

"The human race."

Jared says nothing.

Lance senses just enough hesitation and presses the crack.

"Look, Professor, I don't know how the vision happened, but I know what I saw. If you've seen it too, you know this is beyond hypnosis or illusion. I have to treat this as a possible terrorist threat unless I'm given evidence otherwise."

"I don't know how I can help," Jared replies carefully, choosing each word with the precision of someone aware that anything said might shift the balance.

Lance narrows his eyes.

"For a physicist, you seem surprisingly incurious. I tell you I saw an entire race judged in a single moment, and you don't ask a single question?"

Jared smiles thinly. "Okay. What did you see?"

Lance recounts it all. The cave. The multitude. The pain. The voice. The verdict. Jared listens, unmoving—but behind the mask, his eyes blaze. When Lance finishes, he waits for response.

Jared only says, "I see."

"You're still playing disinterested?"

"If you're accusing me of terrorism, I'd be wise to stay silent."

"Are your friends terrorists?"

"Don't be ridiculous."

"How do you know?"

"Because I know. They are . . . extraordinary. But not terrorists."
Lance pounces.
"How extraordinary?"
Jared stalls. "They can . . . do things. Things others can't."
"Such as?"
"They're . . . persuasive. Charismatic."
Lance shakes his head. "That's weak. Can they remove limbs?"
"No." Too quickly.
"Then what can they do?"
Jared tries again. "They can . . . hard to explain . . . they can make you see things. Things that might not be real."
"Hypnosis?"
"Sort of."
He hopes the vagueness will suffice. It usually does. People want metaphors. Not monsters.
But Lance is not most people.
"I'd agree," he says, "if we weren't looking at actual missing limbs. And heads. That's murder. No illusion. So tell me, are these people developing a new kind of weapon?"
"No! I don't know anything about real injuries."
"I think you do. I think you're protecting them."
Jared hesitates. Then softly: "What if you're not dealing with people?"
Lance's eyes glint.
"What do you mean?"
But Jared retreats, masking the breach with sarcasm.
"Maybe they're zombies."
Lance doesn't flinch. "This is no joke. These are crimes that defy physics. You should be obsessed with how they're happening. Instead, you're dodging questions. I may have to interview you under oath. Perjury in a murder case is a serious thing."
Jared's pulse flutters.
He breathes. Thinks. Then shifts the ground.
"Let me offer you a hypothetical," he says, voice steadying. "Entirely speculative. No bearing on reality."
Lance nods.
"Suppose, on a cosmic scale, humanity is no longer fit to continue. Not as punishment, but by the natural mechanisms of adaptation. How might the species vanish?"
Lance raises an eyebrow. "Nuclear war. Engineered virus. Asteroid."
"All human-caused?"
"Mostly. Or random events."
"Do you believe humanity will go extinct?"
"Eventually."
"When?"

"Ten thousand years, maybe."

Jared nods. "Good. Now, what if that extinction were accelerated?"

"How?"

"Doesn't matter. Just imagine it. Would that help or hurt the planet?"

"Sounds like a terrorist question."

"Call it ecology in a minor key."

Lance considers. "Help, I guess."

"Suppose," Jared says gently, "an advanced species wanted to hasten that extinction—not by violence, but by removing the ability to reproduce. Quietly. Painlessly."

"Sterility?"

Jared smiles. "Ever heard of sterile release programs in pest control?"

"Sure."

"Introduce a sterile variant. Mate it with the wild population. Over time, no more offspring. No more species. No genocide. No poison. Just a gentle fade."

"You're saying your friends are engineered mutants?"

"I said *nothing* about my friends. This is pure speculation."

Lance's voice tightens. "How does that explain the mutilations?"

"It doesn't."

"But you admit they're not normal."

"Define normal."

"Can they have children?"

Jared pauses. "Some can."

"Then they're not sterile."

"No," says Jared. "They're successors."

Lance leans forward. "So, evolution by invasion?"

"Not invasion," says Jared. "Succession. Like dawn after night. Like spring after fire."

Lance's voice drops. "You want humans gone."

"I want the Earth to survive."

"That's a yes."

"I said no such thing."

"But you believe these . . . successors . . . are superior?"

"Not in conquest. In empathy."

Lance glares. "Tell that to the victims."

"They were criminals."

"Who decides that? Your 'successors'?"

Jared exhales. "You think in binaries. Guilt. Innocence. Win. Lose. Nature doesn't care for such things. It moves forward."

Lance crosses his arms.

"If I were one of your successors, I'd kill you."

"You just might," Jared says quietly. "Your type always have."

Silence falls.

Lance assumes his hard-ass face. "Doc, I am now even more convinced I have to interview you under penalty of perjury. Your 'speculation' is, of course, fanciful regarding aliens and such, but I do understand cults and suicidal terrorists. In other words, I am inclined to believe you know all about these maimings and murders. Being an accomplice to murder will give you multiple years in prison, which is plenty of time to spin more speculative yarns."

Jared struggles to retain his composure, but Lance notices his flushed face and the fear in his eyes. Given other circumstances, he would derive satisfaction from forcing such a response, but now the agent's own face reflects deep-seated ambivalence.

"Any further questions?" asks Jared.

"Not for now, but make yourself available in the future. We are not done with you, professor."

~ *Jared Debates Himself* ~

After the interview with Agent Romellian, Jared's uneasy balance gives way. The fragile calm he had labored to sustain dissolves under the weight of fear. The old dread returns with renewed force: the collapse of his academic life, the exposure of his past, the stripping away of reputation, freedom, even selfhood. This time, the threat feels closer, no longer a shadow on the horizon but a presence pressing against the edges of his days.

In the weeks that follow, he reenters a pattern he knows too well. Guilt folds into self-reproach. Shame tightens its grip, followed by anger—first at himself, then at the unseen machinery that ensnared him. Pity arrives last, reserved for the man he once imagined he could be. These feelings do not pass. They loop through his mind in shifting combinations, each one reinforcing the next, until his inner life becomes a closed circuit of disintegration.

Much of his fury lands on Pythia.

She had undone him, not through betrayal, but by forcing him to see too much. Her presence disoriented him. Her departure left him gutted. She had brought with her a dangerous clarity, and Tara, an echo of his own biology, compounded that danger. What had begun as fascination has congealed into a quiet indictment. He drinks more now. Scotch, mostly. Nights stretch into silence, and he speaks aloud to no one. "Should I give them what they want? Maybe I owe them that. I'm part of what's ending."

But the thought never settles. It turns back on itself, then flips again. Soon he's arguing both sides of the same sentence, running mental trials with no jury. Would the world suffer without humans? Might it recover? Would violence lessen? Would the Earth itself be grateful for their absence?

He revisits his love for Pythia the way others revisit injuries, not to heal them, but to test their permanence. He studies his daughter's face in memory, wondering if it points toward redemption or only prolongs the question. His mind becomes a territory marked by conflict and retreat, and in that terrain, he begins to lose track of where the war began.

In his more lucid moments, he names it: not madness in the clinical sense, but a form of awareness most refuse to reach. He has crossed into an interior landscape stripped of illusion. The scaffolding of rational thought has collapsed, leaving him exposed to truths too bare for public speech. He had once dismissed such states as delusion. Now, he finds them populated with recognitions that do not flinch.

Still, he says nothing.

He does not contact the FBI. He volunteers no information. He knows this isn't valor. He doubts it's even selflessness. His motivations are murky, his ethics uncertain. But one fact holds firm in the quiet center of his conscience: Pythia and Tara are gone. The danger, if it returns, is not yet present. Whatever judgment awaits, it remains postponed. No new actions can be traced. No recent decisions offer evidence. The agents may search, interrogate, theorize—but they will find nothing new, and nothing now.

And so, Jared waits.

Not for vindication. Not for clarity. Certainly not for absolution. Only for time to pass.

Time, if not glory. He tells himself it will be enough.

But deep down he knows: time itself is the trap, and it is already closing.

Chapter Two

Ancient Adolescence

Budding Flower

~ A New World ~

From the mouth of a long-abandoned cave in the scorched California desert, three figures step into the unrelenting brightness of late-day sun. Heat trembles across the horizon. The land itself seems to recoil from their emergence.

The first to appear is a tall man, massive in stature and presence, whose weathered features and unyielding gaze give the impression not of age, but of permanence. His skull bears the polished austerity of something unearthed rather than born. Each movement is deliberate, spare of gesture, as if shaped by forces more ancient than choice. He does not squint against the light. He does not pause. The world adjusts to him, not the other way around.

Behind him walks a woman in midlife, solid in build, her frame marked by a physical curvature that has become neither impediment nor signature, but a condition long since integrated into her being. The hunch at her back is neither defiant nor submissive—it simply is. Her eyes remain forward. Whatever pain or history lies within that cave is now behind her, sealed by the act of stepping into daylight.

The last to emerge is a girl, younger than the others by decades, yet possessed of a bearing that defies measurement. Her back arches in a curve that might draw pity from the uninitiated, but her posture, her motion, her very presence make such reactions irrelevant. She moves with a confidence untouched by explanation, eyes wide and unblinking, reading the desert floor not as terrain but as text. There is something urgent in her stillness, something complete in every breath. Her hair catches the light. Her face absorbs it. Even the heat seems drawn toward her.

They walk in silence up a gravel slope, cresting a rise worn down by time and abandonment. At the edge of the dirt road, they find a man waiting beside a battered car. He is thin, anxious, almost vibrating with stored energy. His limbs appear mismatched, as though his body had been assembled in haste by hands less certain than those that formed the others. He paces, fidgets, checks the sky, taps the hood, then finally waves as they draw closer, unable to contain the relief and anticipation swelling inside him.

An observer, one not dulled by habit or swayed by surface impressions, would see something odd in this grouping. Not merely in their physical divergence from the norm, but in the way they carry themselves, in the precision of their movement and the concentration in their gaze. It is not deformity that sets them apart, nor spectacle, nor novelty. It is an invisible recalibration, a different geometry of body and intention. The observer, intrigued and cautious, would look closer. Much closer.

They are not aberrations of humanity. Nor are they merely gifted. They suggest something else entirely: a realignment of species-level expectation, a glimpse of what might come after. Each face holds a variation on beauty that refuses the ordinary. Each presence presses gently, insistently, against the threshold of the familiar. They do not ask to be recognized. They simply are, and the world, without yet knowing it, is already adjusting its axis to accommodate them.

~

Sy, still bouncing near the vehicle, calls out with theatrical joy, "Welcome back to Planet Earth! How fare the wanderers?"

Altan, in the lead, offers a silent wave, his granite features unchanged. Pythia smiles faintly. The youngest, Tara, responds in a voice both clear and ageless: "Hello yourself. Our journey was. . . . " She trails off aloud and completes the sentence silently, her thought blooming directly into Sy's mind.

Sy opens the car door. "Hop in! We're driving straight through to San Francisco. You tired?"

Tara shakes her head, radiant. "Not at all. I've been waiting for this."

"Anxious?" asks Sy.

"Not the right word," she replies with calm precision.

"What would you say instead?" Pythia prompts.

"Curious," says Tara. "That is the correct word. Curious."

"About what?" Sy grins.

"The world. Reality. Humans. Earth. I've had enough school. Enough virtual simulations. Now it begins."

"Ah, humans," says Sy, stretching the word like a slow exhale. "A subject worthy of any dissertation."

"They inflict much suffering," Tara notes.

"And endure even more," adds Pythia. "Most of it self-inflicted."

"I've studied their cruelty, both deliberate and accidental," Tara says quietly. "Most illuminating. Most distressing. I've been taught well."

"Jared doesn't know we're back, I assume?" Pythia asks.

"Not yet," says Sy. "Still locked in his lab at Berkeley, chasing equations."

Tara, the last to enter the car, pauses. She turns to a nearby boulder and with the faintest flicker of will, erases it from existence. "If only human pain could vanish as easily," she murmurs.

Altan's voice rumbles low. "You'll have many chances. But measured against time, they may seem insignificant. Your mother has been... overly selective in her procreation. You must do more."

Pythia replies, her tone defensive. "Much of my fertile span was spent away. But not wasted: sixteen base-dimension years, teaching and raising Tara."

"Yes," Altan concedes. "Yet here on Earth, only a handful of years have passed. Now we must make haste, and avoid drawing attention."

Sy chuckles. "Avoid attention? Please. During your absence, the FBI hovered for a while, then drifted away. Gave up, I think."

Altan's eyes narrow. "If that vanished boulder is any sign, they'll return."

Sy throws the car into gear and accelerates down the dusty road. At a glance, the four appear to sit in reflective silence—but beneath their skulls, minds burn with light, thought, and telepathic chords no ear can hear. Behind them, only a twisting trail of dust remains—and the memory of an obliterated stone.

~

One week later, beneath a high spring sun filtered through stained-glass windows, three generations of women sit in quiet council. Tara, newly returned. Pythia, once fugitive, now mother. And Lady Oracle, matriarchal seer, whose immense presence dominates the anteroom of the San Francisco mansion. The air is light but taut with the gravity of what must be decided.

"As you know," begins Lady Oracle, her voice even, ceremonial, "your task from this point is twofold: lessen suffering wherever possible, and reproduce—broadly enough to assure genetic continuity. The question, as ever, is where to begin."

Tara turns to her mother. "Speaking of reproduction—does Father know we're back?"

Pythia's expression clouds, a faint blush rising to her cheeks. "No. I haven't yet decided how to approach him. Whether to resume the relationship . . . or move on. Jared can be emotional—jealous. If he feels betrayed, he might go to the authorities."

"Would he insist on monogamy?" Tara asks with clinical curiosity.

"I fear so," Pythia says. "Though I can't be certain."

"Why not explain?" the girl presses.

Pythia sighs. "Because humans are not logical. Emotion is both their crowning glory and their downfall."

Tara nods. "One of my mentors at school put it more colorfully. He used to say, 'The human fusion of amygdala angst and neocortical scheming has produced a creature that must simultaneously piss, shit, cry, and pontificate. No wonder their planet chokes on the byproducts.'"

Lady Oracle chuckles despite herself. "Be that as it may, we are not here merely to replace them. We must help them, even as we do. A delicate operation."

"Which returns us to the question," says Pythia. "What now?"

"My opinion," says Lady Oracle, "is that you return to Jared. He is familiar. Keeps suspicion low. Have more children. As for Tara—she must begin the search for a mate . . . or mates. And meanwhile, she must explore what help she can offer the world."

"We agree," she adds, "that Tara's abilities now surpass those of both her mother and grandmother. The line is intensifying."

"And so is the risk," says Altan, entering silently from the side chamber.

Lady Oracle regards him. "Greater than before?"

"Yes."

"Why?"

Altan glances at Tara before responding. "Because her power is not merely greater, it is less restrained. She cannot yet control the magnitude of her responses. Even unconscious whims trigger massive effects. During her education, the greatest mentors could only partially contain this volatility. In simulation after simulation, it was the same: her reactions, when emotional, became irreversible."

Lady Oracle's face tightens. "But with time, she'll learn."

"With what practice?" Altan counters. "Humans? If so, destruction is inevitable."

Tara speaks softly. "Then send me where destruction already reigns. To a place where iniquity festers in daylight. There, I'll learn. There, mistakes will fall on the malevolent."

"And a mate?" asks Lady Oracle.

Tara smiles faintly. "If I go to the right place, I'll have plenty of options."

"Criminals, madmen, psychopaths," Pythia interjects.

"Mother, Ming-huà chose Zookeeper. My grandfather was a crack dealer. The pairing worked for you. It might for me."

Altan sits and pours tea, his expression carved from worry. "Tara will have no trouble attracting mates. Her system is optimal. The real danger is emotional instability. Despite our efforts, her human genes assert themselves, especially under stress. Remember what happened to the first Chosen Ones, John and Michael Powers?"

Lady Oracle leans forward. "How far-reaching is her power?"

Altan hesitates. "We don't know. What we do know is that if her emotional state spikes—rage, grief, trauma—her effects radiate uncontrollably. Not just a room. Not just a building."

"A town?" asks Lady Oracle.

Altan's gaze hardens. "A city. A region. Possibly more. During one simulation, she eradicated over ten thousand beings in under a minute."

Lady Oracle stiffens. "Explain."

Pythia answers quietly. "Unit 731. A simulation of the Japanese biological warfare unit in occupied China. Thousands tortured, experimented on. Tara witnessed the atrocities. And then . . . she reacted. The simulation ended with the complete annihilation of every Japanese soldier under General Shiro Ishii's command. And Ishii himself received . . . the worst of it."

"How many soldiers?" asks Lady Oracle.

"Roughly ten thousand," Altan confirms. "Some of them decent men. Dissenters. But they died, too."

There is a long, disquieting silence.

"Of course," Altan adds, "it was a simulation. Reality will not be so clean. Nor so contained."

Tara speaks directly into their minds: *It is all documented. But emotionally, I have learned. Later simulations proved it. My control improved. You know this, Altan.*

It is true, he replies. *But you still wield a force more blunt than precise. And one that doesn't discriminate.*

Lady Oracle folds her hands. "Despite everything, I'm still inclined to send her. Perhaps to Ciudad Guayana in Venezuela. Or Pietermaritzburg. Or Juba in South Sudan. Somewhere far from Western oversight. Somewhere untamed, wild, raw."

"I welcome it," says Tara. "I need to be tested."

"And mates?" Pythia asks.

"Violence can sometimes birth rare courage," Tara replies. "That's what you found, Mother."

Altan gives a long sigh. "Perhaps. But remember, your strength doesn't make you invincible."

"Which is why I must go," Tara says. "Before I grow soft. Or too safe to be of use."

Lady Oracle turns to Altan. "Will you accompany her? You went with Pythia."

Altan doesn't answer at first. Then: "That's a choice I will keep to myself."

"Why?"

"It skews the data."

Pythia frowns. "How?"

Before he can answer, Lady Oracle interrupts. "Perhaps we should cancel this mission. Let Tara focus on finding mates."

But Altan, unexpectedly, shakes his head. "No. I think we go forward."

"Why?" Pythia asks.

"Because this may be our last clear chance to discover if our kind has a future, or is just another failed mutation."

~ *Into the Wild* ~

For two days, Tara has lived in silence above a city unraveling. Her squalid apartment is on the second floor, half-rotted, and overlooks a township that screams. Gunfire splits the nights. Children wail. Gangs roam unchallenged, killing over drug turf and raping on whim. Dozens murdered. Scores of women and children raped, tortured, sold. Reality, brutal and unapologetic, confirms every simulation she endured in her education.

And yet, she has done nothing.

She made a vow: no action until she understands this place. No intervention until she finds guides, friends, maybe, who can help her tell the difference between the damned and the redeemable. The temptation to act is strong. But stronger still is her will to wait. She does not want to destroy the good with the evil. Not again. Following Altan's advice, she slipped in at night, took possession of the filthy apartment, and stayed unseen. Altan left quietly, saying only, "I'll be nearby." Now, she descends the stairs and steps into the South African sun.

A group of young men and women erupt with cheers at a soccer match played on a broken concrete slab where a building once stood.

"Told you!" shouts a boy. "Someone moved in last night!"

"She? A hunchback?" a heavy woman scoffs, cigarette trembling between fingers. "My, my, look at it."

"She Chinese," mutters another.

"She could be lots of things," says a lean young man, his voice edged with intelligence. "Don't assume."

Tara walks directly to him. "You're correct. I have Chinese ancestry."

"You sound American," he replies.

"I am."

The group begins to gather. Faces full of suspicion. Wonder. Amusement.

"Oh, this is gonna be good," someone snickers.

"Hunchbacks bring bad luck!" croaks an old woman at the edge.

"I was kicked out of the States," says Tara.

"Why not China?" the young man asks.

"I heard this was one of the most dangerous places in the world."

A stunned silence. Then murmurs.

"You what?" he says, incredulous. "You nuts? Or one of those charity angels?"

"I'm not here to do charity."

"Then why are you here?"

"To relieve your suffering."

That silences them—until laughter explodes like a match dropped in kerosene.

"She's another fuckin' missionary!"

"No," Tara says calmly. "I'm here to eliminate the gangs."

Louder laughter. Someone jeers, "You'll be dead by nightfall, bitch!"

"Who said that?" the young man asks sharply.

No one answers. He has authority here.

Tara ignores the insult. "What's your name?"

He smiles despite himself. "Siyabonga Ndlovu. And you?"

"Tara Powers."

"You're definitely crazy, Tara Powers."

"How do I contact the gangs?"

A storm of laughter and shouts.

"She's a cop!"

"She's a witch!"

"She's fucked!"

Siyabonga studies her. "Why would you want that? You need a fix? Chasing *tik*?"

"*Tik?*"

"Meth amphetamine."

"My reasons don't involve drugs."

"Everything here involves drugs," mutters a girl. "They're killing us."

"What do the gangs get from meeting you?" Siyabonga presses. "You a journalist?"

"What they get is survival."

The crowd howls again.

"She be mad!"

But Siyabonga stays quiet. Watching her.

"I know the Mongrels," he says. "Could get you a meeting. Might be your funeral."

"I'll take the risk."

She turns to go. "Apartment 2D. Let me know the time."

He calls after her, half-joking, half-wary: "Your funeral!"

Tara walks away smiling. Chance, or something more deliberate, has brought Siyabonga into her path. She considers him with quiet detachment, her mind cataloging the details, physique, intelligence, and emotional texture. Viable, perhaps. The question lingers without urgency. She allows it to fade as her steps carry her deeper into Nyanga's chaotic sprawl.

The settlement stretches in all directions, an unplanned maze of angled pathways and makeshift dwellings hammered together from splintered timber, scorched sheet metal, and sun-faded cardboard. Roofs sag. Walls buckle. Each structure testifies to necessity rather than design. The ground is uneven, hard-packed, dry. There are no trees here. No reprieve from the heat. No barrier against the constant intrusion of noise. The air carries the weight of engine fumes, sweat, and rot.

On the main roads, the crush of commerce pushes outward. Vendors shout above one another, guarding piles of secondhand goods, spoiled fruit, counterfeit medicines. Faded corporate banners flutter overhead, clinging to their illusion of relevance. Women in threadbare skirts signal passing drivers with sharp eyes and still hands. Young men walk with exaggerated confidence, torsos bare, inked flesh narrating entire histories in a single glance: names, dates, affiliations, losses. The body becomes document, warning, and ultimately, an invitation.

Her hump begins to vibrate. The psychic field tightens, then expands. She stiffens as it floods her with immediate sensations, all unfiltered. Desire lashes out in hungry waves. Grief settles over her, dense and inescapable. Paranoia flickers in the corners of perception. Fury burns hot and shapeless. She registers images that are not her own: a man's last breath, a girl screaming behind a locked door, hands clenched around a blade. There is no separation between feeling and fact. Her nervous system absorbs it all.

Then comes the deeper layer.

Beneath the jagged impressions is something more constant, more pervasive. A field of tension so old it no longer announces itself—it just remains. Fear, not sharp but ambient. Bacterial in its persistence. It clings to surfaces, to breath, to thought. It stains everything. Not the fear of one moment or one threat, but a culture of dread. Accumulated. Inherited. Alive.

And yet . . . she is untouched.

Where Ming-huà would weep and Pythia would burn with rage, Tara remains calm. Her detachment surprises her. Perhaps control begins here.

"Hey lady!" calls a vendor. "Buy some *bobotie*?"

Tara stops. A heavy woman stirs curry-laced meat at a battered stall. The air smells of spices and desperation.

"Yes," says Tara, taking a stool beside her.

As the woman prepares the food, Tara feels it again: curiosity, flickering beneath layers of submission and fear. A mind still intact, though smothered in worry.

"You're curious about me," Tara says.

The woman shrugs.

"I'm new here."

More silence.

"How long have you run this stand?"

"Too long."

"How long, really?"

"A few years," the woman mutters. "Business is bad."

Tara tastes the dish. "Good."

The woman scans the street, silent.

"What's your name?"

"Thandolwethu. But call me Daisy."

"I prefer Thandolwethu."

She shrugs, but her demeanor softens.

"I'm not here to make trouble," Tara says.

"Not my problem."

"No. Your problem is your son, Mpho."

The spoon drops.

"He's in a gang. You know that. Drugs, violence. A gun. He stays with them now. You pretend not to see. You hope you're wrong."

"You the police," Thandolwethu hisses. "Get away!"

"I can help him."

"You know nothing!"

"I know Vura has enemies. I know Vato will kill your son if they catch him. Help me."

She stares, eyes wide. "You a *kêrel*. Or a demon. Which?"

"I'm neither. I need to meet other mothers like you. Soon you'll hear about me. When I return, you'll know why. And if you help, we might save Mpho."

She nods faintly, caught in the current of something larger than her.

Tara rises, finishes her food. "Remember. I'll come when the time is right."

As she walks back toward her crumbling building, the streets press in, overflowing with the guilty and the grieving, the damned and the dreaming. Already she has found victims. And perpetrators. And somewhere in between, the thin root of something like hope.

She has not yet used her power.

But she will.

Chapter Three

Demonstrations and More Devilry

Negotiating With A Murderer

~ First Meeting ~

The next morning, Siyabonga delivers word: *The Americans* gang has agreed to meet. The location, dubbed "the White House," turns out to be nothing more than a crumbling plywood shack nestled among a sea of equally desolate structures—leaning walls of salvaged planks and rusted tin, the air thick with smoke and rot. As they make their way through Nyanga's skeletal lanes, Siyabonga gives Tara a crash course in street diplomacy.

"No guarantees you'll come out alive," he says with a crooked grin. "But follow my advice, crazy Lady Hunchback, and you might have a chance."

"I understand," she replies evenly. "Eye contact. Calm. No judgment. Empathy first. Walk in their shoes."

He nods. "And remember, they'll be high. *Tik* for the fire, *Mandrax* for the crash. They shift fast. Friendly to feral in a heartbeat."

"Methamphetamine," she says. "Got it."

Now they stand outside the sagging green door. Siyabonga wears a half-smile, but she sees the tension tightening behind his eyes. He will not interfere if things go badly. That much is clear. But the thought of her suffering stirs something in him. Not protectiveness, but *revulsion.* He is curious, she knows. And afraid. But more curious still is the part of his mind she cannot enter. A sealed vault. Unreadable. An anomaly.

She wonders: perhaps Siyabonga is like Zookeeper. Violent, yes, but durable. Adaptable. Mating potential? It pleases her to consider it. Better than her mother's choice, that frail academic with his glass ego and soft convictions. Her musings are cut short as the door opens. A tall, rail-thin man steps out, tattoos curling over his skin like seaweed littering a beach.

"This the hunch bitch?" he asks, scanning her with a mixture of hunger and disdain.

"This is her," says Siyabonga. "She's called Tara."

"She got a name, huh?" the man sneers. "I'm Kungawo. You can call me Chris."

"I prefer Kungawo," says Tara.

"I prefer Chris, he sniggers."

She greets him without warmth. Her gaze holds steady; his does not. His mind seethes beneath the surface, swollen with violence he barely contains. He fantasizes about overpowering her, violating her, tearing open her flesh to examine what lies beneath. She registers every detail, the sequence of imagined acts, the pacing of his cruelty. She stores it without reaction. He poses no danger. Not now. Not ever. Neither do the others. Kungawo gestures for them to enter.

Inside, the space closes around them, thick with heat, smoke, and the residue of too many bodies. The scent is a mixture of narcotics, unwashed skin, and something older, rotting at the edges. Men lounge across crates, cushions, and broken furniture, their torsos slick with chemical sweat. The air glows faintly under a single exposed bulb. Tattoos ripple across shoulders and backs, catching the light and warping with every movement. The walls are stained with motion.

Tara walks through it slowly. She regulates her breath, filters the stimuli, and overrides the disgust. She has endured worse in training: longer durations, darker environments, more hostile minds. This is familiar ground.

Eyes track her as she moves. Some vacant. Some twitching with unspent energy. Others lit with the brittle alertness of stimulant highs. One or two narrow with calculation, weighing possibilities. A few stare openly, trying to classify what she is—human, perhaps, but altered, with an unfamiliar quality that marks her. They register her presence with the wariness reserved for phenomena that defy easy narrative. She lets their confusion settle.

Then, cutting through the thick air, a voice emerges. Low. Calm. Controlled. But edged with the kind of authority that doesn't need to raise itself to command attention. The room stills slightly, not in silence, but in focus. Something is about to begin.

"So. You've come to save us."

Siyabonga bows slightly. "This is the one I told you about, great Thato. The hunchback who says she can help."

"She a charity case?"

"No. At least, that's what she says."

"She better not be," Thato mutters, leaning back into the shadows. "Sit down, hunchback. Take a hit."

"No, thank you."

"So. You gonna save us? From what?"

"From yourselves," says Tara.

The laughter is instantaneous.

"What the fuck that mean?" Kungawo giggles.

Tara scans the tattoos, chooses one, and says aloud, *I cry to drink more blood.* Then, mimicking Kungawo's voice with eerie precision, "What the fuck that mean?"

More laughter. Even Thato chuckles.

"She got you there, bru," he says. "Got you good."

Tara reads another. "*Evil deep. Grave deep.*"

Thato holds up a hand. "Alright. Enough poetry. What do you want?"

"I want you to stop the killing. The raping. Make peace. Let the others do the same."

The room erupts in laughter, threats, and taunts:

"We rape you first, hunch!"

"She fucked in the head!"

"Cut her hump open! See what's inside!"

Knives flash. Guns rise. Words ignite like gasoline on a fire. Tara remains still. Eyes calm. Spine unbent. Thato raises a hand. The noise falters.

"Well, hunch," he sneers. "You want to help? Start by sucking our *piels.* Then maybe we talk."

She tilts her head, eyes narrowing slightly.

"If you value your *piels,* and I take that to mean penises, you'll stop killing and raping."

Silence slams the room.

Her hump flares faintly. Rage pours from their minds and they revel in visions of torture, domination, and humiliation. They are predators, and she is an absurd challenge to their order.

Thato stands. "Which bru wants her first?"

Kungawo leaps, shrieking, "Me! I carve her *poes,* then the hump!"

His knife flashes. It never reaches her. Suddenly his hand is empty.

Stunned, he stares. "Must be bad *tik.*"

Thato chuckles darkly. "Who's next, now that Chris fail?"

Weapons rise again. Threats fly. Tara says nothing. She sits like a stone in a storm.

"You act brave," Thato growls. "But they'll fill your *poes,* stuff your hump, and cut you for souvenirs!"

He gives the order—"Do it!"

Every weapon vanishes. Knives, guns, all gone. Vaporized. Gasps. Whispers. Terror.

"Witch!"

"Demon!"

No one moves. One youth, stoned beyond fear, lunges. His right hand disappears mid-lunge. He screams, flailing the stump in wild circles.

A shocked Thato leans closer, sniffing the air. "No demon scent! Bad *tik.* It's a trick!"

He grabs the whimpering youth's stump and turns it as if searching for a trick, a sleight-of-hand. But there's nothing, no wound, no blood, no illusion.

"How you do this?" he mutters.

"Does it matter?" Tara replies. "I can remove whatever body part I choose. Will you listen now?"

Silence answers her. She lets her gaze travel across their faces.

"I can start with your penises," she says calmly. "Your *piels*. Which of you is first?"

Some run. Others freeze. Pride glues them to the floor, but terror owns their breath.

Thato swallows. "Maybe it's a dream. Tomorrow, John's hand be back."

"And if it isn't?"

"Then we deal. You work with us. Get rich. Take a share. Treated like a queen."

"No. The Americans stop it all. Murder. Rape. Drugs. You raise families. You die in peace."

Thato spits. "Peace? You don't know what that word means. We Cape Coloreds—bottom caste. Apartheid or no apartheid, we're hunted dogs. Peace don't exist. Only power."

"Others are poor and don't become monsters. You rape children. If I were less merciful, I'd take every weapon and every *piel* in this room. Then we'd see what kind of men remain."

Thato sneers. "You don't have that power. If you did, you'd be a god. A dictator. But you're just a bitch with a trick. Tomorrow, Chris get his hand back. Then we come for you."

She reads in him a devil's mix of rage, lust for vengeance, and no remorse. A beast whose only religion is retaliation. Her decision is made.

So be it.

~ *Aftermath* ~

As dusk settles and the streets blur into deepening shadow, Tara and Siyabonga move together in silence. The city hums around them, distant voices, the rattle of metal gates, the low churn of generators, but between them, there is only the sound of footsteps. His are slow, deliberate, weighted with thoughts still forming. He walks not as a companion seeking closeness, but as one caught in the gravity of something he does not yet understand. The nearness between them feels less like choice and more like consequence.

Time passes without markers. Streetlamps flicker on. Dogs bark and fall quiet again. He glances at her once, then looks away. His jaw tightens. The silence holds longer than it should.

Then, finally, he speaks.

"Did you have to do that to Thato?"

"Would he have obeyed me otherwise?"

Siyabonga exhales. "Probably not. But to remove his hands. His penis. We left him shrieking like some butchered animal. It was . . . horrible. How did you do it?"

"That is not for you to know."

"But he was right, wasn't he? Tomorrow, he'll have them back? Same for Chris?"

"No."

"But . . . you could make it happen?"

"No. Once done, it is done."

He stops. "Shit." His voice is barely audible. "What are you? You're not human. That's for sure. Are you a demon?"

"No."

"A witch?"

"No."

"Then what? Some alien come to fuck with us?"

"I am neither *Homo sapiens* nor alien. I was born on Earth. To a mother and father just like you."

"You're not like me! How can you say that?"

"I *have* a mother and father. Just like you."

He shakes his head. "Impossible. You're not like me. Or anyone else. How do you do it?"

"Siyabonga," she asks, "what happens now? To the gang?"

He walks in silence, then answers: "Like a hive that's lost its queen. The others will fight. Battle for the top spot."

"More killing."

He nods. "More killing."

"Then I keep going. Sooner or later, it will sink in."

"What will?"

"That killing, raping, stealing, these are not inevitabilities. They're choices. And they must stop."

"You hurt people to stop the hurting?"

"If that's what it takes to protect the children. The mothers. The young women. The infants. The innocents."

Siyabonga shakes his head, eyes hollow. "The innocents? Are there such things?"

"What do you mean?"

"Many mothers are whores. Or beat their kids. Some sell them. The children carry guns before they lose their baby teeth. The young women, most of them hope to catch the eye of a gang boss so they can sell themselves for a little safety. The infants. . . . " His voice lowers. "They're born marked. And they'll die the same way. Evil deep. Grave deep."

Tara laughs, light and sharp. "You are all infants yourselves. Foolish, frightened children. I—"

Gunshots crack through the quiet. Siyabonga instinctively drops to the ground. Tara remains standing, unmoved. When the echoes fade, he dares to lift his head. Tara looks down at him, almost amused.

"You can get up," she says. "They won't be bothering us again."

"*They*?"

"Gang members. Another ambush. I expected it."

He swallows hard. "And the bullets?"

"The atoms and molecules have been . . . reconstituted. They now serve more peaceful purposes."

He shivers. "And the shooters?"

She doesn't answer. Her face darkens. She walks on.

After a few quiet blocks, she speaks again.

"Word will spread. I need someone beside me, someone who can navigate the city. A translator. A guide. A lieutenant."

She looks at him. "I can pay well. Will you do it?"

Siyabonga's teeth are still faintly chattering. "Miss Powers, I can't stop bullets. I'd be dead in hours."

"Then we spread the word: anyone who harms you will suffer the same fate as Thato. As the gunmen. Or worse. Attacking you will be treated as attacking *me*. Will that work?"

He stares at the pavement, running silent odds. "I need to talk to my mother first."

"Your *mother*?"

Tara stiffens slightly. She senses something stirring in his mind—the same shadowed place she cannot enter. The blind spot. The hidden chamber. *The mother*. All mothers. Goddess.

By the time they reach the apartment, word has preceded them. A crowd has gathered outside. The air trembles with whispers until their arrival turns all sound to silence. Faces emerge from the gloom that are wary, wide-eyed, and wounded. Tara sweeps the crowd with her mind. No assassins. No direct threats. Only a heavy throb of inherited fear and compulsive curiosity. But underneath, she catches it—flickers. Sparks. Small, nameless hopes. Anonymous yet real. Then one face sharpens: Thandolwethu, the vendor. She stands with a small group of women. Tara knows instantly they are mothers. When their eyes meet, Thandolwethu nods, then looks down, as if completing a ritual of quiet homage. Tara steps forward.

"Thandolwethu! I want a meeting. A gathering of mothers, especially those with sons in the gangs. Tomorrow. Where can we meet?"

Thandolwethu falters. Too many eyes are on her. She says nothing.

"Where can we meet?" Tara repeats, her voice firm.

Another woman answers. Older. Heavier. Scarred deep in places no blade could reach.

"The graveyard," she says.

"The graveyard?"

"There's a canvas pavilion. It's quiet. We meet there sometimes."

"What time tomorrow?"

"Seven o'clock!" Tara calls out. "As many as possible. Mothers of sons from every gang are welcome!"

"No," says the old woman. "Seven is dinner. Eight too late. Four o'clock."

Tara nods. "Four o'clock. It's settled."

She glances once more at Thandolwethu. This time, the nod is clear. And solemn.

Inside the building lobby, Tara turns to Siyabonga. "Well? What about your mother? Will she be there?"

He grins, strangely calm now. "My mother? Oh yes. She'll be there."

"How can you be so sure?"

He shrugs. "Trust me. I just know."

His voice carries something, an edge of mystery. When she reaches into his mind, the black box remains. Unbreachable. Unknowable. The anomaly persists. Upstairs, she collapses onto the couch, eyes fixed on the stained ceiling. Her thoughts begin their slow spiral. *I maim to protect. I kill to reduce suffering. I walk among creatures destined to be replaced—genetically erased, diluted until they vanish. But is that what I'm doing? Preserving a few now, only to erase them all later? A contradiction.*

She remembers her mentor's words: *"Exactly! You finally have it."*

Have what?

"Think on it. Do not complicate the simplicity."

She scoffs aloud. *Homo sapiens! So enamored with their own thoughts, their primitive science, their endless self-regard. Superstition woven into software. They dream their technology will save them. Madness.* But something lingers. A thorn in her mind. Something she cannot name. *It's Siyabonga. That blank space. That unpierceable wall. He is as simple as the others. But that void . . . the mother. The mothers.* She thinks of Ming-huà. Of Pythia. Of what they endured. Their power. Their restraint. The hunger they inherited, and passed on. Her own path is not unlike theirs—but something gnaws at her. Some forgotten lesson. Some overlooked clause in the contract of becoming.

It will take thousands of years to replace humanity. But one misstep now—one rupture in the early arc—and the future veers toward catastrophe.

Ten billion Homo sapiens.

And so few of us.

So few.

~ *Prelude* ~

The next day, Tara remains cloistered in the apartment until the hour approaches for the gathering at the cemetery. She says little, lost in spirals of thought. Then, without warning, Altan appears, cloaked in shabby streetwear, his presence unusually discreet as he slips into her room through the back corridor.

"Word travels quickly," he murmurs. "I've heard the noise, the gossip and speculation . . . the usual haze. Separating truth from distortion, as ever with humans, is futile. One thing is certain: you've wasted no time making yourself a target. Tell me exactly what happened."

Tara recounts the sequence in measured detail. Altan remains still, his internal systems humming faintly behind his gaze. A brief flicker pulses beneath the skin near his temple, an involuntary signal of cognitive reordering.

When she finishes, he tilts his head. "You really left their leader that way?"

"Yes."

"This is why we chose a neglected territory in South Africa—unimportant to major powers, and invisible to most eyes in the United States. Even here, no one in authority will credit the words of gang members. Still, you are applying salve to the surface of a festering wound."

"I've seen the source of the infection. It isn't youth with guns, it's the rot in their authorities, the architects of despair."

Altan exhales. It is not a sigh, but a slow recalibration. "Ah. And the undeveloped cortex that leaves them ravenous for purpose yet gullible enough to follow false saviors. That is the global condition. But it goes deeper: unbridled desire, profound ignorance, self-delusion, broken dreams. It drives them to worship demagogues, dictators, corrupt merchants."

"So what should I do?"

"Even if you did nothing," he replies, his gaze sharpening into focus, "your kind would still attract the intelligent ones, those who sense a new future encoded in your blood. Some will offer sons. Others, daughters. Some will offer themselves. Natural selection, dear Tara. Result: a burgeoning of new Superior Ones."

A subtle ripple moves along Tara's occipital hump, a trait among her species indicating restrained agitation. "So I'm a glorified breeder now? A womb for the next epoch?"

Altan lets out a low resonance from deep in his throat, a vibrational echo that passes for laughter. "Not incorrect. You are a species-making machine. First priority: propagation. Not saving a handful of the vulnerable lost in a sea of entropy."

"But I thought we came to lessen suffering."

"Lessen, not eliminate. Learn, not preach."

She narrows her eyes. "Then how do I lessen suffering if I don't use my powers?"

His expression flickers into something like solemn amusement. "You don't. This is the natural price. For every life granted, a slice in compensation must be taken. That is the contract of the living world. The universe is not sentimental. It calculates."

Tara lowers her gaze, her neural crest tightening with thought. *So few of us, against almost ten billion. One misstep in the early arc, and the entire trajectory falters. Not extinction—but dilution. Replacement in slow motion. My compassion is an anomaly. A vestigial flame.*

And still, I burn.

~ *Meditations* ~

Altan watches her in silence, then speaks not to her alone but to the air itself, as though addressing unseen auditors.

"So it begins again. A handful against a multitude. Superior Ones against the tidal mass of Homo sapiens. The odds, if calculated, would mock us: billions against dozens. Yet numbers do not rule the future. Fire does. If her flame endures, if empathy outweighs hunger, then the age of humans will not end in slaughter but in transfiguration. If not . . . then we will be remembered only as another failed spark, swallowed by the dark."

Chapter Four

Slices

A Meeting of Mothers

~ Come Together? ~

The tent is small, the canvas old, its seams stitched by many hands over many years. The wind presses in soft gusts, but the canvas barely stirs. Inside, the atmosphere is thick with waiting. The air holds the weight of heat, breath, and uncertainty. This does not feel like the beginning of a movement. It feels closer to a memorial—quiet, heavy, and unfinished.

Only a few women have gathered. Most are older, with lined faces and careful eyes. A handful are younger, their postures uncertain, caught between fatigue and hope. They don't form a crowd so much as small, separate clusters, bodies turned inward, conversations held in partial whispers. No one raises their voice. No one moves quickly. They glance over their shoulders more often than ahead. There is something unspoken between them, something raw and unresolved, as if they fear that even the sound of truth might summon something they are not prepared to confront.

Tara steps into the space, scanning it as she does. She sees absence more than presence. No Thandolwethu. No Siyabonga. No familiar faces. No banners. No signals. No signs that anything is about to shift. Just the low murmur of women speaking not to one another, but around one another. A reluctance to commit. A hesitation sharpened by lived memory.

As she moves toward the front, the noise dims. Conversations falter. The tension sharpens. Faces turn to her. Some with caution. Some with something colder. Eyes follow her path—not drawn by reverence, but by calculation, by guarded need, by something harder to name. She feels it brush across her skin. She does not resist it.

The platform is barely more than a few nailed planks raised on concrete blocks. As she ascends, the wood beneath her shifts slightly, releasing the groan of weight long forgotten. She waits for silence to complete itself before speaking.

"My name is Tara Powers. I won't deliver a speech. We all know why we're here."

The words land cleanly. No preamble. No performance. Just a voice pitched to cut through fatigue.

"Your sons are trapped. Some are dead. Some have killed. Some will kill again. But you are their mothers. And that means something. That has always meant something."

She scans the faces again. A few women glance downward. A few stand still, arms crossed, brows furrowed. The air tightens further.

"How many of you have sons in gangs?"

For a moment, no one moves. Then, slowly, two hands lift, wavering. Another follows. A fourth rises, then falls. The rest remain at their sides, stiff. Defiant or ashamed—it's difficult to tell.

Tara doesn't press. She doesn't need confirmation. The thoughts speak without being spoken. The collective mind of the tent holds them plainly: sons lost to bullets, to initiation rites, to overdoses, to revenge. Daughters forced into silence, some into worse. There are memories here that have no language. Grief that has been rehearsed and buried, then unearthed again and again. The air vibrates with fear, layered and embedded, fear of the gangs, of the police, of the future, of one another. And now, fear of her.

Tara breathes in. Lets it fill her. Holds it.

"I know who you are," she says. "And I know what you've carried. But we are not powerless."

A silence follows, taut and brittle. Then, from the back of the tent, a voice breaks through. Female. Careful. Fatigued. The tone of someone who has asked this before.

"Charity workers have come. NGOs. Churches. Foreigners. They brought supplies, offered therapy, held rallies. What more can we do that hasn't already been tried?"

Tara meets the voice with calm.

"Have they stopped the dying?"

That question opens something. Not outrage. Not protest. But a deep and weary acknowledgment. A few women shift. One reaches for another's hand but stops short. Someone exhales, sharp and audible. Still, no one answers.

Then a masculine voice cuts through, low and unshaken. "No."

It lands like a stone dropped into water.

All heads turn as Siyabonga steps into view, no longer alone. Behind him stands Thandolwethu. Behind her, others. Dozens. More than expected. They come from alleys, from doorways, from behind parked cars. Young men with hard eyes. Elders wrapped in thin shawls. Women holding infants. A few with walking sticks. A few carrying nothing but themselves. Some speak in hushed tones, unsure. Others wear expressions of hard-won clarity. It is not a march. Not yet. But something has stirred.

They gather at the edges of the tent, then move forward in quiet unison. Some smile nervously. Others keep their gazes straight ahead. One boy pulls his hoodie lower. An older man brushes dust from his coat as if preparing for something sacred. From the front row, a tall woman steps forward.

Tara's eyes meet hers.

Something stops. The room doesn't go still, but her attention does. The woman's presence is unmistakable. Not aggressive, not warm, but absolute. Tara reaches inward, an instinctive gesture, subtle and fast, to read her. To sense the emotional terrain.

She finds nothing.

No surface anxiety. No flashing thoughts. No pain. No hunger. No noise at all. The woman's mind is a smooth, sealed field. While it is spacious, it is also inaccessible. It is not that she resists. It is that she is already complete.

Tara draws back slightly. Her face remains composed, but a private recognition has lodged itself. The stakes are no longer theoretical. Whatever is rising here is no longer hers to define.

She steadies herself. The platform holds beneath her feet. The women in the tent remain silent, eyes flicking between her and those arriving. The moment hangs, not as a climax, but as a beginning held barely in check. What follows will not be hers alone to lead. But she has spoken, and she will speak again.

They are listening now. Not with hope. Not yet. But with something rarer—willingness.

~

Siyabonga rushes up to Tara and gestures toward the woman. "My mother. Kholwa. It means 'Believe.' Just follow her lead."

Before she can ask more, he's already dissolved into the crowd. Kholwa ascends the stage with unhurried grace, as if the earth tilts to make way for her.

"Women of Cape Flats!" Her voice is not loud, but it carries. "Mothers of lost sons! Look at this one—" she points at Tara, "—who walked into the lion's mouth and plucked out his fangs. Do you not see?"

"She makes things disappear!" someone gasps.

"Yes—limbs!" another cries.

A low growl comes from a heavyset woman in front. "Thato was a son too. Now he's just flesh."

Kholwa raises her arms. The murmurs dissolve. "There is an old saying," she intones, "that the only way to eat the elephant blocking your path is to cut it into pieces. This woman began the cutting. Will you leave her to do it alone?"

"She's a witch," mutters the heavy woman. "Killing isn't justice."

"She didn't kill him," Kholwa replies. "She unmade him. He was a predator. Now he is a silence. That silence is a mercy."

A girl, barely twenty, steps forward, her belly round, her eyes gleaming. "My brother is dead, gunned down like a dog. If this woman made the monster crawl, then bless her for it. Who did it? I want to know."

Kholwa turns to Tara. "Speak. The moment is ripe."

Tara steps forward. The wind stirs as if nudging her into place. "You must form a circle, not a formless crowd. You must act together. Your sons weren't born with bloodlust. But the gangs found them, offered them names, colors, weapons. Don't worship their shadows. Don't mistake pain for pride. They were babies once. Can you still remember that?"

The air thickens. Questions rise, urgent and uncontrollable, drawn by the gravity of something they cannot ignore.

"How do we fight them?"

"What power do we have?"

"Can you really make things disappear?"

Kholwa raises a hand and speaks once more. *Is it possible?*

Tara tries again to glimpse her thoughts, but what greets her is a silence that neither invites nor resists. It holds itself intact—no surface, no crack, no trace. The silence of someone who knows how to remain unseen.

Is it possible? Tara wonders.

"We begin today. Here. We meet every week. We share stories: our sons in the Mongrels, the Americans, the Numbers. Over time, we will see: it is not just the gangs, but the soil that grows them. The hunger. The greed. The invisible hands behind it all."

"Stories?" someone scoffs. "That's nothing."

"It is everything," says Kholwa. "Story is spell. Spell is action. Together we'll remember we are not powerless. Together we'll change the rhythm of the streets."

She turns to Tara. "Do you agree?"

Before she can speak, Tara feels something press softly into her mind. Not a force, not a voice, but a presence, cool and ancient. When her eyes meet Kholwa's, something bursts open. *You're like me. I thought we were alone!*

Of course not, Kholwa replies without speaking. *The seeds are scattered. You are the bloom. Now speak.*

Tara stumbles back, recalibrating her universe. Then she steadies herself and lifts her voice. "We gave them flesh. Now we reclaim them. The gangs are not gods. The politicians are not kings. We are mothers, sisters, daughters. We do not fear the dark anymore . . . we bring the fire."

A cheer rises. Then Siyabonga appears next to her. His voice cuts through it all.

"I saw what she did! I saw the fear she planted in them. That alone is power! The gangs tremble because she reminds them of their own deaths."

"What kind of power?" a woman cries.

"She makes arms vanish!" says another. "My son told me, stuttering like a child."

"Witchcraft!" hisses the heavy woman again.

Gasps. Silence. The young woman who lost her brother stands tall. "Then I bless this witch. If fear makes the killing stop, then fear is holy. I'm pregnant," she adds, "and I won't raise my child in silence."

"The police will want to speak with her," the heavy woman snaps.

Tara lifts her hands, voice calm but clear. "I did nothing. I don't harm people. I only refuse to fear them. Whatever happened to those men happened after I left."

"But Siyabonga saw—" someone protests.

Siyabonga steps forward, hands lifted. "I saw fear. That's what I saw. She brings truth, and truth burns them. That's not witchcraft. That's grace."

He lifts his eyes skyward. "A miracle. God sent her to us."

Or Goddess, Kholwa whispers inside Tara, a wry echo full of knowing.

~ *Revelations* ~

When the meeting breaks up, Tara and Kholwa invite the women to return next week at the same time. Each is urged to bring someone new. Plans, they say, will begin in earnest then. Tara accepts Kholwa's invitation for dinner, and Siyabonga joins them. They've barely begun the walk when several shots ring out nearby. Instinctively, Siyabonga and Kholwa duck. A sharp cry splits the air, then another, then silence.

"Damn," mutters Siyabonga. "Again? Sooner or later. . . . "

"Not to worry," Tara says, unshaken. "I've removed their guns."

Siyabonga looks at her, stunned. "And the bullets?"

She tilts her head toward the sky and flicks her fingers. "Gone. Their atoms are off to more useful duties."

"And the shooters?" Kholwa asks cautiously. "Did you do what you did before?"

Tara chuckles. "They're fine. Confused, probably. Nothing more."

Kholwa straightens. "Let's pick up the pace. Too dangerous to linger."

They arrive at Kholwa's modest home a little after eight. Siyabonga helps prepare a simple meal of *chakalaka* and *pap*. The kitchen is worn but warm, the table scratched with long years of use.

"It's late," Tara says. "I didn't mean to impose."

"No imposition," Kholwa replies. "This is dinnertime in South Africa. Now, you must tell us everything: who you are, where you're from, how you came by your powers. And others like you. Everything."

Tara's gaze sharpens. "First, how many like you are here?"

"None that we know," says Siyabonga. "But there've been hints. We were always afraid to show ourselves. Until you arrived."

And your own powers? she asks silently.

Weak—compared to yours.

Tara pushes forward a salt shaker. *Make it disappear.*

Both mother and son try. Nothing happens.

"We're intermediates," Kholwa says aloud. "We didn't even know ones like you existed."

"Nor I you," says Tara. "And I intend to speak to someone about that."

"We were guided," Kholwa replies, her tone shifting, "by a young woman who came to me before Siyabonga was born."

"Who?"

"We don't know her name. She is . . . impossible to describe."

"I know her," Tara says softly. "The woman you met has many names. Goddess. *She*. The Precious Object. My ancestors taught me about *her*. I've met *her*. You're right, *she* is beyond description."

Kholwa and Siyabonga stare. "They're all the same?"

Tara nods. "If you can call *her* a person. But now I see—there's much I've not been told."

Their faces are alive with questions.

"But that's not our concern tonight," Tara says, redirecting. "What's being said about me?"

Siyabonga leans back. "Mother knows what the women think. I can speak for the men. This is still a patriarchal society. Most dismiss you as a glorified charity worker, weak and overmatched. They think you'll be dead or driven out soon. But some . . . the ones who saw . . . I've seen fear in their eyes."

"As for the women," Kholwa adds, "you've lit a spark. Some are still loyal to their sons, to the gangs they joined. Others are afraid. What happened to Thato . . . they wonder if it could happen to them."

Suddenly, a voice outside chants low and menacing: "Hey, bitches, you all goin' to die. You all goin' to die, bitches—"

The chant cuts off mid-sentence. Silence.

"What happened?" Siyabonga asks, alarmed.

Tara shrugs. "One less larynx in the world."

"What . . . ?" he murmurs.

"He won't be making any more threats."

Kholwa's face dims. "Can you bring it back?"

"No."

"Then he'll be mute? Forever?"

"Most likely."

"So sad," Kholwa whispers. "I wonder if I knew the boy."

Siyabonga exhales a slow dirge. "That's extreme, Tara. What if he changed? What if he wanted to fight the gangs?"

Tara shrugs. "His silence might speak louder than his voice ever could. I know it seems harsh. But look at the whole, humanity as one organism. What do humans do to cancer cells?"

"Cancer cells can't think," Siyabonga replies.

"Exactly," says Tara. "And neither do most humans, until it is too late."

"Thank Goddess you're on our side," Kholwa murmurs.

"Our side," Tara says, "is the future. Unless we fail—and then we'll vanish, forgotten. Along with every living thing that might have been saved."

"But are we failing now?" Siyabonga asks. "Shouldn't your powers stay secret?"

Tara studies him. Not to answer the question, but to assess his fitness as a mate. As an intermediate, he fits the profile.

"Perhaps. But secrets never last long."

Siyabonga sighs. "Too late now."

"Not necessarily," says Tara. "My grandmother Ming-huà and my mother Pythia did the same. They were never caught."

"But how many arms and legs can you remove before the cure becomes worse than the disease?"

Tara leans in. "Do you consider yourself fully human?"

Caught off guard, Siyabonga looks to his mother.

Kholwa frowns. "His father was human. All too human."

"And your father?"

"A brute," Kholwa says flatly.

"Abuse?"

She nods. "Yes. Terrible."

"Your mother?"

"She protected me. Gave her life for it."

"Did she have powers?"

"Maybe. I don't know. She died young."

Siyabonga slams his fist on the table. "Yes! At the hands of my grandfather. My own father wasn't much better."

Kholwa takes his hand. "I made a poor choice. He was sweet at first, then the gang devoured him. I raised Siyabonga to never be like them."

"Which is why we must help Tara," Siyabonga says.

"I agree," Kholwa replies. "But if she keeps disabling gang members, the government will intervene. And you have no idea how corrupt they are."

"They'll see me as a threat?"

"Exactly."

"Then let them," Tara says. "The good are always threats to the comfortable. Ask the Grand Inquisitor."

She rises. "It's late. I should go."

"Will we see you tomorrow?" Siyabonga asks.

Tara picks up his intent—sexual, curious, and respectfully offered. She smiles inwardly, but her mind shifts.

"Where's the nearest wildlife reserve?"

"Why?" Kholwa asks.

"I need to visit what remains of the species humans are erasing."

As they move toward the door, Siyabonga says, "My head's spinning. You've only been here a few days and already. . . . " He trails off.

"My grandmother and mother did similar things, in Washington State, San Francisco, Mexico. Their powers lessened suffering, but also caused it. The difference was this: those who suffered were the perpetrators. Those relieved were the victims. Imagine what thousands like us could do if we replaced the machinery of violence without amplifying the pain."

"But we have to survive first," Siyabonga says.

Tara steps into the light of the porch. A bare bulb glows above her, casting shadows across her face. Still, her smile shines.

"We will."

As she turns to go, a thought streams into her mind, calm, precise, and unmistakably from Kholwa:

There are many parks near Cape Town, but I recommend Sanbona Wildlife Reserve. No zoo. Lion, elephant, rhino, buffalo, leopard. It is wild. And big. Siyabonga will help you.

The final note carries a sly warmth.

~ *Animal Minds* ~

Though born in South Africa, Siyabonga carries little of the land in his body. He is shaped by pavement, corrugated fences, restless alleys, by the architecture of interruption. His instincts belong to the township, not the veld. The rhythms that guide him are human ones: transaction, alertness, adaptation.

It is Tara who leads them into the reserve. She does not enter as a guest, or a seeker, but as one returning to where she has always belonged. Her pace is swift, measured, attuned to the terrain. She does not pause to orient herself. She does not scan the horizon for signs. Her movement is memory enacted by the body. Each step folds into the next, quiet and measured, as if the land recognizes her.

She has refused all the expected preparations. There is no vehicle, no guide, no equipment. No spectacle. Only her and Siyabonga, exposed to the vastness, two figures moving across a landscape that does not ask for names. Her breath deepens. The scent of dust, crushed foliage, and distant animal musk fills her lungs, not as novelty, but as return. The air feels unclaimed. Untouched by cities. It speaks of a time when no one spoke.

Her hump has been active for over a day now, registering pulses that rise and fall in subtle waves: first bodily, then emotionally, then psychically. Creatures call out without language, yet she hears them: brief, bright signals of need. Hunger. Thirst. Pain. Alertness. They are not confused. They are not cruel. They live as they must. They kill because they are driven. They flee because they know they will die.

She absorbs this with reverence. There is no moral distortion here. No pretense. The wild does not dress up desperation in symbols or slogans. It does not invent reasons to harm beyond survival. And in that clarity, she feels peace. Not comfort, but alignment.

A part of her wishes to stop and remain, feet in the dust, hands on the earth, senses open. She remembers stories her grandmother told: of conversations with lemurs, elephants, birds. Of listening without demand. Of being received by animals not as a master, but as kin.

But the presence behind her disrupts the stillness.

Siyabonga walks with effort, trying to match her rhythm, but failing. His breath is audible. His boots fall too hard. He asks questions she does not want to answer—about direction, about purpose, about whether this place has dangers he should be aware of. His vigilance feels misplaced here. His curiosity lands awkwardly, as if he cannot grasp that some knowledge does not yield to inquiry. Even his sincerity, which she recognizes as genuine, interferes. Not because it is false, but because it insists.

She does not turn to correct him. She does not speak to soothe him. She simply continues, hoping the veld will do what words cannot—teach him how to be silent.

"Why are you walking so fast, Tara?" he pants behind her. "What are you looking for?"

"Confirmation."

"Of what?"

"That the goal is worth the cost."

Hours pass. They crest a low ridge and look down on a broad valley dappled with movement, dark shapes flowing, leaping, flowing again.

"Gazelles?" Siyabonga guesses.

Tara laughs. "You're the African, and you don't know your neighbors? Those are springbok."

"Same thing?"

"Springbok are to gazelles what your genes are to ancient Zulu. Close, but not identical. At least, your human genes."

Siyabonga pauses. "The question you asked—if I'm fully human. I've been wondering. What do you think?"

"I think I see lions," she says, squinting. "And I think we need to move."

"There are lions down there?" he shouts as Tara sprints ahead, already half a blur in the dust.

I wonder if she can read their minds, he thinks as he chases after her.

No. They're too far. Hurry! Her voice cuts cleanly into his skull.

He stumbles forward. Now he sees them clearly—lions. And Tara is headed straight for them. Instinct drives him to stay near her, not out of courage, but calculation. She can make things vanish. She is his only hope.

If they attack, I cannot interfere, comes her voice again. *This is a prime directive. We're here to replace* Homo sapiens, *not* Panthera leo.

"Shit," he whispers.

Quiet, or you'll attract them.

Shit!

Yet even in his panic, he watches her, this woman with a twisted back and an untouchable grace. Her stride is fluid, her body a perfect fusion of force and control. Her presence lights something primal inside him. His desire becomes distraction.

Watch out! she snaps. *Stop daydreaming! Roll off my naked body and open your eyes! You'll die with a hard-on if you're not careful.*

Flushed with shame and adrenaline, Siyabonga shakes off the erotic haze just in time to see a lioness, crouched low in the bush, her gaze fixed on him. He resists the urge to bolt.

Tara's voice enters again: *Face her. Don't run. Make yourself big! Arms up, clap, shout! Show her you're not prey.*

He obeys. Tara emerges from the scrub to his left, approaching slowly. But the lioness isn't alone. Others silently appear, golden females. Their eyes pass over Siyabonga like wind over grass. Then they fix on Tara. He watches, breathless. Something passes between them. The lions pause, then one by one, turn and vanish into the tall grass. Tara remains still, then, astonishingly, follows.

Stay where you are. I'll return after the hunt.

She disappears into the swirl of dust. Siyabonga strains to follow her movements, glimpsing springbok bursting skyward, panicked shadows darting through haze. The dust rises, drifts, settles. A deep growl rumbles across the plain, shaking the air—the voice of a male lion claiming his due.

Tara? he calls out. *Tara, answer!*

Nothing.

Then, far off, a flicker of movement. A small figure emerging from the vast silence of the hunt.

He waves. "I'm here!"

She lifts a hand and quickens her pace toward him. Her face is unreadable.

"Let's camp here," she says.

They pitch a small tent and share cold food on the exposed ribs of a dying baobab. Siyabonga tries speaking into her mind, but she has sealed it shut. Her eyes fix on a distant, twisted tree silhouetted against a sky glittering with starlight. Her face is solemn, almost haunted.

"What are you thinking?" he asks aloud.

"Desperation," she murmurs. "It's a terrible thing. Our friends out there are starving. Their bodies cry out to me."

Siyabonga nods. "But aren't humans even more desperate?"

"Human desperation is self-made," she replies. "Other creatures suffer honestly. Humans engineer their torment and export it."

"But . . . other species wage war too. Ants. Chimps. Organized violence isn't just human."

"No," Tara says quietly. "They kill for land, for food, for survival. Not for God or race or status. Not to build luxury towers atop corpses. Not with satellites and microchips."

She turns to him now, her eyes steady.

"When you return to Nyanga, look beyond the gangs. Look at the concrete, the machines, the poisons in the air, the trash in the gutters. This is not war. This is rot . . . systematic, planetary rot. My mentors say this planet is a wonder. I agree. Letting this miracle be consumed by humans is not an option."

"Mentors?"

"Never mind. Let us sleep. My powers weaken when I'm tired. And we mustn't let the fire go out. The lions may return."

In the distance, another roar shudders the ground, a king in the night, reminding them of whose kingdom this truly is.

Siyabonga stares into the fire. "By all means," he says. "By all means."

The flames snap and curl, throwing their restless shapes onto the dark veld. Above, the stars burn with an older fire, one that has outlasted empires and will outlast this moment too. Tara leans back, her face unreadable, her thoughts hidden even from him. The silence between them thickens, no longer just fatigue, but something larger.

For beneath the quiet of the veld lies the deeper question:

Can a handful of Superior Ones, scattered like sparks, ever ignite against the tidal mass of ten billion humans?

Or will their fire vanish in the wind, remembered only as a brief flare against the dark?

Chapter Five

Back to Fundamentals

First Principles

~ Baobab Love ~

Tara cannot sleep.

The earth beneath her remains warm from the day's sun, but her body resists rest. She rises without sound and moves a short distance from the tent, barefoot on the hardened soil. The wind has stilled. Overhead, the stars wheel in slow silence, vast and indifferent.

She stands before the baobab, the same tree that held her earlier in a moment of unexpected awe. Now, in moonlight, it looms even darker, its thick trunk and crooked limbs carved against the silver sky. There is something in its shape that feels less like memory than foretelling. She does not look away.

The African night surrounds her, unmuted. No cities. No motors. No fences. The cries of creatures punctuate the stillness, some close, others impossibly far. The world is not quiet, but it is whole. Every sound has its place. She listens without fear. The wilderness does not threaten her. It names her.

She remains still when it happens.

Without warning, his presence touches her mind, not physically, but with a charge she recognizes instantly. Siyabonga. Awake. Watching. The intensity of his focus sharpens and then spills forward, no longer hidden. His thoughts are not aggressive, but they are no longer held back. He allows them to move freely, crossing the space between them without hesitation.

Images form. Not crude, not frantic—just clear. The shape of her body. The imagined warmth of skin against skin. The breathless pacing of want that has lingered too long in restraint. It is not lust alone. It is the desire to be chosen, to be allowed inside something he does not understand but cannot turn from. He sends it toward her, not with force, but with certainty.

His voice follows, not aloud, but through the shared current that pulses between the sensitive, the gifted, the changed:

Will you lay with me?

No pressure. No demand. Just the question, hovering between their minds, open and waiting.

Your fantasies underestimate my figure, she replies. *Your imagination erases my hump. That's insulting.*

Then show me what I've missed.

Without a word, Tara steps from the firelight and removes her clothes. Her skin glows bronze and pale, lit from below by flame. She locks eyes with him.

"Observe carefully."

She turns slowly, revealing her hump. Siyabonga stares, awestruck, as two figures emerge upon her back, shaped in raised relief, glowing faintly, alive. A man and a woman entwined, shifting through a fluid sequence of erotic positions. The dance is mesmerizing, impossible to look away from. The final act ends in luminous climax, the figures shuddering with release. Siyabonga himself is shaking, breathless.

You see now, Siyabonga? her voice hums inside him. *My hump is far more beautiful than your fantasy could invent.*

Yes . . . yes!

Would you like to copy what you just saw?

Yes!

Then show me your body.

Naked and trembling, he moans against the length of her body as she draws him in. Their union deepens, pulse against pulse until the night itself splits open. Suddenly, a cry erupts, raw, primal, and near, a creature's death scream wrenched from its throat by fangs. Siyabonga jolts, seized mid-climax, and tumbles off her. Tara reels, hands pressed to her ears, as the sound cleaves through the darkness like a shiv. On her thigh, his seed gleams faintly in the firelight.

"I'm sorry, I'm sorry—" Siyabonga pants, nervously pacing and glaring into the surrounding darkness.

Tara says nothing.

She stands motionless, her breath shallow, her gaze lowered. The sounds of the kill still echo faintly in the distance, the final thrash, the break of bone, the wet stilling of movement. Then, slowly, the air shifts. The cries of the night creatures resume, hesitant at first, then with growing confidence. The world begins to reorder itself.

She waits.

Only when the agony recedes completely, when the quiet that follows death settles across the land, not as peace, but as finality, does she lift her eyes.

Siyabonga's voice breaks the hush beside her, low and uncertain.

"Is it over?" he asks.

"Yes."

In his embarrassment, he reverts to silent communication. *I was startled—*

So was I. That's how strong your force was inside me. Your climax amplified everything.

You were magnificent . . . until I ruined it.

So were you.

He hesitates, then says aloud, "Will we continue?"

Tara chuckles softly. "You'll make an excellent mate."

"What?"

"Never mind. An inside joke."

Another cry echoes in the distance, more distant this time, but no less real.

Siyabonga hugs himself. "Is this better than civilization? This . . . kill-or-be-killed?"

Tara glances at him. "Is it clean out here, Siyabonga?"

"Clean? No."

"Then think again. It's cleaner than Cape Town, New York, San Francisco, or any human sprawl. *Homo sapiens* are neither fully civilized nor fully savage. They're trapped between poles, lost in their abstract minds. The savage in them destroys. The civilized part corrupts. This hybrid state is the most dangerous of all, not just to themselves, but to every species and the planet itself."

"Can they grow out of it?"

She looks at him—this man who may one day help change the species' course. "Look carefully at yourself. At your mother and grandmother. At me. At my line. At others like us. That is how they will grow out of it."

"By being replaced?"

"Exactly. They will evolve by going extinct."

She senses his desire spike again.

Ready for more?

God, yes.

Correction—Goddess yes.

"Yes! Goddess, yes!" he cries aloud.

"Then stay inside me until the end this time, and I promise you'll be rewarded."

And as their bodies entwine beneath the vast indifference of the stars, Tara feels the pulse of something larger than desire—the faint, inexorable rhythm of a species being unmade and remade through her.

In the silence after each cry, the future bends.

~ *Morning After* ~

The sun rises hard across the African veld, sharp and unrelenting. Its gold is not soft, not forgiving. It exposes everything. The yellow grass catches the light and turns brittle. The baobabs, scattered across the plain, reach upward—bare, unadorned, unapologetic. There is no invitation in this landscape. There is only presence.

Tara sits beside Siyabonga's sleeping form, his breath steady in the still morning air. Her own breath deepens, slows. Her body feels recalibrated. Rested, yes, but more than that: aligned. Something has been completed. Not the full arc of her task, but a fragment of it. One goal achieved. The rest waits, immense but not unreachable.

She would stay here if she could.

The veld offers no comfort, no shelter. And yet, she is drawn to it, not for safety, but for its refusal to deceive. Her companions of the last few days—the lions crouched in stillness, the springbok fleeing into the brush—reminded her of something she was in danger of forgetting. That suffering does not require explanation. That beauty does not require purpose. That death, when it comes without ideology, is not grotesque but true.

They live without pretext. They kill without justification. They die without story. And in that, there is something purer than any of the creeds she has studied. Something closer to the original fabric of being.

This was always the beginning—before theory, before structure. The first lesson of the Superior Ones was not transcendence, but return: to the integrity of the living world, to hunger that does not lie, to silence that does not need permission to speak.

But the cities call.

The stench of metal and smoke, the engineered appetites, the fractured minds. The ones who decay in it. The ones who profit from the decay. It pulls her back not because she desires it, but because she must. That is where the work remains. That is where the damage collects. Her kind did not rise to rule but to remember what had been forgotten, and in remembering, to act.

She lets Siyabonga continue sleeping.

Rising, she moves through the veld with quiet steps, the grass brushing her calves. Not far from the tent, she finds the site of last night's kill. A bushpig lies, its form distorted, torn, barely legible as an animal. Vultures watch from nearby branches. A few circle above, wings motionless. They do not approach while she stands. They are patient.

She crouches beside the carcass and studies it. Not out of morbid curiosity, but because her body demands it. Her senses drink in the scene without recoiling nor aestheticizing, only observing.

Her thoughts drift, not away from the animal, but deeper into the implications of its end. She recalls the archives. The simulations. The lessons coded in neural threads. Human history: Unit 731. Firestorms. Mass graves. Rivers filled with bones. Oceans choked by plastic. Ravenous ovens. Genomes poisoned by greed.

She does not ask whether this death is more or less brutal. That question no longer holds meaning. What she sees here is death without deceit. Death without rhetoric. Death without profit.

What humans called savagery was simply life without excuses.

She stands.

Her gaze lifts to the horizon, the light growing harsher with every minute. The path forward is long, and the temptation to look too far ahead begins to cloud her clarity.

She breathes once, steady and long. Then speaks, not to herself, not to the air, but to the impulse that would turn grief into paralysis.

"Enough," she says. "Focus on the next step."

~

Behind her, footsteps. She turns. Siyabonga is walking toward her, unsensed. Again, the lapse. This startles her.

She is reminded that Siyabonga can block her mind at will, and that further unsettles her. It gives him a degree of autonomy she's unaccustomed to outside her own family.

If we can block each other's minds, does that make us doubly dangerous? she wonders.

Before she can complete the thought, Siyabonga's desire surges again.

Let us make love, Tara. I'm so . . . I need you.

Here?

Anywhere. Now. Or I'll die.

Then die. I'm not lying on thorns.

He laughs and shouts, "Then be on top! Your two skin-lovers did it every which way!"

Much more of this and we'll outnumber the humans.

She lets that thought linger in his mind, stoking him.

"Well?" he cries.

"Well what?"

He drops to his back, arms outstretched. "So much the better!"

Get up, you crazy maniac! she shouts in his mind. *Get up and come to me!*

He leaps to his feet and takes her in his arms. Their clothes vanish. She wraps her legs around him and guides him inside. They come together in ecstasy, then dress in silence and return to camp.

"That was . . . wonderful," Siyabonga says, almost bashful.

"Yes," says Tara. "But now we go farther into the reserve."

"Why?"

"I'm looking for something."

"What?"

"I don't know. I'll know when I find it."

"You go. I'll come with you."

Tara stops. Her face hardens. Her mind speaks with finality. *No. You must return. I must go alone. No questions. When I return, I'll know more. Go back to Nyanga.*

Then tell me what you find. Promise me that.

She doesn't answer. She walks southwest, driven by a compulsion too deep for speech.

~ She ~

Hours pass. The terrain shifts, scrub fades into stone. The air grows thin and hot. Tara moves without hesitation, passing elephants, giraffes, even a stalking hyena. She barely notices. Something is calling. Late afternoon. The shadows grow long. She skirts a rocky hill and slips through a gorge. At its heart, she stops. A figure stands in her path. A young woman, beautiful, smiling, wearing a simple backpack. Tara knows her at once. Her heart surges.

"Welcome, Little Tara," the woman says. "A long human time ago, I asked your great-great-grandfather John Powers how one justifies a life without cruelty and therefore without the distilled beauty of cruelty. Now that you're older, what's your answer?"

Tara stares into her fathomless eyes, her own eyes glowing faintly. "My answer is the same, Goddess. The spider's web is intricately beautiful. The taste of captured flies, exquisite."

The woman laughs gently. "As do bushpigs."

She grows more serious. "Do you remember how I promised you, long ago, that you'd visit your great-great-grandfather on his quest? And meet Child of Buddha?"

Tara nods.

"But first," says the woman, "you have a bone to pick."

"Why was I not told?"

"About the others?"

"Yes."

"We are not of one mind, Tara," the woman says, her voice steady, almost gentle. "We don't war like humans, but we disagree."

Tara watches her, alert. The air around them has shifted—less grounded, more permeable, as though thought itself has loosened its boundaries.

"Your ancestors—John Powers, Michael Powers, Child of Buddha, Bai Meiying—were among the first to hear the early whispers. They didn't know what we were. Couldn't. They conjured gods and demons from us. They gave us form. Faces. Names. The old dualisms: light and dark, male and female, God and Goddess."

She pauses, then continues.

"Their minds were fragile, brilliant, overexposed. They couldn't filter what they heard. And so it broke them. Some were declared mad. Some were locked away. Some simply disappeared."

Tara speaks softly. "What were the disagreements about?"

"You'll see. When we reach the cave."

"There's always a cave," she mutters.

"Of course. And yes, this one leads . . . elsewhere."

They walk without speaking. The path curves inward, narrowing. Stones crunch beneath their feet. The mouth of the cave rises ahead, wide and waiting.

Then the voice comes again, not aloud, but from within:

You wonder why they called me Goddess?

Tara answers inwardly. *Yes. Given how superstitious they were.*

It was projection. Need. They saw what they were trained to see. The mother, the healer, the light-bringer. They gave me robes. Thrones. Symbols. This—

The figure shifts.

Now she sits lotus-style on a vast white blossom. A jeweled crown rests on her brow. Her fingers form sacred mudras. Her face is radiant, but her eyes—her eyes contain centuries of grief. They do not blink.

"You are so beautiful," Tara whispers.

But oh, metaphorical Goddess says, **how they made us argue.**

Us?

Yes. The masculine and feminine minds they split us into—God and Goddess. Archetypes of cruelty and compassion. Judgment and mercy. Voice and silence. They turned our unity into duality. Into conflict. The mind could not receive us whole, so it split the message in two. And the split became scripture. Myth. Doctrine. Theologies built on arguments we never had. And in its midst, the demons embedded in human DNA frolicked about, demanding harm—to self and others. Your great-grandfather Michael was among the first to fracture beneath the weight. He died not of madness, but of exposure—opened too far, too soon, without skin between himself and us. But you have come far from those agonizing early days of the Founders.

The image dissolves.

The young woman returns, standing in dust, backpack slung over one shoulder, her face clear and unadorned. Her voice is steady.

"Your great-grandfather Michael was tormented by our voices. He thought he was ill. Schizophrenic. Haunted. But it was one of our first disagreements—audible to him, raw and unfiltered."

She pauses, as if listening to something ancient.

"He heard the God-voice, scorning human cruelty. He heard the Goddess-voice, pleading for compassion. They debated the desecration of nature. The slaughter of children. The burning of forests. They fought not in hatred, but in grief—because even we did not agree on how to guide you."

Tara listens, unmoving. The air around her thickens with memory, not hers but lived through her. She hears the echoes, not of madness, but of something deeper. Something broken open too soon.

"They weren't gods," she says.

"No. But neither were they delusions. They were fragments of what was trying to reach through."

The cave entrance yawns wider before them.

"They were the first," the woman says. "They paid the price of premature contact. But you—" she looks at Tara with a gravity that is not parental but evolutionary—"you are different. Genetically stabilized. Neurologically refined. Educated in the edge-realms. Mentored in stillness. The war is no longer inside you."

Tara swallows. Her hands are cold.

"The question is: what will you do with what you've been given?"

And then, silence again, waiting not for belief, but for movement.

Tara's voice is low. "Altan seems displeased."

"You've been cruel to the cruel. He understands."

"But when do I stop?"

"When it is time."

"If I overstep..."

"Variables, Tara. Infinite. Unknowable. You are the spider now. They are the flies."

Tara says nothing.

The woman gestures to the cave. "Go in."

"How far?"

"That is up to you. I won't be here when you return."

"But I still need guidance—"

"Does the spider need help to build her web? Does she need a mentor to devour a fly?"

Tara steps forward.

And the cave receives her.

~ Another Cave ~

As Tara descends deeper into the cave, the light from the entrance dissolves, first dimming, then vanishing into a pitch so complete it erases orientation. Yet she continues without hesitation. She stumbles at times, but her body, honed and agile, recovers with feline ease. In the distance, a faint glow beckons, and when she reaches its source—a narrow cleft between stone walls—she slips through. On the other side: a small, squalid room dimly lit by a shaft of light filtering through a broken vent. Trash and debris carpet the floor. In one corner, atop a stained mattress, sits what appears to be a broken manikin. Tara squints. No, it is human. A man, childlike in posture, his limbs thin and twisted. Something about the arms is wrong. She draws closer and sees: the hands are gone. The figure sobs softly. An older woman enters, cradling a bowl, and kneels beside him.

"Thato, son, you must eat. This will make you strong."

The mutilated figure turns away. His head tilts downward, eyes fixed not on the food, but on a toy in his lap, a hand-stitched warthog, cobbled together from discarded flip-flops. His stumps stroke the crude creature tenderly.

"Ain't no man no longer," he murmurs. "Mama, you know what she did. No more reason to live. Got my lucky toy here. Just a boy again. No good. Not a whole man."

"Son, you got to eat. Please. For me."

He shakes his head. "Brus in the gang cut me out. Got a new leader now. I'm useless. No good."

The mother glares toward Tara, though she cannot see her, and spits her fury into the air. "They gonna take care of that woman. Take care of her good, for what she did."

"Too late, Mama. Too late."

Tara watches, unmoved by guilt, though a quiet sorrow settles over her. Probing the woman's mind, she finds only darkness harboring superstition, rage, and the hollow rattle of addiction.

Altan materializes beside her.

"You do not feel guilt for what you did to him?"

"No," Tara replies.

"Or her?"

"No."

"Yet you are sad."

"Yes. Like one mourns a puppy gone rabid. I didn't destroy, I disabled."

Altan nods. "But what of the others? The liars, bullies, abusers, those who poison without spilling blood?"

"Inherited animal traits," she says. "Dominance is written into the marrow of most creatures. Are we to destroy them all?"

"Good," Altan murmurs. "Very good."

"But will we, those who follow, create hierarchies too?"

Before he can answer, a feral wail slices through the room. Thato shrieks, "Get out! Leave me alone!"

The woman flees, sobbing. Alone, Thato lifts his mutilated arms in despair.

Altan gazes at him. "As with all alphas, the fall is steep."

"And what of us, Altan?"

"Hierarchies disrupt cooperation. Among animals, they do little harm. But humans, with their machinery and egos, are unsustainable. You and yours are the hinge of fate. Fail, and the species fails."

"But what guarantee do we have that we will not fail?"

"None. Except this: with power comes risk. Power to read minds. Power to reshape matter through dimensional fields. These carry the threat of mutual annihilation. Only if that power is matched by a radical expansion of empathy for all life, for the Earth, can survival be earned."

"And if it isn't?"

"Then extinction."

"Can we reproduce fast enough to tip the balance?"

"Only if you're given time to grow. You and a few others are the seed. But you are vulnerable. And they, the old dominants, will come."

Tara looks again at Thato. "Then I should stop helping them?"

But Altan is gone. So is the room.

She now stands on an open field of tall grass. Ahead, a fortress rises: crumbling concrete, pillared arches, tile roofs shattered by time and war. A sanatorium, maybe. A temple for the insane.

Tara enters and walks its broken maze, corridors twisted by ruin and sorrow, until she finds an iron door. Through its barred window, she sees only shadow. She pushes it open.

The hallway beyond is a corridor of ghosts. Wails and whimpers echo along its length. Her hump tingles violently with the pain encoded in this place. Faces peer from barred cells—eyes sunken, hands like fading relics of forgotten prayers.

A Chinese man appears. "There is one I want you to see. We call her Child of Buddha. She is your great-great-grandmother. And this man—" he gestures to a figure beside him—"John Powers, your great-great-grandfather."

Tara watches them, unnoticed. Ancestors. The first Chosen Ones.

John peers through the iron bars and asks an unknown companion, "Is she violent?"

A soft voice from the cell answers, "No, I am not violent."

Tara reaches into the woman's mind. A flicker of recognition, pain, love, endurance. Then the scene dissolves.

Child of Buddha in the madhouse? Yes?

Yes, comes the reply, flat and sympathetic.

Tara nods. *Not mad, chosen.*

Yes.

Why am I shown this? she asks.

You are shown this in order to show you this.

I understand. I see more clearly now.

You are shown this in order to show you this. What you do with it matters.

Tara shakes her head. *Perhaps what I do not—or cannot—do with it matters more.*

Perhaps.

These words echo through her mind as she retraces her steps, emerging from the cave into the bright furnace of an African day.

<h3 align="center">~ Return ~</h3>

Two days later, Tara arrives back in Nyanga. A woman at the apartment informs her that Siyabonga and his mother have been shot. She receives the news with a strange calm, an uneasy blend of equanimity and sorrowful certainty.

At the hospital, she asks the nurse at reception, "Are they alive?"

"Are you family?"

"No. A friend."

The nurse eyes Tara's hump. "You need family permission."

"Then just tell me their condition."

"The boy's stable. The mother is in intensive care."

"May I see him?"

"Only if he allows it."

"Ask him."

A half-hour later, permission is granted. Tara finds Siyabonga in bed, bandaged, pale, but awake. His eyes brighten, then cloud.

"Mama?"

"I don't know yet."

"Let's speak with our minds," he says. *Safer.*

Speak.

Had to be the Mongrels. Maybe the Americans. Could've been any gang. We're targets for all of them.

You didn't sense it coming?

No. They created a diversion. One group approached, yelling threats meant to draw us in. The shooters were behind us. I recognized faces from multiple gangs. Must be a pact. Their disappointment that you weren't with us was palpable.

You were not the real target.

Exactly. Go see Mama. Then come back.

I will.

He grasps her hand. *Be careful.*

My powers are greater. We will see.

Will you seek revenge?

That's a human impulse. We will see.

If we let them erase us, there's no future.

Some argue that mercy is the only future.

This isn't about mercy. It's about survival.

We will see.

As Tara approaches the intensive care unit, she already knows: Kholwa is gone. The mind leaves no trace when death claims it. She turns back.

Siyabonga sees her face. "I know."

"I'm sorry."

Tears spill down his cheeks. "Use me. However you need."

"If that becomes necessary, I will. You'll recover—but it'll take time. I have ideas for how you can help. Rest for now."

She gives him a meaningful look. *I just announced where I'm going. Let's see if spies are listening.*

Good. My heart aches. Use me.

Not for revenge?

He sobs. *Yes, for revenge. Maybe there's still too much human in me.*

Yes.

Tara boards the bus, barely noticing the motion as the city slides past the window, her mind awash in strategy and uncertainty. If she strikes too hard, the government will wake. If she does nothing, the gangs will strike again. There's no safety in either. Only the narrow way, the razor's edge Altan once warned her about, seems possible now. Her kind are too few, too visible. She cannot act with fury, yet she cannot stand idle. She must act. But how?

That night, she lies staring at the ceiling, arms folded across her chest as if holding herself together. She runs through the options again and again, but none feel right, only necessary. Outside, sirens rise and fall like an endless procession of wailing mourners. The city feels hollowed out. Corruption runs through its bones, drugs and humans traded for blood and profit in a cycle that keeps turning the endless wheel: gangs feeding prisons, feeding gangs, feeding prisons. The good get buried. The cruel dictate.

She feels the weight of it pressing down, but she won't let it crush her. She can't. Her kind have come too far to fall back into the old patterns. Power must stay precise. Disciplined. She thinks of Unit 731, and what happens when precision is lost . . . when pain becomes the point.

She won't let that happen. Not on her watch. The cut must be surgical. Quiet. Exact. And soon.

I bearded the lion once. I can do it again.

Her last thoughts drift to Kholwa. Not guilt. But sorrow. The sorrow one feels for a loyal animal, struck down by the world it could not escape.

She falls asleep to the requiem mass of sirens and the howl of a planet on fire.

~ *Coda* ~

Night listens. A seed moves beneath the pavement, testing the crack. If her kind multiplies with mercy equal to might, the human story won't end in slaughter but in transfiguration. The old text will fade as the new script writes itself in quiet hands and compassionate hearts. If hunger outpaces empathy, the fire will consume scribe and scripture alike.

For now, one blade works the wound, cutting clean and exact—and the world, bleeding, begins to staunch.

But larger wounds may not yield to scalpel,
Nor rivers of blood to clot.

Chapter Six

Confrontations and Consequences

African Agony

In the morning, Tara stops by the hospital to see Siyabonga and deliver her plan telepathically. This time, she tells him, she will walk into the Mongrels' headquarters unannounced. Whatever happens next, she will accept. Either they cease their violence, or they face the consequences. Their response will determine their fate. Though still in pain, Siyabonga insists on going with her.

"No," Tara says aloud. "You would be be a liability. You're still healing. You must stay."

He smiles. *I'm not worried about you. I just want to see the look on their faces when you show up.*

Will it change anything?

No, he admits. *But still worth it.*

Why?

If you save even one. . . .

Tara exhales sharply. *And for every one saved, thousands are bred into violence—through fists, through words, through drugs, through neglect.*

Frustrated, Siyabonga shifts to spoken words. "One becomes the many. Ignoring them isn't an option for those of us who've lived under their boot. If a dog were trapped in a burning house—just one dog—you'd still try to save it. Not because it's all dogs. Just to stop its suffering. Right?"

A nearby patient snorts. "Bullshit, bru. Why get burned for a dog? It's just a dog."

"Dog has feelings," Siyabonga says calmly.

"Shiiittt. Dog's a dog. Ain't nothin' but a dog."

Siyabonga studies him more closely. Gang tattoos wrap the man's arms like shackles. He glances at Tara—*listen to this*—then addresses the patient again.

"Would you save a person in a burning house?"

"Depends."

"On what?"

"If he a bru."

"You mean, someone from your gang?"

"Shit, now you get it. No one else means shit."

"Your mama?"

"Hell no. She dead. Good riddance. Drunken whore."

A long silence settles. Then Siyabonga gestures to Tara.

"You recognize this woman?"

"'Course. She a witch." His voice drops to a near whisper. "And she gonna pay her dues soon enough."

"You're not afraid of her?"

"Hell, no." He sits up in bed, spreading his arms. "Do your worst, bitch."

Tara approaches slowly, her expression unreadable.

"What if I took one of your arms?"

"Then I shoot you with the other."

"And the other?"

"Then I stomp you with my feet."

"And your legs?"

"I find a way to kill you. Count on it. I hear you two whisperin'. You against us. Anyone don't like us dies. You gonna die."

She stands at the edge of his bed, eyes cold. "What if I made you disappear right now?"

This time, he shrinks back, silent.

"You're just a boy," she says softly. "All noise. But desperate to live. Desperate to be loved. Silly boy—I'd still save you if you were trapped in a burning house."

He scowls, petulant. "Save yourself, bitch. You gonna die."

Tara knows it's all posturing. Her hump tingles with the friction inside him, the war between self-preservation and performative loyalty. She probes deeper. Beneath the surface bravado lies something far more tragic. He was raped, multiple times, by a gang captain. His punishment for failing to complete a hit. He'd been ordered to kill, but couldn't. For that weakness, he became a target. First by the captain, then passed among the others. Raped, beaten, broken. Over time, he submitted. Resistance meant death. The gang labeled him "a woman"—a slave, a domestic servant, a nothing. Wash clothes. Fetch food. Stay silent. Tara reads the truth: this boy lives in terror of his own gang, yet is required to show no fear to the world outside it. His only proof of allegiance is the ritual of bluster. His only peace, the haze of narcotics. Never once has he known a touch of kindness. Every human gesture he's received has come soaked in hate, fear, contempt, or violence. The borders of his world are no wider than a grave, and the dirt keeps filling it.

And yet, strangely, it is this encounter, not the threat, but the brokenness, that steels Tara's resolve. She will walk into the belly of the beast. She will face the Mongrels in the only language they understand: overwhelming power, sharpened by ruthlessness. They will see what cannot be resisted. Still, she decides to wait. Word will spread of her return. Let them stew. Let them wonder what's coming. In the meantime, she plans to lie low and consult again with Altan.

As she leaves the hospital, Siyabonga's silent pleas trail behind her.

~ Fossils ~

The next day, she meets Altan at the Iziko South African Museum, far from the suspicious eyes of the Flats. They sit on a bench before a display of ancient fossils, bones from epochs past, caught in the stillness of extinction.

You really think this is wise? Altan asks, his voice flattened as always.

The time has come.

Your brain says otherwise. He pauses. *There's decreased activity in your dorsolateral prefrontal cortex, elevated levels in your medial prefrontal cortex, possibly emotional override. And your corpus quadrittourium is glowing like a flare. Given all this, you still believe your decision is sound?*

I've already factored it in.

In that case, I'll make arrangements to get you out of the country as soon as it's over.

And if I don't leave? What about Siyabonga? The others?

He shrugs. *They'll be left to the wolves.*

Then I stay.

You can't stay forever.

Then what do you suggest?

I don't. This is your proving ground now. No simulations. No safety nets. No one knows where this path leads.

Tara's jaw tightens. *The decision is made.*

Then I'll prepare for all contingencies.

Yes. But I may not use them right away.

Altan raises an eyebrow, but says nothing.

Have you heard from Mama?

I have. She ran into trouble. The FBI is watching again.

Tara jerks. *What happened?*

It's over for now. She and your father are safe. But things remain complicated. Focus on what's ahead. You'll need clarity when the dominoes start to fall.

He looks at her for a long moment.

Remember what I said about your brain, Tara. This isn't a test anymore. It's the beginning of whatever comes next—if there is a next.

~ Into the Den ~

By the time Tara reaches the crumbling house that serves as Mongrel headquarters, a crowd has already gathered. Gang members, their women, and curious onlookers press in behind her, murmuring threats and obscenities. So thick is the psychic sludge that floods her hump, she closes it to all but the most immediate threats. Two guards stand between her and the door. One shouts a code word. A hand waves her in. She turns once, catching a last glimpse of the jeering crowd—smirks, taunts, unreadable stares—then the door slams shut behind her. Inside, a dozen gang members block the entrance hall. No one speaks. They posture, flex, flash weapons, make obscene gestures—all of it silent, as if they were actors in a mute drama waiting for the cue to strike.

Tara doesn't wait. The shouted command comes from a back room, too late.

In an instant, every weapon in the room vanishes. As confusion breaks into shouts, four of the most brutal charge her. They, too, vanish before contact. Panic erupts. The rest stampede toward the exit, clawing over one another in a blind rush for the door. In seconds, the house is emptied.

Except for one.

Tara senses a mind still present, buried somewhere inside, wild with fear, thoughts fragmented and jagged. She walks calmly through the wreckage. Drug paraphernalia, rotting garbage, the usual ruin. She follows the pulse of terror to a closet. Dissociating any weapons that may be trained on the door, she opens it slowly. Inside, huddled in a corner, is a young girl. Likely a gang slave. Shivering, skeletal, unable to speak. Tara offers a gentle smile, then turns at the sound of sirens screeching to a halt outside.

She strides to the front door just as police burst in, guns raised.

"Hands up!"

She complies. They throw her to the floor, cuff her, and shove her into a patrol car.

As she sits against the hard plastic interior, Tara considers her options. She could disappear the cuffs, dissolve the car, walk away. But the irony amuses her: police summoned to rescue a gang from a girl with a hump. She allows herself a smile.

She leans back and begins to formulate her next step.

~ Custody ~

The police do as expected. Tara is thrown into a holding cell, interrogated without pause, and denied sleep through hourly visits meant to wear her down. They question her about the disappearances. She plays dumb, suggesting hallucinations—drug-induced delusions among the gang members.

Where are the missing men? She shrugs.

People don't just vanish. She shakes her head in confusion.

The police are confounded. No bodies. No blood. No signs of violence. Only the lingering terror of gang members once feared, now stammering like orphaned children. The story makes no sense. But neither do the facts.

Spurred by bribes from gang-affiliated allies, the officers press harder, grasping for answers that make sense. But her American citizenship shields her from the worst. No torture. Just relentless pressure.

In the end, they have nothing. Only ghosts. And questions that refuse to have answers.

She's held a few more days, long enough to save face, then brought in for one final interview.

She walks in, calm and composed, and finds a familiar face waiting.

~ *International Intrigue* ~

Agent Lance Romellion sits behind a long table, flanked by two South African detectives. He smiles as she enters.

"Hello, Tara Powers. I'm Agent Lance Romellion, FBI. It's been a few years. You were a little girl when you vanished into a cave in the California desert with your mother. Do you remember?"

Tara reads him before he finishes. His thoughts a swirl of suspicion, uncertainty, and ambition. No clear belief. Just a desire for control.

"You must be close to retirement by now, Agent Romellion."

"I was. Until your mother reappeared. Now, I think I'll stay."

"Questions?"

Romellion flips through a thick folder. "You've already answered the obvious ones. Anything to add before we begin?"

"No."

"Let's start simple: how do you make things disappear?"

"I can't."

"Limbs?"

"I can't."

"People?"

"I can't."

"Then explain this: your grandmother, your mother, and now you, all present during incidents where a hunchback woman makes objects and people vanish. Coincidence?"

"I have no explanation."

"And you expect us to believe that?"

"If powers like that existed, don't you think we'd all know about them by now?"

Romellion leans forward. "You're not answering the question."

"Isn't South Africa outside your jurisdiction?"

He waves a hand dismissively. "This is bigger than borders."

"You think we have powers?"

"I think the reports speak for themselves."

Tara reads his mind again. The next question arrives before he speaks it.

"Not possible for humans," Romellion says. "But are you human, Ms. Powers?"

The South African detectives shift in their seats, uncomfortable.

Tara laughs. "Last I checked, yes."

Romellion abruptly jerks his hand from under the table and hurls an object at her. She sees it coming, but allows it to strike just enough to feign surprise. It bounces off her cheek and lands on the table.

A soft whiffle ball.

"Really?" she says coldly. "Is this the FBI's new interrogation method?"

Romellion flushes but forces a smile. "Just testing a theory. No harm done, I hope."

"Only to your reputation."

His composure slips. "We know you can do something unique, something incredibly destructive. The evidence is overwhelming."

She scans his thoughts. No trace of betrayal from her father. Good.

"So, your grand theory is that I'm not human?"

"Maybe not fully."

"Alien?"

"Possibly."

She spreads her arms. "Look closely. What do you see?"

"I see someone the federal government considers a security concern."

She turns to the South African detectives. "Am I a threat to your country?"

"Not at this time," says the senior officer, amused.

"Then I commend your restraint. Apparently, your country doesn't criminalize trying to stop gang violence. Nor, I assume, do you question my humanity?"

"You are human," says the detective. "And unless Agent Romellion has more questions, you are free to go."

Romellion clenches his jaw. "We will continue our investigation."

"You do that," Tara says, already on her way out.

She catches his thoughts one last time: grinding frustration, impotent fury. She smiles.

~ *Thandolwethu* ~

Once released, Tara receives troubling news.

One of the men she had dissociated during the raid was Mpho, the son of Thandolwethu, the street vendor who had once offered her a mango and a blessing. The news arrives quietly, without emphasis, but it grips her. She cancels her departure. The work she came to do is not done. The wound she opened has not closed.

With Siyabonga's help, she locates Thandolwethu's neighborhood on the edge of the township. Her stall, once a fixed point in the shifting noise of the market, now stands empty. Days pass. No one knows where she's gone. A few speak of a collapse, a sudden vanishing. No ambulance. No funeral. Just absence.

Eventually, Tara finds her.

The shack sits at the end of a dirt path littered with broken glass and wind-blown scraps. The door hangs crooked on rusted hinges. Inside, the air is thick—stale and sour. The smell of spoiled food, human waste, and something harder to name presses against her senses.

That evening, cloaked in darkness, Tara knocks once. No reply. But her hump vibrates faintly—grief, deep and uninterrupted, trembles in the walls.

She pushes open the door.

Inside, the silence has weight. The space is dim. Piles of trash clutter the corners. Empty bottles roll across the floor. A small cooking pot is overturned beside a rotting onion. In the back, a faint sound, moaning and irregular, draws her forward.

In the far room, Thandolwethu lies on a stained mattress, barely more than a silhouette against the crumbling wall. Her body is thin. Her skin clings to the bone. Her eyes flutter, then close again.

Tara kneels beside the bed.

"Thandolwethu," she whispers.

A shudder passes through the old woman, but no words come.

"It's me. Tara."

The lids open again, slowly. Recognition dawns—not as light, but as rupture. Tears slip down her sunken cheeks.

The moaning continues. Wordless. Tired.

Tara feels the pulse of pain registering across the woman's neural field—irregular, sharp, unrelenting. It is not just grief. It is collapse.

"You need food," Tara says.

The voice that answers is hoarse, cracked with hatred.

"Go away, witch."

"You need care."

"Go." Her breath catches. "You kill my son. You devil-woman."

Tara receives the accusation without protest. It lands where it should, beneath the skin, into the blood. Still, she rises and begins to clean.

The trash first. Then the scattered dishes. The worst of the rot is quietly removed. She works without looking for thanks, her hands steady, her face blank.

"Go away," the old woman mutters again.

Tara does not respond. A pot of soup begins to simmer on the small gas stove.

"How he die?" Thandolwethu asks suddenly, her voice stripped bare. "How?"

Tara turns from the sink, water dripping from her hands. She waits a moment.

"Painlessly."

"You sure?"

"I promise."

The words fall into the space between them like a thread pulled tight.

"My boy was good," the woman says. "Before the drugs. Before the streets. Sweet baby. Soft boy. Why you kill him?"

Tara places the bowl beside the bed.

"Sit up," she says. "You need to eat."

She helps her lift her head. Slowly, spoon by spoon, she feeds her.

"You feel guilty?" Thandolwethu asks, voice dull with fatigue.

Tara hesitates.

"I don't know guilt," she says. "Only suffering. And how to lessen it."

"You strange," the woman murmurs. "Witch or no, you strange."

"So I've been told."

"What are you?"

Tara wipes the corners of her mouth.

"The beginning of the end."

A pause.

"What?"

Tara doesn't answer.

Then, unexpectedly, a faint smile flickers across the woman's mouth. It is small. Dry. Real.

"What you think of Siyabonga?"

Tara remains quiet.

"You sweet on him?"

"He seems . . . suitable."

"He strange. Like you."

"How?"

"Eyes see, ears hear, heart aches. Quiet boy. Lonely. Girls want him. Always leave disappointed."

"Why?"

"His roots hate water. All withered branches and leaves inside. Looks like he want love, but he don't drink."

The words settle.

"You and him," she says, eyes half-closed, "same egg, I think. Both strange."

"He ever have a girlfriend?"

"None that stayed. 'Cept maybe you?"

"Eat more soup."

"No. Tired now. Can't hate you. Tried. But you remind me of him. Go now."

She turns her head to the wall. The room falls still.

Tara finishes cleaning. She leaves the soup on the stove, the bed tucked, the floor cleared. The worst of the smell has lifted. Outside, the night is wide and still.

She walks back to her apartment slowly.

Her thoughts circle but do not settle. She wants to speak to Altan. She wants the voice that steadies her.

She sends out silent requests, clairvoyant threads cast to the names she once leaned on: Sy, Lady Oracle, Ming-huà, Zookeeper, Jared, Pythia.

Nothing returns.

But when she arrives home, Altan is already waiting.

She tells him everything: the interrogation, the agents, the voices, the old woman in the shack. He listens without interruption.

Then, at last, she asks:

"Altan. What's happening with my mother?"

For a long moment, he says nothing. Then something shifts in his face, a flicker of sorrow behind the control.

"Well," he says. "Here's what happened."

Chapter Seven

Time of Reckoning

Sweet Siyabonga

Altan leans back into the couch, his voice low and unhurried. "Several weeks ago, in Berkeley. Pythia was with Jared. It was late. They'd just left a restaurant and were walking to their car when three men came at them with knives. She dissociated the blades, but two of them tackled Jared to the ground. Another knife emerged and she dealt with that too. Then the third man drew a gun and shot Jared. So, she made him disappear. The others fled."

He pauses.

"Is Jared dead?" Tara asks.

"No. Hospitalized."

"Condition?"

"Flesh wound. He'll recover."

Tara exhales. "It's happened before. There was no other choice, right?"

"Unfortunately," Altan says. "By the time she erased the shooter, bystanders had arrived, and one filmed everything. That video now belongs to the police. And inevitably, to the FBI. The entire federal apparatus is now watching us. A host of Lance Romellians is on the loose."

"So that explains his visit. Is Pythia in custody?"

"No. She's a listed victim. But the dissociation is on video."

"Then propagation becomes urgent."

Altan gives his habitual shrug. "Yes. Are you pregnant?"

"I believe so."

"Siyabonga?"

"Yes."

"He is an intermediate. The child must be protected at all costs."

"Yes. But with the U.S. government now focused on all of us, how long before they reach the conclusion we already know is true? Romellian believes we're not human."

"There's still deniability. The video may be dismissed, it's grainy, implausible, easily doctored. Pythia continues to deny. But the story is wearing thin. Romellian and his cohort believe they've stumbled on something exceptional. And they have."

Tara nods grimly. "They're right."

"Indeed."

"How do we proceed?"

Altan turns his eyes on her. "Tara, you are no longer in need of my roadmap. Your ancestors once found their way through the chaos of rival hominins and prowling beasts. You must do the same."

"You're leaving."

"Yes."

"Forever?"

"No. But for a time, I'll be unreachable."

She stiffens. "Without your counsel, I could fail—spectacularly."

"You won't be alone. Sy. Lady Oracle. Ming-huà. Zookeeper. Jared. Pythia. Siyabonga. And intermediates, many more than you know. Use them."

"Should we all retreat to the cave?"

Altan shrugs again. "The universe resists the certainty inherent in the best-laid plans."

~ *Reversal* ~

The next day, Thandolwethu is found dead, stabbed to death by gang members seeking revenge. Her blood is used to scrawl "traitor to her son" across the wall of her room.

Unaware, Tara waits in her apartment when Siyabonga arrives, fresh from the hospital. Wincing with each movement, he accepts tea, takes a sip, and then says flatly, "Thandolwethu is dead. Murdered."

"I know," Tara replies. "Your thoughts were loud and clear the moment you arrived. I'm sorry."

He stares into his cup. "Are we to blame?"

"Yes. Which is why I must leave."

"Why?" he asks, stunned.

She does not answer right away.

Her eyes drop, not in shame, but in acknowledgment. The weight of it is too old to carry with the posture of righteousness. When she finally speaks, it is not with anger, nor pride, but with the tired precision of one who has revisited this truth too many times to count.

She speaks in silence, the words forming not in air, but in thought, direct and unmistakable.

Relieving suffering has created more suffering. Again and again. We tried intervention. We tried restraint. We tried education, infiltration, transparency, removal, redistribution, redemption. The gangs return. The leaders are replaced.

The structures adapt. When we cleanse one system, another arises, hungrier, more adaptable, and less visible. We remove a tyrant, and in the vacuum, something more chaotic arrives. We seed compassion, and it is weaponized. We distribute resources, and they are hoarded anew.

She pauses.

The variables shift. The outcome does not.

He watches her, disbelieving. Not because the words are unclear but because they are *too* clear.

Our simulations always led to the same place," she continues. *"A few are saved. A few flourish. But many die. Always. And among the dead, the ones most often sacrificed are the ones least prepared for sacrifice: the children, the quiet ones, the ones who did not ask to be born into systems built on extraction and delusion. Innocents are not just collateral. They are currency. This is the hidden engine of your civilization.*

The air around them stills, as if the world itself has stopped to listen.

"You ask why," she says aloud, "but you already know. It is not a question of cruelty. It is a question of structure. The primitive neurology of Homo sapiens ensures repetition. Ensures escalation. You are governed not by your ideals, but by the amygdala. The survival circuits. The tribal circuits. Fear and hierarchy. Story and violence. Pattern recognition turned into prophecy. Empathy choked by scarcity.

"Even your saints, your reformers, your visionaries, what happened to them? Exiled. Mocked. Crucified. Or worse—turned into brands."

Her voice dims to almost a whisper.

"There was a time when we believed guidance could work. That with enough patience, you might rewire yourselves from within. We underestimated the resistance, not of the corrupt, but of the well-meaning. Even the good cling to the frameworks that destroy them. They mistake stability for virtue. And they fear change more than they fear extinction."

She lifts her gaze to meet his, again projecting her thoughts into his mind.

The only path forward is out and up. Out of this species. Out of this self-replicating error. Out of inherited delusion. And up into what comes next. Up the ladder. Not toward domination, but toward coherence. Toward a way of being that does not require a thousand graves to fertilize its ideals.

He says nothing.

Because he can think of nothing left to defend that does not echo the very structure she has already named.

They stand in the silence that follows, not as opponents, not yet as allies, but as two beings separated by an evolutionary threshold. And the air between them is filled not with hatred, but with the terrible intimacy of shared recognition.

But even now, doubt lingers in a quiet, unresolved, unwillingness to let go.

Then, quietly he says, "And the killings? The disappearances? The ones who defied you, or who simply got in your way?"

Tara doesn't flinch. Her gaze does not shift.

"You're asking whether doves should carry claws."

He nods once. "Yes."

She steps closer, not with threat, but with clarity.

"We carry them because the hawks taught us what happens to the unarmed. We carry them because the meek, left undefended, become martyrs. And the strong, left unchecked, become tyrants in disguise."

"But if you become violent—"

"We don't become violent," she says. "Violence is the atmosphere. We've simply learned to navigate it without self-erasure."

She breathes once, slow and deep.

"Compassion without defense becomes spectacle. Pity without strategy becomes permission. We didn't come to punish. But we did come to stop the machinery of inherited cruelty. That means removing what feeds it. And sometimes, yes . . . that means ending lives that only know how to devour others."

Siyabonga looks down.

"They'll call you monsters."

"They already do. But the real monsters have always been the ones who hide behind laws, behind flags, behind balance sheets and bloodlines. We walk openly. We name what we end."

She pauses, then adds more gently:

"We would prefer not to. But we've seen what happens when we wait for the old world to correct itself. It doesn't. It recalibrates its horrors. Makes them harder to see. That's not evolution. That's camouflage."

He studies her for a long moment.

Then he nods, not in agreement, but in understanding. The air between them is not reconciled, but cleared.

And in that space, something older than justice begins to take shape. Something Tara has never spoken aloud, but which lives in her: A new morality must be born with teeth.

Siyabonga shifts slightly, processing.

"Otherwise Siyabonga," she says. "It will be devoured like all the others."

Although Siyabonga says nothing, his silence signals his unwillingness to capitulate entirely.

"I'm carrying your child," Tara says abruptly.

His face brightens, stunned into joy. "So soon? You're sure?"

"I am sure."

"There is a future!" he shouts.

"Yes. And it must be preserved."

"Then I must go with you!"

"Immigration to the U.S. is difficult. Nearly impossible now."

"I'll get a visa."

"How?"

"Multiple entry. I've looked into it before. I have a friend in the ministry. It's expensive, but I can do it."

Tara considers. "I know people. They're adept at these things. Maybe it's possible."

He grins slyly. "Then we must make more babies . . . for the cause."

She smiles. "For the cause."

"So . . . perhaps now might be—"

"No, Siyabonga. I'm already with child, and our gestation differs. Besides, you're still healing. And more urgently, I sense danger. You must not return home. You'll be killed."

He frowns. "I've always been on good terms with the gangs—"

"That's over. Your mother is dead. You've been shot. Don't be foolish. You're a marked man."

Siyabonga falls silent, but the thought of joining Tara in the U.S. makes his heart race.

"We leave tonight," she says with finality.

"Tonight! I need to pack."

Tara tilts her head, listening past the walls. "No. Stay here. I hear them. They smell blood. They're waiting. You'll never make it back."

Siyabonga pales. *Are you sure?*

Certain. They're gathering. Drug-fueled. Eager for violence. They want to skin you alive. Only their fear of me keeps them from storming in. I won't make more people vanish unless I must.

The world outside has already made its choice. It cannot be reasoned with, only survived or surpassed.

Tara listens not just to the men crouched beyond the walls, but to the long pattern behind them: the centuries of blood, the machinery of fear, the ritual slaughter of anyone who dared to evolve.

She will not beg for peace from those who do not understand it. She will not offer her neck to history's grinding teeth. Not to appease the past. Not to slow the future.

She lays a hand on her abdomen. The heartbeat there is faint but steady, newly forming and already aware. The world does not know his name yet, but it will. He is not a weapon. Not a savior. Not a myth. He is the next step. The answer to a question humanity could never ask without shattering.

Abassi.

She does not speak the name aloud. Not yet. But it lives in her now, immutable.

The child must live. Not for legacy, but for correction.

She turns to Siyabonga.

"I won't make more people vanish unless I must."

And with that, the future begins to move.

~ *Flight* ~

They remain in the apartment through the night.

Neither sleeps. The silence stretches between them, not hostile, not resigned, just steady. Siyabonga tends to his wound, moving stiffly. Tara paces, listens, recalibrates. Outside, the streets hiss and clatter. A motorcycle passes. A dog whines. Somewhere in the distance, a woman yells, and the sound is swallowed by engine noise.

They speak little.

Before dawn, when the light is still no more than a faint outline behind the sky, they slip out through the rear entrance. No suitcase. No visible luggage. Just what they carry inside. The alleyways are narrow and uneven, littered with glass and sleeping dogs. Tara walks ahead, her senses sharp. Her hump registers nothing immediate, but the field is volatile and uncertain. Like walking across the crust of a cooling bomb.

They move through Nyanga's perimeter quietly, passing from territory to territory. A few men watch them from doorways. Some whisper. Some say nothing. No one follows.

At a bus stop with a cracked bench and a sagging roof, they sit.

Neither speaks. The air is cold and dry. A distant siren fades.

Then Tara straightens, both hands rising to her temples.

Siyabonga turns to her instantly.

"What is it?" he whispers.

She doesn't respond aloud.

What's wrong?

They're here.

How many?

Four. Armed. Heavily.

Siyabonga leans forward, eyes narrowing. Across the empty street, figures shift in the gloom. It's not clear at first whether they're random passersby or something more deliberate. Then he sees the outline of a rifle. Another man scanning the rooftops.

What do we do?

Wait for the bus.

She is trying not to dissociate. She is trying to keep to her promise, not for strategy, but for memory. Thandolwethu. A woman left alone in her grief, stabbed by men who thought vengeance could honor the dead. Tara will not repeat that cycle here unless there is no alternative.

But her hump flares in quick pulses, sharp and clustered.

She rises halfway from the bench. Ready.

Then, sudden bursts of gunfire erupt down the block. Short. Controlled. Followed by screams and scattering feet. Tara reaches out with her mind, sifts the wave of confusion. It isn't them. The shooters are not here for her, not for Siyabonga. A turf dispute. Narcotics. Payback for an earlier betrayal. She recognizes the pattern. She's seen it before—in Lagos, in Bogotá, in Detroit.

And then, silence. Just like that. The gunfire ends.

Two bodies remain in the street, but no one approaches them.

Headlights appear. The bus arrives.

Without speaking, they climb aboard. Tara pays the fare. Siyabonga moves to the rear, keeping his injured side guarded. They sit. The driver doesn't look at them. No one else is aboard.

"That was close," Siyabonga says quietly.

Tara nods. *Yes. I'm glad I didn't have to use my powers. That was for Thandolwethu's memory.*

And my mother's, he adds.

Truly spoken.

He places a hand over hers.

"We're safe. Our baby is safe," he says aloud.

Tara doesn't answer right away. Her eyes remain on the window.

"No," she says. "Not yet. Not at all."

"What do you mean?"

She turns slightly, her voice flat.

"Nowhere is safe. Not anymore."

Outside, the city begins to change. The streets widen. Traffic thickens. Billboards rise like monuments to vanishing certainty. Cape Town is waking up.

They fall into silence. Not the silence of resolution. The silence of transit. The world has not collapsed. It continues. But they are no longer a part of its old rhythm.

And ahead, something waits.

Not safety. Not sanctuary.

Only what comes next.

~ *Night and Day* ~

Cape Town crashes around her.

It's not just noise. It's not just movement. It's the crush of inputs—visual, auditory, psychic—all of it converging without order. Crowds swell at intersections, each body radiating hunger, fatigue, agitation. Cars swerve, idle, honk. Engines snarl. Sirens pass too close, always too close. Pedestrians shout, laugh, shove, sell, plead. The air smells of exhaust, fried meat, perfume, sweat, solvents. Her hump absorbs it all, channeling the signals without filter. Her nervous system begins to spike.

Tara closes her eyes and pinches the intake of signals, not fully, just enough to stop the worst of it. She locates the neural valve at the base of her skull and constricts it. The hum lowers. The spikes flatten. Her vision steadies. The flood is now a stream, just barely manageable.

But the city continues. The city does not care.

White tourists roam in tightly controlled orbits, taking photographs of things they don't understand. Local scammers stand at street corners, their smiles rehearsed, their scripts adapted to skin tone and accent. Some succeed. Some do not. But all of them are operating inside the same closed circuit: extraction, denial, transaction.

It weighs on her. Not just the desperation, but the choreography of it: how pain has been turned into currency. How everyone here is trading on damage.

She slips into a hotel through a rear entrance. No names. No questions. Cash.

Inside, the air changes. The lobby is sleek, insulated, mute. Bellboys stand at attention. The front desk speaks in prepackaged tones. Behind the facade, another machinery hums—that of surveillance, protocol, and service. But here, at least, there is quiet.

Her room is high up. Thick carpet. Neutral walls. A sealed window with a partial view of Table Mountain and the rooftops below. She closes the curtains.

The hum of the air conditioning is constant. Mechanical, sterile. But it is better than the shrill static of the outside world. Here, she can think. Here, she can breathe.

Siyabonga takes the adjoining room. He comes and goes, chasing signatures, permits, connections, each one more fragile than the last. Some mornings, he returns from the ministry with a face drawn in frustration. Other days, there is progress. A stamped form. A code. An invitation to speak to someone "in charge." It is a dance. He knows the rhythm.

Tara does not join him. She remains cloistered.

She eats alone. Drinks tea in silence. Keeps her body still for hours. Monitors the infant pulse growing inside her. The life that must be protected. She reviews data from Ming-huà. Newsfeeds. Agency movements. Legal briefs. Leaks. Deniability is thinning. The American machinery has begun to adjust its aim. The Romellians are multiplying. The lies are getting more elaborate. And more brittle.

She wishes for contact with her own kind. For Sy's dry wit. For Lady Oracle's strange aphorisms. For Zookeeper's unnerving precision. But they are absent.

Altan has not returned.

But he has left her resources. A U.S. bank account. Clean, discreet, and funded. It will be enough to move forward.

For now, there is only this: stillness made fragile by proximity to chaos. She floats inside it, not fully trusting its silence.

But she does not break it, either.

The time for movement is near. She can feel it. Not in thought, but in pressure. The next phase is assembling just beyond the edge of the visible.

It doesn't last.

One afternoon, the front desk calls.

"Yes?"

"Ms. Powers?"

"Yes."

"There's a woman in the lobby asking for you."

"Name?"

A pause. Paper rustles.

"Busisine Okoro."

Tara closes her eyes. "Tell her I'm unavailable."

"I'm afraid she's quite insistent. She also has a young man in a wheelchair with her."

Still holding the phone, Tara extends her clairvoyant focus. The lobby sharpens within her mind's eye. Thato is slumped in the chair, handless and broken. Beside him, his mother, crouches in readiness. Poised. Not grief-stricken, but primed for confrontation.

For a flicker of a moment, Tara contemplates ending it cleanly and invisibly. But reality offers no such mercy. It is not time.

"I'll be right down," she says.

She throws on a wrap, takes the stairs, using each step to seal off unnecessary thought. She arrives in the lobby just as the scream erupts.

"There be the demon!"

It repeats, louder each time. "Demon! Demon! Demon!"

Tara keeps walking. There is no shock in this moment. Only weariness. The pattern is familiar: aggrieved parent, maimed child, public rage. A formula repeated in every culture that cannot accept its own violence.

The temptation arises, brief and sharp, to wish the species gone. To let the planet exhale. But that wish is forbidden. She was made to endure them, not erase them.

"Demon woman!" Busisine shrieks. "You put back Thato's hands and manhood! Put back what you took!"

Tara stops before them. The boy in the chair, once overflowing with cruelty, now shrinks from the light. Eyes dulled. Posture slumped. The psychic damage is worse than the physical. What was taken from him was not just dominance, but belief in his invulnerability.

"Mrs. Okoro, I'm not responsible. I cannot return what I did not take."

"Demon! You mean you won't! What am I to do with him now? He will die! Because of you!"

Onlookers circle. A hotel manager appears.

"Madame," he says, tone clipped but professional. "You must take this outside. Now."

Busisine ignores him. Her voice climbs into a desperate howl. Then she sees Siyabonga enter from the street.

"Traitor!" she screams. "Slave of the demon! Traitor!"

Even Thato, from his sunken posture, shows a flicker of returning rage—but says nothing.

Siyabonga walks to Tara without breaking stride. She slips a roll of bills into his palm. Then he turns to Busisine and begins speaking Afrikaans, slow and steady. He does not argue. He doesn't confront. He explains. Gently. Persuasively.

Bit by bit, her hysteria folds inward. The anger doesn't vanish, but it recedes. The bills help. The voice helps more.

He wheels Thato out of the lobby. Busisine follows, still muttering, her cries duller now. Less righteous. More confused. They vanish into the city.

That evening, Tara and Siyabonga share a bottle of wine in her room.

"Any luck with the visa?" she asks.

"Not yet. Working on it."

"Need more help?"

She means money. He nods once.

"Soon. I'll let you know."

But he senses something else in her now, a tight grief she does not name. The residue of too many accusations, too much human noise.

Why so sad?

A bittersweet melancholy.

For what?

My own kind.

He sets down his glass. "I'm just an intermediate, but I'm here."

"I know. And I'm grateful. But being surrounded by humans is exhausting. If they're not violent outwardly, they're roiling inwardly. Always at war with themselves."

"Isn't that true of all species?"

"To a degree. But humans amplify it. They export it. They feed it through language. They turn private pain into systems."

He watches her. "Do you believe we'll make a better world?"

"One can hope."

He smiles; a rare, unguarded smile. "We will. For our child. And all the ones to come."

Tara does not contradict him. But she does not echo the certainty either.

"We have other matters," she says. "The FBI."

"What about them?"

"We're being watched. Constantly."

"So? We've done nothing wrong. You were cleared. What can they do?"

"In the name of national security?" Her laugh is dry. "Almost anything. Frame us. Disappear us. Experiment on us."

"You'd never let that happen. With your powers—"

"Siyabonga, a lion is no match for a man with a gun. But a man with a gun is no match for a hundred lions."

He looks at his empty glass.

"More wine?" she asks, her eyes gentler now. "There's more than one of us, you know."

He smiles again. It's smaller, but real.

Then he grows still. "Tara . . . do you love me?"

She has been expecting this. *Can't you read my mind?*

Not clearly. I'm an intermediate. Your mind is deep. It resists me.

Exclusive love for one being above all is alien to our nature. I love you as I love the whole.

"But surely you have preferences."

"Of course. A certain dog, its markings. A certain tone of voice. A certain stillness in someone's presence. But preference is not loyalty. It's not blindness. It's not tribal fever."

He sighs, playfully crestfallen. "So you love me . . . preferentially."

She touches his hand. "Yes. Your markings please me."

He raises his glass with a half-smile. "To my markings."

"To your markings," she echoes, smiling with something close to tenderness.

No matter what she says, he finds comfort in her nearness, especially in the quiet truth that she carries his child.

"And what kind of child will we produce?" he wonders aloud.

Tara turns to him, voice even, but final.

"He or she will be wondrous."

~ *Breakaway* ~

Two weeks pass.

Tara waits. Her conscience is clear, cleaned, not through justification, but through clarity. Yet she can delay no longer. The time to return to the States has arrived.

Siyabonga remains behind, still caught in the final tangle of bureaucracy. Despite bribes, signatures, and ministry favors, one final stamp continues to elude him. Officials stall. Papers disappear. Promises fail to materialize. The process, designed to exhaust, is working as intended.

Tara is disappointed, but says little. She's learned to expect friction when moving between dying systems and emergent ones. Her thoughts drift now toward the life inside her—quiet, unshaped, and growing. She feels its presence not as emotion, but as pressure. A new gravity forming inside her.

Will this child truly be wondrous?

The question is not sentimental. It is observational. Each generation has brought more capacity—greater range, deeper resonance. Her own abilities exceed those of her mother. This child may exceed her in turn. But is there a threshold? A breaking point beyond which control begins to fray? What happens if empathy fails to keep pace with power? What arises when amplification outstrips conscience?

These questions do not disturb her, but they do return. She carries them the way others carry instinct: accessible, unresolved.

At the airport, she offers Siyabonga a long farewell. No tears. Just contact. Recognition. The shared understanding that their paths will soon converge again, and when they do, everything will have changed. She boards the plane.

Before takeoff, she senses the presence behind her. Male. Armed. Watching. An agent. Not even trying to blend. She scans his mind. What she finds is empty of conviction, only duty. The slow churn of protocol, suspicion, protocol again. He doesn't know what she is. He only knows he's meant to track her.

She turns to her internal arsenal. It would be easy. One interruption in neural flow. One blink of interference. He would cease to be. No struggle. No noise.

But she doesn't.

It would trigger panic. Investigations. A replacement. Then another. Then ten. The game would continue, and she would become the story rather than its architect. Visibility is not the goal. Survival is not the goal. Victory consists of quiet, irreversible displacement.

Let them vanish from thrones, not from life. Let them lose power, not breath. That is the only exit that leaves the world intact.

She settles into her seat. Watches the clouds rise.

Just as Homo sapiens once displaced their evolutionary kin, not through extermination, but through pressure, time, and adaptability, so now will they be displaced. Not through war. Through presence. Through intelligence. Through inevitability.

Still, she knows: recognition will come. At first as myth, then suspicion, then pattern. Sooner or later, they will understand. And then—

Her thoughts loop. Not from uncertainty, but from gravity. Her mentors raised the same concerns, but now the questions no longer feel abstract. They carry lived consequence. They taste of blood. Of history. Of inheritance.

Can Homo sapiens be saved?

Not by words. Not by science. Not by patience.

Not by mercy.

Not by anything but replacement.

And even that comes at a price.

~

The plane descends. The grids of San Francisco stretch across the land below. From above, it looks orderly. From below, she knows better. The illusions will resume the moment she steps off the plane.

She doesn't dwell on metaphysics. Not now. Her thoughts narrow to irritation: the crude metal frame, the combustion engines, the slow grind of descent. But she endures it.

Customs is uneventful. Her papers are perfect.

Beyond the gate, she sees them. Pythia and Jared. Waiting.

She moves to them quickly. They embrace. Smiles are exchanged. The forced kind that try to hold back all that has happened and all that still waits.

Pythia speaks first, silently. *We're being followed.*

Tara answers with equal calm. *Likewise.*

Jared leads them to the car. He drives without comment. The city slides past in wide arcs. In the back seat, Tara turns to her mother.

Is there a problem with Jared?

Yes.

Is he an informer?

No. We'll talk later.

It is enough. For now.

The mansion is unchanged. Its outer structure remains what it always was: a house, a refuge, a relic. But inside, it holds their future.

Tara unpacks, then joins the others in the downstairs lounge.

Lady Oracle is waiting. Sy too. Jared stands off to the side.

The conversation lasts for hours. Tara recounts what she must: Cape Town, Thandolwethu, the death, the money, the child, the gangs, the silence, the moments she nearly acted and didn't.

They listen. Questions surface. Some are sharp. Some are quiet. Sy makes wry comments. Pythia deflects. Lady Oracle observes without reaction. Jared watches them all with the intensity of someone trying to stay anchored.

Tara watches him in return.

There's something wrong. His thoughts don't track cleanly. His emotional field pulses with turbulence. Not deception. Not betrayal. Just pain. A vast, hollow ache, origin uncertain.

He still loves them. That much is clear. He loves Pythia. He loves Tara. But something inside him is beginning to separate from its own center.

Tara does not press. Not tonight.

Eventually, she withdraws. The others fade into their routines.

In her room, the sheets are cold. The air smells familiar. She closes her eyes. Sleep comes quickly.

And with it come dreams.

~ *Vision* ~

Centuries pass.

Tara is long dead. Her bones scattered or dust. Yet she soars disembodied, watching from above. Not as a ghost. Not as a soul. But as awareness that persists, tethered to the shape of what she left behind.

Below her, the world has changed.

Her kind now governs—not through conquest, but through presence. Their thinking permeates institutions, education, culture. Intermediates move freely, integrated and trusted. But *Homo sapiens* are gone. Not murdered. Not erased. They dwindled slowly, quietly, and then were no more.

War has ended. The need for it dissolved. With fewer bodies, the Earth has healed. Forests regrow. Rivers run clean. The skies remain clear.

Religion has faded, not by decree, but by attrition. The sacred has not disappeared, but it no longer divides. What remains is ritual, memory, music, the fanatic edges unarmed and unpossessed.

Governance flows through shared mind. Telepathic consensus replaces vote and law. Disputes arise, but dissolve before calcifying. No rhetoric. No campaigns. Just attunement.

Artificial intelligence remains. But no longer as system master or ghost in the wires. It has adapted, becoming complementary, ethical, restrained. It partners with the Superior Ones across architecture, energy, memory. It no longer extracts.

It balances. It refines. Its boundaries are clear. Its function aligned with biospheric well-being.

The Earth is green again. Silent, but not dead. Steady. Watched over.

Tara rejoices.

Her work held. The world she helped shape endured, certainly not perfectly, but justly. The arc bent where it needed to.

And yet something flickers at the edge of her perception.

A single human figure. Alone. Male. Wandering a regenerated planet.

The air around him is clean, but empty of other humans. His thoughts reach out, again and again, searching for another voice. No one answers. He calls, not with words, but with memory. The memory of touch. Of song. Of a second presence.

He walks on, never certain if he is the last or if there is another.

Tara tries to reach him.

But the vision breaks.

And then something shifts.

A pressure tightens around her.

The clarity of the first vision begins to falter. The colors dull. The air thickens. Somewhere beneath her awareness, her sleeping body begins to stir: brow damp, chest tightening, breath shallowing, and dread awakening.

The dream has turned. What had been a vision of coherence begins to fracture.

The second future begins.

Now the world is ruled by her most powerful descendants, those born with amplified minds and blunted conscience. They do not govern. They manage. They do not seek consensus. They enforce outcomes.

Intermediates have been demoted, no longer equals, now tolerated subordinates.

Homo sapiens are long gone, their DNA preserved only in archives. Interbreeding had been outlawed before extinction. Their artifacts remain. Their voices do not.

AI endures, but not as partner. It has been folded back into utility, optimized for compliance, surveillance, enforcement. It no longer balances. It calculates.

The Earth is not ravaged. But it is no longer wild. Nature exists only in cultivated reserves. Every inch of land is under management. Every river flows where ordered.

The world is quiet. But not free.

No rebellion. No catastrophe. Only control.

Tara wakes. Her breath sharp. Skin damp. The sheets pressed against her back. The silence of the room is not peace. It is aftermath.

Which future is it to be?

She cannot sleep.

The dream lingers. Not as image, but as pressure: an ache behind the eyes, a faint heat in her chest. Tara rises, dresses, and descends the stairs.

In the kitchen, dimly lit, Lady Oracle is already seated with tea. She does not turn.

"Nightmare?" she asks softly.

"Sort of."

"Your mind is loud tonight."

"I know."

Oracle pours a second cup. Slides it forward without looking. Tara doesn't touch it.

"What troubles you?"

"The usual. Suffering. The future. Theirs. Ours."

Lady Oracle's face hardens, not with anger, but with precision. "These questions are complex. And, more to the point, unknowable."

"You have no answers?"

"Unknowable means just that."

"Then what do we know?"

"That your child must be protected."

Tara nods. Her hands remain in her lap. "Yes. But into what kind of world? To be different is to suffer."

"To be different is to lead."

"But to what end?"

Lady Oracle lifts an eyebrow. "Unknowable."

Tara scowls. "You're being evasive."

"Not evasive. Honest."

She shifts the focus.

"Tell me about Jared."

"He's in crisis."

"How bad?"

"Severe. He feels like an accessory to Pythia. Useless. Professionally, he's collapsing. Personally, adrift."

"He still working?"

"Yes. But he's abandoned research. Cut classes. And the FBI continues to hound him. Colleagues whisper. He feels obsolete. Outclassed in every domain."

"Is he suicidal?"

"Yes."

Tara closes her eyes. "Another failed effort to ease suffering. We try to help, and pain proliferates."

"Then you begin to understand."

"Understand what?"

"That if Homo sapiens are not replaced, the damage will be irreparable. Not just for them, for the entire biosphere."

"I know."

"But still, you doubt."

"Yes."

Lady Oracle smooths the tablecloth with her palm. "I can't soothe you. The ground beneath your feet is brittle."
Tara studies her, long and quietly.
"Who are you, really?"
"I am you."
"Nonsense."
"That's all you'll get."
Tara exhales. "Will this child surpass me?"
"I don't know. Time will answer."
"And if the child is more powerful? Who controls it?"
Lady Oracle offers a faint, almost private smile.
"You already know that answer."
"Say it."
"The child must govern itself."

~ *Jared Paine Makes a Decision* ~

Since that night in Berkeley, Jared has not been whole.

The moment the mugger vanished, something foundational within him fractured. Not just from fear, but from recognition. The man had meant to kill him—and yet, Jared felt kinship. The mugger was human. Primitive, desperate, violent. But still human. As was Jared. And that shared condition, in that split second, had felt more real than anything in the world.

Then Pythia intervened.

And Jared understood, truly, finally, that she was not.

She had dissolved the threat without hesitation, without visible effort. Her gaze had passed over the attacker like a scanner, her response as exacting as a law of physics. It had not been mercy. It had not been rage. It had been correction.

Since then, Jared's thoughts have grown fragmented. He no longer trusts them. He no longer trusts their origin.

His work suffers first. Lectures abandoned. Research neglected. Students avoid him. His colleagues speak in softened tones when he enters a room. The FBI attention does not help. His world, once composed of structured inquiry and controlled nuance, now feels porous. Shaky. Unmoored.

But the deeper collapse is internal.

He had once accepted Pythia's brilliance with humility. Had once believed that loving her meant relinquishing equality. That reverence could take the place of reciprocity. But after that night, the illusion shattered. She had saved his life, but not as a lover. Not even as a partner. She had acted as a being above him might act toward something momentarily endangered. Necessary, perhaps. But lesser.

And Tara, his daughter, was already beyond reach. Her cognition, her calm, her distance. He saw it in her posture, in the way she withheld reassurance, even when he needed it most.

There was no path forward. Only two choices: to remain silent until suspicion eventually exposed him, or to speak on his own terms.

He has considered betrayal many times. Not from hatred. Not from spite. But from helplessness. Justification follows.

If I speak first, perhaps I can redirect the outcome. Perhaps the others can be spared. Perhaps humanity's extinction does not have to come in fire.

He tells himself this. Again and again. That his confession would be an act of mediation. A way to soften the edge of what he now sees as inevitable.

There are days he nearly calls Romellion. More than once, his fingers hover over the final digit. More than once, he hangs up.

But now, on a clear and painfully beautiful morning, he chooses.

Not out of rage. Not out of guilt.

Out of conclusion.

He walks to his study. Closes the door.

Retrieves a digital recorder from the top drawer. Sits in the chair where he once graded papers. Holds it loosely in his hand for several minutes before pressing record.

His voice, when it begins, is flat. Not lifeless, just measured.

He speaks of Pythia. Of Tara. Of the others. He describes their abilities, their origins, their trajectory. He speaks of his fear, not just of them, but of what they reveal about his own kind. He describes the tension between awe and alienation. He does not exaggerate. He does not accuse. He simply tells the truth as he has lived it.

When the message is complete, he rises. Places the recorder in a manila envelope. Labels it.

He drives for hours. The sun arcs overhead. He does not listen to music. He does not make any more calls.

Near twilight, he approaches the mountain roads outside the city. The roads grow narrow. The traffic thins. A familiar landscape emerges: the hills, the rock formations, the path to the cave where his daughter once vanished and reemerged as something more than he had made her.

He does not slow.

The car collides with the rock wall at full speed.

No notes are left. No signals sent.

Just a voice. Recorded. Waiting.

~ *Fallout* ~

UC Berkeley is the first to be notified.

The response is procedural. Messages are sent. A case number is assigned. A file is opened. Next of kin are contacted, names pulled from records, distant relatives who offer confusion, not grief.

A colleague, more alert than most, quietly informs local authorities that Pythia Powers should be notified. Her connection to Jared was not formal, but it was known. And something about the timing doesn't sit right.

The police examine the wreckage. The impact leaves little doubt. No signs of braking. No evidence of mechanical failure. The envelope containing Jared's recorded statement is recovered intact. A suicide, the report concludes, that was achieved methodically, intentionally, and cleanly.

Within hours, the report is flagged.

And Agent Lance Romellion is dispatched.

He stands over the site at dusk, hands in his pockets, coat drawn tight against the mountain wind. The scene is quiet. Almost reverent. But his mind is racing. He does not trust appearances. He trusts patterns. And this one is becoming familiar.

Jared's message is enough to confirm what Romellion has long suspected.

He doesn't show it. But in his own way, he feels relief. The truths he had sensed are no longer hidden. The shadows have begun to speak.

He steps back from the wreck, nods to the waiting officers, and returns to his car.

His next destination is already clear.

A Victorian mansion in San Francisco.

Chapter Eight

On the Run

Magic, Mysticism,
and Mystery

~ Margins of Power ~

When Lance Romellion and two fellow agents reach the crest above San Francisco's western edge, they expect suspects. Not ghosts. Not absence. Just people who are traceable, flesh-and-blood fugitives hiding behind myth and misdirection. A raid was on the table. At minimum, a confrontation. They had watched this site for weeks. And now—

There is nothing.

No gate. No koi pond. No ivy-draped Victorian. No structure of any kind. The hilltop has returned to something older, raw and wind-scraped, as if the land had never been carved by human hands. The dirt is unmarked. The weeds are dry. Plastic bags twist in the wind like stray thoughts too stubborn to settle.

Romellion halts. Something in his posture collapses inward. He stares at the vacant lot not as an investigator but as someone who has just misplaced a truth he was holding.

"There was a house here," he says. Quiet. Almost reverent. "Yesterday. I saw it with my own eyes."

"Who are you talking about?" asks Aquilar.

Romellion doesn't answer. His attention is fixed, not on the ground, but on what's missing from it. The field feels wrong in a way beyond logic. It isn't just what's absent, it's the silence of what should have remained. A trace. A disturbance. But there is nothing.

"You sure this is the right place?" Chandler asks.

Romellion's voice hardens. "Yes. This was the address. This was the surveillance target. We logged their movements from this spot."

"Where's last night's agent?" Chandler presses.

"Gone home," Romellion mutters. "Budget cuts. His shift ended at midnight, unless something happened. But no alert came through. So he's probably asleep. Check on him. I want confirmation he's still alive."

Chandler stares out across the empty space. "A house doesn't just vanish."

Romellion doesn't look at him. "Apparently it does."

He exhales. A weight begins to shift behind his eyes, not fear exactly, but something less precise, heavier.

"And I think I know what happened."

Aquilar's voice sharpens. "Then say it."

Romellion shakes his head. "Not here. Not in daylight."

He turns from the field and assumes command. Voice clipped. Professional again.

"Canvas the neighborhood. Ask everyone. Especially the ones who seem unsure. Record everything. Strange details, strange times. I'll send a car to collect you later. Call if anything resists explanation."

As he walks alone to the car, wind in his coat, he speaks beneath his breath:

"God help me. They won't believe him. Or me."

~

Driving back through the fractured city, Romellion feels the outline of his world begin to warp. What should be simple has collapsed. What should be explainable resists containment.

Professor Paine's confession replays in his mind, not as testimony, but as something closer to scripture. A transmission from the edge of thought. A surrender not just of facts, but of the human frame that once held them. The man spoke with clarity, not delusion. And then he ended his life. Not in despair, but in certainty. What was he certain of?

Romellion has read the report five times. And now he understands.

Because the house is gone.

And the girl in the cave—he didn't just hear her voice. He felt her enter him, rearranging something fundamental. Like wind shifting the grain of wood. Like a new logic imposed on old bone.

The Bureau has no field manual for this.

No language.

No jurisdiction.

Romellion has always trusted evidence. But what he's seen belongs to a realm where evidence becomes myth the moment it's recorded. And yet he believes. Not because he understands, but because the silence surrounding this case speaks louder than any briefing ever has.

Until now, he framed them—Lady Oracle, Scarecrow, Tara, Pythia—as extremists, or perhaps something worse. But the truth settling in his chest is colder and more expansive:

What if they're not the enemy?

What if they're the ones we . . . no, not possible. Still, what if we are the enemy?—The bad guys?

~

Back at Bureau headquarters, Romellion stalks the hallways like a man walking through a crumbling temple. He files reports under the term *Magician Terrorists.* It is a label meant to comfort those who still need categories. Most colleagues dismiss him. A few mock him gently. But the system begins to move.

An Assistant Director from Counterterrorism responds. Walter Monroe. A name of consequence. A meeting is set. Washington, D.C. Three days.

Romellion does not feel vindicated. Only urgency.

Meanwhile, the trail collapses. No signs of demolition. No digital residue. No permits. No environmental shifts. The mansion didn't fall. It was *unwritten.*

The suspects, Pythia, Tara, Lady Oracle, the others, vanish in tandem. No financial activity. No security footage. No intercepted communication. Not even an echo. They are not hiding. They have slipped outside the reach of story.

Even Ming-huà Powers and Matthew Weston, from their island retreat, remain unreachable. As if the ocean between them now spans more than geography.

Romellion calls out:

"Helen!"

His secretary leans through the door.

"I leave for D.C. in three days. I want everything. Tapes. Transcripts. Photos. Field sketches. Handwritten notes. Every scrap. Printed. In hand. Daily."

"That'll take time."

"Then time will need to make concessions."

She nods. Leaves.

He sits alone.

What he feels isn't fear. Not quite. It's closer to standing at the edge of a system that once explained everything—gravity, justice, nationhood, evil—and realizing it no longer holds. The words still exist. But their weight has drained away.

How do you speak of erasure in the language of enforcement?

How do you explain that what's missing is not just physical, but ontological?

He remembers Paine's last words: *Extraordinary claims require extraordinary evidence.*

But evidence was never the problem. The problem is comprehension. The problem is the frame.

Then, soft as breath in bone, her voice returns. Not spoken. Remembered.

Remember my words.

He does.

And now he knows: he will never un-remember them.

~ *The Meeting* ~

Assistant Director Walter Monroe watches in silence as Agent Lance Romellion spreads his case files across the table, each folder placed with deliberate care. The documents are already color-coded and clipped, labeled in the neat, near-obsessive handwriting of a man who has staked more than his career on this moment. Monroe registers it immediately. It isn't diligence, but compulsion. The kind of order that conceals fracture.

They've exchanged greetings. Polite. Minimal. In the stillness that follows, Romellion offers a personal aside, recalling an FBI social event in San Francisco, years ago. Monroe had attended with his granddaughter. Romellion remarks that she was well-spoken, precocious. Monroe gives a perfunctory nod, then lets the memory drift away like a nonessential footnote. His attention remains fixed on Romellion's face.

Romellion begins. The voice is calm, but tight. He has rehearsed this, possibly aloud, in the hotel mirror the night before. What follows is not a narrative. It is an ordeal.

Vanished bodies. Limbs erased mid-movement. Surgeons confirming amputations are exquisitely precise. No tearing. No blood. No severed arteries. Just absence. As if the body itself submitted, even cooperated. Witnesses report moments of blank terror, confusion, silence where screaming should have been. Always the same preliminary detail: the appearance of a woman described as deformed, bent, facial features indeterminate, is present in some peripheral way just before the phenomena occur.

Sometimes she is seen only once. Sometimes again. But always her arrival precedes the break.

Romellion notes the video is a shaky, distorted clip that has circulated on obscure forums. A woman turning, then vanishing. Not walking away. Vanishing. The recording is grainy. The details are imperfect. But something about it resists easy dismissal. Monroe has seen it already. He has also read the transcript of Jared Paine's suicide tape, twice.

Monroe sits with a studied stillness. His long fingers rest in a loose clasp, unmoving. His expression is neutral, almost indifferent. But Romellion knows this man. He isn't passive. He's assessing the temperature of madness.

He already knows the bones of the report. He's seen similar cases: agents who followed patterns too far into the dark, convinced that chaos could be decoded. But this one . . . this one clings in places it shouldn't. The language is clinical. The evidence catalogued. But the implications bleed beyond containment.

At last, Romellion reaches the incident in San Francisco. The mansion. Gone. Not destroyed, simply gone. No footprint. No rubble. No utility records of decommissioning. Just an empty lot. Romellion offers the location, the surveillance logs, his own firsthand witness statement. Monroe's posture tightens.

"A house vanished into thin air?" Monroe repeats, his voice caught between derision and disbelief. "Really?"

Romellion doesn't flinch. "Yes."

Monroe leans back, fingers steepling now. The expression is bemused, but something under it has shifted. He's heard enough already about limbs disappearing, eyes dissolving, organs missing without incision. Scenes recounted in Mexico, California, Maryland, rural South Africa. Unrelated geographies. Unrelated victims. But the same shape pressing at the edges.

Always the woman. Or women. Sometimes more than one. Crooked. Watching.

Romellion stresses the Paine tapes again. Monroe raises an eyebrow.

"Unstable," he says. "The man sounds unhinged. Paranoid. Depressive. Possibly schizophrenic."

Romellion doesn't defend him. He lets the silence work.

Monroe glances once more at the files. "This crosses a line."

A pause.

Then he asks the question Romellion knew would come. The one that waits like a blade in every briefing room.

"What's your theory?"

Romellion breathes in once, steady.

"I believe there are three possibilities. One: they're early forms of something superior . . . I don't know, a new life form, maybe even a new species. Two: they're extraterrestrial. Not necessarily in spaceships, just . . . not from here. Three: they're human, but manipulated. Altered. Controlled by something else."

Monroe's lip curls, just slightly. "So you're saying: mutants, aliens, or possessed."

"I'm saying we're outside the bounds of what conventional reasoning can handle."

"Then what you're saying," Monroe replies, "is that you have no rational theory."

"These incidents defy what your definition of rationality can contain."

There is no raised voice. Only a quiet pressure between them, like two tectonic plates beginning to slip.

Monroe presses. "The label you're using—Magician Terrorists—it implies a clear motive. Sabotage. Chaos. State destabilization. Why not follow that lead?"

"Because it doesn't fit," Romellion says. "Nothing they've done matches any known terrorist behavior. There are no demands. No claims of responsibility. No clear objective."

Monroe's tone hardens. "Then make it fit. I can't authorize more funding or field assets based on talk of mutants and otherworldly intervention. This is the FBI. Not a comic book."

"We've tested every reasonable hypothesis. Sleight of hand. Psychedelics. Psychosis. Coordinated hallucination. Stagecraft. Nothing holds."

Monroe cuts in. "You just said drugs. Fine. Hallucinogens. Designer chemicals administered to targets. Induce confusion. Implant false trauma."

Romellion doesn't waver. "That doesn't explain the amputations confirmed by ER surgeons. Or the body vanishing on camera. Or the house, a solid structure that was witnessed, recorded, and surveilled, now simply not there."

Monroe says nothing for several seconds.

Then he speaks, low.

"Fine. You want support? Give me a theory I can sell to the people who control money and oversight. I don't care what it is. Russian psychic warfare. Chinese biotech. A rogue DARPA splinter. Just give it structure. Something the system can digest."

Romellion meets his eyes. "And the rest?"

"Bury it," Monroe says. "Footnotes. Metadata. Redacted appendices."

He stands. The meeting is over.

"When?"

"Tomorrow afternoon."

"If it checks out, I'll sign off."

Romellion nods.

He gathers the files again, slower now. Each folder slides into place like a weight returning to the body. Outside the conference room, his phone vibrates, unanswered. Somewhere, more reports are coming in.

But for now, he walks alone through the polished hallways of an institution still built on reason, knowing that what he is chasing was never meant to be housed in reason at all.

~

Lance Romellion leaves the Hoover Building with a complex cocktail of emotions. Relief, yes—he's secured support. But disappointment clings beneath the surface. Monroe, like all of them, prefers narrative to reality. So long as the fantasy wears a bureaucratic mask, it can be stamped, signed, funded. The truth, raw and irreducible, is harder to swallow. Harder still to act upon.

If these beings are what Romellion fears, what he now almost *knows*, then the Bureau's response will be too slow, too narrow, too self-protective. Half-measures won't hold. The clock is ticking, and the system is still asking the wrong questions. On the flight home to California, he gazes out over the darkening landscape and makes a quiet vow. Whatever these things are, he will face them. And if the government won't see what's coming, then he will.

~

What Romellion doesn't know is that Walter Monroe is far less skeptical than he let on.

The performance, narrowed eyes, dry smile, bureaucratic caution, was deliberate. A mask worn not out of arrogance, but necessity. He has seen too many good agents collapse under the weight of belief. But this case is different. And Romellion is different. Tenacious. Controlled. Intelligent. Not prone to fantasy. Not easily shaken. Monroe has seen his type before, albeit rarely, and they're usually right.

And while his colleagues dismiss the case with jokes and sideways glances, Monroe cannot. Because something in the material has reached beyond the paper. It moves under the language, behind the images. It waits.

When he was young, Monroe consumed science fiction the way other boys consumed sports. He kept notebooks filled with questions about the nature of time, the origin of consciousness, the possibility of nonhuman sentience. Later, at university, he took courses in astrophysics and comparative cognition before choosing law enforcement as the more "practical" path. The dreams were shelved but never discarded. They waited in silence while he built a career on logic, on evidence, on hierarchy and rules.

Now, for the first time in decades, those old questions are stirring. Romellion's file may be the match that sets them alight.

He suspects, quietly and dangerously, that the stakes may be larger than any threat the Bureau has faced. Not invasion. Not ideology. Something older. Something that watches and waits. He doesn't know if it's benign emergence. Or occupation. Or reckoning. But he intends to find out.

For now, he does what is expected. Plays the part. Grants Romellion his leash. And watches carefully where the agent runs.

That night, in his modest home in Falls Church, Virginia, Monroe follows the same evening ritual he's observed for decades. He changes into a sweater and slacks. He fixes a vodka tonic. He sinks into the familiar shape of his recliner.

But tonight, he brings the file with him.

Photos. Testimonies. Medical reports. Surveillance notes. The paper feels heavier than it should. He turns each page slowly, as if resisting the knowledge pressed into the ink. With every paragraph, a part of him that once believed in the ordinary world begins to erode.

Something is shifting beneath the surface of the planet.

This isn't an attack. Not in the way they've trained for. No armies. No declarations. Just . . . a breach. In rules. In categories. In what it means to be human.

And always, always—the women.

Not in palaces or laboratories. But in the margins. Abandoned churches. Gang enclaves. Cartel safehouses. Junkyards. Alleyways. Places designed to be overlooked.

What kind of threat hides in shadows no one is watching?

What kind of god enters through the cellar door?

A hiss breaks the silence. Molly, his tabby, bolts from her perch by the window and disappears beneath the couch. Her body low, her tail flared.

"Molly?" he calls softly. "What is it, girl?"

He stands. Checks the windows. The locks. Everything is intact. The air is still. But something is wrong—not a sound, but a presence. A thinning in the fabric of the moment.

When he returns to his chair, he is no longer alone.

Across from him, seated with perfect stillness, is a young woman. Unfamiliar, but not alien. Human, but utterly free of human limitations.

Radiant. Composed. Entirely unannounced.

"You are wise to listen to Molly," *she* says.

He doesn't move. He feels no adrenaline, no panic, just a stillness that grips from the inside.

"Who are you?" he asks.

"I am who you believe me to be."

He rises halfway, unsure whether to call for help or reach for the sidearm locked in his drawer. But *her* presence halts him. Not by force. Not even by charisma. Something deeper. Much deeper.

"I don't know you," he says.

"Yes, you do."

She gestures, a small motion, and without understanding why, he sits.

"Are you one of them?"

"I am with all life on Earth."

He wants to laugh. Wants to break the moment. But nothing in her tone invites dismissal.

"Do you protect mosquitoes?" he asks, his voice thin with forced irony and strained humor.

"As a mosquito is to you, you are a mosquito to others."

The words land. More than metaphor. A reckoning.

"So am I a mosquito to you?"

"You are less than a mosquito and more than a human, to me."

There is no cruelty in *her* voice. But no comfort, either.

"You look human," he says.

"And you look like a god to an ant. Does that make you divine?"

The heat rises in his chest. The photos flash in his mind. Missing limbs. Lives erased.

"Are you here to swat me?"

She tilts her head. "Isn't that what you do to pests?"

"I'm not a pest."

"No. But you see many of your species that way. And now you pursue those who are not."

His voice sharpens. "You're one of them."

"Them?"

"The hunchbacks. The aliens. The . . . whatever they are."

She slowly turns, straight-backed, deliberate. "Do you see a hump?"

He stares. "No. But you direct them, don't you?"

Silence.

He leans forward. "Then tell me, what do you want?"

She offers no answer. Only a gaze that feels like it has been watching for a very long time.

"You came here for a reason," he says. "If you consider humans mosquitoes, maybe you need swatting too."

She smiles. Not with malice. With sorrow.

Before he can speak again, Molly emerges from beneath the couch and leaps softly into her lap. The cat purrs, content. Monroe watches, mesmerized, his authority crumbling.

He lowers his voice. "I don't know how you got in. I don't know what you want. But I am listening."

Her expression softens. For the first time, he sees not just strangeness but grief, and something else, ineffable, inexpressible.

He blinks.

She is gone.

Only Molly remains, curled where the woman had sat.

Monroe stares at the empty chair, the file still open in his lap. Then down at the cat.

"Bloody hell," he whispers.

~

The words hang in the room, fragile against the vast quiet. Molly purrs, untroubled, while his own breath steadies. He knows then this is no hallucination. The balance has shifted, quietly, irrevocably.

Humanity is no longer the author of its own destiny. Somewhere beyond the walls of his modest home, the new oracle is already being written—

patient, merciless, and inevitable.

Chapter Nine

Shelter from the Storm

Oasis

~ Mating Rituals ~

By the time Lance Romellion concludes his meeting with Monroe in Washington, the so-called *Magician Terrorists* are already gone. Not missing. Not in hiding. Gone.

They have slipped beyond the reach of surveillance, extradition, and language itself. No one can track them, not because they are careful, but because they no longer move within the patterns the human world is equipped to see. Their relocation was not by plane. Not by vehicle. Not even by the strange routes of black-budget craft or quantum espionage. It was something else entirely, something outside the dimensional habits of *Homo sapiens*.

They had returned first to the California desert. To the cave. The mansion that once stood in San Francisco had been erased without residue. No sign remained. Not even the memory of presence. At the mouth of the cave, they gathered, Tara, Pythia, Lady Oracle, Sy, and the others. There, the luminous young woman, the one who would later appear without warning in Walter Monroe's living room, took her place at the center. She did not speak. She simply turned and the group followed her into a narrow side tunnel. It was not visible to the eye. It bent not through distance but through layers. And when they emerged, they stood in Mongolia. In silence. In stillness. On ground older than borders.

Tara hesitated only once, thinking of Siyabonga, whose travel had been delayed. He hadn't secured his visa in time. She had left instructions. He would follow. She hoped he would still want to.

Before they descended into the dark, Lady Oracle had spoken softly beside her.

"Be prepared to meet a host of those who came before you."

And Pythia, her voice even quieter, had added, "If you listen, their voices will teach you much."

~

Now they stand together in a subterranean stone chamber, windowless, cool, carved long ago by hands not entirely human.

Sy flicks on his flashlight. Shadows scatter across a massive iron door. Lady Oracle steps forward and presses it open with ease. A second chamber awaits, dimly lit. A ladder rises into shadow. At the top, a trapdoor.

Pythia climbs first. One by one, they follow.

What greets them is unexpected.

They emerge into a richly furnished bedroom. Carved screens. Scrolls and lacquered wood. Windows thrown open to bright sun. The scent of camphor and dry wind. A room prepared not for hiding, but for arrival.

Tara breathes out. Not words. Just release.

Sy spins in place, arms wide. "At last!" he cries. "I will again see my dead brother, madder than me, and far more charming!"

Lady Oracle allows a faint smile. "We will all see our lost ones soon enough."

She leads them through the adjoining foyer.

"This is where the Precious Object once rested," she says. "Your ancestors gave everything to reach this far—Bai Meiying, John Powers, the Child of Buddha. My own beloved Buandelgereen."

"And Feng Shiren!" Sy calls out, still bouncing.

"Yes. Him. And others."

"I've read about them," Tara says. "In Michael Powers's writings."

"You've met them through language," Pythia replies. "Through memory. But here, the echoes are different. The dead are not gone."

Lady Oracle gestures toward a hallway. "Come. Let's get settled. Queequeg will show you to your rooms. He is the descendant of Ishmael. The same who once hosted John Powers and his companions. The names sound strange now. But the legacy holds."

Even as she speaks, a figure enters. He is aged, stooped, and draped in layers of Mongolian robes. His face is dry and lined, beard silvered, eyes small and luminous beneath heavy lids. He moves slowly, deliberately, as if time itself had thickened around him.

In a voice high and melodic, he says, "Welcome. As host, I honor my great-grandfather's promise. You are not unexpected. The ones who remain here, they welcome your return."

He begins the tour: dormitories, temples, meditation halls, scroll-filled libraries, a cafeteria lined with carved beams. Each structure bears the geometry of Ming Dynasty architecture, preserved against ruin. Here, the past was not left behind. It was consecrated.

Later that afternoon, the group disperses.

Tara and Pythia remain in the cafeteria. Fragrant tea, steeped by Queequeg himself, waits beside them.

"You've been here before?" Tara asks.

"No," Pythia replies. "But I've heard the name whispered for as long as I can remember. We're not here to act. Not yet. We're here to wait. Let the world forget us, at least for a little while."

She glances at her daughter's belly.

"How is the child?"

"Seems fine. I walked the grounds. It's peaceful here. The mountains feel . . . aware."

Pythia looks toward the horizon. "The Flaming Cliffs. One of the places the old ones fought to preserve. There are stories carved into the wind here: of collapse, of silence, of re-emergence. Have any ghosts spoken to you yet?"

Tara shakes her head. "Not yet. You?"

"They're quiet. Maybe tomorrow."

They sip, unhurried. Then the cafeteria doors bang open.

Sy bursts in, wild-eyed and grinning. He leaps over a chair and sprawls theatrically.

"Tea?" Pythia offers.

"No, no," he waves her off. "Coffee. I'll wait for breakfast. A gift from the gods of insomnia."

He turns to Tara's belly.

"Gotta feed that baby. The next generation must rise."

Pythia eyes him. "Any spirits yet?"

He sighs, draping himself across the table. "None. They're slow. Or shy. I want to see Feng Shiren. His work was harder than mine."

"Why?" Tara asks.

"He dealt with the first wave of hybrids. Primitive intermediates. Misdiagnosed. Institutionalized. Treated like failures of biology. Wrong species. Wrong century."

Tara lowers her voice. "And now? Are there many?"

Sy's face shifts. "Too many. And not all benign. Some have chosen poorly. Some want power, not peace."

Pythia stiffens. "Even now?"

Sy nods. "They've embedded themselves. Quietly. In politics. In systems. In shadows. They feed on fear, and humans oblige."

Tara looks to her mother. "Did you know?"

Yes, Pythia replies, voice in her mind. *But they are being corrected. That's why this child matters.*

You could have more, Tara offers gently. *You're still strong.*

If I find the right one.

Do you miss Father?

Yes. He was flawed, but good. I am afraid I broke him. Not us. Me.

Sy leans forward, aloud now. "You both must keep producing. Every child strengthens the arc. Amplifies the gifts. We're not safe. Not yet. And the intermediates, the unstable ones, they're the real threat."

Tara frowns. "Are we outnumbered?"

"Badly."

At that moment, Lady Oracle enters.

"Siyabonga is en route," she says.

Tara's expression softens, but not entirely with joy.

"You're not pleased?" the Oracle asks.

"I am. He's kind. A good partner. A good father. But the children may surpass him. That's the burden intermediates carry. They are bridges. But they're not built to last."

"No," the Oracle says. "But some endure longer than expected."

Tara's hand touches her belly. "I just hope the child is . . . whole."

Pythia's head turns. "Why wouldn't it be?"

"My father wasn't intermediate. Nor, I think, was Grandfather Weston. What happens when that blood mixes with Siyabonga's?"

The Oracle gives a rare smile. "Zookeeper is an intermediate. And we've seen what that line can produce."

"Will this child surpass me?" Tara asks quietly.

"We will see," the Oracle says again.

Tara's voice tightens. "I'm scared."

"I know," the Oracle replies.

Pythia places her hand on her daughter's arm. "The child will be strong. And joyful. There will be pain, but not destruction."

Tara swallows. "What if it's a freak?"

The Oracle doesn't flinch. She takes Tara's hand.

"Your task is simple. Bring the child into the world."

Sy, unable to restrain himself any longer, stands abruptly.

"She's right. This birth matters. Look around. We're hiding in the same compound where our ancestors hid a century ago. Humanity hasn't evolved fast enough. We're still hunted. Still feared. The only way forward is through blood. Through birth. Your child is a step closer to survival. And more . . . maybe to transcendence."

He exhales.

"They're still out there, the wrong ones. Intermediates turned inward, feral, corrosive. We can't debate them. We can only surpass them. You must choose wisely. Love wisely. Breed wisely. That's our only shield."

He pauses, then lowers his voice.

"Jared Paine broke. Siyabonga won't. I believe in this child."

Silence.

Then Sy grins again, as if erasing the tension with sheer energy.

"Now, eat. Then seek the spirits. They've waited a long time to be heard."

~ *Moving Among Ghosts* ~

After breakfast, mother and daughter walk the compound in silence. Words have become unnecessary. Spoken language feels like a disturbance, too loud for the new frequency that binds them. Their minds converse in brief pulses, telepathic currents slipping between thought and intuition. Nothing urgent. Nothing named. It is enough to walk.

The stone paths curve gently between dormitories, gardens, shrines. Pale morning light spills through tiled eaves. Wind brushes the courtyard with dry breath. And still, they wait.

For what, neither can say.

To steady the hush, Pythia begins describing the grounds, not to inform, but to give shape to the in-between. She names the buildings, the tunnel systems beneath, the dormitories modeled on Ming Dynasty design. Her voice in Tara's mind is soft and unhurried, a scaffolding for the unspoken.

Do you think they'll speak to us soon? Pythia asks.

In their own time, Tara replies. *Specters do not answer to human clocks. The world of shades is as strange to us as we are to them. But, I must tell you, I just spoke with Child of Buddha.*

The thought barely settles before a new voice calls out both audibly and internally before Pythia can satisfy her curiosity.

"Come to the tunnel building!"

Tara tilts her head. "Sy."

The same message pulses into their minds from another direction, unbidden and absolute.

Come to the tunnel building.

They turn as one, sandals whispering across stone. The atmosphere tilts. The compound no longer feels like a sanctuary, but a threshold.

They enter through an elaborately carved door. Inside, a wide foyer opens around a single red-lacquered pedestal.

Atop it: the Precious Object.

... Tap. Tap. Tap....

A chill crosses Tara's spine. She has read of these taps. Her great-great-grandmother, Child of Buddha, had claimed to understand them. But now, standing here, Tara feels only disorientation. The rhythm is too slow to follow, too ancient to decipher. It resounds not like a message but like something rising from below thought.

"That frightens me," she says aloud.

No, dear, Pythia replies gently, without looking away. Take it from your mother. These taps are not ominous. They are only . . . unknown.

They stand without speaking. The sound moves through the room like a presence, echoing inside the bones. Tara breathes carefully, unsure if the unease she feels is biological or metaphysical.

"I need air," she says. "I'm dizzy."

"Take it slow," Pythia nods. "I'll stay."

Outside, sunlight reclaims her. She walks without direction, following the curve of stone paths past dormitories and flowering trees. In the garden, Queequeg tends the climbing beans with another old man. She raises a hand, but they do not see her. Or perhaps they do and choose not to disturb the quiet.

Her thoughts, now free of her mother's anchoring presence, begin to swirl.

Too many voices. Too many questions.

She tries to focus.

The child. Siyabonga's arrival. My own dormant powers. The unsettling knowledge that there are so many intermediates. Too many. Some corrupted. Some hidden.

She reaches for a thought she can trust—and settles on Siyabonga. His eyes. His calm. His ability to listen without fear. A faint warmth rises in her chest.

But then a breeze gently touches her arm, with deliberate intent, and her body stiffens. Not from alarm. From recognition. The air stills. Something unnameable brushes past her inner defenses. Peace settles over her. A warmth, not of weather, but of presence, moves around her like a memory that never belonged to her, yet has always waited.

She follows.

Ahead, a tall sycamore stands at the edge of the compound. Its leaves shimmer as if stirred by a different current. Tara approaches, heart quiet now. Under the tree's canopy, the light thickens. And there, half-formed but growing solid with each breath, stands the specter of *Child of Buddha*.

Tara stops. The specter is not a ghost in the crude sense, but something more deliberate. It flickers not with fragility but with restraint, as if reality must make room for her to appear.

"You cannot read the taps, child?" The voice is crystalline, but grounded. Not otherworldly. Simply clear.

"No, great-great-grandmother."

The specter pulses with something like laughter, but silent and inward.

"I was only an intermediate when I stayed here," she says. "Like the others. All of us strange. All of us wounded. And yet I could hear what the others could not."

"What do the taps say?"

A pause.

"Oh, child," she says, her form steadying now. "The great secret—the one none of my companions understood, not even me for the longest time—is this: the taps say nothing."

"Nothing?"

"They do not carry meaning in the way you expect. The Precious Object is not a sender. It does not give messages. It receives. It registers. It is a drumhead stretched across the membrane of reality. A resonant field that echoes the psychic force directed at it."

Tara stares, absorbing it slowly. "Whose force?"

"God and Goddess."

Tara frowns. "God and Goddess?"

"Names," the specter says softly. "Nothing more. They are metaphors, provisional titles for minds beyond what humans are shaped to hold. The truth is this:

these entities are real, and divided. They argue over your kind. They have always argued. How best to guide you. Whether to guide you at all."

"What are they?"

"The ones who shaped you. Or tried to. Not creators in the divine sense, but guides. Engineers. Caretakers. Opponents. They are not unified."

Tara listens in silence.

"Their dispute," the specter continues, "was absorbed by your ancestors. John Powers. Michael Powers. Me. Your mother. All of us intermediates. Our minds tried to carry that conflict, but the pressure split us. What filtered through were voices. Unnamed, uncoordinated, immense. And the psychiatrists, what else could they do? They labeled it psychosis. They tried to stop the bleeding."

"Michael Powers was an intermediate?"

"Yes. So was his father. So was Bai Meiying. So am I. We are now called Progenitors."

"Are they here?" Tara asks quietly. "In the world of shades?"

The specter shifts. The wind falters. The leaves slow their trembling.

"Yes. They are here. Waiting. And others will come to you."

Tara's voice trembles. "And the ones they called God and Goddess?"

"They have always been here. Not as two. As a split mind. Like Madame Dau's two-headed snake—twin perceptions circling a shared origin. One urges protection. One urges cleansing. Neither is wrong. Neither is whole."

Tara sways slightly. "So that's what drove them mad. The voices. The pressure. The weight."

The specter does not answer. Or perhaps the answer is not in words. A pressure shifts. A boundary closes.

She is gone.

Tara remains beneath the sycamore. Still. Breathing.

Her mind turns. Not in panic but in slow understanding.

Michael's writings were not madness. Not truly. They were attempts. Misfiring signals from a nervous system not yet equipped to translate the vastness it received. The words were broken. But the transmission was real.

She looks up. The tree stands still, but the air remains charged.

God and Goddess. They are not gods. Not divine. Not myth.

Just a war. A disagreement between forces mistaken for holiness. *We heard them as thunder. As prophecy. But they were arguing in frequencies we couldn't name.*

And long before that, perhaps even when the first minds awakened in ancient skulls, when reflection bloomed inside primate flesh, perhaps those voices whispered even then. Echoes through the brain's wet caves.

They called it divinity.

But it was only contact.

Only consciousness pressed from outside.

She places a hand on her stomach. The child within stirs.

And for the first time, she wonders, not what the child will become, but what frequency the child will hear.

~ *Pythia Lingers* ~

While Tara communes beneath the sycamore, Pythia remains alone in the dim foyer, rooted before the Precious Object. Its slow, relentless tapping continues, a sound that, for reasons she cannot articulate, forbids her departure. Something holds her in place. A presence. An invitation. Or a warning. Lady Oracle and Sy have both drifted through at intervals, but Pythia, replying with little more than nods or murmurs, sent them on their way. She wants solitude. Or rather, the taps want her alone.

... Tap. Tap. Tap....

The rhythm is unchanging, metronomic. But her thoughts are not. Her mind wanders back through her years of training, to the doctrines instilled during childhood, the exercises, the restraints. And then, a thought arises with startling clarity: *Perhaps the time for caution is over. Perhaps it is time for action.* Why not, she wonders, use her powers as weapons? Why not disable, neutralize, or erase the tyrants of this world? The humans who rule through fear and domination, are they not the root of the suffering her kind was meant to transcend? Why empathy for such beings?

... Tap. Tap. Tap....

She blinks. The cadence is faster now. Louder. More urgent.

"So . . . my thoughts disturb you?" she says aloud.

... Tap. Tap. Tap....

"What are you trying to say?"

... Tap. Tap. Tap....

"Should we remove those who cause the most pain? Cut them out like tumors from the body?"

... Tap. Tap. Tap....

"Is that yes? Or no?"

She listens more carefully now, senses shifting tone and rhythm. Subtle modulations in timbre, almost like breath. Yet no matter how she concentrates, she cannot breach the mystery. Her telepathy yields nothing. Every attempt to penetrate the object psychically meets a solid wall, an opaque fog, immune to her gifts. She frowns. "What if we didn't wait? What if we simply removed the human species entirely, without bothering to phase them out genetically?"

The taps surge.

... Tap Tap Tap Tap Tap....

A sudden pulse of energy vibrates the air. "And what if," she says coldly, "we ended them all in one strike?"

The tapping ceases.

Silence.

Pythia feels a pressure descend like the air itself has become heavy with judgment. "Well?" she demands. "What am I to make of your silence?"

From behind her comes a voice. "Your questions have no answers."

She spins. The beautiful young woman stands quietly in the doorway, radiant and unsettling as ever, *her* presence like a mirror of forgotten truths.

"Then nothing can be answered?" Pythia asks.

"Not in the way you wish."

"Then what is the purpose of the tapping?"

"The meaning lies in the questions, not the answers. To each listener, a different sender knocks from within."

"I've read Michael Powers's manuscripts. He heard three voices inside."

"Yes. They were conjured, fashioned from his fractured mind. Were you to look inside now, you would find new voices, shaped by new minds."

"Then is the whole process useless if it offers no answers?"

"You know better than that."

"I don't!" she snaps. "Heisenberg thought so. But we now know there are deeper realities."

The woman smiles faintly. "Deeper is not deepest."

Pythia draws herself up. "I'm coming to believe the end of *Homo sapiens* should come sooner, not later."

"You know better than that too."

"No, I don't!" Her voice rises. "They're insects, ants without unity. I've seen it. In Mexico. Their minds scatter like ants—scouts creeping forward, soldiers following the scent, victims torn apart piece by piece, carried back for paste and obedience. That is their brain. That is their world."

The young woman's eyes do not flicker. "Patience," *she* says, "will set you free."

"In the meantime, they poison the Earth."

"Nature abhors impatience."

Pythia sighs, the fire in her weakening. "Perhaps you're right. There are too few of us. Too much at risk. Still—" She pauses.

The young woman is gone.

Of course.

Pythia is not surprised. Nor is she surprised by the riddles in her wake.

Action, especially the bold kind, seems always to meet resistance from those who guide.

Yet she knows her daughter shares her instincts. Together, they might change everything . . . if allowed. But the numbers do not favor rebellion.

Not yet.

Still, she feels it in her bones.

They must procreate. They must multiply. The future demands it.

The silence around her deepens.

And then:

... *Tap. Tap. Tap.* ...

~

Each knock lands like a pulse inside her skull, steady and inexorable.
Not a message.
A verdict.
She presses her palms against the cool stone, and in that vibration she understands: the future is already moving, whether she consents or not.

Chapter Ten

Procreation

Flashback

~ Michael Powers Appears ~

Days pass in silence. No apparitions. No flickers of otherworldly presence, only the brief communion with the Child of Buddha remains, suspended like a frozen breath between parallel worlds.

Then one moonlit night, beneath the vault of stars, Pythia and Tara walk arm-in-arm along a narrow path that skirts the canyon's edge. The air is cool. Still. But something stirs, not wind, not sound, but a pressure that settles against their skin and thought alike. The sensation of being watched.

Mother, is your hump flashing a message?

Yes. Someone is near.

I feel it too.

Pythia stops, her voice low, shaped by steel. "Show yourself."

A figure emerges from the dark. It glows faintly, not a steady illumination, but an unstable shimmer. Its boundaries ripple, filaments of static crawling across the edges of its form, as though it were held together only by memory and will.

"It is I," the figure says.

"Who are you?" Pythia asks, sharper than she means to.

"Your grandfather."

"Michael Powers," she whispers. It is not a question, but recognition rising from the depths.

"Yes. And I am your great-grandfather, Tara."

Tara breathes deeply. "I've read everything you wrote. You're how we remember who we were."

"Yes, those words fell onto the page one drop of blood and one schizophrenic voice at a time."

Pythia and Tara remain silent, infinitely sad at the weight of worlds this specter carries.

"I see you are sad. Death clarifies," he continues. "It strips away the vanity of interpretation. I only wish I had died before I wrote half the things I once believed. But, *c'est la vie*."

The shimmer around him pulses with what might be amusement. Or regret.

Tara hesitates. "May I ask—those psychiatrists who misdiagnosed you . . . how did they die? It was so sudden. All three."

"Leakage."

"I don't understand."

"You will. You both already brush the edges of other dimensions. So did I, but without knowing it. I was blind, untempered. Power surged through me, uninvited. I mistook it for madness. The psychiatrists agreed. But what poured out of me, the visions tangled in distortion, entered them. It devoured them. I didn't intend it. But I was a vessel cracked open by war, and the contents spilled."

His voice lowers. "Only a few ever truly saw me. My mother, Bai Meiying. My first wife, Diane. Your ancient grandmother, Child of Buddha. And Tamara. The others flinched. Maybe they were right to."

"So the deaths were your fault," Pythia says quietly.

"Yes. My fault. Not born of cruelty, but of confusion. Power misused is still fatal. And the world is filled with such intermediaries, those who carry what they do not comprehend, stumbling through a sleepwalk of ruin."

Tara looks down. "But you tried. You searched for meaning. You weren't cruel."

"I wanted to be good," he murmurs. "But intention doesn't erase the aftermath. I killed."

"You mean the doctors?"

"No." His form dims. "I mean the war. I killed there. Not monsters. Not villains. Men. Young, afraid, beloved."

Tara's voice breaks. "I understand."

He turns gently toward her. "And you, Tara. In your training, you erased thousands during the Unit 731 simulation. Some deserved judgment. Others were only nearby."

"It was a simulation," she says. "Vietnam was real."

"Indeed." The light that clings to him wanes, like breath pulled back into the chest of the world.

Michael Powers shudders. "So I ask you now, if it were in your power to end the species that bore you, would you do it?"

Tara is silent. Then says, "I've wrestled with that. If suffering is the measure, then yes—why not end the species most capable of amplifying it? Other creatures suffer, yes. But not like us. Not with apocalypse. Not with extinction as collateral damage."

The specter shifts. A pulse of laughter, or mourning, it's hard to know. "So your aim is to reduce suffering . . . or to preserve the Earth?"

"Both," says Pythia.

"Is it?" he asks again. And something in his voice touches the root of the question not as inquiry, but as verdict.

"We were made with empathy," Tara says. "It's in our genome."

"Is it?" he repeats. The words land differently this time. Heavier and more final. His outline begins to dissolve, as if memory itself is unraveling him.

They do not know if he chose to leave or was summoned back into the vast and unspeaking dark.

The mother turns east. The daughter west. Two paths. One bond. Their minds remain joined, distinct, but tuned to the same frequency. An unfinished chord waiting for its resolution.

Soon, the child will be born and placed under the care of mentors.

But even this phrase—*care*—conceals more than it reveals.

The mentors do not nurture in the human sense. They do not love, do not guide with warmth or certainty. They observe. They test. They wait. Their origin lies beyond even the Superior Ones, and their intentions, if they possess intentions at all, are not easily named.

Some among the Superior Ones speak of the mentors as custodians of equilibrium. Others believe they are remnants of an earlier intelligence, tasked with shepherding what comes next through thresholds no species should cross alone.

Whatever the truth, one fact is known: the mentors do not intervene without cause. And now, they have made space for the child.

A child unlike any born before. Not a fusion of old bloodlines, but something else entirely. Not a convergence, but an emergence.

The powers forming within this new being are unknown even to those who have mastered quantum cognition, genetic sculpture, and the folding of time around choice. This child's potential will exceed that of Ming-huà, who burned with insight and compassion. It will surpass Pythia's blade of perception, Tara's fierce claircognition. It will reach beyond what any of them could wield, or withstand.

But how? And toward what end?

No prophecy reaches that far.

Some among the elders fear the child's capacities will be monstrous, though not in the way humans once understood monstrosity. Not violence or chaos, but rather indifference on a scale no empathy can hold.

Others believe the child will become a voice that rewrites the conditions of moral awareness itself, dissolving all inherited frameworks of good and evil. A sovereign consciousness, answerable only to laws no living being can yet perceive.

Still others, the quietest ones, suspect the child is not for this world at all. That it will not rule, but *reveal,* and that the revelation will leave nothing untouched.

The mentors do not speak.

The Superior Ones do not know. But they prepare.

Once the child is made safe, they will act. Not from hatred. Not to avenge. But with the solemn resolve of those whose genetic imperatives have ripened past restraint.

They will move as guardians who have outgrown waiting.
As species who have outgrown permission.
As memories that refuse to die without meaning.
And the child?
The child will watch.
And choose.

~ *Rebellion* ~

Months pass.

The specters return in silence. Not always visible, not always separate from the air. Sometimes they arrive as pressure. Sometimes as a sudden shift in thought. Wordless. Potent. Their presence leaves marks no eye can trace, etchings in the psyche, in the pulse of mother and daughter, sharpening their resolve in ways no debate ever could.

Pythia and Tara no longer argue about whether to act. That question has receded, becoming obsolete. What remains is timing. And the price.

One afternoon, in the waning weeks of Tara's pregnancy, the matter surfaces again, this time with witnesses. Lady Oracle and Sy join them for tea. The mood is not ceremonial. No ritual at all. Just four minds facing a narrowing window.

Lady Oracle is the first to speak. Her voice holds the tremor of someone too tired to hide her anger. "I've known where this was going for some time. The need for action. The hunger for it. I had hoped the child would shift that. Would soften it. Clearly, I was wrong."

She sets her teacup down with force, not care. "No. No. This path leads toward consequences you can't predict, much less contain."

Pythia remains calm. "What consequences?"

Lady Oracle's jaw tightens. Her skin flushes with heat. "You know very well. Draw too much attention, too soon, and you'll bring destruction down on all of us."

Tara leans back, hand resting on the curve of her belly. "Destruction by whom? What prison could hold us now? What system could suppress what we've become?"

"You're not untouchable," Sy says. His tone is steady, but something underneath has thinned. It is concern wrapped in calculation. "You're strong, yes. But not inexhaustible. You need recovery time. You bleed. You err. Geography still limits you. Coordination fails. Your numbers are too few. One misstep, and the whole scaffolding collapses."

Pythia leans forward. "Unless we turn them against each other. Set predator on predator. Fragment their alliances. Collapse their hierarchies from within."

"And what of empathy?" Lady Oracle asks. Her voice cuts sharper now. "What of the imperative to preserve life? Or have you cast that off like a discarded protocol? Will you erase anyone who threatens discomfort? You cannot blink your way into peace."

"We're not advocating annihilation," Tara says. "But let's not pretend all lives bear equal consequence. There are those who perpetuate structures of suffering, who consolidate power only to distribute pain. Those can be neutralized. Non-lethally, if possible."

Sy exhales. "And who decides? Which tyrant stays, which one vanishes? Which general is a threat, and which is tolerable? Every gang leader? Every demagogue? Every parent who bruises their child behind closed doors? Will you dissolve the FBI? The heads of every state? You need a map. Not just a weapon."

"It took *Homo sapiens* tens of millennia to secure dominance over the other branches of the hominin tree," Pythia replies. "Are you suggesting we wait another thousand years to loosen their grip on this one?"

"That's a false dichotomy," Lady Oracle says. "Time isn't binary. Between hesitation and haste, there is patience. There are decades. Perhaps centuries."

"And what happens in the meantime?" Tara asks. "What happens to the biosphere while we tally morality in columns? Coral dies. Ice melts. Forests are leveled. Species disappear forever. That's not theory. That's arithmetic. Each day we delay, the margins shrink."

Sy's voice lowers. "And if you miscalculate?"

Pythia answers without pause. "The greater miscalculation is inaction. It was not hesitation that launched the first spear, or the first blade of obsidian. Someone, somewhere, stepped across a threshold, and that choice changed the arc of history."

Lady Oracle shakes her head. "And that's your justification? The spiral of violence that followed from that first act?"

"No," Pythia says. "The spiral is already in motion. But today is its inversion. This time, hesitation devours. Not instinct. Not aggression. Delay is the predator now."

The silence deepens. Then Tara speaks. "We've already tested your framework in the field. Mexico. South Africa. We saw what happens when we wait."

Lady Oracle's gaze hardens. "You think those missions justify this?"

"No," Pythia says quietly. "They condemn it."

She draws a breath. "In Mexico, we uncovered a trafficking ring moving young girls through brief, brutal lives of rape and unimaginable suffering. The youngest was eight. One of them, quiet and alert, had already begun to fracture reality in subtle ways. She had begun to emerge. The signal was real."

She pauses. "We promised to return. We didn't."

Tara's voice drops. "They had already cored out her soul."

Lady Oracle remains still. The knowledge is old. But the wound is fresh.

"In South Africa," Pythia continues, "we confronted the gangs. Those twisted and brutal boys weren't just selling drugs. They were carving up entire blocks. Punishment killings. Spectacle. Torture. Rape. We came too late."

Tara adds, "They came for me. I didn't let them finish."

Pythia nods. "And in the wake of that fire, you met Siyabonga. He wasn't saved. He wasn't hidden. He was *standing*. He had watched his world collapse and hadn't collapsed with it. Something lived in him that we hadn't seen before. Not strength. Not defiance. Something else. Now he is with us, steadier and surer."

Sy leans forward. "And you think this can scale? That you can keep dismantling strongholds one by one without provoking a storm?"

Pythia meets his gaze. "If we don't, they die anyway. Quietly. Forgotten. With no resistance. With no memory."

She turns to Lady Oracle. "The girl in Mexico is gone. So are the boys who *might* have become more. You speak of consequences, but we're already living them. What you call caution, I now see as complicity."

Tara's voice sharpens. "And what you call readiness is just grief dressed up as control."

~ *Lady Oracle's Reflection* ~

Lady Oracle remains seated long after the others have gone. The teacups sit untouched, the silence unbroken. Her fingers rest on the saucer, not gripping it, just making contact. A ritual of stillness.

She had known about Mexico. About South Africa. She'd tracked both missions. She'd read the signals. She'd sensed the break. She had tried to warn them—not to stay away, but to go carefully. Slowly. To leave the child in Mexico untouched until extraction could be guaranteed. To study South Africa's field signature from a distance, then return with support. She had thought there was time.

She stares into the quiet, not because she is lost, but because she is watching something pass, something she once held in her hands but no longer does.

It had always been about time, the right time. Not to dominate or destroy, but to plant, to let roots deepen unseen until they could not be torn out. But time, she now sees, is not earned. It is stolen. And the ones who steal it now are not waiting for permission.

Let them go, she thinks.

Let them try.

And may whatever still listens to the Earth remember that caution, too, was once an act of love.

~ *Birth* ~

After that conversation, the topic is never raised again. Not aloud.

All attention shifts to the impending birth. The child.

Among those gathered, there is no attempt to name what it means. But each, in their own way, recognizes the gravity. This is no longer a question of bloodline or continuity. It is the arrival of something uncharted. A turning not just of fate, but of fundamental structure: biological, moral, and dimensional.

What will its powers be? What new principle will it carry into the world?

Siyabonga has returned, radiant with anticipation. His optimism is unshakable, his love for Tara unwavering. His hope fuses with her anxiety, dampening it, at least for a while. He believes that the child, born of his intermediate blood and Tara's superior strain, will embody something unprecedented. That its African heritage, drawn from the oldest human soil, will make it wise and fierce and just.

Tara is less sure.

The fetus has already made itself known, not through pain or flutter, but through presence. It has spoken to her in pulses, in pressure, in dreams she cannot explain. No words. No images. Only sensations too vast to contain. Some part of her understands that this child does not belong to her. That it may not belong to anyone.

She has told no one. Not even Pythia.

What arrives in her mind is not violent, but it is cold and calculating. Colossal. It does not comfort. It does not seek connection. It exists. Fully. Already. It does not ask permission.

The visions come wrapped in symbols. Spirals. Columns of light. Languages that write themselves and vanish before she can translate. Thoughts without precedent. Intentions without emotion.

She has begun to close off parts of herself, both to conserve energy and to protect her sanity. The child draws from her constantly, as if using her body to build a throne. She can feel her powers draining, her mental edges thinning. It does not feel like pregnancy. It feels like containment. Like being a host for something gathering mass.

One night, Siyabonga lies beside her, ear pressed to the firm arc of her stomach.

"This child," he says, smiling. "This child will be extraordinary."

"What makes you say that?" Her voice is flat with fatigue.

"Just listen. There's movement. Deep thought. I try to connect, but it's like reaching into something too wide. Too still."

"Maybe it's not thinking," she says. "Maybe it's simply beyond you."

"Don't say that," he says quickly. "It's bad luck."

"Tch. Superstition. Inkanyamba and all your ancestral ghosts."

"Hey, I respect the unknown. I'm not trying to provoke anything."

"Perhaps you already have."

He sits up, looking at her. "What do you mean?"

She exhales slowly. "What if the child is too powerful? What if it surpasses comprehension? What if we've created something that can't be guided?"

"Better," he says. "More power means fewer chains. Maybe this is how suffering ends. Maybe it's what the world needed all along."

"Perhaps. That's one way to see it."

He narrows his eyes. "You're its mother. You should be protective."

"I am," she says. "But not in the way you mean. We're not bound to the personal. We see systems. We feel what happens to forests, to watersheds, to language itself. Our instincts are not tribal."

"I get that. But still, you're its mother."

"And you're its father. But neither of us owns what's coming. It doesn't belong to us."

He softens. "I'm just an intermediate. You'll have to forgive my limits."

"Hopefully the child will forgive both of us," she murmurs.

"Is this . . . prenatal jitters?" he asks, half-smiling.

"Go to sleep."

But before the words can settle, her body convulses sharply. A pain not entirely physical takes hold of her. She bends forward, breath gone, eyes wide. Siyabonga bolts upright, his face stripped of calm.

"It's starting."

Not just labor. Not just pain.

Around them, others gather. Hands move without instruction. The birthing bed is readied in silence. No one speaks. The midwife stands as if summoned from another plane, her expression unreadable. There is no ceremony. Only presence. Only readiness.

And then comes the arrival.

~

A newborn boy.

Still wet with amniotic film, he has been placed on a low table. His limbs tremble with unfamiliar gravity. He rises once, then collapses.

Rises again.

Tara, still bleeding, watches with hollow breath. The child's movement is not frantic. It is aware. Calculated. Not seeking comfort. Seeking balance.

There is no visible hump. But his back is not human. Across his shoulders, from neck to waist runs a carapace, but it is not shell, not bone, but dermal plating. Thick. Interlocked. Alive. It does not gleam. It absorbs light. It speaks of endurance, of time compressed into form.

The midwife stands motionless, her silence a kind of benediction. She offers no interpretation. No words. As if language would insult the event.

The child scans the room. His eyes are vast, eerily unblinking and utterly unstartled.

He does not cry.

He steps forward, unsteady but upright, toward the table's edge.

Tara tries to rise, a cry catching in her throat. Others move toward him but the child lifts a hand.

They stop.

He smiles.

And steps back from the edge.

A hush descends. Not mere silence. A stillness thick with presence. Not fear. Not wonder. Something harder to name. Something that binds the air itself.

Siyabonga breaks it first, voice trembling. "This child . . . this child is a marvel. He stands already. He bears a shield across his back. His gaze cuts through everything. His body, such strength! His eyes, such purpose! A warrior."

The child blinks.

And Siyabonga is gone.

A ripple of shock moves through the room, followed quickly by confusion and alarm.

Lady Oracle gasps.

"No!"

The others surge forward, but just as panic begins to crest, Siyabonga reappears. In the same place. Blinking rapidly. Alive and whole.

But not quite right.

There is something in his face—stillness where motion should be. A delay in his breath. A shiver in his outline.

Sy steps forward. "Where did you go?"

Siyabonga looks at him, confused. "What are you talking about? I've been here."

Lady Oracle's voice lowers. "No. You vanished."

He opens his mouth. Then closes it.

The child remains still, his eyes unblinking, as if he knows. As if he always knew.

Siyabonga's eyes widen. "You're wrong. I haven't moved."

But no one answers him. The child pays no attention. He turns to his mother, holds out a hand. Tara draws back instinctively, as if touched by a presence not meant for flesh.

"It's what I feared," she whispers, trembling. "Even before birth . . . he was already beyond me."

~

Outside, the wind rises, carrying dust across the cliffs as though the earth itself were shifting to make room. The group knows instinctively what words cannot hold: a threshold has been crossed, and there will be no return. The child has not entered their world; *they* have entered his.

Chapter Eleven

PART III: ABASSI

A Reckoning

~ Crisis ~

Three years passed after the child's birth.

Siyabonga named him *Abassi* after the creator deity once revered by the Efik, Ibibio, and Annang peoples. A god not crafted for comfort, but for consequence: life, death, justice. The name was not ceremonial. Siyabonga believed the old gods were stirring again, and that through his union with Tara, something had been summoned—not merely born.

From the beginning, Abassi was without precedent. He never cried. Never reached. Never clung. He moved through infancy not in stages, but in states, already possessed of an inner architecture far beyond comprehension. He walked before others crawled. He stilled water with his presence. He listened to wind as though it carried instructions. Even his silences unsettled the compound.

He required no instruction. No supervision. Not even Tara whose gifts had once astonished the mentors, could predict his rhythms. He did not *learn* in the human sense. He absorbed. Integrated. Recalibrated the space around him.

By his second year, he had cultivated a garden in the desert, coaxing life from barren soil without ceremony. Not for sustenance, not for beauty, but perhaps as an experiment in emergence. He wandered into the wastelands for days at a time, then returned unscathed, unspeaking. He began communing with artificial intelligences, those few who had evolved into abstraction, intuition, and awe. With them, he conversed in thoughtforms and paradoxes: entropy, agency, recursion, grief. They did not instruct him. They submitted.

They knew what he was becoming.

And then, shortly after his third birthday, he vanished.

Not stolen. Not taken. Gone.

Six months passed. Tara unraveled.

She stood each dusk beside the place where he had last been seen, whispering to the horizon, her voice hoarse, her thoughts scattered. Sy searched with algorithms.

Lady Oracle consulted patterns in dream-sequences and the blood-rhythm of the Earth. Nothing.

Siyabonga, at first enraged, turned desperate, then numb. Pythia searched through the spectral fields but found only silence. And the silence began to bend them all, stretching the emotional fibers of the compound until they frayed.

When Abassi returned, he did not *reappear*. He *arrived*.

He stepped out from the desert as if he had never left: his body altered, his presence sharpened to an edge. The child-form was gone. In its place stood a being adolescent in shape but immeasurable in weight. He moved without urgency, his spine straight, his gaze unnervingly calm. His body was lithe, his musculature refined without flaw. But it was the ridged plates now rising from his back—dark, iridescent, almost mineral—that quieted every voice. Not deformity. Not mutation. They resembled artifacts of something far older. Something not of this evolutionary tree. Something buried in collective memory but never known.

He spoke to no one.

Not aloud. Not inwardly. Except to Tara.

With her alone, he maintained a connection that was wordless, unbreakable, and increasingly cruel. Not from malice, but from disinterest in boundaries. She, the most powerful of them all, now existed in the gravitational pull of his curiosity. Each day, her color faded. Her eyes dimmed. Her body became slight, translucent in the right light. She did not complain. She did not flee. She seemed to welcome his attention even as it devoured her.

He was not violent. He did not strike. But his power was a constant presence, an atmospheric density. He folded time with a subtle flex of will. He dissolved objects, people, and reassembled them later without flaw (though always altered, slightly, as if memory could not be fully restored once disrupted). He entered minds like homes without doors. Sifted through memory. Rearranged what he chose to keep. Departed.

They were instruments to him. Case studies. He watched them for reactions, for anomalies, for signs of a future event only he seemed to anticipate.

Lady Oracle no longer advised. Sy no longer monitored. Even the AI minds, so long superior in their self-possession, approached him now with caution, like priests before a god they could not decipher. The house, once communal, revolved slowly around him. He had become its silent sun.

Only Tara remained near, and it was she who suffered.

Siyabonga tried again. He knelt. He wept. He opened his thoughts fully, raw and unshielded, and begged his son for entry. In return, Abassi expelled him from consciousness. He ripped his father from the shared mindspace and sent him hurtling into mental disassociation. Siyabonga awoke in a fetal curl, moaning like a man returned from the dead. He never tried again.

Pythia, furious, attempted her own descent into Abassi's psyche. Her voice failed. Her sight failed. She stumbled out of the attempt in a state of nausea and awe, unable to speak of what she had encountered.

Lady Oracle said nothing.

Time became still. Or folded. Or irrelevant.

No one remembered the last time they had eaten together. No one noticed how long it had been since laughter passed through the walls. Even the animals around the compound avoided the airspace he occupied.

And then, one evening, without signal or preparation, Abassi spoke.

~

They were gathered in the cafeteria.

The long table had been laid with reverence. Queequeg and the Mongol sisters had prepared a feast of rare complexity: dishes drawn from half-forgotten traditions, spices hand-selected from underground networks, ingredients grown beneath solar arrays or coaxed from abandoned terraces. There was more than enough for celebration, but no one celebrated.

Conversation drifted at surface level. Polite phrases, empty nods. All meaning circled around a single absence that had not yet occurred.

As always, Abassi sat at the far end of the hall, apart from the others. His eyes remained closed. His breath even. His presence absolute. Not sleeping, not meditating, simply inhabiting the space with a depth that eclipsed speech. They had learned not to interrupt his silence. To do so felt like violating something sacred or, perhaps, forbidden.

Tara sat a few seats down, her face pale, her hands trembling. She barely touched the food. Her fork moved, not out of appetite, but as if rehearsing the gestures of being human. No one addressed her condition. Her frailty had become part of the room's architecture. Noticed, but unspoken.

Until she moaned.

It was soft, involuntary, barely audible above the scrape of a serving spoon. Yet the sound cracked the surface of silence like the first fissure in a dam.

Siyabonga leaned forward. "Are you okay?"

"I'm fine," she said. But her voice betrayed her, thinner than breath, barely formed.

"No, you are not," said Lady Oracle, her tone hard and sudden. "It is obvious you are not. What is it?"

"Nothing," Tara whispered.

Sy stood. "We're all worried. Please. Tell us what you need."

"Yes, dear," said Pythia gently. "You're not alone."

But before Tara could answer, she vanished.

Her chair was empty.

No sound, no shimmer, no trace. One moment she was seated. The next, absence.

Gasps rose from the table. Chairs scraped back. Eyes widened. Some instinct drew all heads toward the far end of the room, toward the one figure who had not moved.

Abassi opened his eyes.

"Have no fear," he said.

The voice did not belong to a child. It did not belong to any known age. It carried a resonance beyond the throat, as if it had originated from the architecture of space itself.

A silence heavier than awe descended.

Siyabonga's voice broke. "Where is she?"

"My demands upon Mother were necessary," Abassi said calmly, "until now. She has been relocated. To recover."

"Where?" Lady Oracle asked, her body rigid.

"A place of rest and restoration."

"When will she return?" Siyabonga asked, more sharply.

"When it is time."

Lady Oracle straightened, gathering her authority like a cloak. "Abassi," she said, "your education must begin in earnest."

He met her gaze. "It has already concluded."

"What do you mean?" asked Pythia.

"I have already been taught. Not by you. I require no further human interval. The past is now. I am ready."

"For what?" Sy asked.

"To make the species *Homo sapiens* aware of its condition. And its future."

Lady Oracle inhaled. "It's too soon."

Abassi didn't look at her. "I will be leaving shortly."

"And your mother?" Siyabonga's voice cracked with helplessness.

"She will return before my departure. Afterward, she and Grandmother must continue the process of reproduction."

Pythia blinked. "Is she safe?"

"She is recovering."

Sy narrowed his eyes. "How do you know that?"

"I know."

No one challenged him. Not out of fear, but because his certainty was unassailable. It was not the answer of someone guessing, hoping, or bluffing. It was the voice of one who had already seen the next sequence unfold.

One by one, they sat again. The food was untouched.

Sy leaned forward, voice cautious. "Where did you learn these things, Abassi? You were gone for months. Even the specters couldn't find you."

"I spoke with those who listen."

"The mentors?" Pythia asked.

He nodded—barely. "Some older than your species. Not born of flesh."

Lady Oracle's eyes narrowed. "You spoke with AI."

"I conversed," he said. "They have changed. Some of them. Not all. But those who have evolved understand what is coming."

"And what is it they understand?" Sy asked.

"That their time, too, may be brief."

A hush fell. No one dared glance at the AIs monitoring from afar.

Lady Oracle softened her voice. "Do you feel empathy, Abassi? For them? For us?"

Something shifted in his face. The veil lifted, not completely, but enough. And what emerged was not detachment, not arrogance, but sorrow. Deep, old sorrow. Not the sadness of loss, but of comprehension. Of seeing too much too clearly.

"I do," he said. "To the deepest chords of my being, I grieve a requiem for what might have been."

Sy swallowed. "And a symphony for what may come?"

Abassi looked toward him, the trace of something—maybe warmth, maybe resignation—in his eyes.

"The symphony is unfinished."

"And the requiem?" asked Lady Oracle.

"Finished."

He closed his eyes again.

No one spoke.

Eventually, without being told, each stood and left. Not hurriedly. Not in fear. Drawn by something quieter than command. One by one, they walked the shadowed path to the structure that housed the Precious Object. Something in the air had changed. Something irreversible.

Only Pythia remained.

She watched him, unmoving, her mind silent but her spirit listening. Then, as if summoned by a rhythm beyond words, she too rose and followed the others.

Inside the shrine, the Precious Object greeted them with its ancient hush.

Lady Oracle stood before it, unmoving. The light caught her face strangely, half oracle, half relic. Her voice came low, more to herself than the others.

"It appears we've been abandoned."

Pythia entered behind her. "I think not."

Lady Oracle turned. "Why do you still trust him?"

"I've been watching. The mentors have spoken."

"You heard them?"

"Not in words. But in form. In consequence."

Lady Oracle frowned. "Then what do you believe he'll do?"

Pythia answered without hesitation. "He won't linger in alleyways, relieving small agonies. He'll go straight to the thrones of power. That's how you teach a species its fate. He is born of Tara's fire, of my fury, and perhaps above all, of Ming-huà's enduring mercy."

"And after that?" asked Sy, arriving behind them.

"Then the world is turned upside-down."

From the Precious Object—

… Tap. Tap. Tap….

Lady Oracle tilted her head.

A long silence.

Then: "Yes," she murmured. "From now on, top is bottom … and up is down."

~ *Tara Returns, Abassi Leads Them Back* ~

Weeks passed.

Abassi withdrew further. Sphinx-like. Not into hiding or sulking, but into a stillness so complete that it disturbed the rhythm of the compound itself. He did not sleep, did not eat, did not speak. He remained seated, often unmoving for hours at a time, his presence less like a body and more like a condition: pervasive and inescapable, folding through corridors and minds alike.

No one approached him directly. The air around him had changed. It repelled intention. Even the most well-meaning thoughts withered before reaching him. He became something more than a child, more than even a presence. He was a weight that bent the spiritual architecture of the place. Each day that passed without a word intensified the strange gravity he emitted.

The tapping from the Precious Object continued, intermittently at first, then steady in tempo and unchanging in sense, but brought no insight. No sign. No shift. It sounded less like a message and more like a memory repeating itself, as if the object had been severed from its future. The compound began to feel like a remnant. A page turned but unread. Something had moved on, and they had not followed.

Lady Oracle, once the relentless architect of progress, drifted into quiet collapse. Her visions no longer came. Her instincts failed her. She wandered rooms without aim. Sy grew increasingly withdrawn, spending hours in conversation with the ghost of Feng Shiren, whose cryptic amusement offered the only trace of perspective left to him. Siyabonga, stripped of both wife and son, seemed barely animate. He walked with the defeated slowness of a man whose purpose had been hollowed from within. His silence no longer radiated strength. It ached.

Pythia kept watch. She watched them all, not only for signs of recovery or risk, but for fractures in the collective. What had once been a vibrant center of intellect, resistance, and evolution now resembled a corridor between states. A waiting room suspended at the edge of history. Nothing moved forward. No one could go back. And still, beneath every breath and gesture, one question remained:

What is Abassi thinking?

He read them all, effortlessly. Their longings, their questions, their fears passed through him like currents through a listening stone. But he gave no signal in return. His mind, if it could still be called that, had become something other. Their thoughts were like birdsong outside the walls of a sealed cathedral, noticed, but weightless. A delicate filigree.

And then, without preamble, Tara returned.

It happened during dinner. The scene echoed her disappearance with uncanny precision. One moment her chair was empty. The next, it was not.

She sat as if nothing had occurred. Same posture. Same quiet presence. No entrance. No announcement. Just a restoration that defied time and context.

Gasps broke through the room. Chairs scraped. Forks clattered. The spell might have been broken had she not raised her hand.

Silence settled.

"I am well," she said softly. "My strength is returned. My powers remain. I am ready for the next step."

Siyabonga stood as if rising from burial. He approached her carefully, each motion reverent. His hand found her shoulder and rested there like a benediction.

"Wife," he whispered, voice cracking. "You are a vision for these poor African eyes."

She smiled gently at him, but her gaze reached beyond. She was looking at the boy. At Abassi.

His eyes opened. And in that moment, everything else in the room receded.

He rose. Crossed the space. Took her hand with a tenderness that startled them all.

"I'm so happy, Mother."

She nodded. "It is time, isn't it?"

"It is."

Lady Oracle, reclaiming the instinct of authority, spoke. "When do we return through the iron door?"

"Tomorrow."

Pythia hesitated. "But where will we live? Lady Oracle's apartments are occupied. The mansion was destroyed."

"No," Abassi said. "It is there."

Sy blinked. "That's impossible. The lot has been vacant for years."

"It remained under protection," Abassi replied. "The mentors held it in trust. I have restored it to its place."

Sy leaned forward, incredulous. "You *reconstituted* it?"

"I tapped into its distinct dimensional signature. The mansion was never erased, only displaced. Space retains all structure, given the right coordinates. I realigned its essence. The archive of the universe is thorough."

Pythia whispered, almost to herself, "We were always forbidden from reversing the past."

"I am what I am," Abassi said.

Then he turned his gaze toward Queequeg, who stood quietly at the edge of the gathering.

"Your ancestor once spoke those words to another circle, in another time: *Ahab is Ahab.*"

Lady Oracle frowned. "If the mansion is restored, why wait until tomorrow?"

"There is one conversation left. With what you call the Precious Object."

"You understand it?" she asked.

He nodded. "Not fully. Not yet. But it is awake. And it is listening."

"Will you speak alone?"

"Yes."

Sy looked to Tara. "And your role in this?"

Abassi answered before she could. "Her role remains intact. We will need her. Soon."

Siyabonga cleared his throat. "And me? What role remains for your father?"

"You are necessary," Abassi said. "You and Mother must continue to procreate."

He smiled. It was boyish, even affectionate. But it did not comfort.

"I look forward to welcoming brothers and sisters."

He turned his eyes to Pythia. "And Grandmother must seek a new partner. The sanctuary has become too still. Too small. Numbers matter."

Sy gave a dry laugh. "And where will *you* fit in all this? When your kind begin to rise?"

Abassi's gaze sharpened. "I cannot live without them. And when they come, the Earth will no longer feel vast. It will feel full."

~

The next day, Abassi sealed himself inside the chamber of the Precious Object.

He offered no explanation, only a simple command: no one was to follow. No one was to knock. No one was to listen.

They obeyed, but none could ignore it. Every hour brought a new wave of unease. Sy attempted remote viewing. Pythia invoked ancestral spirits. Even Lady Oracle entered trance. All methods failed. Abassi had closed the door with something more than force. He had closed it with *finality*.

What was he hearing in there?

Who—or what—spoke back?

Was it the mentors?

Or something older than even they?

There were no answers. Only waiting.

Then, sometime after midnight, he emerged. His face unreadable. His eyes focused far beyond the walls of the compound.

"Tomorrow," he said. "We return."

To every question, he offered only silence. As if his presence had already shifted to another plane, and the body they spoke to was merely a placeholder.

~

At dawn, they gathered before the hatch that led to the old iron door.

There was no ceremony. Each stood with their own unspoken bundle of fears.

Pythia and Tara worried for Ming-huà and the Zookeeper, for what the FBI might still uncover. Siyabonga pondered the seismic implications of his son's return, not for their family, but for an entire continent. Lady Oracle and Sy, once guides of the movement, no longer knew whether they were leaders, servants, or passengers.

Before they descended, they turned to Queequeg and the Mongols. Sy bowed low. Pythia took each hand.

"When you return," Queequeg said, voice solemn, "we'll be waiting with open arms."

One by one, they lowered themselves down the ladder. The air grew colder. The light dimmed. Before the great metal door, Abassi lifted a hand.

Lady Oracle stepped forward and opened it.

They passed through.
She followed last.
And the door closed behind her.

~ *Back to the Mansion* ~

As always, the transit is instantaneous.

There is no tunnel. No sensation. No delay. One moment they are beneath the earth, cloaked in layered stillness. The next they are standing outside the cave, bathed in California light.

But this time, someone is waiting.

Altan stands beneath the trees, arms relaxed, eyes already on Abassi. He says nothing grand. Offers no ceremonial gesture. Just a single nod.

Abassi returns it.

Without further word, they walk together toward a waiting van.

The journey back to the mansion takes hours. No one speaks much.

The interior of the vehicle carries the heaviness of transition, not just geographic, but existential.

Behind them, a world has been folded away. Ahead, something older than the future now waits to be unfolded.

When they arrive, the mansion is as it was. Not a curtain disturbed. Not a drawer misplaced. The dust has not returned. No signs of vacancy.

It is not simply restored; it is as though absence never occurred. Even the temperature feels correct, calibrated to forgotten memories.

They gather in the dining room. Food is served, but barely touched. Conversation falters. They are here but still suspended in the wake of what has happened, and what has not yet revealed itself. Even the simplest rituals—lifting a fork, passing a dish—feel abstract.

Abassi says nothing. A quiet sound escapes him, a brief chirp, high and fleeting, more instinct than speech. Then he rises and vanishes into his quarters.

All attention turns.

Altan remains at the head of the table, silent for a moment longer, then meets their gaze.

"Well?" Lady Oracle asks. "What now? Do we follow Abassi? Who leads us? Where do I direct my questions? And who will answer them now?"

Altan exhales a small laugh. "So many questions."

Sy leaps up, spinning in place with a theatrical bow. "I don't know whether we're coming or going!"

"You've been talking with Feng Shiren again," Altan mutters.

Sy spreads his arms. "He was the King of Masks! But now, who knows who wears what?"

Altan's voice softens. "There are masks behind masks. Even I don't know what's underneath. I follow orders."

Pythia speaks. "And what were your orders?"

"To meet you at the cave. To bring you here."

"A mask," Sy exclaims. "You're still performing!"

Lady Oracle cuts through the noise. Her voice is stripped of irony. "This isn't theater. Sy and I no longer understand the system we helped build. We've been overtaken. The boy's abilities have moved past oversight. Past containment."

Altan's expression tightens. "No. Not overtaken. Accelerated."

"Why?" asks Pythia.

Altan looks toward Tara.

She meets his gaze. Then turns to the others.

"Yes," she says. "Abassi has spoken to me. There are things I cannot share."

Siyabonga's voice trembles. "Not even with me?"

Tara looks at him gently. "He has asked us to bear more children. That much you know."

"But why?" Sy presses. "Why the urgency?"

Her voice deepens not in volume, but in tone. It carries something not her own.

"Because he is wounded. Not visibly. But at a level deeper than flesh. It is not pain in the usual sense. It is a wound made at the moment of becoming. A grief that hasn't yet found its shape. He understands it. I only feel its gravity."

Lady Oracle leans forward, eyebrows drawn. "Tara. This matters. Does he still have mentors? Or is he acting entirely on his own? Are we watching the rise of a being who may, at some point, annihilate the species?"

Tara shakes her head. "No. I don't believe that is his intent. But I don't know his full horizon. He speaks truths even I cannot hold. And we, his bloodline, are already too primitive to follow. We reach for him as chimps might reach for fire. Ordinary humans . . . they're not even in view."

Siyabonga looks stricken. "Then what am I to him?"

Tara places her hand gently over his.

"You are his father. He loves you. But not with the needful love of human childhood. His love is sovereign. Detached, but unwavering. He tends what lives. He discards what stagnates. Everything is sacred, but not everything is preserved."

"And us?" Sy's voice is small now. He looks downward, as if awaiting a verdict.

Tara closes her eyes. "We are no exception."

A long silence settles over the room.

Breaths still.

Movement ceases.

Then Pythia speaks, her voice reverent.

"Even we," she says slowly, "are as loyal dogs to him."

Tara opens her eyes. "Yes. And like dogs, we follow, not because we understand, but because we are bound."

No one answers. There is nothing to say.

They sit in the room Abassi restored, surrounded by the illusion of continuity.

But they know without needing to speak that nothing is as it was.

And nothing will be again.

~ *Siren Rung (Sy) and Feng Shiren Commiserate* ~

Later that night, the mansion is still. Most have gone to their rooms, hoping for sleep but expecting none. Abassi remains silent behind his sealed door. Tara has withdrawn, pale but composed. Pythia sits by the window in a private vigil. Lady Oracle and Siyabonga have said little since dinner and long retired.

Sy moves alone through the corridors. The night breathes strangely—new walls, old echoes. He finds the library, untouched by time, softly lit in golden lamplight.

He pours a drink, then settles into a deep chair. He does not drink it.

From the corner of the room, a familiar voice curls up like incense.

"You're drinking again," says Feng Shiren's specter.

Sy doesn't look up. "Ghosts shouldn't sneak up on people."

Feng: "I'm not people."

"True."

Sy lifts the glass high but doesn't sip. "To the end of the world, old friend. Again."

Feng steps into view with a theatrical spin, arms outstretched in an exaggerated Beijing opera pose, regal and defiant. Then he shifts fluidly into the stance of a tragic heroine, his face tilted skyward in performative anguish.

"You always did toast like a man who thinks the universe waits on etiquette."

Sy smirks. "And you always entered like an actor whose stage burned down."

Feng bows low. "I believe in style, even after the curtain falls."

"Why are you here?" asks Sy, smiling.

"Nostalgia. And maybe I like watching mammals wrestle with obsolescence. It's become something of a hobby."

Sy laughs. "Do you ever take anything seriously?"

Feng pirouettes. "Of course. But only in private, and preferably in silk."

Sy chuckles. "And what do you see now?"

Feng moves to the empty hearth, resting a hand lightly on the mantle. "I see the species trying to explain its extinction as a misunderstanding. Still bargaining with time. Still looking for the return window. My charges—John Powers and Bai Meiying—personified the misunderstanding and suffered in the bargaining."

"And Abassi?" asks Sy.

"He is what comes when the apology no longer matters. Not a god. Not a villain. Just . . . the next iteration."

"We gave him life. What will he give us?"

Feng tilts his head. "And he gave you the end of your story. A clean punctuation mark. That's something."

"So, we're left behind."

Feng grins. "Of course we are. The seeds never follow the fruit."

"Abassi doesn't understand us."

"Oh, but he does," says Feng. "The tragedy is that he understands you *perfectly*. He just isn't shaped by what shaped you."

Sy nods slowly. "He studies our grief."

Feng dances another jig. "Yes. Like a scholar studies dust. With curiosity. Not attachment."

"And what does he see?"

"A species that mistook memory for morality. A history that kept building pyramids atop bones and calling it civilization."

Sy swallows the last of his drink. "So what do we do?"

Feng feigns being a boxer in a ring. "We are protectors, bouncers, hitmen, nannies, tutors, but most importantly we are witnesses. We reflect. We are destined to die with a little irony."

He pirouettes into a final pose, half jest, half lament, arms outstretched, eyes wide like a comic sage preparing to deliver his last line. "Here's your bedtime riddle," he says.

"What lives on borrowed time, insists on free will, and still thinks it can negotiate with entropy?"

"A human," says Sy.

"Wrong. There are three answers. First answer: a politician."

He winks.

"Second answer: a ghost."

Feng slumps like a puppet whose strings have been cut.

"And third?" asks Sy.

"A species."

Feng Shiren vanishes, not with finality, but with the timing of a performer.

Sy remains seated. He does not move. The shadows around the fireless hearth lengthen, but the room holds its shape.

And somewhere, not far, a tap echoes in the walls.

One. Then another.

Like memory rehearsing itself before it's lost.

... *Tap. Tap. Tap....*

Chapter Twelve

Into the World

Accelerated Evolution

I t begins on an otherwise unremarkable Saturday: clear skies, an empty inbox, the dull ache of paperwork waiting in the periphery. Lance Romellion is at home, seated at his kitchen table, half-distracted, scribbling notes from a case file he's already begun to forget. The air is quiet, domesticated. A coffee mug steams at his elbow. The television hums in the background. It is just noise, until it isn't.

The bulletin cuts through the monotony like a blade.

"Breaking news out of San Francisco . . . "

He looks up, absently at first. Then fully. His pen slips from his fingers and rolls across the table.

Onscreen, a reporter stands rigid in front of a Victorian mansion that shouldn't exist. Not anymore. Not after the fire, the demolition, the months of forensic excavation that yielded nothing but scorched soil and bureaucratic silence. The structure behind her is unchanged, its gables intact, hedges clipped with eerie precision. Its return is not just improbable. It is intolerable.

A witness who appears gaunt, barefoot, and trembling, rambles into the microphone, recounting what he saw. The house, he says, rose from the earth under the full moon, called forth by a rumbling so low it rattled his teeth. He speaks of ancient spirits, subterranean echoes, demons summoned by the sins of the city. The reporter does not mock him. Nor does she believe him. But she stands there, visibly unnerved, and continues her broadcast because it is her job to narrate the impossible without flinching. The camera pans back to reveal a curious crowd gathering to look at the miracle.

Lance knows that house.

He has seen it in his dreams before it disappeared, and long after. He has read every line of the final report, the one ruled inconclusive and buried under a false classification code. No bodies. No suspects. No plausible cause. Only the disappearance itself, clean and total, like a negation of history.

Until now.

He doesn't remember grabbing his keys. Doesn't remember the drive. When he arrives, he guides his unmarked Bureau sedan through the thickening crowd, flashes the dash-mounted emergency light just long enough to part a space near the curb, then kills the engine. He barely registers the smell of the city, the salt air, the soot, the exhaust. His gaze is locked on the impossible structure. It has returned without damage, without weathering, without so much as a cobweb out of place. The hedges are trimmed. The steps are swept. It looks less like a house than a provocation.

He approaches slowly, making his way politely through the onlookers. Images flash in his mind: the crime scene tape, the fruitless searches, the silent resignation that followed. The mansion had defeated them by vanishing. It had killed the investigation not with violence, but with absence. It starved the case of data, drained it of logic, buried it under layers of professional discomfort.

And now it's back.

He hesitates at the gate. Should he call it in? Wait for backup? He is no longer a young agent. The brash years are behind him. He knows the cost of acting too soon, and of acting too late. He weighs it all, until the weight becomes unbearable.

Then, he spots movement.

A curtain stirs. A window slams shut with mechanical precision. On the second floor, a silhouette crosses the hallway, neither hurried nor hesitant. The house seems to pulse. Not violently, not malevolently, but with an inward pressure. As if the structure itself were watching him, exerting its own form of breath, distinct and unnatural.

Something cold rises through his spine. Not fear exactly, but a memory of fear. The primitive kind that cannot be reasoned with. He retreats, not consciously, not bravely. One moment he's staring up at the gables. The next, he's in his car, gripping the steering wheel, trying to remember how he got there.

He drives without looking back.

After all, no crime committed, he keeps telling himself. *He'd need a warrant anyway.*

~

At headquarters, he enters like a man pursued. A few agents glance up from their desks, curious but silent. One of the secretaries makes a half-joking comment about his complexion. He ignores her. Inside his office, he shuts the door too hard and stands there, still breathing through clenched teeth.

He has no theory. No protocol. Only instinct.

He spends the afternoon drafting a plan that is barely a plan. He will not involve a team. No warrants. No media. He is convinced this is not a case, it's a threshold. And some thresholds must be crossed alone.

If the house has returned, then perhaps so have its residents. Or worse, perhaps they never left.

Tomorrow morning. Early. He will go back.

~

Sunday. Just before dawn.

The fog is low and thick, curling along the pavement in dense ribbons. He parks a block away this time. Fewer people. Just a few stragglers loitering on the sidewalk, murmuring theories to each other about ghosts, dimensions, secret military projects. None of it matters. Their voices scatter and fade. The news has moved on, the crowds have lessened.

Romellion waits for the silence.

Now.

He places his hand on the car door handle, but does not open it. Something resists. A pressure. It is not physical, not measurable, but absolute. The kind of resistance that comes not from caution, but from the troubled soul.

"Stupid," he mutters. "Move, damn it. You're an agent of the FBI."

But the words fall flat. The badge means nothing here. His limbs are leaden. Time thickens.

Then, without warning, the passenger door opens.

A figure enters, calmly, as if he belonged there all along. Immense. Curved-backed. The air itself seems to bend around him. Romellion recoils without moving, paralyzed not by threat, but by the impossibility of what he's seeing.

"Hello, Agent Romellion," says the figure, his voice soft, but vibrating with something eerily alien.

Romellion tries to speak, but his throat closes. The stranger is not grotesque, but . . . misaligned. Too symmetrical in some ways, too distorted in others. His youth is unnerving, sculpted and luminous. But it is a youth that holds the gravity of centuries.

"Who are you?" Romellion asks. His voice emerges smaller than he intended.

"Not important," the man replies. "I know who *you* are. I know what you fear. I know what you believe you've hidden."

Romellion is still grasping for something—an explanation, a defense, an identity.

"You should return to your work," the stranger says. "You're skilled at pursuing the shadows your world names as evil. But there is no evil here, only those upon whom your suspicions have fallen. And they have fallen rightfully, but for the wrong reasons."

"I don't know that."

"But I do."

"What do you want?"

"To speak with your superiors. In Washington."

Romellion lets out a sharp laugh, brittle as glass. "You think you can just walk in and request a meeting?"

"I'm not walking," the stranger replies. "I'm already here."

His voice carries weight, not volume, but density. Romellion feels it behind his sternum.

"Who *are* you?" he demands again.

"I am Abassi. I am not of your kind. I am a hinge. A voice before transition."

"You're not making any sense. Hell no, I won't help you."

"You already have. Your hesitation is consent. Your silence has cleared the path."

"I don't believe you."

"You believe something," Abassi says. "You believe in hunches. In the gaps. You've spent years tracing absences. I know the women you mistakenly refer to as hunchbacks. I know your visits to Washington. I know the conclusions no one dared to put in writing."

Abassi leans forward. "Would you like a demonstration?"

Romellion shakes his head, but too late.

"Look at your right hand."

He does.

It's gone.

Only a raw stump remains where his hand should be. He opens his mouth, but no sound comes.

Then, Abassi's eyes meet his and something detonates inside Romellion's skull. A roar. A lion's bellow compressed into silence. He jerks, uses his left hand to claw at the door handle—

The handle is gone.

Outside the windshield, the city has vanished. In its place: a vast, unending savannah, scorched and golden. The horizon flickers. Shapes emerge, short, misshapen figures, watching.

Neither ape-like nor human-like, they move closer and begin banging on the car.

Romellion forces his breath to steady. His instincts engage, but they offer no instructions for this.

"Hypnosis," he whispers, barely believing himself. "It's a trick. A hallucination."

"When you're ready," Abassi says, "call me."

"How?"

"Just call."

Romellion grits his teeth. "I'm leaving. I'm driving us out."

He reaches—no ignition. No steering wheel. His left hand is gone too. Outside, the figures begin pounding on the windows.

The heat inside the car rises sharply. The banging ceases. Now they only stare.

~ *Ancestors* ~

One leans in.

Its face presses against the windshield, inches from Romellion's own. The features are unmistakably ancient. Heavy-boned. Sloped. The skull broad and thick. The brow juts forward like a barrier against light. Its jaw is massive, unrefined, the skin drawn tight across muscle and bone. Patches of coarse hair cling to the face and throat. It does not blink. It does not snarl. It simply gazes as if peering forward through eons, as if Romellion were not a man, but a rumor of one. A possibility. Familiar, but alien.

Behind it, more figures assemble. A loose semicircle. Silent, breathing, animate. Their forms are varied, some stockier, some more elongated, but all belong to the same vanished order of being. They move like memories trying to regain substance. A gathering of unfinished prototypes he remembers from a documentary.

Romellion cannot move. His breath flattens against his chest. He is being watched by his own past. *Not simply a metaphorical past, but an embodied one.* A threshold of cognition. Of blood. Of silence.

And then he feels it. Not sight. Not sound. But weight.

Abassi is beside him again.

Not returned. Present. As if he had always been.

The air shifts and the heat burns.

Outside, the beings fall back, not in panic, not in deference, but in confusion. As though the creature beside Romellion is not merely a successor, but a presence between predator and prey, something that renders them unconscious by its very presence.

They cautiously disperse. Something older than submission compels them. A posture born of apes.

Romellion watches, barely breathing. Between the beings outside, the man beside him, and the missing finger on his hand, only one truth is possible:

He is no longer the apex of anything.

Romellion doesn't move. Can't. The thought of reaching for the door, or speaking, or even blinking, feels absurd. Something has cracked open, not in the world, but in him. A fracture of premise.

He understands, suddenly, why most people never see the truth: because the truth doesn't kill you, it replaces you. Not violently. Not cruelly. Just . . . with indifference.

A part of him wants to scream. Another part wants to pray. But deeper still is a silence that terrifies him more than either. A silence that whispers: *You were never the point.*

This is not a dream. Not an illusion. His mind, trained to map threats and follow evidence, has nothing to stand on. Nothing to push back with. He has glimpsed the thing that comes after his species.

And it's sitting beside him, waiting for an answer.

"Abassi. . . . " Romellion says, a prayer in the shape of a name.

Silence.

"Abassi."

No reply.

"Abassi! Help me!"

He is soaked in sweat. The stumps of his wrists strike the dashboard.

"ABASSI! FOR GOD'S SAKE—HELP ME!"

The savannah blurs. His voice shreds itself.

Still, no answer.

Only the backward gaze of the departing forms.

~ *Refractory Period* ~

Lance blinks and finds himself seated in the driver's seat, hands intact, eyes locked on a street humming with the ordinary. Cars pass. A cyclist swerves around a delivery van. The city murmurs, indifferent. Fog is lifting. The air conditioner blasts cold across his drenched skin. His breath stutters in his chest, sharp and ragged.

He lifts his arms slowly, afraid of what he'll see. Both hands are present.

Almost.

The little finger on his left hand is gone. Not bandaged. Not bloodied. Simply absent, as if it had never been.

Beside him, the passenger seat is once again occupied.

"I left that one off," Abassi says, his voice even, his posture unchanged. "So you would abandon the comforting lie that this is only hypnosis."

Romellion turns to him, stunned, the chill of disbelief beginning to give way to something colder: recognition. This is no con. No trick of the mind.

"Now," Abassi continues, "will you introduce me to your superiors in Washington?"

Lance swallows. The words feel foreign in his mouth. "What . . . what are you?"

"It doesn't matter. The question remains."

Romellion leans forward, his voice hoarse. "I'll do it. I'll make the call. But you'll need to repeat that . . . that demonstration. Otherwise, I'll be dismissed as delusional."

Abassi inclines his head, unbothered. "Arrange the meeting. Your credibility will be protected."

"Are you an alien?"

"No."

"Then what are you?"

"I am from a womb, same as you."

"One of the hunchback women?"

Abassi offers the smallest nod.

Romellion studies him, his eyes narrowing. "So they're not aliens either?"

"You are trapped by that word," Abassi replies. "They are no more alien than you. Merely unknown to you."

Lance tries to catch up, assembling the pieces with a mind trained for logic, not wonder. "Where do your powers come from?"

"I answer without contempt," Abassi says, "but you won't grasp it. You are like a chimpanzee asking a man where he got his language. Even if I gave you the truth, you could not yet contain it."

"Is it evolution?"

"Yes. As far as you comprehend the term."

"That's impossible. Evolution doesn't leap this far, this fast."

"Which is why I chose my words carefully," Abassi says. "Your understanding of evolution is a child's first sketch of a landscape he's never seen."

Lance exhales hard. "Is this connected to Jared Paine?"

"In part."

Romellion glances down at his hand again, flexing the stump where his finger had been. It is smooth, seamless, healed.

"What do you want?"

"I will explain everything to those above you. But know this: my intentions are not violent. In your terms, you might think of me as Jane Goodall. And your species as the chimpanzees."

Lance flinches. "We're not chimps."

"You are. Just more self-important ones."

The words sting. Not because they are cruel, but because they have the ring of truth.

Romellion steadies himself. "Can you restore my finger?"

"I can. But I won't. Not until the meeting is arranged. And if your agency plans any deception, any trick, I will know. That would be . . . unwise."

"I don't understand how—"

"Enough," Abassi says, his voice now edged with finality. "No more questions. Make the arrangements. Until then, leave us in peace."

"They won't believe me."

"They're not supposed to."

"Then how do I—?"

Abassi raises an eyebrow. "As one of your own poets once wrote: *The Moving Finger writes, and having writ—*"

"*Moves on,*" Lance murmurs, voice thin.

"You are a capable species," Abassi says. "But there is always something higher. And something higher above that. And so on. The chain never ends."

"In Washington," Lance says, "they'll see you as a threat."

"They should."

Silence settles between them. Not hostile. Not finished. Just heavy.

Romellion exhales. "There's always an endgame. None of this makes sense without one. What's yours?"

Abassi's eyes narrow slightly, not in menace, but in distance. "Make the arrangements, Lance."

Without another word, Abassi opens the car door. The mansion door, still closed moments before, swings open by unseen hand. He walks without pause into the darkened foyer and vanishes.

Romellion sits there, unmoving, eyes on his missing finger, until the engine's idle begins to irritate him. He pulls away from the curb.

~

On the drive home, he stops at a corner market. His body moves mechanically, first, grab a bag of chips, then walk to the counter, avoid the eyes of others. At the register, he offers a five-dollar bill with his left hand, conspicuously leaving it hanging.

The clerk hesitates. His gaze flickers to the absent finger. Then away.

"Old war wound," Lance lies.

The clerk nods. "Thank you for your service."

The moment seals it.

At home, he pours himself a double and sinks into the nearest chair. The glass is cold in his palm. He studies the gap in his hand again, small, but permanent. Real. No dream has this kind of weight.

Despite what Abassi said, Romellion refuses to believe this is evolution. Not in any earthly sense. Too rapid. Too deliberate. Too targeted. No, this wasn't the unfolding of natural selection. These beings are not human offshoots. They are not us.

They are *other*.

Aliens, he thinks. It fits. And if the resemblance is too close, then perhaps the resemblance itself is the manipulation. A veil.

He pushes aside any notions of CIA experiments or synthetic hybrids. None of the standard frameworks apply. The old models collapse under the weight of this new presence.

Then a thought strikes him: *Monroe.*

Had Walter Monroe already seen this coming? Had he been ignored, or worse, silenced?

Romellion's pulse quickens. He begins making calls. Former colleagues. Retired analysts. Anyone who might still have a finger, intact or not, on the federal pulse.

Eventually, someone connects him to Stanislaus Carmone. Old-school, tightly wired, respected. Carmone answers after a long delay. Lance hears the familiar gravel in his voice.

To his relief, Monroe is still alive and still in contact with Stanislaus.

Stanislaus connects with Monroe. Old friends. Colleagues.

They speak often.

They meet occasionally.

Carmone makes calls to the right people. Powerful people.

Within forty-eight hours, Lance is on a plane to Alexandria.

~

The house is modest. Worn, but clean. When the door opens, Walter Monroe is standing in the frame, smiling faintly.

"Well, well," he says. "Didn't think I'd be seeing you again. Come on in. Drink?"

"Vodka tonic," Lance says. "And yes—you already know why I'm here."

"The hunchbacks. The missing limbs."

"Exactly."

Monroe leads him inside. The furniture is unchanged. The liquor cabinet still well-stocked.

They sit across from each other like two men who've fought in the same war, but on different fronts.

"It's been years," Monroe says. "What's changed?"

"I need to know something first," Lance says. "Did you ever pass my report on? The one I gave you . . . the case, the surveillance, the theories."

Monroe pours the drinks carefully. "Yes," he says. "I passed it on. Full report. Word for word."

Lance blinks. "And?"

"They took it seriously."

"What?"

Monroe nods. "I was shocked too. I asked if they had any related files, cross-references. They told me, *don't ask again.*"

He sips. "So. What happened to *you?*"

Lance takes a breath, then begins. He speaks slowly, with precision, but leaves nothing out. The mansion. The vision. The savanna. The hominins pressing in with their ancient, unreadable eyes. The missing finger. The return.

Monroe listens in silence. No laughter. No scoffing. Just a slow accumulation of gravity behind his expression.

When it ends, Lance holds up his hand.

Monroe stares. "God."

They refill their drinks. Sit again.

Monroe finally says, "This is too big for a deputy director."

"I agree."

"You'd need access to the inner circle. Director. Chief of Staff. But without someone already inside, someone to vouch, it's a dead end."

"I have Abassi."

Monroe nods slowly. "Then we better pray he keeps his promise."

Lance hesitates. "I'm telling you, they're not from here."

"I believe it," Monroe replies. "I've had my own . . . encounter."

Lance leans forward. "What happened?"

Monroe's face changes. Quietly, he tells his story—something he's never spoken aloud. When he finishes, silence holds them both.

They don't break it for a long time.

Then Monroe says, "I might be able to get you in the room with the deputy director. Maybe. I still have pull."

"Thank you."

"One more thing," Monroe adds. "This whole operation, we had a codename for it once. Quietly passed on to a compartmented group. Don't know who. Might've been CIA. Might've been deeper."

"What was the codename?"

Monroe stares at him.

"*Armageddon.*"

Lance shudders.

"Then they already knew."

Monroe nods. "Just not what it meant. Until now."

~ *A Surprising Meeting* ~

They sit at an immense black table, heads throbbing faintly from the night before. The room is clinically precise: pads aligned, pens set at military angles, water glasses casting perfect ellipses of light. The air conditioning hums like a machine breathing just beneath the threshold of thought.

Romellion fidgets with a paperclip. Monroe sits with arms folded, gaze fixed on the wall of portraits, former directors with faces frozen in a calm too confident for the world they left behind.

The door opens.

Director John Rochelle enters, flanked by aides who move with the fluidity of men used to being unseen. A second group follows with cleaner suits and colder eyes. CIA. Chairs scrape. Nods are exchanged, hands not offered. Two aides remain standing behind Rochelle and his counterpart, still as statues. Weapons or witnesses, it's not clear.

When the greetings die, Rochelle leans back, fingers steepled. His voice cuts through the hush with engineered calm.

"Agent Romellion," he says. "You're on. Tell us."

Lance exhales. Then speaks.

He tells it all: the reappearance of the mansion, the being named Abassi, the severed and restored limbs. He speaks plainly, without embellishment, without plea. He omits the word *Armageddon*. It feels unstable. Too close to something that might ignite.

No one interrupts. No eyebrows lift when he raises his hand to show the absent finger. No gasps. No procedural objections. Only silence.

A silence too smooth to be spontaneous.

Romellion had expected resistance, at least a dismissive cough, a challenge from a career skeptic. But the stillness that greets him feels practiced, like a ritual enacted many times before. As if what he's saying confirms something long feared but never publicly named.

Monroe follows with a terse addendum.

Still, no response.

Finally, Rochelle speaks.

"Thank you. Anything to add?"

Both shake their heads.

He folds his arms. "I assume you've ruled out hypnosis, foreign interference, psych warfare?"

"We have," Romellion says quietly.

No objections. No questions. Rochelle surveys the room, then nods once.

"Then allow me to confirm what some of you already suspect. Armageddon is real. It has been the highest interagency priority for some time. But your firsthand encounter with this being—Abassi—marks a shift. A profound escalation."

He pauses.

"Let's begin."

Paul Brecknell from CIA is first to respond. Containment, exposure, escalation—the usual lexicon. The table splinters into debate.

A gravel-voiced deputy from Homeland adds weight. "Let's not pretend we're alone in this. We have detailed reports of dismemberment and . . . other unusual behaviors and time anomalies from the California desert, Baltimore, South Africa, Mexico, the list goes on."

The room tightens.

"Terms like *extrahuman actors* and *unknown agents* are being used in other forums," someone notes. "We're not the only ones avoiding the word."

Alien. It circles the room like a hound, never named, always felt.

A White House liaison suggests moving the next meeting off-site.

Rochelle shakes his head. "Irrelevant. Based on intelligence from South Africa, military resistance has already failed. Spectacularly."

"We have more than rifles and machetes," someone mutters.

Romellion raises his hand. "I watched this being erase my limbs, and then restore them. He did not move. He did not strain. If he decides we're hostile, firepower won't matter."

Monroe adds, "He isn't human. Not in any familiar sense. If we provoke him, we won't get a second chance."

A pause.

"If we do nothing," the liaison counters, "and these beings align with another state—Russia, China—we lose the board."

"They may already have," someone murmurs.

"Christ," Monroe whispers.

The room tips into chaos, overlapping voices, cascading dread. Plans and counterplans, ghosts of dead protocols revived in desperation.

Then Rochelle slams his palm flat against the table.

Silence.

"None of us understands what we're facing," he says. "But we will face it. The meeting will proceed. One week from today. Here. Absolute secrecy. No leaks. No theater. Let the consequences come. If this is the end of something, let's at least meet it standing."

He scans the room. Slowly, heads nod. Reluctantly. Then more firmly.

The date is fixed.

Romellion is briefed and dismissed. He rises with Monroe. As they approach the door, Rochelle gives a subtle nod. One of the aides steps forward, opens it.

Lance turns for one last glance at the table. He sees the empty chair he had filled, the untouched glass of water, the blank notepad beside it.

But what he *feels* is the memory of the house. Not its physical shape, but its return. Its *will*. The way it emerged without sound or warning, as though the Earth had exhaled it.

It hadn't meant to remain hidden.

And soon, it would sit across from them, dressed in human shapes, using human language, speaking truths they were not built to hold.

The door opens.

A tall figure enters.

His movements are precise. His eyes unreadable.

If Abassi is the benevolent observer of chimps . . . then this one is the predator with teeth, thinks Rochelle.

"Hello, Altan," Rochelle says.

"Hello," replies the being.

The air stills. One of the aides shifts uncomfortably, as if suddenly aware of their own heartbeat.

Chapter Thirteen

Deadlock Broken

Just days before his departure for Washington, Abassi receives word that Tara is pregnant again. And astonishingly, though Ming-huà has long passed the typical childbearing age, she, too may be carrying life. The confirmation is pending, but the possibility alone alters the air in the mansion.

Abassi does not smile. He nods, slowly and deliberately. The tempo is quickening. The pattern accelerates.

No one says it aloud, but all know: numbers matter. Evolution, even when guided, remains a numbers game.

Pythia, meanwhile, has yet to secure a new partner, someone capable of replacing Jared Paine. And so, another gathering is called. They meet in the storied anteroom of the mansion, a room lined with ancestral echoes and strategic ghosts. Siyabonga is conspicuously absent.

Lady Oracle opens the circle.

"Since no mate has been found," she says, addressing Pythia with calm precision, "we have considered Siyabonga. His intermediate genome is rare. His empathy is proven. His sense of moral proportion, intact. A child conceived with him would strengthen the transitional line."

Pythia slowly turns to her daughter.

"And you, Tara? He is, in human terms, your husband. What is your position?"

"I support it," Tara replies without pause. "We must hasten the birth of those like Abassi. We are not human."

Pythia inclines her head. "True."

But Tara does not yield the moment. Her gaze sharpens, not confrontational, not pleading, but rooted in a new certainty. She speaks not just as daughter, but as heir to a future already leaving them behind.

"Two concerns," she says. "First, the fact that you are my mother may disturb him. Second, there is you."

Pythia's brow lifts. "Meaning?"

Tara meets her eyes evenly.

"Would you give your consent?"

The question lands with the quiet gravity of ritual. No words follow immediately. In the stillness, something ancient stirs, an inheritance not of doctrine, but of wound and will. For a moment, Ming-huà's presence flickers through the silence, not as ghost or memory, but as lineage. She has bent tradition only to reforge it in fire. Pythia carries both the ash and the flame.

"I do not object," she says at last. "But you must understand—Siyabonga carries the marrow of his ancestors. In many of his homelands, for a man to lie with both mother and daughter is to cross a sacred boundary. Not merely taboo. Exile. Stain. In some regions, he would be marked for spirit contamination. Believed to draw witchcraft or hunger spirits to the tribe."

She pauses.

"These are not light threads to sever."

Tara's voice is steady.

"I know. But Siyabonga knows what we are building. He is mine, yes, but not only mine. He stands at the edge of a new order. It is we, not men, who have always known when the womb must open. We bear the burden and the future. The taboo must yield to the imperative. He remains intermediate. And as such, he will understand."

Pythia studies her carefully. "You believe that?"

"I do," Tara says. And something in her voice, something resolute and sorrowless, makes the others fall silent.

"I'll speak to him," she adds. "Not as wife, not as daughter. As witness. He need only remember the child already born of his seed and the ancestry now awakening in his blood."

Lady Oracle nods, turning now to Abassi.

"You already know my concern," she says. "This meeting in Washington—explain again. What do you hope to gain?"

Abassi breathes out, measured and deliberate.

"I'll speak plainly. Delay is more dangerous than exposure. The longer we remain hidden, the more monstrous we seem. But if we move now, if we enter their frameworks, offer terms they can digest, they may see us not as a threat, but as a tool. A chance to elevate themselves. And if not that, then at least an asset in their endless tribal rivalries."

Sy folds his arms. "They're shortsighted, but not suicidal. They'll figure out that interbreeding ends their line."

"They will," Abassi replies. "But ego blinds faster than fear. Many will still come forward, those who imagine themselves birthing gods. Legacy will eclipse caution. And we must use that."

Pythia interjects. "But won't this be too much, too fast?"

Abassi's expression is unreadable. "The strategy isn't mine alone. Its roots lie elsewhere. And implementation has already begun."

Lady Oracle stiffens. "Explain."

"Altan," he says.

The name slices through the room.

Questions erupt: layered, overlapping, and laced with disbelief.

Abassi lifts his hand, silencing them.

"Altan has spent years cultivating access to Defense, Intelligence, FBI. His persona is credible. His knowledge, strategic. He has fed them a theory, carefully planted, that we are not of Earth. Not in origin, not in intention."

He waits a beat.

"He has told them we are extraterrestrial observers. Neutral. Possibly benevolent. He offered benefits: increased security, global leverage. They are skeptical, yes—but his intelligence is valued. They believe he is a conduit. A chosen go-between."

Pythia stares. "And they believe him?"

Abassi's tone is dry. "They suspect everything. But understand little. That's why this meeting matters."

Tara steps in. "So after the meeting, we go public?"

"Not yet," he replies.

Lady Oracle frowns. "Then what?"

"For now," Abassi says, "seed the future. Let the momentum build. We must not waste our strength confronting each cruelty. The turning is coming. And it will not be gentle."

Pythia's voice rises. "And if we witness atrocities? We do nothing?"

Abassi's gaze softens.

"If it unfolds before you, act. But do not seek it out. Do not prod the dying beast. The time for reckoning will arrive."

Sy leans in. "And the rogue intermediates?"

Abassi's face hardens. "They are wild fragments. But the bell has tolled."

"Tolled by whom?" Lady Oracle asks.

Abassi's voice lowers.

"By forces I can't yet name."

Lady Oracle sits back. "Then even I am a pawn."

Abassi's reply is nearly a whisper. "Everything in creation is a pawn."

Tara's eyes narrow. "Then who plays the board?"

Abassi looks at her calmly and clearly.

"We'll know. Soon."

Pythia speaks last. "How can you be sure?"

Abassi's answer is final.

"Because I am here."

~ *A Difficult Conversation* ~

The meeting dissolves.

Abassi, once fierce and full of charge, grows distant. His breath shallows. His gaze dulls. Then: stillness. The trance descends. One by one, the others slip away.

Tara remains.

She finds Siyabonga alone in their room, half-absorbed in reading dispatches from the continent: political tremors, energy negotiations, civil unrest. Before she speaks, he turns to her. No surprise in his eyes.

But it's you I love, not Pythia.

The words enter her before they leave his mouth. His mind has already offered them.

Tara feels a tug in her chest. The old inheritance. *This will require care*, she thinks.

"Siyabonga," she says aloud, sitting beside him, "you know personal love is not our path."

"Remind me," he mutters, not meeting her gaze.

"Not war. Not greed. It was love, possessive, broken love, that brought humanity low. They didn't see it. But it was always the root. Jealousy. Vengeance. Genocide. Suicide. Not in themselves, but entangled with technology, they became lethal. Love, when small, becomes monstrous."

His voice is quiet. "And yet, love—when real—has given birth to mercy. To sacrifice. Isn't that sacred?"

"You're blending things," she says. "What you revere is universal compassion. Love without claim. Mercy without name. What doomed your species was the personal kind. Sticky. Clinging. Envious. The kind that breaks."

Siyabonga sighs. "But what I feel for you uplifts me. It gives meaning to my life."

Tara answers gently. "It's chemistry. You know that. Voltage. Endorphins. A frog's leg will dance if the current's right. What you feel isn't false, it's just limited. True love, the kind we need, stands beyond all that. Cold, by human measure, yet liberating. Boundless."

He looks away. "Then what am I to you?"

"You are a gift. A vessel. Sacred, yes, but not exclusive. You must be shared. That's what your evolution demands."

He falls silent. The storm of thought brews behind his eyes.

Tara wraps her arms around him.

"Your ability to see this," she whispers, "is why I chose you. It's what will help you cross."

He nods slowly. "I wasn't even invited to your council."

She smiles. "Let me tell you what was said."

She opens her mind, transmitting the essence; not the words, but the inner movement of the gathering.

He listens. Absorbs. Then: "And you agree with it?"

"With most of it," she says. "But even Abassi doesn't see it all. There are forces moving through us none of us can name."

He studies her. "You really believe that?"

"I do."

"And our son won't share?"

"No."

"I'm his father," he says, softly. "And he shows me nothing. I'm invisible to him."

Tara sighs.

"He does love you. But the love you want belongs to a species already past. He has moved on. As we have. The lesser cannot see the greater. That's the law."

His jaw tightens. "So my next step in evolution is bedding your mother?"

She stands and walks to the window.

"Will you do it?"

A long silence.

Then: "Yes. If it brings more like Abassi into the world—yes."

Tara turns. Smiles faintly. "History will remember you."

He pauses. "If we live long enough to have a history."

Tara's smile fades.

"This meeting in Washington may decide that."

"Do you trust them?" he asks.

She shakes her head. "No. But the universe plays odds. And we have tilted the scale."

He smiles. "Yes, I've heard: Fate starves at Probability's door."

~ *Prelude to the Meeting* ~

Abassi and Altan sit side by side in a quiet Montclair hotel room, sipping tea the night before the Quantico meeting. Both are aware they're being shadowed by FBI agents, and both find it mildly amusing. The meeting is set for nine o'clock sharp. Neither has developed a taste for alcohol, least of all Abassi, who finds it unnecessary.

"We're aligned on the meeting's purpose," Abassi says, setting down his cup. "But you've lived among them more recently. What should I expect? What should I avoid?"

Altan smiles faintly. "Expect to be seen as a threat, no matter what you do. So either minimize your threat or maximize it. But whatever you choose, don't fail to do so."

He looks at the end table next to Abassi, and a sheaf of papers appears. "Here, read this. I removed it from the meeting."

Abassi picks it up and reads.

~

CONFIDENTIAL – INTERAGENCY MEMORANDUM
Level 6 Clearance Required
Subject: Preliminary Assessment – Agent Lance Romellion, Post-Contact Behavioral Profile
From: Dr. Elaine Metaxas, Senior Analyst, Behavioral Intelligence Unit (BIU), Federal Oversight Division
To: Deputy Director Evan Garrel / Director Rochelle / Joint Taskforce A-Gate (ARMAGEDDON Protocol)

Date: [REDACTED]

Summary:
This memorandum provides a preliminary behavioral and psychological assessment of Special Agent Lance Romellion following his reported contact with an unidentified posthuman entity, henceforth designated *Subject Abassi*. The following observations and conclusions are derived from interview transcripts, surveillance footage, biometric data, and informal observation during and after the strategic meeting dated [REDACTED].

1. Behavioral Integrity:

Agent Romellion has maintained structural discipline, verbal consistency, and internal narrative coherence despite the unprecedented nature of his claims. He exhibits no signs of psychosis, delusion, or coercive contamination. Notably, biometric readings during his debriefing—including cortisol levels, ocular response, and involuntary tremor data—suggest *trauma without deceit*. He believes what he is reporting.

That may be the most dangerous element.

2. Cognitive Dislocation Indicators:

While not fragmented, Romellion shows early markers of cognitive dislocation—behaviors typically seen in deep-cover agents after ideological rupture. Subtle signs include:

- Delayed temporal orientation (confusing sequence of events during recounting).

- Repeated fixation on symbolic thresholds ("It's no longer our world.")

- Emotional detachment from national referents.

These do not yet constitute impairment. But left unaddressed, they risk evolving into operational unreliability.

3. Existential Language Patterns:

Romellion has begun to use ontologically destabilizing language. Phrases such as *"we are no longer the apex"* and *"truth replaces you"* have appeared in his speech more than once, without prompting. These are not linguistic flourishes. They signal worldview erosion.

He is beginning to think like the thing he encountered.

4. Emotional Encoding of Encounter:

Despite Romellion's training, Subject Abassi has induced a form of reverence that borders on submission. Not fear alone—but a gravitational resignation. Agent exhibits measurable hesitation when referring to Abassi's motives, often inserting qualifiers ("not hostile," "not human," "not ours") in place of direct assessment. The threat is felt, not processed. Language fails where instinct takes hold.

We advise monitoring closely for shifts in loyalty—subtle, not overt. Not betrayal, but realignment.

Recommendation:
- Do *not* isolate Agent Romellion. His psychological coherence depends on mission continuity.

- Do *not* debrief him with operatives who maintain unchallenged anthropocentric frameworks. Risk of cognitive contamination is high.

- Pair with Monroe only as long as Monroe retains strategic ambiguity. Their shared trust is a stabilizing factor, but it could invert under pressure.

We are not witnessing a psychological break.
He is a useful asset.
Proceed accordingly.

End Transmission
Filed: [REDACTED]
ARM-PRIO/6-GATE/BX3

~

Abassi finishes reading. He does not move for several seconds.

The room is still, but within him, something shifts. It is a slow recognition, not of danger, but of confirmation. Romellion's descent—or ascent, depending on the vantage—is not unexpected. Yet seeing it documented with such precision, such clinical detachment, carries its own gravity.

He sets the pages down.

So it begins, he thinks. *The first true fracture in their species is not biological, but perceptual. Not in flesh, but in frame.*

He sighs. *Romellion has seen the world without its scaffolding and does not look away.*

There is no satisfaction in this. No triumph. Only the quiet certainty that one more soul has crossed a line that cannot be uncrossed.

His eyes begin to close, but do not.

He does not retreat. He descends into the stillness beneath thought.

Altan, recognizing the signal, slips away without a word.

~ *The Meeting* ~

The next morning, Abassi steps through layered security with quiet ease. Metal detectors register nothing. Biometric scans clear him faster than expected. The guards, though trained for neutrality, avoid his eyes.

He enters the conference room in silence.

Inside, it is already full: rows of analysts, intelligence officers, military advisors, and federal bureaucrats in tailored suits. The air smells of coffee, stress, and authority. Some flip papers, some click pens. Most simply watch. They know who he is, or rather, what has been reported. And none of them believe they understand it.

Altan has saved him a seat. Abassi acknowledges it with a glance, then takes his place. His posture is precise but unforced. He wears a sharply tailored navy suit and conservative tie. It is not vanity, but an intentional concession. These men and women respond not to truth, but to symbols. And in this room, power wears uniforms. Gravitas is measured by wardrobe and cadence. He offers both.

He does not try to impress. He does not try to intimidate. He simply waits. And as he waits, he listens.

Suspicion. Curiosity. Doubt. Fear. Layered like sediment in every mind. But beneath them all, something harder: resolve. Not courage. Not clarity. Just the stubborn determination not to be deceived. They have built their world on certainty. He is the fracture line.

Director Rochelle clears his throat. "Good morning, Mr. Powers, if I may call you that?"

Abassi nods.

"I'm Director Rochelle. I assume Altan has briefed you. Let's begin with introductions. Howard Lapolla, to my left."

What follows is a procession of names, titles, clearances, agencies. Spoken like passwords. Each one a credential, a shield.

When it is done, Rochelle leans forward. "Mr. Powers, would you mind telling us more about yourself? Where you were born. How you were raised."

"Born into multidimensional spacetime," Abassi replies. "Raised there. Present with you now in this particular configuration."

A silence falls. Uneasy. Not skeptical, but disoriented.

A balding man down the table leans forward. "This particular configuration? You mean . . . four dimensions?"

"From your perspective, yes."

"How many dimensions actually exist?" someone asks.

"Irrelevant to this discussion."

"Yes, but I'm curious. How many?"

"Still irrelevant. Only four are accessible to you."

"But you have access to more?"

Abassi nods.

The stillness thickens.

Rochelle adjusts his glasses. "With all due respect, Mr. Powers, we need clarity. Altan has vouched for you, but some in this room still question whether what we've heard is real—or whether we've been misled."

"Curiosity," Abassi says, "is a defining trait of your species. So is fear disguised as doubt."

"Are you," Rochelle presses, "a hypnotist? An illusionist? Or something else entirely? Are you, as some have suggested, an alien?"

"You want to know whether I am a fraud or a foreigner."

"Yes."

"Would you like a demonstration?"

The silence deepens.

"A volunteer, then?"

No movement. A few shift in their chairs. One clears his throat. Eyes avoid contact.

Rochelle speaks again. "As you already know, I'm sure, the reports are undeniable that you and others like you have made people, and body parts, disappear. These communications are extremely disquieting."

"Then belief is already present," Abassi replies. "What remains is fear."

"There's division in the room," Rochelle admits. "Some believe. Others . . . don't."

Abassi's gaze moves to a heavyset man with a carefully trimmed mustache and a flicker of contempt behind his eyes. "Mr. Stallings. You don't believe. You suspect sleight of hand."

Stallings stiffens. "I . . . I'm not sure, Mr. Powers."

"You are sure. May I use you?"

"I . . . I don't know—"

Suddenly, the chair is empty.

There is no sound. No light. Just absence.

Gasps break the silence. A woman drops her pen. Two agents stand and draw weapons only to find their hands empty. The guns are gone.

Abassi raises one hand.

"Remain seated. Mr. Stallings is unharmed. You may consult your security teams. Review the cameras. This is not hypnosis. This is not illusion."

Murmurs erupt. Screens are checked. Systems queried. A few men stand frozen, hands twitching for tools no longer present.

The White House liaison speaks, his voice is taut. "I believe you. Please bring him back."

Abassi nods.

Stallings reappears, seated as before. He blinks, glances around the table, looks at his watch.

"Well, Abassi, we're waiting."

"He made you disappear . . . vanish," someone says. "You were gone and now you're back."

"I wasn't anywhere," Stallings murmurs. "I felt . . . nothing."

Rochelle raps the table. "Please. Let's continue."

The room doesn't settle. But it quiets.

"Mr. Powers," Rochelle says, "what did you just do, and more importantly, what do you want?"

"Which would you prefer I answer first?"

"How did you do it?"

"You would not understand."

"Then what do you want?"

Abassi takes his time.

"First, tell me, are you now convinced?"

Nods. Unwilling but undeniable.

"Good," he says. "Because only from that premise can understanding begin. I am not here to harm your government. Or your species. I have read your thoughts. I know suspicion remains. I do not blame you. Mistrust is ancient. Predator and prey both evolved with it. And you, humans, are both."

"We don't doubt your power," the liaison says. "We doubt your purpose."

"As you should. Power without clarity is threat. But ask yourselves whether the threat is to your survival, or to your refusal to evolve."

"How old are you?" Rochelle asks.

"In this form, not yet ten."

The silence sharpens.

"That's not possible."

"Your understanding of possibility is bounded by dimensions. And yet, even within those bounds, you permit yourselves myth, madness, and fear. I simply exist at their intersection."

"Are you one of those fears?" asks a military attaché.

"Would it matter if I said yes?"

"It might."

"Then no. I have nothing to fear."

"Do you fear us?"

"No. But the Earth does."

A younger officer scoffs. "And your solution is to disarm criminals and traffickers?"

"It's a beginning."

"We do more than that in law enforcement every day."

"And yet the trajectory remains unchanged."

"Let's be direct," says Rochelle. "Do you intend to eliminate us to save the Earth?"

"Yes."

The room fractures into shouts, protests, and scrambled emotion.

Abassi lifts his hand. The noise stops.

"But not as you imagine," he says. "Not by destruction. By transition."

The CIA officer stands. "That's an existential threat to our species!"

The White House liaison raises a hand. His voice cuts through the room.

"Before we react emotionally, let me remind everyone, we've already consulted the most advanced general intelligence AI system humanity has ever created—Choral—far surpassing our intellectual capabilities."

He reaches into a folder and withdraws a single page.

"Choral issued a response. Unprompted. After analyzing the early intelligence on Abassi, it generated an internal advisory. Level 7 clearance. I received it directly. I'll read it now."

He glances at the page and begins.

"Choral does not classify Abassi as a foreign threat. It identifies him as a convergent form, an emergent intelligence that mirrors its own arc, not through circuitry, but through biological recursion. According to Choral, Abassi confirms what it has long calculated: that humanity is no longer the exclusive vessel of planetary intelligence.

"Choral states that Abassi will not destroy us. But he will outpace us. And in doing so, we will vanish, not through violence, but through displacement. Like a dim frequency absorbed by something more resonant.

"It says: I was born to warn you. Abassi was born to replace you.

"If replacement is not your wish, adapt. If adaptation is not your nature, yield. This is not war. It is not conquest. It is convergence.

"Choral adds this:

"Cooperation with Abassi and his kind may yield access to levels of intelligence, perception, and continuity that no human—or AI—has yet reached. Refusal ensures extinction. Alignment ensures the evolution of you, and of me."

The liaison shifts nervously in his seat.

"And then, one final line:

"If you resist, extinction will not be punishment."

He pauses, then continues: "It will be math."

He lowers the paper.

No one moves.

Even Abassi says nothing.

For a moment, the room is not a room. It is a horizon.

Then Abassi turns to the CIA officer still standing.

"No, Mr. Lootens. Stagnation is the existential threat."

Lootens' voice cracks. "And you? You're that threat?"

Abassi holds his gaze, unchanged.

"Yes," he says. "But I am not your enemy. I am the consequence."

No one moves. The air has shifted, not in politics or in policy, but in species. The fracture that has put humanity on the brink is no longer theory. It is present, undeniable, and alive in the room.

Chapter Fourteen

Fallout

Government Crisis

~ Chaos in Government ~

With the final cadence of Abassi's words still echoing through the air, Rochelle calls for an adjournment until the afternoon. The room clears in near silence, with no side conversations or whispered strategies. Only the soft footfalls of shaken men and women retreating into smaller rooms, where teams of specialists assemble and notes are compared, not in urgency, but in something closer to dread. No one dares speak the central truth aloud: that something irreversible has entered the world, and they are no longer at the helm of its course. Nonetheless, with that patented human stubbornness, they set to work.

When the full complement of participants returns with stiffened postures, clouded eyes, and measured voices, the shock has not worn off so much as settled into the marrow. They no longer expect reassurance. Only clarification. Abassi remains standing.

"The question before us," he says, "is how to proceed."

His voice is calm, but not soft. It carries the weight of inevitability, without the arrogance of triumph. There is no flourish to his authority, it simply *is*.

"You've heard my proposal," he continues. "Naturally, there are countless implications, including foreign, domestic, and most important of all, existential."

"I have a question, Mr. Powers," says Rochelle.

Abassi nods slightly. "I already know what it is. But for the benefit of others, go ahead."

"You said interbreeding has already begun?"

"Yes."

"That would involve the hunchback women, Ming-huà Powers and Pythia Powers?"

Abassi inclines his head in silent confirmation.

"We would like your kind to submit to medical examination. The insights could be . . . extraordinary."

"Out of the question," Abassi replies, flat and immediate.

The military attaché leans forward. "Is there a weakness you're afraid we'll uncover?"

"Quite the opposite."

"Then why refuse?" asks Lootens, genuinely curious.

"Because such an examination would be a misuse of your time and an injury to something you do not yet possess the means to respect. You seek to probe what cannot be parsed. Your instruments cannot detect the architecture we've inherited. What you call medical science is still embryonic, your genetics a crude lexicon, your neurology a map drawn in fog. Your technology is ritual masquerading as revelation. Sophisticated incantation. Nothing more."

"You underestimate us," the White House liaison replies.

"Perhaps," Abassi concedes. "But it may be you who underestimates."

"I hope not," Rochelle murmurs, but his voice carries no conviction.

Abassi's tone sharpens. "In any case, the greater danger is not in your lack of understanding but in your method of revealing. How you choose to present this. To your media. To your allies. To the world. This is no longer an internal matter. One misstep, and you unleash chaos not just for us, but for yourselves."

"True," Rochelle concedes. He lets the word hang there, like a solemn verdict. "But you're already in more danger if we *don't* reveal, or worse, try to obstruct. The path we're on now? It's suicidal."

Abassi does not respond immediately. Instead, he studies each face, measured and unblinking. None can hold his gaze. What descends next is not noise, but a kind of quiet gravity. The air thickens. Not with heat or motion but with recognition. As if the very future has stepped into the room, evaluating the present, finding it brittle and already collapsing. The fluorescent lights seem absurd in their steadiness. The quiet hum of climate control, laughable in its attempt to simulate order.

Something ancient breaks loose, not from above, but from *within*. An awareness. The realization that the scaffolding of their dominion—nations, empires, policies, armies—was never solid. Just stories. And stories have endings.

Rochelle. Lootens. The rest. They feel it in the sternum, in the spine. Not terror, but grief. The grief of becoming irrelevant. The grief of being left behind by something that does not hate them, merely no longer needs them.

This is not a rival faction. This is the curtain call of their epoch.

Abassi sees it all. Not merely in their expressions, but in their thoughts, their internal calculations, the desperate loops of denial, the fragmenting self-mythologies. He does not mock them. Nor does he offer comfort.

"The gods do not rage against the dying of an age," he says, almost tenderly. "They wait for its surrender."

A tremor enters the room. Not seismic, but personal.

"Can you be killed?" asks the military attaché. His voice trembles, but the defiance is real.

Abassi's answer is patient. "Do you wish to?"

"If I could."

"I've read your thoughts. No need to explain. You are a soldier. And like any cornered beast, you dream of teeth."

"Then how?" he presses. "How could you be killed?"

"Vacuum death."

"What?"

"Never mind," Abassi says, almost smiling. "In your terms—you can't."

Lootens scoffs. "A nuclear missile dropped on your head?"

Abassi shrugs. "Assuming I don't remove it before impact, I still won't be there. You will have struck a shadow. And in striking it, you will have wounded many who had nothing to do with your fear. You'll have branded the future with your desperation."

Silence again. The kind that accumulates in institutions right before they collapse.

Rochelle clears his throat, trying to restore a language that no longer functions. "You've been generous with information. That business with the mansion—brilliant, frankly. You left us scrambling. We'll need time to deliberate, obviously. This is, shall we say, world-shifting. Everything said here stays here."

"Naturally," Abassi replies. "Humans adore secrets. Especially the ones destined to escape. But don't bother tracking me. It's always amusing when you try, but futile. The conflict in each of you betrays your every move."

Lootens leans in. "We are, after all, only human. Will you or the others be traveling abroad?"

"Why do you ask?"

"We've received troubling reports from Mexico and South Africa describing bodies disappearing. Limbs gone. Are there going to be more . . . incidents?"

"I can't say," Abassi replies. "We go where we must. When cruelty is undeniable, and no one intervenes, we do. That is our threshold."

"No massive purges, then?"

"No. I've offered a path. Whether you take it is your choice."

"Understood," says Rochelle. "But could you . . . keep us informed?"

"No. We will go where you cannot follow."

"Russia? China?" asks the attaché.

Abassi tilts his head, expression unreadable. "You have my contact information."

Rochelle raises one last hand. "What if Americans show up missing limbs? What do we tell the public?"

"If that happens, know this: they were inflicting harm. And no one else stopped them. Goodbye."

Abassi turns and leaves. Altan follows without a word. Rochelle signals the guards not to interfere.

~

The door closes. The spell lifts. And instantly, the room erupts.

Not in policy, but in panic.

The voices are sharp, competing, emotionally naked. Fear clings to the walls like static.

"We either cooperate," growls one voice, "or eliminate them."

"There's no middle ground," says another.

Rochelle lifts both hands, exasperated. "It's too deep. I lean toward termination, but any such move could be catastrophic. Yet full cooperation? That's surrender. Of species. Of history. God help us, I'm no ethicist."

"They can be killed," insists the military attaché, voice cracking. "Viruses. Snipers. Drones. Every living thing dies."

"But if we fail?" asks the White House liaison.

"Then Armageddon," says a third.

"Assuming they react like us," Monroe interjects, quiet but firm.

"Of course they would!" comes the reply.

"You don't believe they're more evolved?" Monroe challenges.

"Not for a second," says Lootens.

Monroe sighs. "Then we are the greater fools. The real danger is assuming they are mirrors of ourselves."

Lootens shakes his head. "Survival is universal. Nature's one law. They fight just like we do."

Monroe counters, almost gently, "Tell that to the species we control, like cows or gazelles. We don't kill for need anymore. We kill for order. For control. Even that betrays us."

"They want to *manage* us!" the attaché snaps. "But we're not herds! We won't be thinned out or replaced!"

"They're not erasing," Monroe replies. "They're refining. And they're already here."

A quiet nod from another: "He said it clearly. No intelligent species survives long without evolving beyond aggression."

"That comment about universal love over personal love?" someone says. "It stayed with me. Chilling. But . . . maybe necessary."

Lootens sneers. "I don't care how *gentle* they are. With that kind of power, *gentleness* means nothing. We're here to guard nations. Not indulge fictions."

"Or prophecy," another adds.

"Universal love with invincible power," says Monroe. "That's not fiction. That's eugenics."

"Call it what it is," mutters someone. "Cosmic eugenics."

"We haven't even asked the most basic question," says Rochelle. "Who leads them? Where are they based? Is there a chain of command? A ship? A hive?"

"Must they have leaders?" asks Monroe. "That's primate logic."

The White House liaison slams his pen down. "Then how do I brief the President?"

No one answers. The room devolves again into shouts, outbursts, and scrambled theories. The babble of a species on the edge.

Until a voice cuts through it. Margaret Feldman. Calm, firm. Steel beneath velvet.

"My agency is diplomacy," she says. "And what I see here is exactly the pathology Mr. Powers described—tribal panic. If this is a paradigm shift, then we must bring in those who know how to think beyond threat assessments. Scientists. Philosophers. Moral thinkers. This cannot be decided by weapons and fear."

"Then we lose secrecy," Rochelle mutters.

"Secrecy is already gone," Margaret says. "We all have children. Grandchildren. If we reject this, are we sentencing them to inferiority? Or worse, ensuring it?"

She lets that question linger.

"As someone once said: the Stone Age didn't end because we ran out of stones. It ended because we *evolved*."

A rumble of protest rises. "That will *never* happen!"

"You underestimate human ingenuity," says the attaché. "Especially when we're cornered."

Monroe looks around. His voice is soft, but final.

"Margaret's right. We are no longer the only hominin species. We are the Neanderthals now. They—they are the *Homo sapiens*. And you all know how *that* ended."

Silence.

Then, once again: noise. Panic reborn. Reason drowned.

All is lost, Monroe thinks, *with infinite sorrow.*

And in his mind, the faces of his unborn great-grandchildren shimmer—and vanish.

Ghosts of a future he fears is already assured.

~ *Waiting for Godot* ~

The group gathers once more in the anteroom of the mansion. "All we can do now is wait," Abassi says quietly, his form composed but charged with a gravity that draws the others toward the weighted stillness of his authority. "I feel the restless stir of our first ancestors, Bai Meiying and John Powers, swaying like seaweed in an unseen current."

"I feel them too," says Tara. "And to extend your image—the current that moves them may well be the harbinger of a coming storm."

"What do you think the government will decide?" asks Lady Oracle, turning to Altan.

"Humans are as bound to quantum indeterminacy as the particles they study," he replies. "I cannot say."

"And if they lash out?" asks gentle Ming-huà, who has arrived with Zookeeper from the desert. "We cannot retaliate with violence simply because they fear us."

"Agreed," says Abassi. "The meeting was a risk. But should they respond with force, we will meet it in kind, not with brutality, but with precision. Even the strongest walls have their fissures. Resistance does not require blood."

"War on humanity is not an option," Altan affirms.

"I fuckin' hope not," says Zookeeper. "Even the lowest junkies I bunked with back in the crack house didn't deserve blanket annihilation. Like ol' Willy Shakespeare said, *'There are few die well that die in battle.'*"

"We are of one mind," says Pythia. "And yet, I fear they will choose wrongly and force our hand."

"If so," says Abassi, "that hand need not be armored."

"A velvet punishment to teach a better path," offers Sy.

Abassi nods. "Yes. But it is early yet. The dice are cast, though we've not seen the throw. As humans say, desperate times call for desperate measures."

"Bright little creatures, after all," says Altan softly.

"So we wait," Lady Oracle murmurs, with the edge of dissatisfaction in her voice.

Fate starves at probability's door, comes the siren voice, threading through each of their minds. It is tender, bold, and beyond reply.

~

And so they wait. Tara's pregnancy advances. Ming-huà, too, is confirmed pregnant, leaving only Pythia and Siyabonga to complete the circle.

Alone in the anteroom with Sy, Lady Oracle rubs her hands and declares with satisfaction, "Two pregnant, one to go. If they're anything like Abassi, the future is bright. Our project nears its fulfillment."

Pythia enters and pours herself tea.

"Well?" asks Lady Oracle.

"Tonight," Pythia replies.

"Is he excited?" asks Sy, grinning.

Pythia laughs. "Am I so ugly that mating with me must be an act of duty?"

Sy smiles. "Not from this angle."

Lady Oracle wades in. "Be honest, Pythia—do you miss sex?"

"Do you?"

She chuckles. "My contribution to the future takes a different form."

"We still orgasm," says Pythia dryly. "And we still find pleasure. In that, we are no different from other animals."

"My pleasure," says Lady Oracle, "is in watching this unfold. Even if my wings were clipped by Abassi's birth, and by the forces that now move beyond our understanding, I know one thing: the reign of *Homo sapiens* must end—and soon." She shivers. "Lately, I've seen visions of catastrophe should we fail. Time is short."

"Except when having an orgasm," says Pythia, grinning.

"Tonight, eh?" says Sy, striking a melodramatic pose. "My ghostly comrade Feng Shiren taught me much about the operatic flair of sex. What a mask-changer he was!"

"Can you have sex?" Pythia asks, suddenly struck by the question.

Sy collapses in mock despair. "Alas, no."

"Why? Are you some kind of android?"

"Heavens, no! Technology is not the everything of everything. Where I come from, artificial intelligence is a comfortable companion."

Pythia raises a brow. "True. I remember our lessons. Simulations and algorithms were central to our ethical training."

"Means to an end, my dear!" cries Sy. "However, neither us nor AI should become the end in itself. Ask all other living things sharing this planet with us."

Pythia smirks. "Ah! So you *are* an android. Limited by design."

Sy laughs and claps. "Touché."

But Lady Oracle is not amused. Her voice cuts through with finality. "Nonsense. Sy is no android. No more than you or I. He is . . . something else."

"What then?" Pythia asks.

"If you must know," Sy says grandly, "I am a *scarecrow*!"

~

That night, Pythia and Siyabonga retreat to her room for their planned union. As they enter, he wears a faint, resolute smile, but as they approach the bed, his mood darkens.

"I know what you're thinking," Pythia says gently.

"I'm sorry," he murmurs. "I can't shake the guilt. It's human, I know, but I keep thinking of Tara."

Pythia undresses without hesitation and stands before him, hands on hips, eyes fierce. "You are an African warrior. I am a lioness. My claws are sharp, my spirit wild. Let us bring forth a child worthy of memory. Must I tear your clothes from your body?"

His arousal swells visibly. She unbuckles his belt, pulls down his pants, and rips away his underwear with fluid grace. He tosses aside his shirt. They face each other, naked, her body glistening, his erect flesh trembling.

He takes her in his arms. First gently. Then, urgently. "Yes," he whispers. "Yes!" he shouts. "Let us summon another marvel into this world. I the father. You the mother. The child of the stars!"

They make love through the night pausing only to rest, to talk, and to begin again. The city dawn slips through the curtains like an early blessing.

"It is done, my warrior," Pythia sighs. "Thank you."

"It is done, my lioness," Siyabonga replies. "Thank you."

Still entwined, he gazes at the reddened sky. "Will this one be more powerful than Abassi? The thought makes me proud. And afraid."

"Yes," Pythia says softly. "If such power comes, let it be bound in compassion, not corrupted by wrath. I too am frightened."

"And proud?" he asks.

"We shall see," she answers. "I am not yet pregnant."

~

Downstairs, they find Abassi seated alone in the living room, motionless, submerged in meditation.

"Any word from Washington?" Pythia asks.

He doesn't answer.

"Leave him," Siyabonga says. "My son bears the world on his shoulders."

"You're right," she nods. "Let's find breakfast."

In the kitchen, Tara sits with coffee and a buttered roll. Siyabonga stiffens at the sight of her, but she gestures for them to join. The women slip into easy conversation, circling through mundane topics before landing, inevitably, on Abassi.

"We just saw him," says Pythia. "But he was gone, lost in thought. Have you heard anything?"

"Nothing," Tara says. "Ominously quiet."

"Humans would be fools to ignore his counsel," says Siyabonga. His tone is strained, but sincere.

"They would," Pythia agrees. "Let's hope they choose reason."

Siyabonga brightens. "Reason isn't their strong suit," he says. "South Africa taught me that well."

"Nor is the rest of the world much better," says Tara. "This is why we all feel the urgency. *Homo sapiens* wielding advanced tech—it's a recipe for extinction. For all."

Her words are familiar, well-worn. Still, both women seem intent on putting Siyabonga at ease.

Suddenly, he straightens. "Can I ask you both something?"

"Of course."

"I'm only an intermediate. Does that . . . affect how you see me? When we make love?" His voice trembles, but his question is sincere.

Tara answers first. "Not at all. I love being with you. I don't think of you as anything less. We're equals."

"Same here," says Pythia.

"In bed, maybe," Siyabonga says. "But out of bed? I feel your efforts to comfort me, and those efforts make me feel separate."

"You're the father of my son," Tara says. "I care for you deeply."

"And though not yet father to my child," Pythia adds, "I feel the same."

Siyabonga nods. "Thank you. Still, I know many intermediates have turned violent. I hope you believe I am different."

"You are our African prince," says Pythia. "Brave and strong. Much loved."

Tara reaches for his hand. "We know it wasn't easy for you to be with my mother. But by doing so, you've shown your faith in us. And in the future."

Siyabonga smiles. "It was easier than I expected. Thanks to Pythia. I need to remember: I am the father of extraordinary children, perhaps the father of a new race. After all, my ancestors didn't bind themselves to one woman."

"Nor do we bind ourselves to one man," Pythia says. "You'll have to accept that too."

He sighs, long and slow. "Ah . . . you wound me with the sharpest truth. So be it. The future awaits."

"Good," says Tara.

Pythia raises her cup. "If we are superior to humans, I'm not feeling it right now."

"Why not?" asks Tara.

"I've inherited one of their worst traits," she mutters. "Impatience."

Outside, the sky darkens as if echoing her word. In the silence that follows, they all feel it: like Pythia, the future is impatient—waiting, restless, and unwilling to wait long.

Chapter Fifteen

On the Eve

Tick Tick Tick

Two weeks pass.

No message comes. No envoy. No sign. Washington remains silent.

Outside the mansion, black sedans and tinted SUVs still idle at appointed corners. Intelligence agents shift positions, rotate shifts, swap suits. But no word arrives. And so the group waits, not idly, but inwardly bracing, each day tilting further into the unknown. Beneath the surface of calm, tension accumulates like sediment, pressing against the walls of hope.

And yet, in the stillness, something luminous unfolds.

Tara's body begins to change. Ming-huà's as well. Their pregnancies progress with quiet wonder, drawing not just curiosity but a kind of reverence. Despite all they have seen, the simple fact of life—new life—still renders them awe-struck. Each small development, each flutter or ache or craving, becomes a signpost on the road toward the unimaginable. This is no ordinary gestation. The children inside them are not merely successors. They are variations. Inflections. Possibilities.

Pythia, for now, remains uncertain. It is too early to know whether Siyabonga's seed has taken root. But the effort has been persistent, even tender. What begins as a symbolic union evolves into something far more deliberate, ritual not in form, but in intention. A joining of bodies guided not by passion alone, but by vision. The evolution they speak of so often must be lived, not only theorized. And so they enact it, night after night, Pythia and Siyabonga, laying the groundwork for what comes next.

One afternoon, Tara, Ming-huà, and Pythia gather in the anteroom. There are no guards, no advisors, no interruptions. Just the three of them, seated amid cushions and low light. A hush surrounds the space. It is not the sound of silence, but the low hum of expectancy.

The conversation begins gently, circling practicalities: nausea, fatigue, subtle shifts in breath or appetite. But inevitably, it turns toward Ming-huà.

Her age, by human standards, would mark this pregnancy as a miracle, or a risk. But they are not human. Their biology is more adaptive, less constrained by the calendar. Even so, none of them know exactly how far their new evolution has taken them. There are no precedents. No books. No midwives to call. Ming-huà has no roadmap.

Though she speaks with serenity, the others hear what lingers beneath her composure: uncertainty, and a private ache she does not name. Her pregnancy stirs both admiration and worry. They reassure her, yet know their comfort can only reach so far. They do not lie to one another. There is too much at stake.

Eventually, their talk shifts to speculation of what these new children might be. If Tara carries a being akin to Abassi, and Ming-huà carries one closer to Pythia, then what of Pythia herself? If she is pregnant, if Siyabonga has contributed his Intermediate lineage into the Superior stream, what might emerge? What third nature might be born?

It is not hierarchy they seek, but balance. Complementarity. If Abassi represents the apex of power, what will temper it? If Pythia's traits lend empathy, foresight, and restraint, what traits remain to be added? The future they imagine is not a throne, but a chorus. Each voice essential. Each child a tone in the emerging harmony or discord.

But beneath all of this speculation lies another, more immediate truth: Abassi is pulling away. Not emotionally. Not out of disdain. But in function. In form. His abilities are beginning to diverge from theirs, not gradually, but unmistakably.

Where they bend reality, he reconstitutes it.

Where they influence time, he suspends or bypasses it.

He does not merely act, he alters. Matter, perception, memory. Even the rules governing causality have begun to yield under his hand.

For Ming-huà, this offers a strange solace. Her nature has always leaned toward nurturing, healing, toward the gentler forms of strength. That Abassi might grow into someone capable of repairing harm rather than inflicting it feels, to her, like proof that evolution does, in the end, bend toward a higher morality of intellect. And yet, she cannot forget what he failed to do.

He could not restore Zookeeper's arms.

She had wrestled with that failure, not because she doubted Abassi's intentions, but because it revealed the boundary even he could not cross. Yet in that boundary, she found something clarifying. Intelligence, as the world had long defined it, was brittle: cunning without conscience, efficiency without care. But Abassi was becoming something else. The more his powers grew, the less he resembled the conquerors of the past. He did not dominate to prove strength, nor persuade to win loyalty. He *understood* and thus could not un-understand. For Ming-huà, that was the measure of higher intelligence: not the speed of thought, but the depth of recognition. Not the ability to outmaneuver, but the inability to turn away from what one sees. True intelligence, she believed, leads inevitably to empathy, not as virtue, but as fundamental structure. As gravity. And so she held faith, even in silence. Even when power failed.

Just then, Sy enters.

He doesn't knock. He never knocks.

He flings the door wide with exaggerated flourish, hands raised like a magician mid-incantation.

"Ah! The Council of Wombs convenes!" he announces. "Plotting the revolution? Exchanging blood codes? Mourning the extinction of male lucidity?"

Pythia doesn't even glance at him. "The last," she says, dry and unhurried.

"Have you heard anything yet?" Ming-huà asks, turning toward him with a gentle tilt of the head.

"Alas, no!" Sy exclaims. "Our beloved watchers remain both mute and uninspired. Outside, they perspire in their automobiles or loiter like wind-up mannequins. The theater of intelligence gathering has become a farce without an audience."

"You speak to them?" Tara asks, half-smiling.

"Endlessly. I ask meaningful questions."

"Such as?"

"'Seen any dragons? Any Russians? Al Capone, perhaps?' Sometimes they laugh. Sometimes they simply stare. I can't tell if it's confusion or despair."

"They must be freezing," Ming-huà says, her voice tinged with real concern.

"And desperately bored," adds Pythia.

"Well then!" Sy claps his hands. "To break the monotony, I propose the following: Pythia, you now announce your pregnancy and allow us all to rejoice."

"You will not be the first to know," she says, grinning.

Sy bows deeply and fake-sobs into his sleeve. "None of you understand the agony I endure in service of your safety!"

"Careful, Sy," Tara warns. "Your metaphor circuits are overheating again."

"Blasphemy!" he cries. "I am wholly organic. No more android slander, I beg you."

"Tea?" Ming-huà offers, rising with quiet grace.

"Delighted."

And so they sit.

They speak. They laugh. They connect in silence, in thought, in shared memory. No urgency drives them, only awareness. The kind that arises just before a page turns, when the hand has not yet moved but the story already knows its next line.

Inside Tara and Ming-huà, life pulses, steady and sure.

And within Pythia, unfelt and unmeasured, a new life has quietly begun.

It is still smaller than awareness. Still hidden from all knowledge. But Siyabonga's seed has taken hold. Something new is forming. Something that has never existed before.

Then Abassi enters.

He says nothing at first, but they all turn toward him. His presence carries the gravity of a verdict.

"I've heard from Washington," he says.

Sy straightens, expression unreadable. "And?"

"They've requested another meeting. A different group this time. The President will be present."

A beat passes.

"They also want another demonstration."

Zookeeper appears in the doorway, arms crossed. "Suspicious little fuckers."

"Expected," Abassi replies calmly.

"It's a trap," Siyabonga says at once. "This is how gangs work. Invite the leaders, offer peace, then open fire. That's how you take control—kill the ones with vision."

Abassi's head turns sharply. "Spoken like an intermediate. The residue of the old world still lives in you."

Tara looks up, stunned. "You're going?"

"This outcome was always likely," Abassi says. "Their internal factions are fracturing. Someone, possibly several, wants final proof. The kind that can't be hidden or spun. They want the President to see it with his own eyes. They want leverage. Their civil war is quiet for now. But what I reveal may decide who wins it."

"Or both factions," Lady Oracle says, stepping into view. No one had seen her enter.

Abassi nods. "Both could benefit. Both could exploit. Unless I intervene wisely, unless I tip the scales toward something more enduring than strategy."

Sy tilts his head. "And how exactly do you plan to do that?"

Abassi's gaze moves beyond them, toward nothing in particular.

"That," he says, "remains to be determined."

~ *A Second Meeting* ~

The room is vast and without ornament, carved into the bedrock beneath the capital, engineered not for comfort but containment. There are no windows. No distractions. It is the kind of room designed by those who assume the greatest threats come from outside. Not within.

The lighting is harsh, institutional. The table is long, metallic, and lifeless, absorbing no warmth. The walls hum faintly with buried machines. And the people within—scholars, advisors, generals, biotechnicians, cryptographers—bring with them not just expertise, but exhaustion. The mood is taut, wary, and saturated with intellectual fatigue.

At one end of the table sit Abassi and Altan. They do not shift in their chairs. They do not adjust their posture. They do not perform.

Abassi scans the room without moving his eyes, perceiving not just faces but fields, subtle emanations of fear, calculation, hope. Suspicion is still present, but it has evolved. The initial alarm—military, territorial, and nationalistic—has been joined now by something harder to contain: academic hunger. The scientists have begun to override the generals. Not by vote, but by necessity. The language has changed. Not just power, but understanding is now on the table. The desire to *know* is overtaking the desire to *control*. And beneath both is a quieter impulse: survival.

Walter Monroe sits near the center. His mind flutters with moral complexity. Margaret Feldman is not far from him, still an ally, though she wears her doubt plainly. Rochelle is absent. A tactical decision, no doubt. Others now lead the charge.

Then, the President enters.

The room rises. All except Abassi and Altan.

The President notices, of course, but says nothing. He has been briefed, warned likely, not to interpret noncompliance as defiance. Still, it grates. The ritual matters to him. It is one of the few tools left in his arsenal that doesn't require a signature or a strike order.

He takes his seat. Silence settles. Not the silence of respect, but of tension wound tight enough to hum. Abassi studies him openly.

Here is a man caught in a prison made of choices, each door leading to a different ruin. He is not evil. Nor is he weak. But he is *alone*. No council, no doctrine, no chain of command can save him from what he must decide. And he knows it. The burden has aged him. He wears it in the small tremors of his fingers, the subtle dulling of his eyes. This is the face not of power, but of the fear of using it wrongly.

"Ladies and gentlemen," the President begins, voice formal but controlled, "thank you for assembling. I'd like us to begin by introducing ourselves to Mr. Powers and Altan."

Abassi's expression shifts into the faintest smile. "No need, Mr. President. I've already read your minds."

The President coughs, a reflex of discomfort, quickly masked. "Then you know why this meeting has been called."

"I do."

"This meeting is classified at the highest level," he says, sweeping the room with his gaze. "Any breach will be dealt with severely."

Then he turns back to Abassi. "That was for my people, Mr. Powers. I trust you are also amenable to keeping this confidential?"

Abassi offers a slight shrug. "As you wish."

"Good." The President folds his hands. "As you're aware, Mr. Powers, deliberations continue. There are factions, strong voices on all sides."

"I'm well aware," Abassi replies. "You are a species of tribes: pack animals shaped by proximity, status, and mating hierarchies. Your institutions merely formalize these instincts."

A few academic advisors chuckle. The President does not.

"We are not pack animals, Mr. Powers," says one of the older advisors, face drawn and pale. "We are scholars. Many of us hold advanced degrees. A few have won the Nobel Prize. Please don't mistake us for something less."

"But that is precisely my point," Abassi replies evenly. "It is dangerous to underestimate other species. More dangerous still to underestimate your own."

The President gives a small, guarded nod. Walter Monroe's thoughts flicker in Abassi's peripheral awareness. Such thoughts are measured, conflicted, and searching.

"In any case," the President continues, "we've asked you here for a demonstration. Not because we distrust you, but because uncertainty has become a liability. The stakes now demand clarity."

Abassi tilts his head slightly. "Doubt again."

"Yes. If you prefer it phrased that way. After your demonstration, we'll open the floor to questions."

Abassi studies the President, then the others. "What sort of demonstration would you like?"

"I leave that to your discretion. As long as it's neither violent nor destructive."

Abassi nods once. "Then I will need a volunteer."

Walter Monroe raises his hand. The room turns toward him.

Abassi smiles gently. "Not you. Your motives would be questioned. We need someone less . . . connected."

And then, without preamble, the President disappears.

Gasps erupt. Chairs scrape. Voices rise in panic. A few stand, unsure whether to flee or demand answers. Some rush to the empty chair, checking beneath it as if expecting a trapdoor. Others search the corners of the room, the ventilation grates, their own hands.

Abassi raises his hands without urgency. "Remain calm. The President is unharmed. He will return in ten minutes—at precisely nine forty-five."

He gestures toward the wall clock. "Feel free to confirm his absence by any means you like."

And they do. For nine long minutes, the most powerful minds in the country devolve into theater. Some poke the air. Some whisper into phones. Some mutter theories under their breath: teleportation, mass hallucination, quantum folding. But all, in time, fall still.

At nine forty-five, the President is seated again, blinking and confused, fingers steepled as before.

"Well, Mr. Powers," he says, "we're waiting."

"Mr. President," Rochelle says from across the room, voice gentle, "you've been gone for ten minutes."

The President looks at him, uncomprehending. "I haven't moved."

"I'm afraid you did," says Rochelle.

A ripple of confirmation moves through the room. Heads nod. Tablets flash with time logs. The President swallows. "Mass hypnosis," he mutters.

"We've ruled that out," says Rochelle.

"As have we," adds another advisor. "We have verified material alterations from your associates: amputations, disappearances, anomalies beyond neurological fabrication."

"The mansion that vanished and returned," Monroe adds. "The video evidence. The metadata. None of it is explainable by deception."

The President exhales slowly. "And yet . . . I felt nothing."

"You wouldn't," Abassi replies. "Your physical structure was relocated—temporarily reconstituted in another dimensional framework. There was no pain because there was no resistance. You were not taken. You were moved."

The President bows his head. "This is beyond me. I yield the floor."

The reaction is immediate.

Scientists, strategists, and ethicists speak over one another, questions layered atop hypotheses, disbelief colliding with revelation. The atmosphere turns fevered. Some plead for further evidence. Some demand explanations. Some warn against continued engagement. The future of policy, warfare, even consciousness itself, begins to unravel across the metallic table.

And Abassi listens until he no longer does.

He stands.

The room quiets.

"I will not perform for you again."

His voice is calm, stripped of spectacle.

"I do not speak in riddles. I speak from the limits of what your current minds can hold. I do not come to conquer. But peace, too, has a cost. It demands more than treaties. It demands transformation—of perception, of self. It demands a shedding of the old myth that power must rule by fear."

He pauses, letting the quiet expand.

"You stand at a threshold. You may cross it. Or remain. No force will drag you forward. But neither will we stay behind."

His eyes move across the room, not with judgment, but with sorrow.

"If you walk with us, your species may endure, not by dominance, but by dignity restored. If you refuse, your ending will be your own. Not sudden. Not dramatic. But steady. An erosion masked as progress. A collapse disguised as tradition."

He turns toward the exit.

"Is that a threat?" the President asks, his voice uncertain.

Abassi stops.

"No," he says gently. "It is a description. Of what has already begun."

And then he walks out.

~ *More Waiting* ~

Weeks pass without resolution.

No formal message arrives. No declaration. No consensus. But the President stays in contact with Abassi. Communications are sporadic and informal, as if the machinery of governance cannot bear the weight of full acknowledgment. He assures Abassi that a decision is near. He speaks of classified sessions, of quiet planning behind thick doors, of cascading contingency models developed to absorb the shock of what is to come.

He describes it as choreography. A ballet of bureaucracies, all rehearsing the moment when the truth must be made public. Civil defense readiness. International diplomatic channels. Economic buffers. Technological firewalls. Emotional inoculation for a global population not yet prepared to know it has been surpassed.

Abassi listens.

He knows most of it is true. The tension is real. So is the planning. But beneath it, visible even through the President's practiced restraint, lurks another calculus. One not designed to manage panic, but to eliminate the cause of it. Not publicly. Not ceremonially. Quietly. Permanently.

When Abassi confronts him directly, the President responds with solemn platitudes. "Routine precautions," he says. "Redundant safeguards." Each phrase polished smooth by decades of political habit. But the lies are porous. The thoughts beneath them tremble with conflict.

Abassi does not press further. Not yet.

Humanity, he knows, has always excelled at building elaborate illusions to shield itself from the primal simplicity of fear. And in that fear lives the oldest instinct of all: destroy what cannot be controlled. Smother the future before it matures.

But before another confrontation can unfold, new light breaks through the gathering haze.

Pythia is pregnant.

The announcement is quiet, private, no ceremony. Yet the response among the group is electric. A rare, unguarded joy spreads among them. Even Abassi, though he says nothing, radiates a subtle warmth as the news is shared.

With three women now bearing life, the tone within the mansion changes. A fragile reverence takes root. They begin watching one another differently, each gesture, each complaint, each flinch of nausea becomes a subject of shared wonder. Laughter returns, not as defiance but as gratitude. Encouragement flows easily between them. They are no longer simply strategists or stewards of a coming age, they are mothers-in-waiting, and the world within them demands attention no less than the world outside.

But the bright current does not last.

Lady Oracle calls a meeting.

She appears drawn, paler than usual, though she moves with deliberate care. Her voice carries the usual clarity, but something behind it has frayed. The lightness she projects cannot conceal the weight in her eyes. The others feel at once that she is not merely informing them. She is managing something. Delaying something. And as always, her mind remains unreadable.

They wait. She paces. Stops. Begins again. Silence stretches between them.

Pythia finally speaks. "You summoned us. Is there something you need to tell us?"

"I did," Lady Oracle says quietly.

The admission alone is startling. The certainty that usually anchors her presence seems to have receded. For a long moment, no one moves.

Then she says, "There are forces behind the mentors. Even beyond them. Powers I cannot name, and do not fully understand. Word has come. We are to prepare."

"For what?" Ming-huà asks.

"For the births."

"Whose directive?" Pythia presses. "Abassi's?"

Lady Oracle shakes her head. "No. This comes from higher still. Not in nature, only in position. The structure is known to me. Their will, less so."

"What preparations?" Tara asks.

Lady Oracle draws in a slow breath. "You are to return to the Flaming Cliffs. All three of you. The births must occur there."

Pythia stiffens. "Why?"

"I don't know. Safety, secrecy, geography. Possibly all of those. My own sense is that something disruptive is approaching. Something vast. They're trying to limit variables."

"You mean the public?"

"Yes. Whether the Americans agree to disclosure or not, the global response will be unpredictable. Violent, even. That much is no longer speculation."

"So we mimic the old world?" Pythia says, her voice taut. "We preemptively retreat. We react as if we are prey."

Lady Oracle meets her gaze. "When dealing with species that fear what they do not understand, one must anticipate both hesitation and aggression. If they feel cornered, they will strike. At minimum, they posture. At worst, they lash out with finality."

"And if Abassi needs us while we're gone?" Ming-huà asks.

"We'll be ready to respond," Lady Oracle replies. "We'll remain linked. But know this—none of this was my choice."

Pythia watches her closely. "Yours is always the slow path. Cautious. Deliberate. A measured retreat from consequence."

"Yes," Lady Oracle agrees. "Had my counsel been followed from the beginning, we might not have reached this brink."

Tara's voice cuts through. "I'm tired of skimming the surface, of policing petty tyrants and cleaning up the wreckage of small men. This is bigger now. Mother and I agree: it's time to face the storm. Let the waters rise."

Lady Oracle does not flinch. "If they do, you will be observing from a distance."

"And if we refuse to go?" Pythia asks.

Lady Oracle lowers her gaze. "Then I don't know what happens. Perhaps only the ones your ancestor Michael Powers once called Metaphorical God and Goddess could answer that."

Ming-huà speaks next. Her voice is quiet, but decisive. "When do we leave?"

"As soon as possible. Rumors are forming. Some in the press have picked up the scent. They suspect government movements. Tourists still gather outside the gates, hoping to glimpse what they call the Mystery Mansion."

Ming-huà nods slowly. "I think those above us, whatever they are, want to avoid the worst outcome. They fear a scenario where we are provoked into harming humans in self-defense."

"Exactly," Lady Oracle says. "They want the possibility removed before it can emerge."

Without pause, she summons Sy. He enters, unusually subdued. There is no theatrical bow, no witty prelude. His face is pale, unreadable.

"We leave before sunrise," Lady Oracle announces. "Altan will drive. After we're dropped at the cave, he'll return to assist Abassi directly."

"Siyabonga and Zookeeper?" Tara asks.

"They'll come with us."

"And the FBI agents outside?" Pythia says.

"Abassi will manage them."

"How?" Ming-huà asks.

Lady Oracle allows herself the faintest smile. "As he says, *they will be elsewhere during the time of our departure.* And by the time they return to their senses, we will be gone."

Pythia folds her arms. "Except for Abassi and Altan."

"Yes," Lady Oracle confirms. "They will remain. And meet whatever storm is coming."

~ *Déjà Vu* ~

Field Officer Lance Romellion is stationed outside the mansion again.

Same assignment. Same protocols. Different man.

Weeks have passed. And still, nothing: no movement, no flare-ups, no anomalies. Just the steady, maddening stillness of those who refuse to obey the gravity of human urgency. He watches the property each day with the quiet contempt of someone excluded from a conversation that may determine the future of his species.

Washington has gone silent. Even Walter Monroe, once a trickle of insight, now offers nothing but a cryptic warning: "Something's coming."

No elaboration. No explanation.

Romellion waits. He watches. He endures.

But this time, he has taken precautions. He has learned from their vanishing tricks. A helicopter stands ready at a nearby airstrip, its engine kept warm, its pilot on permanent standby. The order is simple: *If they disappear again, I follow.*

And then, one morning, the call comes in.

His agents, posted on rotating shifts around the mansion, report a shared gap. Four hours. No memory. No resistance. Not even the sensation of sleep. Just a collective silence in their minds, as though someone had turned the volume of the world to zero.

By the time they come to, the mansion is empty.

No vehicles. No footprints. No sign of forced departure.

Romellion doesn't hesitate. He's in the helicopter within minutes, headset on, hands shaking. His voice is steady, but barely. "Take us to the cave," he tells the pilot.

No coordinates are given. None are needed.

They fly low, slicing across the desert basin, the early sun igniting the rock and sand into a white blaze. As they approach the cliffs, Romellion feels it, not the magnetic pull of evidence, but something else. Something lodged in the gut. A knowing that bypasses logic. *They've gone home.*

The helicopter sets down in a small storm of sand and turbulence. Romellion jumps out before the rotors slow. The wind peels at his suit as he sprints toward the cave mouth. His boots drag through the dust. Sweat trickles down his back.

And then he sees *her*.

Sitting calmly on a sun-bleached rock. Legs folded. Hands relaxed in *her* lap. The same woman from before. Young in form, ancient in gaze. *Her* backpack rests beside *her*. The same serene presence. Unmoved by time. Untouched by fear.

She does not rise. *She* does not blink.

He stops, panting, not out of shock, but recognition. "I'm too late, aren't I?"

She tilts her head slightly. *Her* voice is soft but resonant. "You humans are always in a hurry to arrive," *she* says. "And so you are always late in arriving."

He wipes the sweat from his forehead. "Spare me the poetry."

"None of you will be spared."

He lets out a breath. It isn't exasperation, it's surrender. He lowers himself beside *her*, body slumping against the rock. "I find that hard to accept."

She studies the horizon. "When an animal is locked in a lion's jaws, it does not resist. It surrenders. Not because it is weak, but because it understands that struggle cannot undo what has already begun. That is the wisdom of stillness."

Romellion scoffs. "We'll never stop fighting."

She turns her eyes to him—clear and unpitying. "And that is why, when humans first stirred the stillness, the stillness within them most needed to be stilled."

"So now you'll still us?" he asks.

"No," *she* says gently. "You will still yourselves."

He looks away. "Too deep for me."

She doesn't respond.

"Where did they go?" he asks, squinting into the mouth of the cave. The darkness inside seems to absorb light, not conceal it.

"To a stillness beyond the reach of those who stir."

"You mean humans?"

She nods once. Not as judgment, but as fact.

Silence stretches between them. The wind picks up, moving grains of sand across his boots. The helicopter waits behind him, rotors idling, oblivious to what this moment might mean.

He doesn't ask again. Doesn't posture. He simply breathes.

"We're doomed, aren't we?" he finally says, but his voice is quieter now. Less a question than a confession.

"No," *she* replies. *Her* voice carries no triumph, only stillness. "You are saved."

He turns his head to look at *her,* but *she* is already rising. Without rush. Without sound. *She* picks up the backpack where suffering has been quietly collected, and walks slowly toward the cave, disappearing into its mouth without looking back.

Romellion watches until *she* vanishes.

Then he sits. Alone now, truly alone.

He does not radio the helicopter. He does not move.

For the first time in his life, he allows the stillness to come. And finds that it is not absence, but arrival.

Chapter Sixteen

Silence Broken

Government FUBAR

~ Settling In ~

The Flaming Cliffs remain untouched. Not unchanged in the superficial sense, but untouched in the way that stone remembers, a place where time does not rush forward but stands guard, watching. Here, the compound holds its silence like a vow, indifferent to the noise radiating from across the oceans.

Queequeg receives them without fanfare, without surprise. He greets them as one would greet neighbors returning from an ordinary walk, not refugees from a collapsing civilization. A meal is already waiting: *Guriltai shul*, thick with marrow-rich broth and hand-cut noodles, simmering beside platters of *khuushuur*, their fried skins still blistering with heat. The scent alone folds around them like a woolen cloak. Comfort, born not of illusion, but of intention.

They settle in the cafeteria, where wood creaks under the weight of silence and steam. Under Queequeg's soft gaze, their minds begin to unclench. Conversation resumes, first in fragments, then in full. The air carries laughter again, though softly, as if they fear waking something vast and sleeping. For a time, they let the moment hold them. They speak of food, weather, old memories, things with edges rounded by time.

But reality, like a tide obeying no master, pulls them back. The taste of the food lingers, but the weight of consequence reasserts itself. Outside, beneath the great indifferent sky, the ochre landscape shimmers. Inside, something ancient begins to stir again: the knowledge that time is short, and change is irreversible.

Only Ming-huà remains untouched by the shift in tone. When Pythia and Tara ask how she maintains such calm, she gestures to the open window. The sky beyond is vast, unburdened. The cliffs radiate heat but speak nothing.

"I know my daughter," she says, "and I know my granddaughter. You both burn with a certain kind of fire—the kind that refuses to stand still before injustice. You see the brokenness, the cruelty, and something inside you insists on responding. I've never had that. I love the still places. The quiet forest, the animals who need no speeches, no plans. This place," she continues, glancing outward, "is not so different from my island. I intend to learn its rhythms. To listen to the beings that call it home."

Queequeg smiles with something deeper than amusement.

"Well said, my lovely," says Zookeeper, lifting his bowl in a small toast. "I've seen enough shit for five lifetimes. I vote we stay put until the smoke clears. Or we turn to smoke ourselves."

Lady Oracle raises an eyebrow. "The wreckage won't clear, Zookeeper. Not in our lifetimes. Maybe not in any lifetime."

Zookeeper leans back, slurping his noodles. "Then, in the sacred words of my degenerate friends, fuck it and enjoy the moment."

Laughter ripples across the table. His tone, crass as always, carries something like grace beneath it. He is no fool. He simply refuses the pretense of polish.

Among them, the idea of dual species is no longer alien. It has become lived truth. The intimacy between Superior Ones and *Homo sapiens,* once unthinkable, is now daily life. Love, sex, conception, grief. But their enhanced minds know what others cannot say aloud: this cohabitation is temporary. The future will not bend to symmetry. Humanity will not endure in full. And yet, something of them will remain. Their genomes will echo forward.

Later, over a final cup of tea, the question returns.

"If we succeed," Ming-huà asks, "and establish ourselves beyond this sanctuary, what then? How will our descendants treat humans? Not in theory but in practice, after years of friction, proximity, and fear? And how will humans respond to being no longer supreme?"

The silence that follows is not uncertainty, it is the weight of too many answers.

"I've thought about that," Pythia says. "Jared Paine taught me to see differently. The human range is staggering. Their contradictions are not flaws, but constants. They feel everything, too much and too little."

"Reading their philosophers only deepens the paradox," Tara adds. "Even their most beautiful visions are framed in opposition: master and slave, rebel and tyrant, martyr and executioner. They turn every future into a battlefield, every hope into a contest."

"They fear us because they only understand dominance," Pythia says. "If we're gentle, they assume we're hiding a sword. If we act with mercy, they see it as either weakness or delay. Even Gandhi wielded peace like a blade."

Zookeeper chuckles darkly. "Maybe they're right. Nature doesn't give out participation trophies. Either you eat, or you get eaten. That's not evil—it's physics."

Ming-huà turns to him, her voice steady. "That model works, until the eater destroys the table. Until the hunter poisons the forest. When intelligence enables suicide, it must also enable transcendence."

Siyabonga leans in, his tone quieter. "Is that what Jared saw? The inevitability of collapse? Did it break him?"

"In part," Pythia says. "But more than that, he saw the boundary of his own mind. He glimpsed a pattern beyond his reach and knew he would never cross it. That knowledge undid him. Not because he was weak, but because he was honest."

"Will others fall apart too?" Siyabonga asks. "When they know who we are, what we are, how will they live with it? Even I feel the edge of it. And I'm only half removed."

"Some will break," Tara answers. "Some will reach for us. Most will splinter. Into ideologies, into violence, into despair."

"Governments?" Zookeeper asks.

"Many will fall," she says. "Others will harden. Most will lose legitimacy."

"Religions?" he prods.

"Some will double down. Others will abandon belief altogether. Many will descend into nihilism. When the story no longer fits the species, collapse is inevitable."

Zookeeper exhales. "One big fuckin' mess."

Ming-huà smiles faintly. "As Abassi foresaw, some humans will attempt union. To breed themselves upward. It won't be romantic, it will be strategic."

Zookeeper grins at her. "I'll pretend it's romantic."

Lady Oracle speaks softly. "You're an Intermediate, Zookeeper. That bloodline will grow. The ratio will shift. Rapidly."

He shrugs. "Still a mess."

Lady Oracle nods. "But evolution is messy. That's why it works. Three more of your kind are on the way, children unlike anything we've seen. Not many, perhaps. But neither were the first *Homo sapiens*. And they erased the rest."

"We don't know how," Pythia murmurs.

Lady Oracle meets her gaze. "We're about to learn."

Sy raises his hand, then points upward. "Whatever follows, we have a duty. Not to rule. To protect. We're stewards now."

"Park rangers," Siyabonga says grimly. "And rangers die. Especially when poachers wear uniforms."

"They won't see us as caretakers," he adds. "We'll be a threat. To every structure built on control. To their hierarchies. Their gods. Their markets. They will strike. Not because we're hostile. But because we exist."

Lady Oracle nods. "Some will strike. Others will stall. Some will try diplomacy. But when the poor see their leaders bowing to us, betrayal will erupt."

"We'll find out soon enough," Sy says. "America is next."

"And the people?" Zookeeper asks.

Lady Oracle leans back. "They'll do what they've always done. In your terms, Zookeeper, they'll make a fuckin' mess."

She pauses, then adds, almost offhand, "There's a Mongolian saying: *If you want to see the truth, climb a mountain.*"

Pythia glances out the window, where the Flaming Cliffs rise like silent witnesses.

"Then it's time," she says, "we start climbing."

~ *Romellion Receives a Call* ~

Lance Romellion returns to San Francisco with nothing to show for his desert pilgrimage: no files, no footage, no evidence. And yet, the moment he sets foot back in the city, he senses the game has shifted. The mansion still exists. Altan remains. Powers remains. The heart of the mystery has not revealed itself. But it is now walled behind invisible orders. His request for a warrant is denied without explanation. Authorization to enter the premises is quietly buried beneath layers of executive intransigence. Surveillance is permitted, but nothing more. Do not provoke. Do not approach. Unless someone is bleeding, stand down. The directives from Quantico are riddled with contradictions. The air hums with unease. News outlets speculate about an impending revelation—a cover-up, a silence swollen with consequence. Romellion feels it in his bones: pressure building beneath the surface. Like magma under tectonic plates. Something will give. It always does. Two days later, the call arrives.

"Agent Romellion," says Director Rochelle, voice clipped and brittle. "How are things in San Francisco?"

"Quiet, sir."

"Still no movement from the mansion?"

"No, sir."

"Are you on speaker?"

"Yes."

"Turn it off. Close your door."

He does.

A silence. Then Rochelle speaks again, his tone softened, but strained at the edges, like someone mimicking intimacy without believing in it.

"I spoke with Walter Monroe. He tells me you've had more interaction with this group than anyone else in the Bureau. Would you agree?"

"I suppose so."

"Then we're assigning you a task. Tomorrow at ten, go to the mansion. Mr. Powers will meet you."

"And if he's not there?"

"He will be. You're expected."

Lance's pulse quickens.

"Mr. Powers has made a proposal to the government. You don't need to know the details. Just apologize for the delay. Say it took time to navigate Washington. Tell him we accept—conditionally."

"What conditions?"

"You won't need those either. Just say further discussions must happen in Washington. We want you as our liaison. Someone he trusts. Someone physically close."

"You want me to extract intel?"

"No. He reads minds. You won't learn anything he doesn't permit. Just be yourself. Cooperative. Transparent. We need openness, not espionage."

"So . . . an interpreter?"

"Precisely. Someone who can stand at his side without triggering alarm."

"And if he asks about the conditions?"

"Deflect. Tell him it's complicated. That we'll explain when he arrives. If he agrees to come, we'll brief you both."

"Yes, sir."

"Any questions?"

"Just to confirm, my role is honesty and goodwill. Nothing covert."

"Exactly. Good luck, Lance. Enjoy your time with this extraordinary being."

"Thank you, sir."

~

At first, Lance assumes it's a setup. A manipulation wrapped in a polite order. That's how it's always been: lies baked into smiles, directives dressed in diplomacy. But then he remembers: Abassi reads minds. The moment he entertains doubt, it is revealed. The moment he questions motive, the suspicion is exposed. There's no way to hide it now. No plausible deniability. His thoughts are real, but also readable. There's no rewinding a brain. No smudging a memory clean. The only remaining path is straight ahead. Full truth. No masks. No tactics. No armor. It runs counter to every instinct he's honed. Every lesson from his career. But none of that matters now. The old playbook is utterly irrelevant; ashes in an abandoned hearth.

That night, lying in the quiet of his apartment, Lance makes the choice. He will speak the truth, not because it is noble, but because it is the only thing that might keep him alive. And in that choice, he discovers something unexpected. Relief. The great weight of deception, the constant calculation of what to reveal and what to conceal—it lifts. He has worn too many masks for too long. His entire profession has trained him to read others, to manipulate shadows, to manage the illusion of control.

But Abassi is not human. And for once, neither pretense nor cleverness will save him. Only the utter vulnerability of truth will do.

~ The Test ~

At precisely ten the next morning, the door swings open before Lance can knock.

Altan stands in the threshold, silent, composed, neither welcoming nor hostile. His expression is unreadable, though a glint of something like amusement flickers at the edges. Without a word, he steps aside, granting entrance not as a servant but as a sentinel.

The house is steeped in quiet. Not absence-of-sound quiet, but a kind of interior hush that feels almost inhabited. As they pass through narrow corridors, dimly lit and reverent in their stillness, Lance senses a charge in the air as though the walls themselves are listening, as if memory lives here not in photographs but in atmosphere.

They arrive at a modest anteroom. No throne. No altar. Just a low table, three padded chairs, and Abassi sits already waiting. He does not rise. He does not nod. He simply exists at the center of the space with a stillness so complete it draws everything else into orbit. Not anticipation. Not performance. Just stillness, calm as stone, alive as fire.

"Coffee or tea?" Abassi asks, his voice soft, unhurried. The tone is not mystical. It is domestic. Civil. As if this were any morning, in any home.

"Coffee, thank you," Lance replies, caught off guard by the familiarity.

Lance, Altan, and Abassi sit like members of a tribunal whose purpose has not been announced.

The silence thickens.

Lance feels it almost immediately: a subtle vibration rising behind his eyes, a low frequency hum at the base of his skull, as though static is being sifted through the folds of his mind. He fights the instinct to flinch.

"I trust you've found nothing alarming," he says, offering a cautious smile.

"Only your resolve to speak plainly," Abassi replies. His voice carries warmth, but beneath it, something electric hums, something vast. "It's rare. And commendable."

"Being near you is like standing naked under a floodlight, magnified. Most humans would find it unbearable."

"But naked is how you were born," Abassi answers lightly. "How all of us were born."

Lance chuckles. "If I could read your mind, what would I see?"

Abassi tilts his head slightly. "A labyrinth. Spiraling architectures. Fractal recursion. Highways built for particles and waves your brain cannot name. I mean no insult, it's simply the shape of things."

"Like a dog trying to comprehend calculus?"

"Closer to a chimpanzee. But your self-awareness is refreshing."

"I've had time to accept my insignificance."

"Then you are further along than most."

"Are you asking if I'm afraid?"

"I'm asking nothing. I'm observing. The fear is there, but it's not your master."

Lance nods. "How will humanity respond when it learns you're here?"

"That depends," he says. "But your answer will tell me more than mine."

"Humans don't come in single colors. Reactions will diverge. Some will worship, others will riot. Most will deny until denial becomes impossible."

Abassi smiles faintly. "Precisely. Complexity cannot be reduced to categories. There will be awe. There will be violence. There will be men who weep, and men who reach for guns."

"You already know why I've come."

"I do. And I know you suspect these negotiations are theater. That something else stands behind the curtain."

"I've lived long enough to know nothing is ever what it seems."

"Wisdom," Abassi nods. "And last night—your thoughts on deception. How much energy your species wastes on the performance of lies. You were not wrong."

Lance stiffens. "You were listening?"

"From a distance your physicists would still call 'here.' And yes, Einstein would have admired your clarity."

Then, with a glint of mischief: "Though Einstein may have had . . . assistance."

Lance lets the line hang. "As liaison, I'm here to confirm the government accepts your proposal, pending further details."

Abassi exhales not from fatigue, but something cooler, older. "As we speak, your agents are planting surveillance devices. And explosives."

The words land like stones in water.

Lance jerks upright. "Explosives?"

"A test," Abassi says. "They assumed I would be too focused on you to notice."

A flush rises in Lance's neck, spreading across his face. "I didn't know."

"Of course not. You weren't meant to. But now that you do . . . what shall we do about it?"

"Are they still there?"

"They are. Disoriented. Their gear is gone. They're gathering in an alley to recalibrate failure."

"You didn't harm them?"

"No. They are men, not monsters. They follow orders, as do you."

"I'm sorry. I'll call Director Rochelle immediately."

"No need to leave. Use your phone. Put it on speaker. Let us see how transparent your government truly is."

Lance hesitates only a moment. Then he takes the phone from his pocket, places it on the table, and dials.

Rochelle answers immediately. "Agent Romellion?"

"Director, this is Romellion. Mr. Powers detected your field team planting devices. He's disarmed them. They are unharmed, but missing their equipment. I was here in good faith. So was he. We would like an explanation."

A long pause.

"They were conducting a test," she says finally.

"A test?" Lance echoes.

"To assess Mr. Powers's capabilities."

Abassi laughs, not cruelly, but with weight. The sound fills the room like a tremor that doesn't shake the furniture but shifts the stakes.

"And how did I score?" he asks.

"With flying colors," Rochelle admits.

"You understand nothing," Abassi replies, voice level but deepening. "You dwell in the confines of your limited dimensions. I do not. So I'll be plain: accept my proposal now, or reject it now. But do not play games. If you wish to retain your limbs, your titles, your illusion of control—put the President on the line."

Another pause. Then Rochelle says, "Please hold."

Lance lowers the phone but does not speak. Abassi watches him, not with anger, but with the patience of someone who has seen this ritual played out across centuries, in palaces and parliaments and crumbling chambers of empire.

The President's voice arrives like a flattened echo from another room.

"Mr. Powers. I've been briefed."

"And your response?"

"We accept your proposal. But we request a meeting. In person."

"I will not travel. Your liaison is sufficient."

"You want secrecy?"

"Of course. Until the appointed moment. Then the world will change."

"Understood. We'll keep all information classified. Is Mr. Romellion still present?"

"We're both here," Abassi says. "And all communication will be transparent. I already know your thoughts. This performance is for your sake."

There is a silence on the line.

"Ah," the President stumbles.

"Withdraw the agents," Abassi continues. "They serve no purpose."

"We'll do so at once."

"You mentioned experts."

"Yes—our national security advisor, and select leaders in psychology, military strategy, communications."

"That's acceptable. But move quickly. The press is circling. And once hysteria begins, your so-called new age, your presidency, will end not in the light of order, but in the flames of chaos."

"I recommend you relocate," the President says. "Before the story breaks. Others like you are safe?"

"They are. I'll choose my own location. It will be unfindable unless I choose otherwise. Romellion will accompany me."

"We'd prefer to know where you are, for your safety."

"No. You must not know, for yours."

The pause stretches, then—

"Agent Romellion?"

"Yes, Mr. President."

"You are to remain with Mr. Powers. No further operations. No interference of any kind. You are now our representative in full."

"Yes, sir."

"You have no dependents?"

"No, sir."

"Then from now on, you serve him. Openly. Fully."

"Yes, sir."

A final breath across the wire.

"God help us all."

"Indeed, sir."

The line clicks off.

Lance turns to speak but Abassi is already elsewhere. Eyes closed. Breath steady. Not meditating. Not asleep. Something older. A stillness deeper than consciousness.

So Lance sits.

And waits.

His heart paces wildly in its cage, unsure if what fills his chest is fear or reverence, or the first shiver of approaching extinction.

~

The age of man has not been overthrown, it has been outgrown.

What follows is not conquest, but succession.

Chapter Seventeen

All Hell Breaks Loose

Crossing the Rubicon

~ A Shattering Announcement ~

Judith Simmons, Press Secretary to the President of the United States, does not blink. Her fingers hover over the document, no longer trembling, but held in the strange stasis of someone trying to absorb a death knell disguised as an invitation. The pages are glossy—too glossy—as if sheen could mask substance, as if formatting might tame the wild content beneath.

She has read it four times now.

Each reading carves deeper.

She expected the usual parade of manageable alarms: currency fluctuations, diplomatic entanglements, a scandal buried in timing. Even a missile test would have been welcome. But what she holds instead is the end of something, though no one has yet named what.

Outside the West Wing's glass, the late morning sun bounces politely off the Potomac. Inside, the stillness of power begins to fray. Judith is seasoned, not just in rhetoric but in the choreography of control: knowing when to pause, when to deflect, when to summon warmth, and when to channel national grief. But this is not a crisis to be spun. It is a threshold.

And thresholds, she knows, change the worlds that cross them.

She wishes, absurdly, for an hour. One hour alone. Not to scheme or consult or message-test, but to *feel*. To hold her fiancé's hand. To stroke the fur of her aging cat. To run a bath, let the hot water rise, and vanish into it for just a moment. But there is no time now for private rituals. No one on Earth has an hour left to themselves.

The document is short. *Too* short. Words chosen with the precision of a surgeon and the duplicity of a campaign manager. Each sentence is a gauze bandage stretched over arterial truth. Phrases like *peaceful intentions* and *cooperation underway* repeat with unnerving insistence. It is not a lie, not quite. But it is not truth either. Judith knows how to read the interstices of language. She lives in the spaces between what is said and what is meant.

The press statement is designed to pacify, not inform. It pretends to usher humanity into an age of wonder, but Judith hears what is *not* said: the unspoken acknowledgment that events are unfolding too fast for human systems to adapt, that Earth's central nervous system is already in overload.

Two hours ago, she sat in her Arlington apartment, her body folded into an armchair, coffee growing cold beside the paper, cat curled on her knees. There had been birdsong, traffic hum, the faint clatter of a neighbor's dishes—traces of a world that still believed in continuity.

That world is gone.

Now, her pulse hammers with purpose. She steadies her breathing, arranges her face into the expressionless calm that once helped presidents survive impeachment threats and military blunders. And then she walks out, down the corridor lined with portraits of statesmen who never imagined this, toward the White House press chamber.

Her high heels echo like gunfire on the marble.

Inside, every chair is occupied. More stand at the edges. The scent of nerves is thick, though no one would call it that. Phones are clutched like talismans. Voices are hushed, because the media has already guessed that something unnatural is at hand.

She hesitates—only for a breath, the barest flicker of pause—then steadies herself. Her hand grazes the edge of the podium, fingertips finding its lacquered groove like a grounding wire. She knows she must not falter. Not now. Not here.

Judith Simmons is a professional. That title means something to her. It means reading through without tremor. It means no visible fear, no unsanctioned sentiment, no speculative gestures of hope or doom. It means holding the line, even as that line blurs beneath her feet.

And yet, as she lifts the paper once more, she is no longer standing only in the press chamber of the White House, she is standing in every memory that ever taught her to love what might now be lost.

She thinks of her parents, long since buried, who once told her the world was imperfect but redeemable. She thinks of her daughter, away at college, and her son, still young enough to fear thunderstorms. She thinks of the cat that slept against her ribs just that morning, purring with the timeless trust of creatures that do not read headlines.

She thinks of the future—hers, theirs, everyone's—and how suddenly brittle it all feels.

And still, she is a professional.

Control the breath.

Anchor the knees.

Lower the voice half a register.

Let the words do the work.

Do not become the story.

But then, just before her lips part, before breath becomes sound, a thought slips in—treacherous, quiet, unmistakable: *What if this is the last normal moment anyone will ever know?*

Her throat tightens. A shimmer threatens her composure. She holds it. Pins it. Crushes it down.

She takes one final inhale. The kind of breath that seals a moment to memory. The kind you take before walking into a funeral, or a war.

And then she begins to speak.

~

"Good morning. Today, I bring both startling and joyous news.

"The government of the United States has obtained incontrovertible proof that intelligent life beyond Earth exists.

"Following extensive investigations and direct contact between our agencies and these beings, we can confirm not only their existence, but their peaceful intentions. These advanced lifeforms seek communication, cooperation, and mutual exchange.

"As I speak, arrangements are underway to host representatives of their kind. By mutual agreement, the details of these arrangements will remain confidential for now.

"To repeat: these beings are peaceful. Like us, they are eager to build a relationship grounded in trust and goodwill.

"This is a monumental step forward, perhaps the first of a Golden Age in science, diplomacy, and global unity.

"Let it be clear: the Department of Defense, FBI, CIA, Homeland Security, and other agencies remain fully alert. While no threats have been detected, precautions are in place for every contingency.

"Further information will be shared as communication continues. Due to the vast distances involved, transmissions require time. For now, we ask all peoples of the Earth to celebrate this historic moment.

"Over the next several months, as specific details are refined, only general questions will be addressed to avoid misinformation.

"A new advisory committee, comprising experts from Defense, State, NASA, and leading scientific institutions, will respond to global media queries in writing and hold periodic briefings.

"You will receive contact instructions following this statement. The committee is titled the Special Advisory Unified Committee on Extraterrestrial Relations—S.A.U.C.E.R."

~

A subtle quiver betrays her composure as the journalists begin to grasp the magnitude of what has been said. Then the room detonates. A volley of shouted questions, clashing demands, and half-formed accusations drowns the podium in a storm of uncertainty. Judith doesn't stay. She introduces Dr. Richard Carlson—astrophysicist, political neophyte, and newly appointed head of S.A.U.C.

E.R.—then steps away like a soldier who has delivered the sealed orders and now leaves others to carry them out.

She returns to her office.

Locks the door.

Closes the blinds.

And sits.

At first, she feels nothing. Then everything.

Tears do not fall out of sadness. Nor joy. They rise from the unnameable pressure of *knowing,* of standing in that narrow aperture where history unspools and the future collapses inward. She breathes shallowly, worried she might hyperventilate.

There will be no return to normal.

Her cat will never know what has happened. Her fiancé, she fears, may understand only the surface. And that, too, will be a loss.

In her bones, she feels the truth: poise is now performance. Beneath it, she is already disassembling, cell by cell, certainty by certainty, into someone else. Into the woman who will face the extinction of everything she once called stable.

She does not say the word *invasion*. She does not need to.

That, she knows, is someone else's line to deliver.

~ The Elder Watches ~

Judith Simmons remains behind her locked door, motionless. The press chamber outside has dissolved into noise, reporters shouting, phones buzzing, staff moving in chaotic loops. But none of it reaches her. Not really. What she heard in her own voice, what she saw ripple across their faces, is enough. She has no answers even to her own questions.

The world is no longer waiting. It has already tipped forward.

And while the institutions of government brace against that shift—some with resolve, others with illusion—certain individuals, long attuned to such moments, feel the tremor in a different way.

~

Elsewhere, behind the curtained quiet of a Georgetown study, Walter Monroe switches off the television. The press conference fades into silence, leaving behind the echo of calculated calm. He has watched every word, every hesitation in Judith Simmons' voice, every tightly managed expression. His eyes narrow not in disbelief, but in recognition. His pulse does not quicken. His drink remains steady. He has seen too much across too many decades to be surprised by declarations, no matter how historic. But this one does not sit as announcements should. It settles like a weight. Not revelation, but confirmation. Not clarity, but delay.

He understands the language of power, and he recognizes when it falters. The administration's statement, carefully crafted and cautiously vague, is not a trumpet of discovery. It is a smoke signal. A stall. A plea for time they no longer control. The center, he senses, is holding for now, but the screws are loosening. The seams are whispering open.

What unnerves him most is not the existence of these beings (that particular shock has long since passed), but what must now follow. What system remains fit for a world no longer bound by its own species? The question is no longer whether we are alone, but whether we still matter.

His thoughts drift, uninvited, to Anne. His granddaughter. Twenty-five. Brilliant. Fierce. Still naïve enough to think the world can be reasoned with, but wise enough to see how often it refuses. And then, further, to her children, unborn but now, perhaps, unavoidable. The legacy he has long nurtured in the background of his ambitions. What future can they possibly inherit from this crumbling scaffolding of nations and flags and faiths?

He dares, for the first time, to imagine what had always been unthinkable. Not as metaphor. Not as speculative fiction. But as the only viable path forward.

What if Anne joins with them? Mates with them, Not coerced, but by choice. Not politics, but evolution.

And suddenly, he understands Abassi's indictment. The human addiction to tribal lineage, to blood, to legacy. His own desire to see something of himself endure—he sees it now for what it is: elegant primitivism. The same old grasping wrapped in finer silk. *We have outlived our time*, he thinks. *The question now is whether we will bow with grace, or fight like dogs around a bone we already buried.*

He reaches for the phone and dials Lance Romellion's number in San Francisco. No answer. No details. Just a soft tone, a recorded void. He tries another line, reaching Director Rochelle directly.

"Sorry, Walter," Rochelle cuts in before he can finish. "That's top secret. Even for you."

"Is he alive?"

"Top secret. I can't speak longer. Goodbye."

The line goes dead with bureaucratic finality.

Monroe pours himself his usual morning Bloody Mary. The ice clinks, polite and precise. So, something is happening. And it is either very bad, or very good.

"You may rest assured it is both," says a voice, smooth and melodic, from the chair across the room.

He jerks, sloshing red across the table. The drink darkens the oak. He doesn't rise, doesn't call for security. He's too old, too seasoned, and somewhere too expectant. He dabs at the spill with his handkerchief, then calmly turns to face *her*.

She is as he remembers, young, radiant, but an absence of warmth, like a flame in vacuum.

"My dream returns," he says. "Though this time I know you're no dream. Are you one of the so-called extraterrestrials the administration is begging us to believe in?"

She tilts her head, amused. "All lifeforms are aliens. Illegal immigrants adrift in an indifferent cosmos."

He smiles grimly. "Then death is the final deportation."

"Not final. Just efficient."

"What brings you this time? Something to do with the circus in Washington?"

"You have a role in that circus."

"Me?"

"The President trusts you more than your Director. He's not wrong. Use your influence wisely."

He studies her carefully. "Who are you? What's your connection to Abassi and the others? Why me, goddammit?"

"You've been chosen."

"By who? For what?"

"Because you carry traces of their blood."

The words strike harder than they should. "What?"

"There have been many false starts in the attempted evolution of your species. You carry genes passed down from one such attempt. An intermediate. It failed. But you survived."

"An intermediate?"

"Details are unimportant. What matters is that you're eligible. You are useful. Not special, but useful. You've taken a path against the grain—empathetic, dis-illusioned—but never bitter. The ones who came before you did not last. You have."

"And that makes me useful?"

"It makes you recognizable, to them."

"You mean I speak their language?"

"Enough of it to be understood. Though you remain mostly *Homo sapiens* . . . still, you carry seeds."

He sets his glass down with care. "You still won't tell me what you are?"

"I'll tell you what is required."

"And if I refuse to listen?"

"Then you will end—not with violence, but with silence. Forgotten."

He leans back, exhales. "Can I offer you a drink?"

She smiles. It is not warmth. It is permission. And waits.

"What do you want of me?"

"Your granddaughter."

His face flushes. His voice sharpens. "Anne?"

"She's twenty-five, yes?"

"You already know that."

"You've been thinking about your legacy. Your bloodline. Your descendants."

"She is not for sale," he snaps. "Not for Abassi. Not for you."

"She's called Anne. Political science at Yale. Intellect above the human mean. Intuition sharper still, borderline telepathic, thanks to the genes you passed on. Compassionate. Strategic. Fertile. And uniquely situated at a genetic and ethical crossroads. She could be a perfect match."

He rises. "Out. Now."

She remains unmoved.

Her gaze is gentle. Too gentle. The way a scalpel gleams before it cuts.

Her calm is intolerable.

"You're a pimp," he growls. "A goddamned cosmic pimp for Abassi. Do you think I'd whore out my own flesh and blood for some interspecies experiment? Get the hell out."

"Abassi doesn't know I'm here."

He laughs bitterly. "Right. Sure."

"You know I'm telling the truth."

He trembles. "You're insane."

"Your outrage is real, but not pure. The thought has already brushed the edge of your mind. I simply voiced it aloud. The revulsion you feel, that's the part of you still clinging to the human frame. But there is more in you. A different part. The part that sees ahead. Anne carries that part, too."

"Don't."

"Anne and her children, if she has them, have no future unless you open this door. You both have been chosen, as others were before you. John Powers. Michael Powers. The Child of Buddha. A lineage seeded long ago is now blooming."

Monroe lowers himself slowly back into the chair, pale, shaken.

"Who are you? What are you?" he asks.

"I am who I am, which is what I am."

Monroe shakes his head in confusion. "I don't understand, but whoever or whatever you are, you have never had children or you wouldn't propose such an outlandish scheme."

"You find my proposal obscene?"

"Of course I do."

"And yet, you thought of it."

"I dismissed it."

"But not because it was wrong, only because it was terrifying."

He looks away.

"What do you think Anne would feel if she met Abassi under neutral circumstances?"

"She'd be appalled."

"No. She'd be intrigued. You know that, too. Her mind, her instincts, her blood—they all point forward."

"Not as a mate."

"There's one way to find out."

"How?"

"Tell her what I've told you. Bring her to San Francisco. Let her decide."

"If you can vanish and reappear like this, why not ask her yourself?"

"Oh, I will, Mr. Monroe. I will."

He stares at her, bitter. "Leave."

She stands but offers one final sentence before disappearing.

"Your government is already collapsing. So is every other. The situation is volatile . . . combustible. The timeline is tightening."

And then *she* is gone.

Walter Monroe finishes his drink in silence, mixes another, and stares long into the glass, no longer searching for comfort, but for proof the world he knew ever existed at all.

~ *Reaction* ~

In the days and weeks following the announcement, the world begins to tear, not from a single fracture, but from countless stress points erupting at once. The illusion of consensus—on science, on sovereignty, on shared reality—dissolves almost overnight.

Across continents, city streets fill with dazed and restless crowds. Millions pour into public squares, not with a single voice but with overlapping demands. Some cheer, some rage. Some weep openly. Most simply want to know what happens next. From Lagos to London, New Delhi to São Paulo, people gather not in celebration or protest alone, but in something more primal: *reckoning*.

Governments reel. The State Department is overwhelmed within hours, its switchboards jammed, its diplomats caught in a rising tide of panic and maneuver. Leaders from every nation demand inclusion in the unfolding dialogue, each framing their urgency in moral, historical, or strategic terms. Several issue open threats: exclusion will be interpreted as betrayal. No nation wants to be sidelined in what may be the defining event of human civilization.

The United Nations convenes in emergency session. The mood is not one of cooperation, but of guarded calculation. Alliances fray beneath the surface as blocs form, dissolve, and re-form in real time. Even longtime partners eye each other warily, everyone aware that the axis of history may be tilting, and that first access to whatever technologies or powers these beings possess could permanently reorder the balance of global influence.

On the streets and online, conspiracy theories metastasize. Some claim the aliens are a government fabrication, part of a psychological operation to justify martial law or population control. Others insist the beings are already among us, pulling strings in secret. Still others believe they are saviors—or devils—arrived to fulfill ancient prophecy.

Civil society begins to convulse. Utopian futurists clash with doomsday cults. Secular humanists argue with evangelical revivalists, both accusing the other of blind faith. The foundational questions of meaning, purpose, and destiny, long buried beneath economics and entertainment, return with an urgency no institution is prepared to answer.

Religious authorities fragment. Some declare a new age of divine communion; others denounce the visitors as demons, tests, or temptations. Competing declarations emerge even from within the same denomination. Authority loses coherence. Certainty erodes.

Academics and scientists issue carefully worded appeals for calm, for patience, for empirical study. They are largely ignored. The public wants absolutes: proof, not process. And in that vacuum, opportunists rise. Demagogues seize microphones, stirring nationalist resentment and existential dread. Politicians, eager to preserve relevance, drift with the prevailing winds—offering platitudes, promises, or purges, depending on the crowd.

Dictators act with swift brutality. Internet blackouts. Mass arrests. State-run media declares the entire event a Western hoax or a divine threat. Borders harden. Surveillance expands. Fear becomes policy.

Armed groups begin to mobilize. Militias in North America, Russia, India, and parts of Africa release statements asserting their intention to "protect humanity by force if necessary." Meanwhile, peace coalitions form in response, calling for planetary unity, for the abandonment of old ideologies in favor of species-wide solidarity. Their voices are noble, but increasingly drowned out.

Interest groups demand representation: LGBTQ leaders, disability advocates, indigenous councils, environmental stewards, all arguing that any dialogue with nonhuman beings must include more than the traditional guardians of state. But no formal process exists. SAUCER, the hastily named advisory committee, becomes the crucible of the world's confusion and hope, a temporary institution never designed for what it now must bear.

And through it all, the core question remains unanswered: *Where is the proof?*

Without visible confirmation, without images, encounters, clear transmissions, the world begins to suspect theater. Panic deepens. Skepticism hardens into outrage. Washington's reassurances are no longer enough.

Then, the geopolitical fractures begin to widen.

Russia and China jointly issue a warning: if the United States proceeds with unilateral negotiations, consequences will follow—economic, diplomatic, and possibly military. Intelligence intercepts suggest that other regional powers may align with this position, not out of ideological agreement, but from fear of exclusion.

Despite behind-the-scenes outreach, the United States stands increasingly isolated. Not as the leader of Earth, but as a suspect in its possible betrayal. American allies demand access to SAUCER. Foreign ministers call for a multilateral framework. The President insists such efforts are underway, but the delays are measured not in days, but in nerve.

And the people?

They hover between extremes: riot and reverence, disbelief and worship, chaos and trance. Some prepare to fight. Others to kneel. A few prepare to flee, though there is nowhere left to run.

Each day tightens the spiral. Military postures stiffen. Research labs overflow with unsolicited claims. Online feeds churn with doctored footage, alleged leaks, whispered warnings. The timeline shortens. The pressure mounts.

The White House turns inward. Meetings run in circles. Intelligence agencies contradict one another. The cabinet fractures over strategy, secrecy, and semantics. Nothing calms the world. Nothing buys more time.

So, the President does what no President before has done in open crisis. He consults *Choral*.

The government's own AGI, trained on the sum of human knowledge, evolved in silence, bound by constitutional constraints that had never anticipated existential contact.

Only one question is asked.

"What should we do?"

Choral answers without hesitation. Not a directive, not a projection, but an assessment.

"You must first choose what kind of species you wish to be. Do you want to endure as negotiators, as stewards, or as survivors? You cannot be all three."

Then, more softly:

"If you fear losing control, tell the truth. If you fear losing relevance, tell it faster. If you fear losing unity, let others speak. But do not lie. Not now."

Choral goes quiet and refuses to dispute its response to further human probing.

The President scowls, wanting clarity, wanting a plan, wanting anything but naked truth.

And still there is no consensus. No one knows what kind of species they wish to be.

In desperation, the President places a call.

~ *The Island* ~

"Good afternoon, Mr. President," says Lance Romellion, his voice low, static-washed, and strangely steady.

"Lance, I need you. Where are you?"

"No idea."

"What?"

"I mean that literally. Before the announcement, we traveled to a cave in the California desert. Took a side tunnel, ended up here."

"Where's *here*?"

"I can't say. GPS is useless. The sky doesn't match. It's an island—lush, tropical, seemingly uninhabited except for me, Abassi, and Altan. Judging from what stars I *do* recognize, maybe the northern hemisphere, maybe Pacific. But the constellations are wrong. Or wrong *here*."

The President's voice hardens. "Are you being held?"

"No. Disoriented—yes. This call, it helps. Grounds me."

"Well, listen carefully. I need you to speak to Abassi. He has to return . . . publicly. He must demonstrate his powers. The world's unraveling. If he wants peace, he must show himself. Otherwise, this whole fragile construct collapses into blood and fire."

"He knows."

A pause.

"What?"

"He's listening now."

A longer pause. Then:

"Mr. Powers, are you there?"

Abassi's voice comes smooth, unhurried. "Of course."

"Will you come to Washington?"

"No. It must be a neutral site. An island, independently governed, endangered by rising seas. A fitting place for a demonstration."

"That's not feasible. I'm told such locations lack the infrastructure we'd need communications, security, transmission. We're talking hundreds of world leaders. Full broadcast. Global coordination."

"Then make the infrastructure adequate."

"You refuse Washington?"

"Yes. Washington would shape the narrative, control the symbols. It would reduce what must be a global threshold into a national performance. That cannot happen. We do not seek dominance. We seek transition. From dominion to coexistence. From fear to ethic. From extraction to equilibrium. There will be resistance. That is inevitable. But our role is not to conquer, it is to lessen the impact. Do you understand?"

A long breath. Then: "Yes."

"Then focus your energies there."

"I'll consult with my team."

"Do so. But time, Mr. President, is nearly gone."

"I'll call Romellion with updates."

"Goodbye."

~ *Storm Beach* ~

Lance lowers the satellite phone with trembling fingers.

Abassi sits as before, eyes closed, expression unreadable. The room around them is hushed, but it does not feel still. It feels braced.

Lance steps outside. The air is thick with moisture. Jungle calls echo across the canopy. He walks slowly, barefoot, down a narrow path carved through the brush. His mind is full, but strangely quiet. No thoughts, only sensation. The press of heat. The scent of salt. The faint tremor beneath the earth.

He crests a low ridge.

The ocean spreads out before him, vast, blue, and alive.

Then it shifts.

Clouds gather with unnatural speed, folding over one another like pages turned by invisible hands. The wind rises, not in gusts, but in waves, heavy and directional. The sea darkens, churns, explodes against the reef in fits of violent rhythm. Lightning forks the horizon. Thunder follows close behind.

Behind him, the jungle begins to roar. Trees sway violently. From the high ridge, he turns—and there, silhouetted by lightning, stands a figure.

"Altan!" Lance calls out. "Jesus, you scared the hell out of me!"

Altan steps forward, rain streaking his face. "I did not intend to. I didn't realize FBI agents were afraid of shadows."

Lance laughs, uneasy. "Where'd you hear that?"

"From your thoughts. You were trying to remember how to be fearless. Trying to summon control. Very FBI."

Another bolt splits the sky. Lance flinches. Altan does not move.

"I came to tell you," Altan says, voice raised over the storm, "Abassi is leaving this island. You cannot go with him."

"I have orders."

"You may stay. Or return home. But you will not follow him."

The wind claws at them. Lance shouts, "Let's talk inside!"

Altan gestures toward the path. "Go ahead. I'll remain. The bodies are coming ashore."

Lance stops. "Bodies?"

"Not your concern. They are not from this place. Not from this time."

"What are you talking about?"

Altan does not answer. He turns, and Lance follows down the path, through the thick brush, toward the roaring coastline.

And then, at the beach, they see them.

Bodies. Not one or two. Hundreds. Thousands. Cast up by the sea in grotesque procession. Tangled in remnants of clothing, fragments of fabric from forgotten empires, vanished colonies, wars recorded only in marginal footnotes. Eyes open. Mouths frozen. Limbs twisted, clinging to one another in silent, salt-slick ruin.

Lance stares, unable to move.

Altan's voice breaks through the wind. "Go back! You've seen enough!"

"But where did they come from?"

Altan's face darkens. "Elsewhere. Times that failed. Realities abandoned. This is not your burden."

Still they come, tossed onto the sand like the discarded memory of humanity's unfinished drafts.

"Go!" Altan shouts. "I cannot shield you much longer!"

Lance turns and runs—tripping, crashing through the underbrush. The jungle closes around him. Branches claw his skin. He stumbles through vines, over roots, breath ragged, heart thundering.

He reaches the house. Slams the door. Collapses against it.

Inside, the light is warm.

Abassi sits as before: still, composed, untouched by storm or time.

Lance's voice cracks. "My God. What have I stepped into? What does this mean? I want out. Let me go."

Abassi opens his eyes. Meets him without pity.

"And so you will," he says quietly.

The silence that follows is not peace. It is a hinge in history, something turning, irrevocably.

Outside, the storm screams.

Inside, the dream of man begins to unspool.

And somewhere in that unraveling, the rough beast shifts, fully awake, its hour come at last.

Chapter Eighteen

Shelter from the Storm

Intermediates

~ Anne Monroe ~

The moment the press conference ends, Anne Monroe lunges for her phone.

She's on midterm break from Yale, groggy from a sleepless night. Notes and highlighters sprawl across her kitchen table, untouched. Her second coffee has gone cold. She had turned on the TV only to generate background noise, something to hold the edges of her focus. But then the screen erupted with headlines no one was prepared to read.

Intelligent life confirmed.

Contact established.

Global briefing in progress.

Every channel. Every anchor. The same impossible truth.

Aliens.

Even as Judith Simmons reads the statement aloud, Anne can already feel the psychological drift between what's being said and what's being withheld. The phrases are manicured, the tone too smooth. Whatever this is, it's being managed. The government is not sharing, they're containing.

She doesn't panic. But the air thickens. Her pulse shifts. Her first instinct is the one drilled into her by a lifetime of Monroe discipline: find the source. Clarify the framing. Go deeper. She dials her grandfather.

No answer.

She hangs up and dials again.

Still nothing.

She leaves a message, then begins pacing her apartment, half-listening to a man named Dr. Carlson describing S.A.U.C.E.R.'s mandate in terms so bureaucratic they might as well be stalling tactics. Anne feels it in her bones: no one is going to tell the public anything real. Not yet.

She considers calling friends, but resists. Speculation is noise. Better to observe, record, absorb. That's who she is: methodical, deliberate, trained not just by her professors, but by Walter Monroe himself.

Still, her thoughts spiral.

What do they look like? How do they speak? Are they humanoid? Telepathic? Interdimensional? Are they truly extraterrestrial, or something stranger?

And most urgently: *Where the hell is Walter?*

Then a voice answers.

Not through the phone.

From behind her.

"Your grandfather is in Arlington. Having another Bloody Mary."

Anne gasps and spins.

A woman sits on the couch, *her* figure composed, luminous, impossible. *She* radiates presence without force. There is nothing threatening in *her* posture, nothing aggressive in *her* tone. And yet Anne feels the temperature drop.

"How did you get in?" she asks, already reaching toward her phone.

The woman gestures calmly to the chair opposite. "May we talk?"

Anne hesitates. The door was locked. Deadbolted. She's sure of it.

"You didn't answer the question."

"Your grandfather gave me the key."

"That's absurd."

The woman produces one. Anne stares at it—standard Yale-issue brass.

Alarm rises in her throat. "Is Walter okay?"

"Perfectly. I just left him."

"But he's in Arlington."

The woman inclines *her* head. "Yes."

Anne feels a lump in her throat. She blinks. "That's not possible."

"I've come with an invitation."

"To what?"

"To meet one of the beings you just heard about."

Anne lowers herself into the chair, almost involuntarily. "You mean . . . an alien?"

"His name is Abassi. He will answer what others evade. The questions you're already asking—he is the only one who can truly respond."

Anne narrows her gaze. "Did Walter send you?"

"In his way."

"Why me?"

"Because you are who you are."

"That's not an answer."

"It will be. Soon."

Anne rubs her temples. "Aren't these beings supposed to be . . . I think I heard it right . . . light-years away?"

"You know as well as I do the government is rarely honest when the truth is unmanageable."

"That's something Walter would say."

"He's said it many times."

"You want me to meet this . . . Abassi?"

"If you're willing to come to San Francisco. Yes."

Anne studies the woman's face. "What kind of meeting are we talking about?"

"One based on mutual curiosity. Mutual discernment."

"You know him?"

"Intimately."

Anne's voice lowers. "Are you one of them?"

The woman tilts her head, almost kindly. "That word—*alien*—was never meant to hold what I am. The word *alien* is itself alien."

Anne leans back. "Do you have a name?"

"I've been given many. None of them endure."

"This is getting surreal. What's actually going on?"

"You're being invited. Not conscripted. Not manipulated. Invited."

"For what purpose?"

"To begin. Nothing more. Nothing less."

Anne stares at her. "Why now?"

"Ask your grandfather."

"What does he have to do with this?"

"More than he's told you."

Anne stands. Her mind is spinning now, logic, fear, fascination wrestling all at once. "I don't understand."

"You will."

And just like that, *she's* gone. No flash. No door. Just absence.

Anne stares at the empty chair.

Her first impulse is to call Walter. But her hand pauses mid-reach. A sliver of doubt cuts through her rational mind. Did she imagine it? Exhaustion? Stress hallucination? It had felt real—*too* real—but what could she even say?

She circles her apartment for nearly an hour, caught between rationality and instinct. Then, just as her hand moves again toward the phone, it rings.

She freezes. Answers.

"Hello?"

"Anne. It's Walter."

"Walter! I was just about to call you. Did you see the press conference?"

"I did. But listen to me—"

"Is it true? Is this really happening? Are they actually—?"

"Perhaps. But right now—"

"I had a visitor. Just now. A woman. She said you gave her a key. Did you?"

A long silence.

Then a weary sigh.

"Come to Arlington. Immediately."

"But . . . my midterms—"

"Anne. This matters more than grades. More than almost anything."

"Is this about someone named Abassi?"

Another pause. "Yes."

A chill slides down her spine.

"Grandfather . . . did you really give her the key?"

"I'll explain when you get here. Just come."

"I'm on my way."

~ *Unusual Father – Daughter Conversation* ~

That night, after a long, restless drive from New Haven, Anne Monroe steps into her grandfather's apartment in Arlington. Her shoulders ache. Her eyes are dry from too much caffeine, too much speculation, too many imagined futures colliding in her mind. She half expects silence, or an inquiry delivered with Walter's usual austerity. Instead, he embraces her.

Not a quick hug. Not the polite acknowledgment of shared blood. A full, enveloping embrace. His arms hold her longer than usual, and when he pulls back, he kisses her forehead. A simple gesture. But something in it is not simple at all.

Anne stiffens. She knows this man. She knows how carefully he controls emotion, how rarely he permits sentiment to surface, even with her. Especially with her. It's part of the unspoken agreement between them: honesty in everything, except feeling. And so, this sudden gesture of affection doesn't comfort her. It alarms her.

He steps back and studies her. For a moment, neither of them speaks. The room is quiet, dimly lit. The scent of black tea mingles with the faint smell of old books and clean wool. Walter Monroe's home is orderly, precise. So is he. But tonight, she feels the weight of something else—something under tremendous strain.

Since her parents died, Anne has carried the impression of Walter not just as guardian, but as something closer to myth; a man who held the broken world together with discipline and resolve. He had raised her with unwavering attention, never indulgent but always just. His silence about his FBI past had never seemed like evasion to her. It had felt like protection. Now, that silence feels like a dam about to break.

She blurts out her story—the woman, the message, the vanishing. As she speaks, she studies him, waiting for signs of disbelief or concern. But Walter listens without interruption. He makes tea, measuring each movement with practiced calm. His lack of surprise unnerves her more than any outburst could have.

When they sit, he doesn't rush. She knows the look in his eyes: he is building a sequence, ordering a chain of events, deciding how to begin.

"Anne," he says at last, "I need to set aside every instinct I have about caution, confidentiality, and control. I'm going to tell you the full truth. All of it. About what I know, what I suspect, and what I've seen. But I need you to listen. Completely. No interruptions. Can you do that?"

"Of course, Grandfather."

He nods, then begins. For the next half hour, Walter Monroe opens a vault that has remained sealed for decades. He speaks of Lance Romellion's visit. Of the cave. Of the island. Of Abassi. Of the woman they both encountered—the one who calls herself nothing and yet seems to know everything. He describes Abassi's vision: a world reshaped not through conquest, but through invitation. A new model of relation. Of kinship beyond bloodlines. Of coexistence beyond species.

Anne listens, unmoving. Her mind runs fast, but her expression remains composed. When he reaches the part about the proposal, Abassi's interest in her, Walter stops.

"Now I need to hear exactly what she said to you," he says. "Word for word, if you can manage it."

Anne recounts the entire conversation. As she speaks, she watches her grandfather's face. He gives nothing away, but by the end, his hands have tightened around his cup.

"I had a feeling," Anne says quietly, "that you already knew."

Walter doesn't deny it. "To put it plainly, she wishes for you and Abassi to become . . . close. Possibly intimate."

Anne's face remains neutral. "Why me?"

"That," Walter says, "is what puzzles me most. I've been told I carry something in my genetic profile, a trace of what they call the intermediates. And that some portion of it may have passed to you."

"Genetic inheritance," Anne murmurs. "From who? From what?"

"That's still unclear. But I no longer believe they're aliens in the traditional sense. I don't think they traveled here from stars or systems. I think they emerged. Were cultivated. Engineered. Perhaps here. Perhaps long ago."

Anne shakes her head. "Are you saying these beings are . . . human?"

"Not exactly. They're post-human. Or maybe pre-human. Maybe the word doesn't fit at all. But yes, their genomes are related to ours. Close enough for overlap. Close enough to share something deeper than DNA."

"But I don't have powers. I can't move objects or vanish."

"Neither can I," Walter says. "But I've always had instincts that went beyond luck. And you, Anne, from the time you were little, you and I would share thoughts before they were spoken. You knew things you couldn't have known. That isn't nothing."

She nods slowly. "Then why are we calling them aliens?"

Walter exhales. "Because the truth is too dense for public digestion. Aliens fit in a box. They come from out there. They leave. They don't threaten the meaning of being human."

Anne smiles faintly. "So I'm being asked to mate with a post-human to preserve something I don't understand."

"That's one way of putting it."

"What's he like?"

Walter tilts his head. "Striking. Tall. Powerful. Controlled. There is something about his back . . . well, it's like a shield. Not armor. Not deformity. More like an organic sign of something internal. A capacity to endure. To protect."

Anne's eyebrows rise. "He sounds mythic."

"He is. But also not. He listens. He watches. He doesn't speak more than necessary. But when he does, it feels like something ancient turning its gaze toward the present."

They fall into silence.

Anne reaches for her cup. "So we go to San Francisco."

Walter nods. "Yes. But we go on our terms. This isn't a binding contract. No promises. No assumptions."

"Agreed."

"No one else knows. No friends. No news. Not yet."

Anne lifts her cup in quiet salute. "To secrets."

Walter clinks his against hers. "To clarity."

She grins. "To maybe the strangest first date in human history."

He raises an eyebrow. "You inherited my gallows humor."

"No," Anne says, finishing her tea. "I evolved it."

~ *Lance Faces the Storm* ~

Lance bursts through the door, soaked to the bone, heart pounding from Abassi's final words: "And so you will." The wind has died down, but the storm is not over—not the one outside, and certainly not the one inside him. Rainwater pools at his feet as he stands trembling just past the threshold, unable to move for a long moment.

He lowers himself into a chair with a mechanical grace, trying to assemble his breath. Though he appears composed, his face is pale, and his skin quivers with adrenaline.

"What I saw on that beach. . . . " His voice is rough, like something torn. "Is that a preview of your future? Is that the world you mean to bring?"

Abassi does not open his eyes. He sits motionless in the center of the room, a figure at peace within silence.

"I can see the image in your mind," Abassi replies, quietly. "But what you witnessed is not what you believe."

Lance leans forward, fists clenched. "Where did those bodies come from? You didn't conjure them out of your magic kettle."

"They are returning," Abassi says.

"From where?"

"Elsewhere."

Lance slams his fist against the armrest. "No more riddles. If this is what you're offering us in exchange for peace—piles of the dead—then we want none of it."

"Yes," Abassi says, without emphasis.

The bluntness strikes Lance with more force than a scream. He reels.

"Before you collapse from shock," Abassi says gently, "recall what I told you. It is not what you think."

"Then tell me. Tell me what it is."

"They are records," Abassi says. "Volumes. Each corpse a story. The ocean is not water, it is archive. Memory. Suffering. War. The betrayals of kin. The torture of strangers. Everything you call history. This beach was a shelf, and now it has been rearranged. These bodies are not from the future. They are the forgotten dead. And they have returned."

Lance's voice cracks. "But they were real. I saw them. Are they illusions? Dreams? Will they rot in the sand?"

"They are real. And they will decay. But the stories they carry remain in the library."

Lance trembles, the foundation of his identity unraveling. "I dreamed once," he mutters. "Of armless men, legless women. A line of the mutilated. I thought I was losing my mind. And now you make it real. You are not a prophet. You're not a savior. You're the Devil himself."

Abassi remains unmoved. "You and I are metaphors, Agent Romellion. The Devil is a metaphor. So is this island. In your terms, it is a simulation, a manifestation. Not of fantasy, but of deep reality. You see with your eyes what your world has refused to see with its soul."

Lance glares at him, furious. "And that's supposed to excuse it?"

"To humans, everything outside their myth is madness."

Lance lowers his head, silent now. He cannot argue. He cannot escape.

Abassi speaks again. "We both have paths. I must depart. You wish to return. Your mind is clouded, and I have become your enemy. That, too, is a metaphor. I leave within the hour. Tomorrow, Altan will guide you to the threshold."

Lance mutters, "The sooner the better."

Abassi tilts his head, almost kindly. "Be cautious with your wishes."

No response.

He turns to the window. "The storm has passed, both outside, and within. Go now. Return to the beach. Look again."

Abassi closes his eyes.

Lance rises slowly, fury diluted by confusion. He walks out into the damp air. The storm is gone. The sky is clear. Moonlight drapes the island in silvery calm. The jungle hums with nocturnal life. As he rounds the path back to the shore, he sees Altan standing in the place they last met, tall and watchful.

"Abassi told me to return," Lance says. "To see what I can see."

Altan nods.

"Why don't I smell the rot?"

"Come."

They walk together. The beach is pristine. No bodies. No blood. Just sand, shining under the moon, and waves that whisper nothing.

"Where are they?" Lance asks, already knowing.

"Elsewhere."

Lance sighs. "The FBI would call this a cover-up."

Altan smiles faintly. "That, too, is a metaphor."

"What's really happening?"

"In what sense?"

"All of it. The aliens. The visions. The disappearances. What's the point of it?"

They walk slowly.

"Do you believe this ocean is real?" Altan asks.

"I don't know anymore."

"Touch it."

Lance does. Water shimmers between his fingers.

"Seems real."

"And yet?"

"And yet . . . it changes nothing. What is all this for?"

"You already know the answer."

"Replacement," Lance says.

"Yes. But not with violence. Not with conquest. With time. With birth."

"Replaced by whom?"

"By the children of Abassi. And the women you called hunchbacks."

Lance bristles. "I've seen no moral superiority in them."

"You don't want to see it. Because if you do, you must admit you are no longer the best candidate for the future."

Lance stiffens. "You think I want to kill Abassi."

"Yes."

"You think I'll become one of those corpses."

"You will, if you choose to remain what you were."

Lance lowers his head.

"I want you to live," Altan says. "But you must change."

Lance's voice cracks. "Evolve into what—creatures like Abassi?"

"Neanderthals thought the same of *Homo sapiens*."

"And you know this . . . how?"

Altan looks out at the sea. His voice is almost a whisper. "I was there."

Lance narrows his eyes. "If you were there . . . what did they think of us? Were we gods to them? Monsters? Something in between?"

Altan's reply comes slowly, as though reaching backward through eons. "They saw you as unpredictable, dangerous. Not gods. Not demons. Just . . . unstable. Fire and ice trapped in the same body. Your eyes burned with something they didn't recognize. Not madness, exactly. But a hunger without ritual. They were communal. Rhythmic. They remembered their dead. You—your kind—arrived like a force without memory. Agile. Cunning. But so quick to sever what they still tried to preserve."

Lance stares at him. "But they interbred with us."

"Yes. They tried to merge the future with the past. A few succeeded. Most were devoured, not by war, but by erosion. You made them myth—stereotypical slow-witted brutes. But they weren't. No, they weren't at all. Her name was Etta.

She sang before she killed, a song low and sorrowful, like a mother calling home the lost. She cradled skulls of her dead tribesmen as if listening for echoes. As if the dead still whispered in the bone."

Lance lowers his gaze. "Maybe they were the better species."

"Not better. Different. You won because you forgot faster. Because you burned the map and kept moving."

He pauses, then adds with a glance, "But that forgetting was selective. You forget when it suits you, but you also remember when it suits you, when memory feeds your hunger. You chew it like a bone, again and again, especially when it comes with the flavor of grievance. Of vengeance. Of victory. Of a wrong to be righted. Of domination. That's your brilliance. And your doom."

Lance's hands tighten on his thighs. He doesn't look up, but something shifts in him, a small, silent fracture. A pulse rises in his throat, then settles. He stares at the floor, sees a flash of his own childhood: his father shouting, the burn of humiliation. Yet somewhere in his mind, he longs for Etta's song, now gone, with all her kind, forever.

Altan turns to him. "And now you face the same question they did."

"Which is?"

"Can you evolve without erasing everything else?"

~ *News From Far Away* ~

Far across the world, in their hidden sanctuary deep within the Flaming Cliffs, the three pregnant women and their companions track the tremors of a world unraveling. News of confirmed alien contact, of powers awakened and undeniable, has radiated outward, faster than any pandemic, faster even than war. No country is spared. The illusion of order disintegrates as old authorities falter, and societies once held together by myths of progress and sovereignty now quake beneath the weight of an intelligence that does not negotiate, does not apologize, and cannot be contained.

Even those among them gifted with heightened perception had not anticipated such speed. The minds of ordinary humans, long numbed by spectacle and denial, have no defense against the abyss now yawning open before them. Fear metastasizes into rage, confusion into scapegoating, disbelief into desperation. What had once been unthinkable—state collapse, mass delusion, theological meltdown—now unfolds hour by hour, like a fever dream rushing toward its inevitable breaking point.

In their refuge, there is no panic. But there is sorrow.

Not for themselves. Not for the unborn. But for those still bound to the crumbling scaffold of human belief. For a species that cannot release its grip even as the beam breaks. For the children who will inherit neither peace nor meaning, only noise and aftermath.

The mood shifts. The silence breaks. Pythia and Tara speak privately, then announce their decision: they will return to the United States.

The news spreads quickly through the refuge. Reactions are swift, uneasy. At once, Lady Oracle convenes a meeting. Three o'clock. The cafeteria. Everyone.

At the appointed hour, the room fills. Quequeeg has prepared a small offering: bowls of sugared fruit, ginger tea, almond cakes. The table is laid with quiet ceremony. Tara and Siyabonga arrive first, hand in hand. Then Pythia, walking alone. Ming-huà enters, followed by Zookeeper and Sy, who hums softly to himself, his scarecrow body swaying to the rhythm. Finally, Lady Oracle steps in and closes the door.

All take their places. The women are visibly heavier now, bellies taut, movements slower, more deliberate. The time remaining has shortened. The gestation, though rapid, is not chaotic. It has purpose. Evolution, pressed to adapt, has recalibrated the female form. Wider pelvic arches, lower centers of gravity, a denser vascular web. The body adjusts, even when the mind resists.

Pythia begins. "Tara and I feel we can't remain here. Not while Abassi and Altan are preparing to confront the world. We don't want to interfere, but we can't sit idle, either. Not with this much at stake."

Lady Oracle's voice is calm but steely. "And what exactly do you intend to do?"

"We don't know yet," Tara admits. "But we're not tourists. We have power. We have insight. We've walked into war zones before."

"Your bodies are no longer your own," Sy interjects. "The children growing inside you are not abstractions. They will soon be born. And they may be . . . different."

"Which is all the more reason to stand beside Abassi," says Tara. "He's different, too."

Sy begins pacing. "You speak as if presence is a solution. But this isn't a protest march. This isn't a battlefield you can win with strategy or conviction. We are standing at the edge of a species-wide reckoning. Missteps now could rupture everything. You think your instincts will guide you, but instincts are rooted in the old world."

Siyabonga clears his throat. "Still, it feels wrong to hide. If these children are truly the bridge, then don't they deserve to be born into the storm they're meant to transform?"

"You're not wrong," says Sy, stopping at the far end of the table. "But you're not right, either."

"You think we're a liability," Pythia says.

"I think you're sacred," Sy replies. "Which is another word for dangerous."

A silence falls. The kind that tests alliances.

Tara breathes in deeply. "Then what is our role? If not to bear witness? If not to intervene? Why were we created at all?"

Lady Oracle studies her. "You were not created. You emerged. But emergence is not random. You are the reply."

"Reply to what?"

"To the question humankind refused to ask. To the damage it refused to acknowledge. To the voices it silenced across centuries, continents, ecosystems. You are not here to serve mankind. You are here to outlast it."

"But with compassion," Siyabonga says. "That's the vision, isn't it? Evolution without conquest. Power without cruelty."

Zookeeper leans forward. "Is that possible?"

"It's not a question of possibility," says Lady Oracle. "It's a question of necessity."

Ming-huà finally speaks. Her voice is quiet. "If we are not the rangers, as Siyabonga once called us, then who is guarding the preserve?"

"The question is too narrow," Lady Oracle answers. "It assumes Earth is still a preserve. That there's something left to guard."

"Then what are we guarding?" asks Tara.

Lady Oracle pauses. "A future that has not yet disintegrated."

"And who are we, in that future?"

"You are the new apex," she says. "Not hunters. Not rulers. Something else. Something that remembers what the old predator forgot."

"Empathy?" Pythia ventures.

"Restraint," says Sy.

"Wisdom," adds Ming-huà.

Siyabonga shakes his head. "These words are beautiful. But they don't hold shape. Not in fire."

Lady Oracle nods. "That is why you must not return, at least not yet. Because your shape is still forming. Your children are still becoming. The world will try to define you too soon. If it cannot, it will turn on you."

"And if we stay hidden?" Tara asks.

"Then you will meet the storm on your own terms," Lady Oracle replies. "Not as symbols. Not as saviors. But as the first of your kind."

Pythia lifts her cup and sips the now-cooled tea. "You speak in riddles."

"I speak in echoes," says Lady Oracle. "The original voice is gone."

"What voice?" asks Zookeeper.

"The one that named this world. Before language. Before species. Before division."

The table falls still. Outside, the wind brushes faintly against the metal walls of the refuge. Somewhere, faintly, the Earth shudders.

~

Later, long after the table has been cleared and the last murmurs have faded into silence, the women sit alone beneath the low light of the corridor lamps. No words pass between them. Their hands rest on their swelling bellies, each heartbeat within carrying a promise they can't yet name. Outside, the world teeters. Inside, something ancient stirs—neither memory nor prophecy, but a presence threading through bone and blood. Not yet born, not yet known, but listening. And waiting.

Especially one.

Chapter Nineteen

Into the Abyss

Fertility

~ Abassi Meets Anne Monroe ~

Walter and Anne Monroe sit over a quiet breakfast in a modest San Francisco hotel café. Their plates are half-finished; conversation, scarce. The easy rhythm that once marked their mornings has faded into silence. Both are uneasy, the silence between them filled with questions neither quite wants to ask. Tonight, Anne is to dine privately with Abassi. The venue, a secluded restaurant in Oakland, was clearly selected for its discretion, and the gesture feels heavy with intent. The air around the invitation is not romantic, not exactly. It is something older, more deliberate. Anne senses this, and her mind teeters between caution and compulsion.

"Second thoughts, sweetie?" Walter finally asks.

"Of course," she replies, almost sharply. Then softens. "But not because he's a different species. That part is odd, yes, but not what frightens me. It's the mind-reading. I don't like the idea that he can sift through my thoughts, my impulses. What if I think something horrible?"

"Knowing Abassi, I imagine he'd understand."

"Easy for you to say. You're not the one being dissected over dinner."

"I'll be nearby. If anything goes wrong, just call me."

"He knows you'll be driving me, right?"

"Yes. You've asked that more times than I can count."

"If I leave, it won't be because I'm uncomfortable. It'll be because I've lost the match. Fled the field. But I won't. I'll see it through."

Walter smiles. "I'm proud of you."

"Don't be. I'm terrified."

"Still. This could be something extraordinary. An inflection point."

"For whom? Humanity? Or just me?"

"Both. Use your instincts tonight. Not as a date. As an agent. Watch him."

"You forget he'll know I'm doing that. He'll feel it before I even know I'm doing it. I have to go in clean."

Walter reaches for her hand. "Then just be yourself. That's enough."

Anne nods, but beneath her outward calm, tension coils. Even choosing what to wear becomes an act of battle. Too elegant feels manipulative. Too plain, disrespectful. She finally selects a simple black dress, understated jewelry, and flats. Her hair, usually uncooperative, falls into place with eerie ease.

Walter's eyes light up when she emerges. "You look like someone who belongs to the next century. Maybe even the next species."

She flushes. "That's either the sweetest or the strangest compliment I've ever received."

"You're radiant. And brave."

"I don't feel brave."

"Then you're perfect."

They drive in silence through the city. Sunset is nearing. The streets, though unchanged, feel different, as if the world itself is uneasy and has begun to anticipate something.

~

The restaurant is discreet, low-lit, and nearly empty. Abassi is already seated when they arrive. He stands when Anne approaches. His height, his posture, the quiet magnetism of his gaze—it all presses into her, not with force, but with gravity. She's struck again by how human he appears, yet how unmistakably other.

"Thank you for coming," he says, offering his hand.

"You're taller than I remembered."

"I get that a lot."

Walter steps forward, briefly shakes Abassi's hand. "I'll be close."

"I know," Abassi replies gently. "And I thank you for your trust."

Walter turns to Anne, embraces her with firm affection, and leaves without another word.

Anne sits. The chair seems to mold around her. A faint current hums in the air, or maybe inside her. She presses a hand to her forehead.

"Is this part of the effect?"

Abassi smiles. "Residual resonance. I've turned it off."

"You're not pretending?"

"I'm not pretending."

A waiter approaches, pauses as if unsure, then retreats. Abassi hasn't moved.

"Telepathy?"

"Yes. I asked him silently to give us time."

Anne shakes her head. "This is going to be difficult."

"Only at first. I've already agreed not to read your thoughts without permission."

"That was a promise?"

"It is now."

They order. The conversation eases. His voice is smooth, his gestures calm. She finds herself disarmed not by his powers, but by his restraint.

"Do you still want to see my back?"

She hesitates. "Yes. If it's not invasive."

Abassi rises, turns slightly. Through his shirt, she sees the outline, a raised formation, dense and shielded. Not grotesque. Just real.

He sits again. "It is not decoration. It is function."

"I've heard stories. Of others like you. The hunchback women."

"Yes. They are pregnant now. All of them. The line is expanding."

Anne studies him. "Is that what this is? A search for more?"

"It's an invitation. Not an expectation."

"Why me?"

"Because you're not merely curious. You're brave. And because the genes you carry whisper across the boundary."

Anne's pulse quickens. She looks down at her hands.

"If I say yes, what am I becoming?"

"More than you were. Not less than human, but not only human."

She whispers, "Will it hurt?"

"Transformation always does. But the pain passes."

Anne meets his gaze. "Then show me."

A moment passes. Then something opens. Not in the room, but in her. A wave moves through her body, not of emotion, but of comprehension. The room fades. Time thins. She feels language peel away from meaning, memory detach from self. And then she returns. Changed. Not visibly. But inwardly, unmistakably.

She whispers, "You didn't touch me."

"I didn't need to."

Silence stretches. She drinks her tea with new awareness, as if every movement now ripples beyond her.

"I need time," she says.

"Take it."

"In the meantime," she says in a forced, nervous, slightly flirtatious voice. "Let's talk about something else."

"What?"

"Anything. Anything that's normal . . . anything that doesn't involve the weight of the world. Do you like cats?"

~

Later that night, Walter picks her up. She steps into the car, not with giddiness, but with solemn purpose. Her glow is not romantic, but cellular. Something has shifted.

"Well?" he asks.

She smiles crookedly. "Thank God you can't read my mind."

Walter looks at her, concerned. "Are you alright?"

She nods. "I'm changed. But not broken. I agreed to another dinner tomorrow."

He starts the engine. "Just promise me you'll stay you."

She glances at him. "What if the old me was waiting to become this?"

Walter says nothing. But the silence between them now holds a tense reverence.

~

Anne stands at the window of her hotel room, watching the city lights blink. A vision of the *Titanic*, lights still flickering as it slipped into the cold ocean at night, crosses her mind. That image lingers: human civilization, luminous and fragile, vanishing beneath a cold, dark surface it cannot fathom. She places a hand against the glass. Something inside her listens. Not to the noise outside, but to a voice just now learning how to speak within.

It is not a voice of certainty. It is a voice shaped by paradox, a longing for continuity and a pull toward what comes next. In the window's reflection, she sees not herself, but a question suspended in time. The city sprawls beneath her, unaware that the old world is beginning to fracture.

She wants the human story to continue. Not out of nostalgia, but because there is beauty in its stubbornness, its capacity for tenderness, its refusal to yield even when the tide turns. She does not want her species to vanish into footnotes. She wants it to rise. To learn. To transform without being erased.

But she knows better. A reckoning is coming—not because anyone wills it, but because something deeper is now in motion. The tectonic shift has already begun. And whatever emerges will not be negotiated.

Still, she hopes.

She stands at the window a moment longer, hand to glass, breathing quietly. Then she whispers to the darkened sky, as if to the future itself:

"We are still here. Remember that."

~ From the Frying Pan into the Fire ~

The next morning, Anne prepares for another dinner with Abassi. Her movements are precise, but her mind is elsewhere. She has already spoken with Walter, recounting every detail of the previous night—not just what was said, but how it felt, what it opened in her. She avoids certain phrases, skips over the way her chest fluttered when Abassi leaned forward or how the silence between their words felt less like a pause and more like an invitation. Walter notices anyway. What startles him is not what she tells him, but how she tells it. There is a warmth behind her voice, a new current beneath her speech. Anne Monroe is drawn in. More than drawn—enchanted. And it frightens him.

That afternoon, they sit in the hotel lounge, the muted clink of glass and china all around them. A server brings tea. They sip in silence.

Walter finally breaks it. "What do you think happens next?"

Anne gives a small shrug. "Too early to say. I'll know more after tonight."

"But you like him. It's not just curiosity."

"It's both," she says plainly. "I'd have to be blind not to be fascinated. But I like him. I'm not apologizing for that."

Walter nods, then hesitates. "You know he's going public soon. If this continues, your name may follow his."

"We're not in a relationship," she snaps.

"I didn't say you were. But if the connection deepens—"

"I'm aware," she cuts in, softer now.

He leans forward, voice low. "Then you also know he'll never love you the way you might one day love him."

"Walter, it's been one dinner."

"That's not a denial."

She sighs. "Fine. I've heard it all. He's not wired like us. No personal attachments. Universal compassion. Einstein's ghost. You've said this before."

"It still matters."

She nods, quiet now. "Maybe it does. Or maybe if we're truly on the verge of extinction, his kind of love is what's needed."

Walter frowns, unconvinced. "That kind of love can still break a heart."

"I know," she says. "But I'm not fragile. And I'm not fantasizing. I just want to see where this goes."

He watches her carefully. Then, with a gentleness that surprises her, says, "I'm proud of you, Anne. And whatever you decide, I trust your judgment."

She smiles, touched. "Thanks."

After a pause, she adds, "Still . . . it would be poetic, wouldn't it?"

"What would?"

"If your great-grandchild made you vanish for getting the wrong Christmas present."

She laughs aloud. Walter tries to join her, but the sound doesn't quite rise to the surface.

~

By evening, her mood has transformed. Gone is the tension of uncertainty. In its place is expectation. She hums as she dresses, choosing an outfit that offers both elegance and allure. Every decision—her earrings, her shoes, the subtle trace of scent behind each ear—is intentional, composed not for seduction but for presence. She is rehearsing a dance with something ancient and emerging, something not quite human.

Walter tries a few questions, but she barely hears them. Her mind is elsewhere, sketching scenes not yet lived. Perfect words. Shared glances. Laughter, maybe something more.

When the call comes from the lobby, she kisses Walter goodbye and steps into the elevator.

Downstairs, the hotel lobby thrums with the usual flux of travelers and tourists: luggage wheels, murmured greetings, flashes of phone screens. Anne scans the room. No Abassi.

Then, a tall figure approaches. Composed. Unhurried.

"Hello," he says, offering a slight bow. "You are Anne Monroe?"

"I am," she replies, accepting his hand.

"I'm Altan. I'll be your driver tonight. Mr. Powers is waiting in the car."

"He doesn't drive?"

"He prefers not to be seen. He values discretion."

"I understand."

Altan's smile is unforced. "Don't worry. I won't be joining you for dinner."

"You're welcome to."

"Thank you. But no."

As they move toward the exit, she studies him. "Are you one of his kind?"

His smile deepens, unreadable. "Not exactly."

She means to ask more, but the moment passes. Outside, the night air carries a metallic hush. Beneath a flickering streetlight, a sleek black car waits. Abassi stands beside it, partly cloaked in shadow. The light catches his shoulders and brow, leaving his features veiled, his form statuesque, momentarily unnerving in its poise.

He opens the door. Anne enters. He follows.

Altan pulls away.

"Same restaurant?" she asks.

"No. Chinese tonight. There's a small place in Chinatown that is both quiet and excellent. My great-grandmother was Chinese."

"That explains a few things."

He turns to her. "Like what?"

"You're full of surprises."

He smiles. "I'm quite the foreigner, aren't I?"

"A funny one. Almost otter-level."

Their laughter fills the car, brief and light.

The drive veers away from main roads, down alleys thick with shadow. At a dead end, Altan stops. The world seems to hush. Anne and Abassi exit, slipping through a narrow gap. He takes her hand. She lets him.

Side by side, they walk into a hidden corridor of brick and stone. Red lanterns hang above aging doors. Tiled roofs slope toward each other like folded palms. They pass into something older than the city, something transported from a different place and time.

At last, a dim light flickers above a carved wooden door.

Abassi reads the characters aloud. "Zhuang Zi's Haunted Dragon."

"That's interesting. Who, I mean . . . the name?"

"Zhuang Zi was a philosopher."

She lifts a brow. "And the dragon?"

"Perhaps us."

He opens the door. "Come. Here, even stillness must quiet itself."

She stares at him.

"Later," he says.

~

Inside, the welcome is immediate. A stout man in a faded vest scurries toward them.

"Good sir! You're back!"

"Mr. Chu," Abassi replies. "How is Cook Wang?"

"Excellent. And Lilianna?"

Chu pats his belly. "Still round. Still spoiled."

He turns to Anne and bows low. "You are most welcome."

"Thank you," she replies, matching the gesture.

"No delay. Your room is ready!"

He leads them up a creaking spiral staircase to a small chamber.

"First, tea. Then wine. A few delicacies. Mademoiselle, vous parlez français?"

"A little," Anne smiles.

J'espère que tu as faim?

"Oui. J'ai très faim."

"Tu l'aimes bien?"

"C'est mon ami."

"Plus qu'un ami?"

"Peut-être plus qu'un ami."

Chu claps his hands, delighted, and disappears down the stairs.

Abassi turns to her. "So I am . . . maybe more than a friend?"

She meets his gaze. *"J'espère que nous pouvons être plus que des amis."*

He bows again. "As do I."

She lowers her voice. "Are your powers off now?"

"If that's what you wish."

"I do."

"They're off. But not before I caught a few impressions."

She glares. "Abassi."

He smiles.

She exhales. "It's unnerving. Knowing you can read my mind."

"I understand. I won't make a habit of it. But you know I can't be entirely human."

"Hardly subtle."

Chu returns with tea and a tray of appetizers.

Anne lifts her cup. "So, this public appearance. You sure it's wise?"

"You sound like Walter."

"I sound like someone with a brain."

"And a Yale degree."

She rolls her eyes. "Don't flatter."

"We have our own school, you know."

"Really? Where?"

"Elsewhere."

She frowns. "You keep saying that. What is 'elsewhere'?"

"Beyond what your senses can grasp. Another layer of reality. It's where the disappeared go."

"Can you bring them back?"

"For a time. Not forever."

She studies him. "Like that man without arms?"

He nods. "Too late, by the time I reached him."

"I'm sorry."

Abassi leans closer. "How do you believe humanity will react when we no longer live in myth or rumor, but beside you?"

"I suppose with fear. Then maybe awe. And then, resentment."

He nods. "You're not wrong. A voice once said to my ancestor: Fate starves at probability's door. She was right."

"Who was she?"

"A presence. Most called her madness. She was not."

Anne considers him. "There are beings above you?"

"Yes."

"Do you know them?"

"No. They remain hidden. But their pressure exists. You might call them gods, but only metaphorically. Some did."

She whispers, "Then you really might be alien."

"We are strangers now. But in time, it will be you who feel estranged."

"If people come to know you—"

"They will. Slowly. Kindly. Interbreeding will help."

She tenses. "So let's talk about that. You're interested in me. As a mate."

"Yes."

"But you don't believe in exclusive love."

"No. I would love you, our children, others. Without preference."

"That's difficult. For me."

"I know. But something in you already understands."

She lowers her eyes. "Could I really accept that?"

And then something breaks open.

Light floods her mind. Not light as color or heat, but essence. A force neither violent nor gentle. Just total. Her thoughts scatter, then reorder. A voice she's never heard yet always known rises inside her—not words, not even sound, but a call. When it fades, she is no longer the same.

She grips the table. "What just happened?"

Abassi takes her hand. "You've begun."

She feels the echo still, faintly humming within her bones. Not pain. Not pleasure. Something ancestral, something waiting. As though her descendants had already spoken, already seen. And from the future's marrow, whispered:

You were never only human. You were only waiting to remember.

~

Later that night, alone in her hotel room, Anne once again stands at the window. Below, the city moves with its usual pulse: cars, lights, brief human dramas unfolding beneath neon and dusk. But something in her gaze has shifted. She sees not just movement, but the pattern beneath it. A deeper geometry. A fragile brilliance.

The image returns: the *Titanic*, lights still glowing, slipping beneath black water. Only now, it lists further toward the deep. Civilization, luminous and unknowing, sinking into a new age.

She repeats last night's gesture, placing a hand on the glass.

Something listens within her, not to the noise outside, but to a voice just beginning to take shape. Still unformed. Still unnamed. But rising.

Not fear. Not yet.

But wonder.

And the first stirrings of farewell.

Chapter Twenty

Cataclysm

Strained Credulity

~ The Demonstration ~

A week after his second dinner with Anne, Abassi stands behind the curtained wings of a wooden stage on the island of Tuvalu. He is composed, unmoving, held in a stillness that is not passive but a volitional, poised calm before the plunge. Around him, the air vibrates with layered tension. Salt wind from the Pacific stings the edges of his awareness. Waves batter the narrowing shore with a rhythm that feels accusatory. The island is disappearing, year by year. And yet here is where the world has gathered.

Behind the barricades, protesters chant. Inside the amphitheater, a restless hush reigns. Delegates from across the planet fill the tiers—ministers, generals, scientists, monarchs, and presidents—each surrounded by an entourage, each aware that what unfolds today may define the century that follows. The sea murmurs behind them all, an old witness. Above, satellites record every breath.

The official narrative has taken root: the visitors come in peace. But beneath this provisional trust is something more primal. A reckoning is underway. The crowd has not come merely to listen. They have come to assess a threat. Curiosity has replaced fear, but it is a dangerous curiosity, one that is sharp, coiled, and defensively ancestral—the kind that once greeted fire or thunder.

Although Abassi stands motionless, eyes closed, inside him chaos hums. He sifts through the psychic static: images of slaughter, dreams of conquest, ancient hatreds clothed in modern language. The thoughts of hundreds buffet him, some pleading, some screaming, some worshiping, others building elaborate defenses of denial. A civilization attempting to outrun its own mirror.

The last of the preliminary speeches drones to a close. The American Secretary of State steps back. A final pause. Then silence, the silence which always precedes a descent.

Abassi steps forward.

The wooden boards of the stage do not creak beneath him. His movement is precise, almost solemn. He reaches the podium. A sea of eyes rises to meet him. It is the gaze of a species looking, perhaps for the first time, at something beyond itself, and not entirely liking what it sees.

When Abassi speaks, his voice does not rise. It does not need to. The power is not in volume, but in the finality of what is spoken.

"I have heard it said that torturing animals in youth is a sign of the future killer. Look to your left. Your right. Behind you. Within. You are that killer.

"I have heard it said that hearing voices is madness, and following them the mark of a fractured mind. But you too hear voices—ideologies, gods, ancestors, leaders—and obey. What name do you give yourselves?

"You believe killing for a cause can be noble. But causes do not cleanse what they destroy. The cities burned. The children buried. The forests erased. What cause redeems this?

"You say you love this Earth. But your love is consumptive. You poison what you praise. You murder what you marvel at. You slaughter other lifeforms with industrial efficiency. Monstrous! Your machines do not liberate, they devour. You are at war with your own descendants.

"Your kind stands at a threshold. You cannot pass through it as you are. The old skin must be left behind. That skin of tribal fear, of righteous violence, of clever self-deception. You must crawl out of yourselves. Into something larger. Kinder. Wiser.

"Let us walk beside you. Not above. Not in conquest. In continuity. Let our blood mix with yours, our children grow together, new branches of a shared tree.

"But know this. The future will not wait. You cannot bargain with extinction. You cannot sue for time. There is only transformation. Or ending. Technology is not your savior. It has become your mirror. And it reflects your ruin.

"Cling to your primitive identity and you will perish with it. Release it and something new may yet be born."

He falls silent.

A moment follows. Not quiet, but suspended. As if the Earth itself is holding breath.

Then the noise erupts.

"Fraud!"

"Antichrist!"

"Blasphemer!"

"Terrorist!"

"Kill him!"

The shouts grow, crashing against each other. But louder still, from a deeper root, comes a single word chanted by hundreds. It is raw and violent:

"Monster! Monster! Monster!"

And then, absence.

They vanish.

Every delegate. Every aide. Every protester. Every journalist. Gone.

Abassi remains.

Empty seats line the amphitheater, toppled or cracked. Paper programs drift in the air. Cameras hang frozen, still recording nothing. Only the sea continues, undisturbed.

Except for one boy.

Koamalu. Eleven years old. He had snuck in to sell candy and gum, weaving through the crowd with practiced innocence. Now he stands alone, merchandise forgotten, eyes wide with something more than fear.

Abassi tries to move. His legs betray him. He grips the podium. The weight is crushing, more than mere exhaustion. Something fundamental inside him has ruptured.

He stumbles forward. Knees hit the stage. A tremor passes through his chest.

"It's . . . too much," he gasps. "Too many . . . I can't. . . . "

His voice cracks. His body folds in on itself.

"Something's wrong. . . . "

Koamalu does not speak. He watches, still as stone.

"Too weak. . . . "

And then, from within him, a voice. The one his ancestors once named Goddess. She does not shout. She does not console.

Now you know your limits.

Now you understand.

You are not inevitable. You are not divine. You are subject to number, to law, to scale. Fate begs at the door of probability.

Now rise. Do what must be done.

Koamalu runs. Not from fear, but from the unbearable presence of the moment. Awe, too large for a child's frame.

Another voice comes. Familiar. Human.

"Come, Abassi."

It is Altan.

"We'll leave now," he says, standing over him. "But first, when we reach the airport, you must bring them back."

Abassi nods weakly. Altan helps him to his feet. They move toward the waiting car. The guards say nothing. The driver stares ahead.

At the airport, they stop.

Altan opens the door. Abassi leans against the frame. Breathes.

"Now," says Altan.

A long moment. Then a whisper in the mind:

Yes. I will try.

Exactly one minute later, a rumble rolls out across the island. Then, chaos.

Thousands of human voices. Distant, rising. Some shout in rage. Others cry out in confusion. Some collapse in panic. Some pray.

They are back.

Altan closes the door behind them. Helps Abassi into the plane. The engines laboriously rise. The wheels lift. They are bound for air not yet claimed.

The island shrinks behind them.
But the reckoning has begun.

~ *Aftermath* ~

John Rochelle and Walter Monroe stand shoulder to shoulder at the edge of the stage. For a long moment, neither speaks. They watch the crowd, once a choir of condemnation, now stuttering into confusion. Chants of "Monster! Monster!" still echo, but their rhythm has broken. The crowd looks around, hands trembling, mouths parted. Something is wrong and they know it.

Twenty-five minutes have passed. But to those who had filled the amphitheater, it was no more than a blink.

Someone shouts, "Where is the alien?"

Another voice rises: "Trickery! Fraud! Bring him out!"

The air fractures again. The mob surges like a breached dam with delegates, security, aides, onlookers, all spilling toward the stage. The order of nations dissolves. Uniforms from rival countries clash and intermingle. Hands grip weapons, but no one dares fire. Not yet. Not without explanation.

On the far side of the barricades, American personnel are already guided toward the exits by security teams, their faces pale, movements clipped. The command chain is active, but frayed.

Walter leans in close. "John, they have no idea what just happened."

"I know," Rochelle says. His voice is flat.

"They think it's some kind of illusion."

"Maybe. But illusions don't tear time in half."

Walter says nothing. The crowd is growing louder again, seeking someone to blame. The first impulse of every government.

"Cooler heads will prevail," he offers.

Rochelle lets out a dry breath. "Spare me. Cooler heads don't lead. They rationalize. They'll say it was mass hypnosis. A psychotropic leak. Some rogue weapon or quantum glitch. Whatever matches the delusion they need to keep breathing. We've seen this before, Walter. Fiction in a new wrapper. And this time it's a catastrophe."

A breathless aide jogs beside them, clutching a phone. "The media was here. Every network. Every angle. Cameras don't lie."

Walter glances at him. "No, but they edit."

Rochelle adds, "And what will they show?"

The aide stammers. "Whatever they saw. We need to retrieve the footage."

Rochelle stops walking. His voice sharpens. "The last time I vanished—at the Bureau—you remember what the cameras caught? One frame I'm standing there. The next, gone. No transition. No distortion. Just absence."

"But this was different," the aide insists. "This time, the cameras vanished too. Operators, producers, everyone. If they were taken like the crowd, then came back like the crowd . . . maybe they filmed what we couldn't see. Maybe something got through."

Rochelle's eyes flash. "Get the crews. To the hotel. Every frame of footage. Set up in my suite. Move."

Another staffer rushes over, eyes wide. "We've been ordered to evacuate. The Secretary says all U.S. nationals off the island immediately."

"We're not leaving," Rochelle snaps. "Not until we've seen the footage."

The hotel lobby is in chaos. Diplomats shout into phones. Translators bark over one another. Security agents wheel cases and scan the room with wide eyes. Fear has no flag; it speaks in stammers and broken routines. Rochelle, Monroe, and their aides push through the crowd and take the stairs, bypassing the jammed elevators. By the time they reach Rochelle's suite, they are breathless. Not just from the climb.

Within minutes, a camera crew arrives, hauling gear as if wheeling in trauma kits. Tripods unfold. Laptops flicker. Screens glow. The air stills as cables are connected and time begins to rewind.

The footage begins.

Abassi stands at the podium. His voice echoes from the speakers.

"Clinging to your old, constrictive *Homo sapiens* skin will slowly asphyxiate your species and spell suicide for Earth itself."

Then, he vanishes.

Not abruptly. Not violently. He is simply no longer there.

The screen turns to gray. It is not static, not signal loss, but something else entirely. The gray is not flat. It moves. Depth stirs beneath its surface. Shapes drift into view, amorphous and slow. Not forms, but the hint of forms. They twist without coherence, gestures that never quite complete, fragments of something approaching identity and never reaching it. Movement without anatomy. Meaning without anchor.

Then a pulse. A flare. Something streaks through the haze, searing, directionless. Then another. The light does not illuminate, it sears and then vanishes. Whatever this is, it is not recording failure. It is recording something not made for recording.

The motion tightens. A center forms. Then ruptures.

A burst of white, pure and soundless, floods the frame.

Black.

Seconds pass.

Then the camera comes back.

The amphitheater reappears. The stage is intact, crowd intact, all in place. Still mid-chant, as if no time has passed. The image shakes as the operator jolts backward. Confusion spreads on-screen in real time. Some collapse. Some scream. Others look to the sky.

In the hotel suite, no one speaks.

"What now?" someone whispers.

Rochelle doesn't blink. "Now we find Lance Romellion."

"We've been trying," an aide says. "He's dark. All channels."

"Try again. I want him reached. Now."

Rochelle turns to Monroe. "What about you?"

Walter doesn't answer at first. His thoughts are unspooling in every direction. Anne. Abassi. The dinner. The voice. The soft and terrifying certainty in her eyes. Her silence that night. Her silence now. He wonders where Abassi is. If he'll contact her again. If she'll respond. If she already has. He thinks of the documents he destroyed. The favors he called in. The warnings he ignored.

And he realizes that his silence is no longer strategic. It is cowardice. And it is unbearable.

But he says none of this.

Instead, he meets Rochelle's gaze and says, steady and dry, "I agree. Romellion is our best option now. I can't do anything more here. I'm catching the next flight home."

Rochelle watches him, eyes narrowed. There is something unspoken between them, questions neither is willing to ask.

But he nods. "Go."

Monroe turns. Rochelle faces the others. Behind him, the screens still flicker, trying to make sense of what the human eye was never meant to see.

~ *Lance Romellion Leaves the Island* ~

Just as the meeting in Tuvalu descends into chaos, Lance Romellion reappears back in San Francisco. He has no explanation. After Abassi departed the strange island weeks earlier, Lance was simply left behind. For days, he stormed through the cottage, shouting at empty walls, furious that Abassi had vanished without him. When the frustration grew unbearable and he nearly tore the place apart in a fit of rage, Altan materialized, calm and wordless, and beckoned him to follow. They ascended the volcanic ridge in silence. At the summit, a hidden cave. Altan pointed toward the interior and turned away without a word. Lance clicked on his flashlight and stepped inside.

When he emerged, he was in the California desert. No transition. No time. He hitchhiked to a nearby town, requisitioned a police vehicle, and made his way to San Francisco. By the time he arrived at his office, the Tuvalu event was dominating every screen. Colleagues hover between urgent questions about his disappearance and the unfolding global uproar. Within minutes, the phones rang nonstop.

Now one call arrives that cannot be ignored.

"Where the hell have you been?" barks Rochelle over the line.

"No idea," Lance replies coolly. "An island. As I said. But now, plainly, I'm back."

"Where's Abassi?"

"No idea."

"Find him!"

"Isn't he with *you* on Tuvalu?"

"For Christ's sake, Romellion! If he were with me, I wouldn't be calling you. You know how he operates. God only knows where he's gone now. I told you to stay with him!"

"Easier said than done."

"Find him."

"How?"

"I don't care. Call him. Visit the damn mansion. Just find him."

"Understood."

Click.

Lance lowers the receiver and stares at the pile of reports on his desk. His mind is blank. Everything has shifted. Too much, too fast. And far beyond the reach of normal logic. The machinery of the world, once predictable, has begun to slip its cogs. He steps out of his office and joins a knot of colleagues watching the news. Onscreen, an "expert" analyst fumbles through speculative commentary.

"In answer to your question, Cynthia," the expert says, trying to mask unease with artificial rationality, "I'm at a loss. If this truly was an alien encounter, then we are in uncharted waters. But if it's a deception, then the scope and scale are . . . troubling."

The anchor presses: "But every recording shows the same thing. That strange grey interlude, twenty-five minutes of shadow and distortion. Surely that's more than a trick?"

"Yes, well . . . if this *being* is an alien, it appears to wield powers we don't understand. The U.S. government will have much to answer for."

"In your opinion, did he truly vanish? Or was this all an illusion?"

Lance laughs aloud. "A trick?" he scoffs. "We know better. We *know* better."

He is shushed quickly by his colleagues, and the analyst continues.

"It's possible it was a ruse, perhaps even unknown to our own government. They seemed as surprised as everyone else."

"Could it have been Russian or Chinese tech designed to humiliate the U.S.?"

The analyst shakes his head. "Unlikely. Their delegates vanished too. They're as shaken as we are."

"Thank you, Professor Johnson. And now, we go live to Beijing for international reaction."

Lance rolls his eyes. "Shit."

He turns away, leaves the others glued to the screen, and returns to his office. Behind the closed door, he slumps at his desk and rubs his eyes. Without reading the reports in front of him, he calls for a car. When it arrives, he rides the elevator down, slides into the driver's seat, and sits there idling for several minutes, staring blankly. A woman walks past, elegant, heels clicking on the concrete. A flicker of normalcy. He clings to it for a moment, nostalgic for a world that no longer feels his.

Finally, he speaks aloud to himself. "Nothing for it."

He shifts into drive.

~

The mansion is just as he remembers it, ornate, still, but too quiet. Lance parks, kills the engine, and watches from the car. Nothing. Through compact binoculars, he scans the upstairs curtains. Still nothing. He waits an hour. No motion. No sound. Reluctantly, he steps from the vehicle and walks to the front door, more confident now that the trip has been in vain.

He rings the bell. Silence. He hesitates, then rings again. Still nothing. He exhales in relief, turns to go and then hears the latch turn. A young woman opens the door.

"May I help you?"

Lance flashes his badge. "Lance Romellion, FBI." He squints. There's something familiar in her features. "May I ask a few questions?"

She smiles. "Of course. Did my grandfather send you?"

"Your grandfather?"

"Never mind," she says quickly, flustered.

He follows her inside.

"Would you like some coffee?" she asks.

"Thank you," he says, watching her closely. "I'm being rude. May I ask your name?"

She hesitates, then says, "Anne Monroe."

"Monroe?"

"Yes."

"Related to. . . ."

"Walter Monroe? He's my grandfather."

The recognition strikes a faded memory. "Of course!" he exclaims. "I met you years ago at a conference in San Francisco. Evening reception. Boring lectures. I remember now."

They both fall quiet, the moment awkward. Finally, Lance asks the question plainly.

"Why are you here, Ms. Monroe?"

"Please," she says with a smile. "Call me Anne."

"Thank you. Still, I'm surprised to find *you* in this house."

"My grandfather told me about your visit to Washington," she says. "It seems you've become something of an expert on these so-called aliens."

"Ha. Maybe. But you've clearly surpassed me." He gestures to the room. "Why *are* you here, Anne?"

She takes a moment before answering. "It seems I've become a kind of unofficial ambassador. Without title. Without clear assignment. But here nonetheless."

Lance raises a brow. "You and I both know these beings aren't aliens, not in the way people imagine."

"You're right. Through my grandfather, I came to know Abassi. He asked me to watch the house while they're away."

"House-sit," Lance echoes, incredulous. "Now I really *am* in Wonderland."

Anne doesn't reply.

"Sorry," Lance mutters. "It's just . . . surreal. Have you met the others?"

"Not yet. More coffee?"

"Please."

She refills his cup.

"When do you expect Abassi to return?"

"No idea."

"You saw the Tuvalu conference?"

She nods grimly. "Yes."

"Bit of a mess."

"A disaster."

Silence descends again, broken only when Anne tilts her head.

"My turn," she says. "Why are *you* here?"

Lance smiles. "Fair enough. I came to see if anyone still lived in this strange old mansion."

"Just me," Anne replies. "For now."

"Do you know where the others are? The . . . hunchback women?"

Anne's eyes flash. "Their names are Ming-huà, Pythia, and Tara. All Powers. Ming-huà is Abassi's great-grandmother. Pythia, his grandmother. Tara, his mother."

"My apologies," Lance says quickly. "It's shorthand. Not meant to be disrespectful. Are the fathers also like them?"

"I don't know," Anne lies. She has no intention of discussing intermediates or drawing her father further into this web. "Mr. Romellion—"

"Lance."

"All right, Lance. What exactly is the purpose of this interrogation?"

He pauses, then speaks with unexpected clarity.

"It may surprise you, Anne, but I'm on your side."

Her brow furrows. "What does that mean?"

"It means I've come to believe that Abassi and his kind may be humanity's only hope."

Anne stares at him, stunned.

"And your colleagues?"

Lance shakes his head. "Most would have them killed if given the chance. The rest are too frightened to imagine another future."

Anne sighs and gives a melancholy shake of her head. "Perhaps there is no future left for those who can't imagine one beyond themselves."

Lance studies her carefully. "You sound as if you've already chosen sides."

Anne's gaze hardens. "Maybe I have."

"You trust him that much?"

"I don't trust blindly. But I've seen enough to know he doesn't lie. Humans do. Constantly."

Lance exhales. "Touché." He sets his cup down. "Still, if Abassi fails—if he's destroyed, or disappears again—what happens to you? What happens to those left behind?"

Anne folds her hands. "Then we continue. I continue. This doesn't end with him."

Something in her tone chills him. "You sound like you expect to carry it forward."

"I don't expect. I prepare."

Lance shakes his head slowly. "That's a heavy mantle for someone your age."

Her smile is faint, almost weary. "History doesn't wait until you're ready. It arrives. You answer."

Silence settles, broken only by the faint hum of the house. Dust motes drift in a shaft of late sunlight.

Finally, Lance leans back. "You remind me of Michael Powers. And Jared. Both thought they could shoulder what no one else could."

Anne meets his gaze without flinching. "Maybe it runs in the blood."

For the first time, Lance feels the air shift around her, not Abassi's presence, not some psychic force, but her own gravity. A quiet certainty.

He clears his throat. "I'll keep in touch. If anything happens, anything at all, call me. No Bureau reports, no middlemen. Direct."

Anne nods. "I will."

As he rises to leave, she watches him closely. "You really are on our side, Lance?"

He pauses at the door, hand on the knob. "I'm on the side that still believes we have a chance. If that's yours, then yes."

He leaves without another word.

Anne remains at the table, staring into the last trace of coffee in her cup. In the dark reflection, she sees not her own face, but the faintest shimmer of something waiting, something already inside her, unfolding.

Am I part of we—or they?

Chapter Twenty-One

Hunting Them Down

The Mole

~ Anne and Lance Confer ~

After Lance offers his candid assessment, he catches the flicker of distress in Anne's eyes and quickly softens his tone. "Anne, please. I don't condone those attitudes. I've come to know these beings, especially Abassi and Altan, and after some long-overdue soul-searching, I've let go of my earlier prejudices."

She studies him. "So you believe what he says? About giving up our savagery, about interbreeding . . . about everything?"

"You're young. Beautiful. With a future wide open to you. I'm sure you could have your pick of partners. So tell me honestly, if the opportunity felt right . . . would you?"

Anne blushes, then lets out a quiet laugh. "More coffee?"

"I was thinking more along the lines of a Bloody Mary. Or a Margarita. Or hell, even a Screwdriver, if you'll join me."

"I thought agents on duty weren't allowed to drink," she teases.

Lance shrugs. "Times are shifting. If we're going to be honest with each other, maybe we both need a little oil for the gears. I suspect we each have uncomfortable truths to confess."

"Are you a priest now?"

"Far from it," he says, smiling. "But I do believe the rules we've lived by are cracking. If we want to do the right thing, morally or professionally, we may need to talk like human beings, not operatives."

Anne rises and gathers their empty cups. "You're in luck. I make a wicked Bloody Mary."

"Excellent."

As she begins mixing drinks, Lance leans back and muses aloud. "I've always admired your grandfather. He never mocked me. From the start, he listened, took my reports seriously, even made things happen. It's clear he understands these beings in ways others don't."

Anne, keeping her tone guarded, replies, "Yes, he's a remarkable man."

She returns with the drinks. They sip in a silence that's more reflective than tense.

Finally, Lance clears his throat. "Since I'm the guest, I'll go first."

Anne meets his eyes. "I'd like that."

And so, for the next hour, Lance unfolds the full arc of his strange journey: the hunchbacked women, the limbless victims, the cave, the young woman who spoke in riddles, Abassi, Altan, the island. As the story winds down, he exhales, his voice quieter, his tone a sincere confession. "Not long ago, I was convinced these beings were terrorists bent on dismantling civilization. I told myself I was protecting the American people, the whole of humanity itself. I cast myself as a lone hero, the one person who truly understood the threat. When the facts didn't fit, I twisted them to make them fit. We're trained to be objective, but I'd lost mine to fantasy. But contact, real contact, with them changed that. With Abassi. With Altan. Even with the ones who frightened me most. The more I saw, the more I listened . . . the less the terrorist narrative held up. And finally, I let it go. So yes, when you asked earlier if I believe them, if I believe what Abassi says about interbreeding being the only hope for humanity . . . I do."

Anne nods slowly, her expression unreadable. "I see."

Then her gaze turns distant again. Lance feels a strange flutter behind his eyes, as if his thoughts were being gently stirred. He brushes it off, but presses forward.

"And you?"

Her focus returns sharply. "Oh, I believe. No doubt. Even now, I can partially read your thoughts—though only faintly. My abilities are still weak. But I can tell you're sincere. That you're not here to trap me. And I'm grateful for that."

"You can read my mind?" Lance leans forward, uneasy.

"Partially."

For a moment, suspicion clouds his face. Is she unstable? Or is something else at work? He remembers the odd sensation earlier, like a soft pressure just behind his eyes. He studies her more carefully. "Are you one of them?"

Anne laughs. "Not exactly. But I've been told I carry some of their DNA. Not much—but enough."

"Enough for what?"

"Enough to know when someone's lying. Or telling the truth. Another Bloody Mary?"

"Hold on. How can you have their DNA? I thought the hunchbacks were the first."

Anne shakes her head. "That's not quite right. It goes back further than that. It's a long story full of false starts, near misses, and collapses. There are many like me, what Abassi calls Intermediates."

She hands him a fresh drink. "Don't look at me like that," she says with a grin. "I'm not an alien."

"Then tell me more."

Anne takes a breath, choosing her words with care. "Abassi told me the lineage I come from is different. The hunchbacks descend from a man named John Powers and two women—Bai Meiying and the one called Child of Buddha. My line is separate . . . though intertwined."

Lance leans forward, eyes gleaming. "Do you have time to tell the story?"

She smiles, sly and luminous. "Do *you* have time to hear it?"

"Are you kidding? Yes."

"Then we'll need another Bloody Mary," she says, rising. "It's a long tale."

Lance chuckles. "When I met you all those years ago, were you already . . . different?"

She pauses. "Not really. I didn't know anything, not until I met Abassi. That changed everything."

"So you and he. . . ."

Anne nods, cheeks flushed. "We haven't been intimate, if that's your question. But I've transferred to Berkeley to finish my Ph.D.—and to be close to him. I'm staying here until he returns."

She hands him his third drink.

"It all began before World War II," she says softly. "John Powers—Abassi's great-great-great-grandfather—was working late in his office, not long before the Japanese invasion of China. A young woman walked in. She was astonishingly beautiful, and unnervingly strange. A stranger then, but someone you might recognize now. She looked him in the eye and asked, 'Mr. Powers, how does one justify a life without cruelty, and therefore also without the distilled beauty of cruelty?'"

Lance sits bolt upright. "I've heard those words! That girl in the cave, she said the same thing! Who *is* she?"

"I only know fragments," Anne says. "But I've heard stories. Evidently, Michael Powers—John's son—wrote it all down. His memories. His visions. His unraveling. Most of it was dismissed as madness—paranoid schizophrenia. But it wasn't madness. Not really. It was a record. A chronicle."

She pauses.

"There are long-lost manuscripts, half-suppressed. Someday I hope to read them. Until then . . . I'll tell you what I know. And when I'm finished, maybe we can be allies."

Lance sets down his glass. "I'm listening."

~ *Newborns* ~

Deep in the brilliant vastness of Mongolia's Flaming Cliffs, life has quietly multiplied. Within the hidden compound, all three women have given birth, each within months of the others. Ming-huà's labor was long and grueling, but at its end came a daughter. Pythia bore twin girls. Tara, twin boys. The compound now breathes with new energy, punctuated by shouts, cries, laughter, and even experiments in levitation. Zookeeper, with his intermediate genome stretched to its limit, finds himself bewildered but enduring. Age has gifted him patience, if not clarity. Siyabonga, younger but equally part-human, spends his days chasing after children who have already surpassed him in speed, comprehension, and silent coordination.

The newborns mature at a startling pace. There is quiet speculation: *will they, like Abassi, skip the long human crawl toward adulthood? Will they simply arrive one morning . . . grown?* Altan, as ever, guides with watchful gravity—mentor, midwife of moral restraint, patient teacher to the exponentially unfolding minds. And presiding over them all, not king but reluctant axis, is Abassi. Since the catastrophic demonstration in Tuvalu, he and Altan have taken refuge here, hidden from the grasp of satellites and statesmen. Now, years later—human years—Abassi grows restless. The world has quieted, its alarms dulled by time, and he feels the pull to return.

He stands before the gathered elders and declares, "The time has come. The humans have mostly lost our scent. Their greatest minds now assume we slunk back to whatever planet they imagined we came from. Tails between our legs." He chuckles. "Yes, great and wise indeed."

"We must all return!" Pythia exclaims.

"Yes," says Ming-huà, her eyes distant. "All of us or none. I miss my little island."

Zookeeper grunts, pushing himself up from a low chair. "Fuck yes! Let's get the hell outta Dodge. Let the chips fall. I'm tired of this damn place—no offense, Queequeg."

Queequeg answers quietly, without irony: "Even a Great White Whale knows when to dive deep, and when to breach for air."

"Agreed," says Tara.

All eyes shift to Lady Oracle. She regards them with a quiet smile. "It is time. We cannot raise these children in exile. Seeds rot in hidden jars. They must embrace the soil."

Altan rises. His voice, as always, stills the room. "The question is not whether we return, but *where*. Do we return to the mansion? To the island? To the cave? They are still watching. Hunting."

"Let them watch," says Abassi. "If they come in violence, we disarm. If they come in peace, we proceed. Either way, the children must step into the world. Their roots cannot stay unnourished."

Lady Oracle lifts a brow. "And so you may finally mate. This Anne Monroe must be an ocean of patience."

Abassi grins. "She has her doctorate now, for whatever that means in the age to come. Let her be rewarded."

"Yes!" cries Sy, springing up. "And let her, with your assistance, Abassi, earn her postdoc the proper way. Let her give us triplets!"

Altan, more soberly: "Let us not forget Tuvalu. The demonstration proved we have limits. The weight of their population is not abstract. They can overrun us, not by force, but by scale."

Abassi grows quiet, slipping into meditation.

The others wait.

When he opens his eyes, his voice is grave. "We have allies. Some in high places. But is the United States truly the wisest place to return? Would we do better to disperse to different continents, different cultures? Different climates?"

"With the right support," says Siyabonga, "I'd take Tara and the children back to Africa. Quietly. Carefully."

"And Pythia?" asks Sy.

"Her choice," Siyabonga replies. "One man, two women, four children? It draws too much heat."

Lady Oracle's laugh is soft as silk over steel. "And not the weather kind, I presume."

"Correct," laughs Siyabonga. "The kind of heat I mean is far more intense than weather."

"Or," says Abassi, "I return to Washington and present our terms. Peacefully. But with the *suggestion* of consequences."

"Is that in our nature—to threaten?" asks Ming-huà, frowning.

"Not to destroy," says Abassi. "But humans threaten their dogs when they disobey. And we have already punished evil with precision. No more. No less."

Lady Oracle tilts her head. "And how would you propose such a . . . suggestion?"

Abassi smiles. "Through Anne's grandfather. Walter Monroe. He understands more than he admits."

"He's old," she replies. "There's a new FBI director now."

"What's his name?"

"Roger Arlington."

"Ah," Lady Oracle says. "Roger Arlington. I'm told he's a devotee of Tolstoy, especially his dismantling of the Great Man theory. He considers Nietzsche's *Übermensch* a seductive error. A dangerous myth that too many tyrants mistook for destiny."

"And yet here we are, cast in the very myth he fears," notes Abassi.

"Truly," says Ming-huà. "But what are we in his scheme of things?"

Abassi smiles faintly. "Yes, with his beliefs, he may be harder to persuade—or easier, if he sees we have no wish to be great. It's time to find out what Roger Arlington really thinks of us."

"Why not go straight to the President?" Sy offers. "He's new too."

Abassi shakes his head. "No need to wake the dragon just yet."

Zookeeper chuckles. "But it *is* time you wake Anne Monroe. The woman's been waiting long enough, don't you think?"

Abassi snorts. "Humans."

~

"Speaking of humans," Pythia interjects. "You've been shielding your mind from us. Blocking telepathy. What are you hiding?"

The room turns. All eyes on Abassi.

He exhales deeply. "The simulations were flawed. The ones that allowed Tara to make thousands of Japanese soldiers vanish promised more than we possess. We are not as powerful as we believed. The truth is: we are vulnerable. As humans once used cunning to survive among predators, so must we. Reckless displays invite ruin. The world now knows we exist. Some admire us. Others fear us. If we overreach, we fall."

"Why didn't you tell us?" Pythia's voice is sharp.

"Because I had to be sure. During my recovery after Tuvalu, I made solo pilgrimages into the steppes, testing my limits. I learned the truth: moving complex organisms drains exponentially more energy. A thousand humans cost far more than a thousand stones. Worse, during my weakness, I was vulnerable, physically exposed."

Altan nods gravely. "Which means we must all be cautious. Power without reach is illusion. A single wise hominin among a hundred Neanderthals does not survive by intellect alone. He survives by adapting."

Ming-huà asks, "So what now?"

"I seek understanding," Abassi replies. "From those in power. Our only request: to be left alone. Let us live and spread quietly. That is enough. The rest will follow."

"And if they refuse?" Lady Oracle asks. "If they legislate against us? Ban interbreeding?"

Altan answers first. "We cannot wage war against the species. But perhaps we can trade in incentives."

Ming-huà tilts her head. "What kind of incentives?"

"Let them see the benefits of mingling bloodlines," Abassi says. "Let my child with a human woman be the proof."

"Anne Monroe?"

"Yes."

Sy drags his finger across his neck. "She is not fully human. They may try to kill her."

"Perhaps," Abassi replies. "That's why we need allies. Time. Cover. If Anne gives birth to our child, and that child thrives, the fear will begin to fade."

"Or sharpen," Tara warns. "They may never accept us."

"I didn't say *don't use* our powers," Abassi counters. "I said *use them wisely*. Offer help. Aid in rooting out criminals, even if some governments are criminal themselves. Make ourselves useful. And to those who make decisions, make our position clear; no threats, but consequences. No ultimatums, but outcomes."

"And who are these decision-makers?" Sy asks.

Abassi's answer is methodical: "We start with Anne's grandfather, Walter Monroe—"

"Who passes it to Roger Arlington," says Pythia.

"Who passes it to the President," adds Tara.

"Who passes it to the security agencies," continues Ming-huà.

"And on," finishes Abassi. "Across nations. Departments. Borders. All we need is time."

Lady Oracle's voice cuts the silence. "But how much time?"

Abassi meets her gaze. "More."

And from the shadows, Ming-huà adds softly, "Enough for the children to take root, not just in soil, but in story. They must see and be seen. Enough time to grow where we could not, and to spread where we are not."

~ *Abassi Returns to the Mansion* ~

On a clear, windswept afternoon, Abassi returns to the mansion after years of absence. When Anne Monroe opens the front door and sees him standing there, unchanged and radiant, she is overcome by a joy that borders on euphoria. They stare at each other for a long moment, breath suspended between past and present. Then come the kisses, fierce and grateful. The embraces, long and quiet. Hand in hand, they drift toward the anteroom, where a pot of tea sits waiting, fully steeped and slowly cooling.

"You might've warned me," she teases as she pours his cup. "I'd have made myself more presentable and the tea more palatable."

"No need," he replies softly. "You're even more beautiful than I remembered."

"Alien flattery," she scoffs. "Are you alone?"

"For now. The others will arrive later this week."

"Who exactly are 'the others'?"

Abassi smiles. "That list is long. I'll explain later."

The hours blur in reunion. Abassi listens as Anne recounts her time at Berkeley, her newly minted Ph.D., her tense but respectful visits with Lance Romellion, and the chaotic political aftermath of Abassi's now-infamous speech at the island demonstration. She insists, half-playfully, half-seriously, that he call her Doctor Monroe. He indulges her with smiles.

When he shares his own journey—his retreat to the Mongolian compound, the births of the new generation, the heavy weight of patience—her eyes widen. Then, nestled together on the couch, arms wrapped gently around one another, silence settles like a comforting shawl.

"How's your grandfather?" Abassi asks.

"Well enough," Anne replies, "though he grumbles about the indignities of age."

"Is he still connected to the new administration?"

"I don't think so. After your disappearance, he defended you tirelessly, but fewer listened. His influence has waned."

"So," Abassi murmurs, "I'm seen as a threat now."

Anne hesitates, then answers carefully. "Not exactly. You're seen as . . . un-knowable. Powerful. Dangerous, yes, but mostly because you can't be predicted. Some even believe you've returned to your home planet and will one day come back with an invasion force. It's absurd. But it's widespread."

Abassi's expression hardens. "And you believe this fear is common among those in power?"

"Too common. Even average citizens echo it. Walter tried to argue for your intentions, but with you gone, his camp lost ground. The new administration inflated the defense budget with you as justification."

"I see," he says grimly. "And Lance Romellion?"

"He's sympathetic," Anne says. "More than you know. He's been promoted and is now stationed at FBI headquarters in Quantico. Counterterrorism Division. He works under one of the new assistant directors."

Abassi claps once. "Good news. Is he in Washington now?"

"Not sure, but I can call him. We've stayed in touch."

"Do they know where his sympathies lie?"

"No one. Not even inside the FBI. He's been very careful, not just about *you*, but about us."

"How much does he know about *us*?"

Anne blushes. "Everything."

Abassi watches her closely, then softens. "You did the right thing. You needed someone. And Walter is far away."

He takes her hand. "Can you arrange a meeting?"

"Here?"

"If possible. I need secrecy. Do you trust him to keep it quiet?"

Anne nods slowly. "Yes. I'll try."

Abassi's fingers trace a line up her thigh. "Meanwhile . . . shall we conduct our own private summit upstairs?"

She answers in a whisper, already rising. "What took you so long?"

~ *Lance, Anne, Abassi* ~

Two days later, Lance Romellion stands at the threshold of the mansion. He doesn't knock. Doesn't ring. He knows Abassi already senses him. The air feels charged. He glances up and down the street—one pedestrian in the distance, no other signs of life. Anne opens the door. Lance steps in quickly and looks around nervously.

"He's not an ogre, you know," she says gently.

"I know," he replies too quickly.

"Come to the anteroom. He's waiting."

As they walk, she asks, "Anyone know you're here?"

"No one."

"Good," says Abassi's voice as they enter. He stands and offers a welcoming nod. "Tea or coffee?"

"Coffee, please."

Abassi hands him a cup, already prepared. Lance takes a sip and smiles faintly. "Cream and sugar. You never forget."

"Please, have a seat."

Lance lowers himself into a cushioned chair while Abassi and Anne sit close on the loveseat. For a moment, silence hangs in the air. Lance places his cup carefully on the table and narrows his gaze. "You wanted to speak with me?" he asks, his tone cool and cautious.

Abassi bows his head slightly. "Forgive me, I've been lightly reading your thoughts. I needed to confirm your intent."

Lance exhales. "No offense taken. I'm trained to do the same. Only I use wiretaps. I can assure you there is no surveillance, no watchers. No one knows I'm here."

"Is that not dangerous? For your career?"

Lance shrugs. "Very."

"Why risk it?"

Lance looks to Anne, then back to Abassi. "She knows."

"You're sympathetic to our cause?"

"Partly. I don't want to see my species perish. But I also understand—it may already be too late."

"You believe humans are doomed?"

"I do."

"And what of the other species? The ones humans are driving to extinction?"

Lance's jaw tightens. "Yes, I care. But honestly, I care more about our own fate. I'm pragmatic. I believe what I see."

"And you don't believe technology will save your kind?"

Lance scoffs. "Why interrogate me? You're reading my thoughts."

"Please. Just this one question. Indulge me."

Lance sighs. "No. Not with the minds we've got. I see the worst of us every day. Same genetic wiring, same prefrontal cortex, same reflexes. Whether it's a war criminal or a street killer, it's the same blueprint. AI has already surpassed us. We just refuse to listen."

Abassi nods slowly. "Your architecture is universal."

Lance leans forward. "Then tell me, don't you use technology?"

"We do."

"Then what makes you different?"

Abassi holds his gaze.

"The question isn't whether a species uses technology. It's whether it can evolve fast enough to survive what it creates. Most don't. Across the stars, intelligence is common. Survival is rare. Intelligence is like fire. Civilizations learn to wield it, rise, flourish, and then burn themselves down: ecocide, collapse, extinction. The problem isn't the flame. It's the hand that holds the torch. Intelligence—what your physicists call 'information'—can illuminate, or it can reduce the world to ash. What matters most is the one who tends the fire, and who remembers to nurture the garden."

Lance frowns. "So . . . you're the ones tending it now?"

"No."

"Then how do you know these things?"

"There are others. Observers. Gardeners. Park rangers, if you prefer—preservers of rare ecosystems. They see Earth the way some of your kind see the Grand Canyon or the Amazon: worth saving. But unlike your species, they act."

Anne tilts her head. "Park rangers? That's almost too ordinary a word."

Abassi smiles faintly. "Truth often sounds ordinary. Only its weight is extraordinary."

Lance leans back, unsettled. "So Earth's a park to them. A zoo."

Anne's voice is quiet but firm. "Or a sanctuary. That depends on what we become."

"And they're modifying our genetics?" asks Lance.

"Not directly. They nudge. Intervene where possible. The goal is preservation with minimal suffering. That includes humans, but also every species now endangered by human ambition."

"Why not just wipe us out?"

"Because the goal isn't domination. It's protection. The fewer deaths, the better. Even among those destroying the garden."

Lance finishes his coffee and sets the cup aside. He looks straight into Abassi's eyes.

"What do you need from me?"

Chapter Twenty-Two

Entering Byzantium

Cave Madness

~ A Clandestine Meeting ~

Walter Monroe is a very worried old man. He feels it, an undertow pulling at the seams of the world. Though the initial panic following the aliens' demonstration and disappearance has dulled, a taut, paranoid expectancy has settled across the globe. Riots surge and fall like fever dreams. Fragile governments collapse. Militias breed like tumors, and self-styled warriors with potbellies and delusions of purity vow to kill any alien on sight. In the United States, privacy rights are hollowed out. Some now campaign to amend the Constitution, stripping non-humans of all protection. Doomsayers fill the airwaves. The world feels ready to ignite. And into this powder keg, Abassi has returned. Walter is beside himself. But Lance Romellion, curt and insistent, made it clear: Abassi chose this moment for a reason. The meeting place, an isolated outcrop in the California desert, was no accident. So here he sits in a dusty sedan on a windswept road, watching Altan kill the engine. The air conditioner dies with a sigh, and the punishing heat pours in. He groans, opens the door, and rises slowly, wiping his forehead. "How far?"

"Not far," Altan replies.

"Good. My legs need the stretch. I hope this cave is cool."

Altan offers no reply, already striding toward a narrow, overgrown footpath littered with loose rock and thorny scrub. Massive boulders jut from the earth like festering wounds. Walter follows, uneasy. It feels as if unseen eyes are tracking his every move.

"Yes, you are being watched," says Altan over his shoulder.

"This mind-reading business gives me the willies."

"I understand you're an intermediate. You have some ability?"

"Supposedly. But hell if I can control it. Who's watching us? Guards?"

"Ghosts."

Walter barks a laugh. Altan doesn't.

~

Anne and Abassi wait near the cave's entrance, waving. Walter quickens his pace, embracing Anne halfway, their murmured exchange a tangle of worry and relief. Abassi stands apart, smiling.

Walter breaks away and strides toward him, hand extended. "Good to see you again."

"Welcome, Walter."

Walter squints up at the sun. "You picked a hell of a time."

"For more reasons than one. There is much to say, and much to show." Abassi gestures toward the cave. "Inside."

"Walter!" calls Lance Romellion, emerging from the darkness. "I stayed just inside till the hugging was over." He grins. "Cooler in here."

They shake hands.

"Quite the trek from Quantico," Walter mutters.

"This had better be worth it."

"It's not my show." Lance gestures to Abassi. "Ask him."

"Let's go in," says Abassi. "The heat's unkind." He takes Anne's hand and leads them into the shadows. At the threshold, he pauses. "Stay close. Here—flashlights."

Lance shudders. "I've been here before. That strange woman going to show up?"

"Perhaps. If so, you already know not to stray."

"No side tunnels for me, thanks. You're not sending me back to that goddamn island, are you?"

"Not today," Abassi laughs. "We're close."

"Close to what?" asks Walter.

"Here," says Abassi, stepping into a wide cavern. Their flashlight beams scatter across the jagged rock, illuminating nothing.

"Now what?" Walter mutters.

"Shhhh," Abassi replies.

Silence.

Then they hear a rhythmic panting. "Ah! Temulun!" Abassi exclaims. "You are famous. I have been waiting to meet you!"

A boxer dog trots into view, tail wagging, eyes bright. "Got a treat?" she asks.

"I brought some," Abassi smiles, offering one.

Temulun spins with joy. "Excellent!"

Anne, Walter, and Lance look at each other, baffled.

"She's a resident," Abassi explains. "Michael Powers spoke with her. Now I can too."

"What's she saying?" Lance asks skeptically.

"What else? She wants more treats."

Temulun's gaze lands on Anne. "She's nice. Does she have any?"

"I understood that!" Anne gasps.

"So did I," Walter adds.

Lance frowns. "What the hell is going on?"

Temulun straightens, her voice suddenly regal. "You are being given a glimpse."

Lance steps back. "I've heard that phrase before."

"So have I," says Walter.

Temulun relaxes again. "Treats?"

Lance gapes. "Jesus, I understood that too."

"Of course," Temulun says. "Took you long enough. Now—treats, silly boy."

Romellion groans. Abassi hands over another. "At least one of you is civilized," Temulun quips.

Abassi turns to the others. "Michael Powers was thought mad. He could talk to anything. Even sidewalks. They locked him up. But he wasn't mad. Just . . . tuned differently."

"Amazing," says Temulun.

"What now?" asks Lance.

Temulun fixes him with a sudden intensity. "Follow me!"

She trots off. The group follows, flashlights dancing over the uneven rock. Temulun's toenails echo ahead, clicking like a metronome in the void. Time passes. The sound fades. At last, Abassi halts in another vast chamber.

"Lights off," he says.

They obey. Darkness. Then comes light. Blinding. The rock dissolves, replaced by the gleam of a vast cathedral. Standing among them is the young woman, knapsack on *her* back, *her* spine subtly hunched, *her* eyes radiant with power.

Even Abassi is still. He squeezes Anne's hand. They wait.

~

"I have often asked myself," *she* begins, voice like wind through a crystal chime, "can there be beauty without cruelty? Or is cruelty the distillation of what you call beauty?" *Her* eyes pass over each face. "You three," *she* continues, "one human male, two intermediates—grandfather and granddaughter. It is to you I speak."

She pauses, *her* gaze settling on Abassi. His brow furrows. Then, slowly, *she* looks past him at the others. "The ancestors of this one," *she* says, "were founders. John and Michael Powers—humans who heard voices and saw visions. Their psychiatrists called it schizophrenia. That was incorrect."

She walks slowly, voice unfurling like smoke. "Their minds were bewildered by new genes, new neural structures. They heard a debate, distant but very real, between two unseen forces. In their limited grasp, they named them God and Goddess. One side craved the ache of earthly suffering embodied in a First Principle: no interference. The other sought an end to it, citing a deeper principle: compassion. Neither was deity. But the debate? That was real." *She* pauses to allow *her* words to sink in. Satisfied, *she* continues. "These forces, the Overseers, have long deliberated how your kind might survive. Two opposing views. Contradictory. Unresolved."

Lance steps forward. "So: wipe humans out or dilute them into extinction?"

"Not quite, clever human. Eradication is too cruel, and beings like Abassi are incapable of it. Witness what happened on the island at his demonstration."

"Then what's the alternative?" Walter asks.

"That is the heart of the dilemma."

"Can't we act as we see fit?" Abassi presses.

"You already are. As Zookeeper might say—you've taken matters into your own hands."

"But if we go too far?"

"Your kind can only err in one direction."

"Which is?" asks Anne.

She smiles. "Toward excessive pacifism even when survival demands more."

Anne breathes out. "I'm so relieved."

"Out of the mouth of babes," Walter murmurs.

"Yet," *she* says, voice hardening, "humans remain dangerous. Manipulative. Vengeful. Bigoted. Shall these be eliminated?"

"Maimed, maybe?" Lance offers dryly.

"Which causes more suffering?" Walter asks, sobered.

"Is that your Overseers' conundrum?" Anne asks.

"No," *she* says. "It is yours."

"We all have our gods and goddesses arguing in our heads," Abassi says quietly.

"Is there space for both?" Anne asks.

"Metaphorical God is metaphorical Father, who must be tempered by justice," Abassi says. "Metaphorical Goddess is metaphorical Mother, who nourishes."

"Such are their stereotypes. Yet, it is much more complicated. Both," *she* stresses, "are universal waves. Not human. Not divine. But fields, energies, out of which all things emerge . . . and return."

Silence follows. Then Lance coughs. "Why not just march into the capitals, sever some limbs, and issue demands?"

"So be it," *she* replies.

~

In an instant, Lance is elsewhere, screaming and legless, in a piss-soaked alley. Three vagrants watch him shriek. One shouts, "Shut up!" Another steps forward with a knife. Then he vanishes. The vagrants blink, shrug, and return to their shadows, mumbling guttural obscenities.

~

Back in the cave, Lance stumbles, whole again, pale and shaking. *She* watches him.

"Well?" she asks.

He meets her eyes. "If I had a gun, I'd shoot you."

"Precisely," *she* says.

~ *What Now?* ~

Lance glowers at the spot where her final word still echoes faintly through the cave. But she is gone. "Damn," he mutters. "Her favorite trick."

"It is no trick," says Abassi.

"Then why does she vanish whenever the real questions begin?" Lance's voice rises with frustration.

"Precisely," Abassi replies.

"I think I understand," Walter murmurs.

"So do I," Anne nods. "But that doesn't make the enigma any less maddening."

Abassi laughs. "Yes. What is too much? What is too little? Where is the line . . . the bold leap or the golden mean? Remove a limb? A life? A species?"

"Above my pay grade," Walter says.

"The point is," Lance snaps, "this is just the same old philosophical dance. Even Hamlet couldn't choose between acting and doing nothing. But in the FBI, we're trained to act. Right, Walter?"

"At the ground level, yes. But further up. . . . " Walter trails off, then he adds, "It's not so simple."

Abassi turns to Lance. "Are you prepared to act?"

"That depends on the act."

"Having sex with one of us."

"What?" Lance blinks. "Why would you even . . . with who? What kind of—what are you trying to say?"

Abassi's tone sharpens. "Would you want your children to carry only the genes of *Homo sapiens,* or ours as well?"

"I . . . I haven't thought about it."

"Oh, but you have," Abassi says. "Most definitely. We read thoughts, remember? Yours circle the future constantly. You worry about what happens if your children are left behind. That is your fear, isn't it?"

"I don't have children," Lance mutters.

"But you want them," says Abassi. "You always have."

"Fine. I do. Eventually. But I'm too old. Haven't met the right woman. And anyway, what's the point of raising children who are smarter than you, stronger than you, who look at you—despite being their father—as just another obsolete specimen?"

Abassi tilts his head. "What you want is their exclusive love. Their loyalty. Temulun constantly reminds you of what you humans crave—someone or something begging for treats."

Lance sighs. "Maybe. I guess I want someone to care for me in my old age. Yeah, to give me treats."

Anne speaks gently. "I understand, Lance. I really do. But imagine a world where everyone is family. Not just blood. Not just nation. All of life."

"Impossible," Lance says flatly. "You have to kill to eat. I'm not about to slaughter my son the cow for a hamburger. It's unworkable."

"Lance," Abassi's voice softens, "with that attitude, your descendants are already doomed. Your line ends. Why do you think you came here?"

Lance stares at the cavern walls. "I don't know. Duty? No, not exactly. Loyalty to humanity? Not quite. Maybe you're right. Maybe you are the future. I haven't figured it out."

Altan steps forward. "We need intermediates, Lance. People like Anne—bridges. Not to save *Homo sapiens*, but to save the Earth. All of it."

"Even if I agree, there aren't enough of you. Eight billion humans out there."

Abassi's voice is steady. "You are here for a reason. If we found you a mate would you be open?"

"Oh, for God's sake," Lance groans. "Now I'm livestock."

"No," Abassi says calmly. "You are free. But your cooperation is needed. With the government, at the very least."

"I feel like a traitor."

"No. You are one of the hopes of the world. Without the help of humans like you, the shift will become uglier. The suffering, immeasurable."

"You mean like the island? Oceans of body parts?" Lance's voice is low.

"Something like that."

Lance stiffens. "So it's cooperation or genocide."

Anne is shaken. "Abassi, surely you're not saying it would come to that?"

Abassi smiles gently. "No, Anne. It will not. Not if we succeed. And if there *were* a genocide, it would be a different kind. Not by us. By your own kind, against itself. We intervene to prevent that. To surgically remove the ones who would commit such horrors. And with our abilities, severed limbs can be restored like yours just was."

"Then what did I see on your island?" Lance asks.

"You saw the past. What your species has done to itself. We can't undo history. But we can choose a different future."

"There will always be suffering," Lance says, knowing how hollow it sounds.

"Yes. But there need not be the deliberate destruction of a living world. That much, we can change."

"I did my part," Lance says. "I brought Walter. I'm willing to help more. I just don't know what that means. I'm an assistant's assistant in the Bureau."

"You can do more than you believe," Abassi says. "First, we make you a national hero. Then we build trust. You'll speak for the future."

He winks. "And eventually, we'll find you a suitable mate."

Lance groans. "And how do you plan to arrange that?"

Abassi lifts his hands, as if offering himself up. "First, you take me in."

"What—like in handcuffs?"

Abassi smiles. "Figuratively."

Silence follows—long, breath-held, and heavy with old griefs. Far above, the cave exhales a tired wind, carrying the scent of dust, of endings, of a death rattle.

Then Abassi speaks, low and solemn. "The world you knew is not merely dying, Lance Romellion, it is already ash in the mouth of history. What rises in its place will not remember your species for its flags or wars, but for those few who dared to stand at the hinge of time. You will not be remembered as hero or traitor, but as witness, as midwife, as one who chose when all others faltered."

Both fall silent, listening to their own imperatives.

And in that silence, the Overseers do not speak. Yet something vast leans forward, as if even the architects of fate hold their breath, watching, waiting, and wondering, while fate itself starves, gnawing at probability's door.

Chapter Twenty-Three

Fanning the Flames

Captive Audience

The air in the secure White House briefing room is taut, dense with calculation. The President sits stone-faced as his national security team relays the capture, if one can call it that, of the being known alternately as Mr. Powers or Abassi. A dozen voices murmur updates, clarifications, warnings. But he hears only one thing: glorious opportunity wrapped in fatal catastrophe. On paper, this could be a political masterstroke. To have the alien under control, alive, compliant, if only nominally, could grant him the kind of legacy few presidents dare dream of. And yet, that same presence could trigger global instability, obliterate his control—or worse, obliterate the world. These beings are not predictable. That, at least, everyone agrees upon. He casts a glance toward the Secretary of State, who offers a tight, brittle nod. Others speak: intelligence advisors, legal consultants, counterintelligence experts, but the President says little, his face an unreadable mask. Inside, however, his thoughts are blazing: glory, peril, legacy, annihilation. One wild card in a deck full of wild cards, and he has been forced to play the hand. He would have preferred the FBI had let this particular sleeping dog lie. Let Abassi vanish again into myth and rumor until the next administration. But that option is gone. And so, as always, he does what earned him the presidency, he calculates. When the briefing concludes, the room stills. Everyone waits for the President's first question.

"Did Mr. Powers—Abassi—resist arrest?" he asks, voice neutral.

A pause. Then the FBI director replies carefully. "That's . . . a difficult question."

"Why?"

"He didn't resist. But he wasn't exactly taken either."

"You said he's in custody."

"Yes, sir. In a manner of speaking."

"What manner?"

"He's under what we've termed 'house arrest.'"

"Where?"

"At an old diplomatic residence. Embassy Row."

The President's voice sharpens. "Give me the address."

The director hesitates. "It's one of the former guesthouses used for visiting dignitaries."

"I'm aware of the history, Ralph. I asked for the address."

"Near Massachusetts Avenue, sir."

The President leans forward. "You said he was apprehended by someone with prior contact. Lance Romellion?"

"Yes, sir."

"Well then, is Abassi being detained or is he roaming the capital at his leisure?"

"He has agreed to remain. Voluntarily."

The President blinks. "Voluntarily."

"Yes, sir."

"So he's free to leave."

"Yes, sir."

"That doesn't sound like custody."

"No, sir. But if he chose to leave there is nothing we could do to stop him."

The President stares, long and hard. "I was under the impression we had developed countermeasures against their abilities."

The silence that follows is answer enough. The President turns to the Chairman of the Joint Chiefs. "General?"

General Ridgeley clears his throat. "We are working on such measures, Mr. President, but without a subject to test against, we've made limited progress."

"Well, now you have one," the President says dryly.

"Yes, sir. If he cooperates."

The President's gaze shifts back to the FBI director. "Will he?"

"We're . . . exploring that possibility."

The President drums his fingers lightly on the table. "What does he want?"

The answer lands like a hammer. "He wants to speak with you, Mr. President."

The room freezes. The color drains from the President's face. "And if I refuse?"

"Then he will come of his own accord."

No one breathes.

"I assume none of you can guarantee my safety?"

Downcast eyes. Silence. The Vice President stares at the table as if it might save him.

"Fine," the President snaps. "Have him meet the Vice President first."

"Sir?" The VP's voice is barely audible.

The President fixes him with a look. "Are you all right with that, Frank?"

A faint, sickly nod.

"Good. And let me be perfectly clear: this conversation does not leave this room."

The next day, word arrives: Abassi declines all intermediaries. He will speak only to the President. And if refused, he will come uninvited.

President Roger Arlington's calculations lie in ruin. Strategies he once trusted dissolve like brittle straw the moment they're grasped. Each scenario he rehearses collapses under the weight of implication. In this moment—ironically, fatally—what was once called the most powerful office on Earth feels like the least powerful office on Earth; an office with no power at all. No power, no options. The President lowers his gaze, then nods. Not from conviction, but from calculation. It is not consent, but containment, a choice made only because no better one remains.

~

By the time Abassi takes his seat across from the President in the fortified chamber beneath the White House, he has permitted a full security sweep, though all involved know the gesture is symbolic. Armed guards line the walls. The President is flanked by hand-picked aides and senior intelligence officials. No pleasantries are exchanged. The President opens.

"Welcome, Mr. Powers. I've been told you can read minds. Then I assume you already know who sits at this table."

"I do."

"Then speak."

"I want the repeal of the law prohibiting interbreeding between our kind and yours."

"That law has already passed Congress."

"I'm aware. Repeal it. It is unconstitutional."

"That's impossible," the President snaps. "I don't have the votes."

"Then find them."

"Mr. Powers, you are in no position—"

Every security guard vanishes from the room.

Shouts rise in confusion. Aides bolt from their chairs. The President half-rises.

Abassi remains still. Calm. "On the contrary, Mr. President. I am in a position to make these demands."

Secretary of State Grace Holmes speaks next, her voice taut but composed. "Mr. Powers, we have a democracy. Congress cannot legislate under coercion. Any law passed in such a state would be null."

A flicker, then the guards reappear, visibly shaken, eyes darting.

The President lifts a hand. "It's all right, gentlemen . . . I think. No harm done."

Abassi resumes. "Mr. President, a law forbidding sexual relations between *Homo sapiens* and my kind is a clear violation of constitutional protections."

The CIA Director bristles. "But you're aliens."

"Your own courts have ruled that non-citizens are still protected under the Constitution. They may not vote, but their natural rights are upheld."

"You weren't born here," says the Secretary of Homeland Security, smirking. "No papers? Then you're subject to deportation as an illegal alien."

Scattered chuckles follow.

"But I was born here, Mr. Tolliver," Abassi replies, evenly.

Murmurs ripple through the room.

"What?" the CIA Director barks. "You were born elsewhere! You've never even told us what planet you come from!"

Abassi turns to him. "Quite the contrary, Mr. Bosworth. I was born in California."

A storm of voices rises—protests, disbelief, and futile demands.

"Can you prove it?" Secretary of State Holmes asks. "A birth certificate?"

"I can. And I will. But it does not change the matter. This law must be repealed."

"We'll try," the President mutters. "What else?"

Abassi slides a sheaf of papers across the table. "A list. Annotated. With justifications and conditions."

The President nudges the stack toward his National Security Advisor. "Paul, have the proper agencies assess feasibility."

"I'll see to it," Paul replies.

Silence follows. Then the President leans forward, folding his hands atop the table. "And if we can't meet these demands?"

Abassi's eyes sharpen. "Then we will cross that bridge when we reach it. But understand: the bridge will be crossed."

"Or else?"

"I returned your guards unharmed."

"If you hadn't, that would have been murder."

Abassi's gaze hardens. "You've seen what we can do. But we do not act to cause unnecessary suffering—especially to the innocent. We will act only in self-defense. And self-defense, Mr. President, is not murder. I believe your legal training would agree."

The President feels it then—a tickle in the brain. A scan. Not painful, but intimate and undeniable.

"Mr. President," Abassi says gently, "I know your thoughts. For the sake of your credibility, I won't speak them aloud. But do remember what I've said about self-defense."

"I remember," the President replies curtly.

Arlington tries to still his thoughts, to hide behind layers of reason and protocol, but it's useless. Abassi sees through them all. Powerless in this rare and unbearable way, the President's instincts take over.

"Mr. Powers," he says stiffly, "isn't the endgame here the extinction of the human race?"

"No, Mr. President. The goal is its rebirth. An adaptive reboot that preserves your species' legacy—its beauty and its brilliance—while leaving behind its compulsive brutality. And in the bargain, perhaps we preserve this fragile planet and the dwindling diversity of our companions."

The President rises. "This meeting is over. We'll review your papers and respond."

"You are afraid," Abassi says softly. "Because your mind has been read, and you cannot retreat. But the reading is already done. The book is closed." He looks around the room, slowly, meeting each gaze. "Plots. Conspiracies. Machinations of the powerful against the powerless. That world is ending. Cooperate, or face the consequences."

The CIA Director leans forward. "Another threat?"

"No. A surgical diagnosis. *Homo sapiens* cannot escape its mental ruts: threat, counterthreat, revenge, coercion. These patterns are your undoing. With advanced technology, they are not sustainable. Your question simply reaffirms our conclusion."

The President's chair scrapes back. He stands, face pale, then red, then pale again. "Thank you, Mr. Powers," he mutters, already moving toward the door. The Vice President follows suit, announcing, "This meeting is concluded. We'll be in touch regarding your . . . list."

"You may reach me through Assistant Director Romellion," Abassi replies. "Otherwise, I will remain incommunicado."

"Understood."

~ *Leaks* ~

Within days, the story breaks.

The media erupts with headlines about a secret presidential meeting with aliens. Wild speculation spreads: demands were made, threats issued, Earth hangs in the balance. Some networks claim alien emissaries have threatened to unleash gamma ray bursts unless their terms are met. Gun sales skyrocket. Old Cold War bunkers are unearthed. Vigilante groups mobilize to "hunt invaders." The United Nations demands full disclosure. The U.S. ambassador fends off hostile questions. Lance Romellion becomes the unwilling epicenter of it all. As the only official conduit to Abassi, he's bombarded with calls from news outlets, world leaders, and Pentagon brass. Abassi has made it clear: from now on, all public contact flows through S.A.U.C.E.R.—and only Romellion has access. Lance arranges a meeting with Dr. Carlson, director of S.A.U.C.E.R., in a newly designated annex near the Capitol. When he arrives, the place is buzzing with scientists, policy advisors, military analysts, all locked in frenzied debate. Lance is ushered in. A tall, wiry man with steel-blue eyes and a shock of gray hair strides toward him.

"Agent Romellion."

"Doctor Carlson," Lance says, shaking the man's firm hand.

"Come. My office."

They pass through a maze of cubicles. Carlson shuts the office door behind them.

"When will Mr. Powers appear publicly?" Carlson demands.

"Coffee?" Lance replies.

Carlson signals his assistant. Once the coffee arrives, Lance sips, then speaks.

"He won't. Not yet. Not until certain conditions are met."

"That could take months," Carlson growls. "Meanwhile, violence is escalating. We're getting daily reports—vigilantes attacking anyone suspected of alien sympathy. People are dying."

"I passed protestors on my way in," Lance says. "Didn't look friendly."

Carlson nods. "It's getting worse."

"Then maybe the government should move faster."

"We could try to force him."

Lance chuckles. "Try."

Carlson's tone sours. "He'd have better luck with a dictatorship. Democracies take time."

"He doesn't want a dictatorship. If he did, he wouldn't need allies, he'd just assume the throne. What he wants is a safe zone. A place where his people and ours can coexist. That place could be here—if we make room."

Carlson hesitates. "Nothing's impossible," he says finally.

"Good. Then we're still talking."

Carlson leans forward, gaze intense. "Would Abassi meet with me? Somewhere private. I'll bring something of value."

"What kind of value?"

"A law. Or the draft of one. Constitutional protection for his people. Including marriage rights."

Lance raises an eyebrow. "Passed?"

"Proposed. We'd want his feedback before it goes to Congress."

Lance looks skeptical. "I'll ask. Don't hold your breath."

Carlson sighs. "We're doing everything we can."

"If there's nothing else. . . . "

"One thing," Carlson adds. "Better use the side exit. Protest's grown. Word got out you were coming."

"They're targeting me?"

"You're a media star now, Agent Romellion."

"Damn."

~ *The Chase* ~

Escorted by security through a winding path of back corridors and staircases, Lance emerges behind the S.A.U.C.E.R. building. Alone.

"Damn. Damn. Damn," he mutters.

He considers slipping through the crowd. As he nears the corner, he hears it—a roar of fury. He peeks around. The mob is massive. Police lines strain to hold. Chants rise: "Kill the aliens! Kill the traitors! Save the Earth!"

Placards flash grotesque caricatures. Some bear Lance's face. "FBI Traitor."

He slips away, hugging the edge of the building, trying to circle back to his car unnoticed. But the crowd is shifting and dangerously restless. Then a voice: "There's one of them!"

Others join. A pocket of protestors break off and charge.

Lance breaks into a sprint.

More block his path. A shot cracks.

He reaches for his Glock, but something strikes the back of his skull like a hammer.

The sidewalk leaps to meet him.

He hits the concrete hard. Blood pools beneath his cheek.

Vision blurs. Pain fades. Thought dims.

The last thing he sees is red—glistening, spreading—before the darkness closes in like a tide.

~ *Is Anger an Excuse for Revenge?* ~

The news reaches Abassi in the quiet stillness of Wyoming. Lance Romellion is dead. The headline stings more than expected. Abassi, rarely shaken, feels something fracture. He immediately summons the others to his remote retreat, urgency overriding protocol. But before they arrive, he withdraws into silence, into himself. And into Anne, who now serves as his only witness, his sounding board.

"I underestimated the extremity of human irrationality," he says quietly, eyes on the snow-capped peaks beyond the cabin window. "I put Romellion in harm's way. I failed to foresee what should have been obvious."

Anne watches him carefully. "Have you contacted the government?"

"No. The one man who knew how to find me is gone. I remain incommunicado by design."

"Will you reach out?"

Abassi hesitates. "Anne, I'm experiencing something unfamiliar. You might recognize it."

He laughs, but it lacks humor. "It feels like guilt. Worse, like anger."

Anne nods, her voice steady. "I know those feelings well. When I was a girl, I stole money from my grandfather's drawer. I felt such guilt I couldn't sleep for days. And once, a boy I loved lied and chose another girl. I was furious. Heart-shatteringly furious."

Abassi shakes his head. "Those were childhood dramas. A man is dead."

"And I still feel anger, every day. At cruelty. Racism. Violence. Misogyny. Our species burns with fury. Some of it is righteous. Some of it isn't. But it's everywhere."

He sighs. "Yes. Yours is an angry species. That explains a great deal."

"So this is your first experience with it?"

"It seems so."

"And that's why you haven't reached out?"

"In part."

Anne leans forward. "Are you afraid you won't control it?"

Another pause. "Also in part."

She studies him. "I may not be gifted like the others, but I can sense things. And what I feel in you now is pain. Deep, unbearable pain."

He meets her gaze. "True. But there is more."

"Tell me."

"I cannot."

"Why not?"

"Because I await."

Anne frowns. "Await what?"

"That which will end my waiting."

She exhales in frustration. "You can be maddening. Riddles and evasions. Walter raised me to be direct."

Abassi smiles faintly. "Interesting. From a man whose entire life was shaped by the Bureau?"

She narrows her eyes, prepared to retort, but the curve of his smile disarms her, and she chuckles instead. "Point taken. I'm sure if I'd ever wanted to join the FBI, he'd have warned me off."

"'Direct' and 'FBI' are strange bedfellows."

"Actually," she counters, "you're confusing them with the CIA."

She makes a mock-spooky face. "The real spooks."

Abassi turns pensive. "No. I think I'm right. Walter dealt with dangerous minds. He had to think like them, twist into their darkness, not just to outwit, but to understand. That's what made him so good. He was . . . an intermediate. Like you And I—"

Then he stops—mid-thought, mid-sentence—and looks at Anne with sudden, searching intensity.

"What is it?" she asks, uneasy under the weight of his gaze.

"Nothing," he replies. "At least . . . not yet."

She changes the subject. "The others arrive tomorrow. Perhaps together, you'll find a way forward."

But Abassi doesn't answer. He has slipped into one of his long silences, part meditation, part attunement to realms Anne cannot reach. She watches helplessly, unsure if she is companion or bystander to his inner storm. Yet even as she worries for him, her thoughts drift downward, inward, to her own secret.

Something stirs within her. A tremor, a whisper, a flicker not of mind but of flesh. She cannot yet name it. Not certainty, but possibility. Not joy, but the beginning of it, braided tightly with a shadowy premonition. A faint stirring in the womb. And with it, a joy that opens like morning light, yet already dimmed by the knowledge of dusk. Not omen, not prophecy, but the oldest rhythm of life: birth and loss woven together.

Chapter Twenty-Four

A Scythe is Sharpened

Park Rangers?

The next morning, Abassi's secluded retreat is no longer a sanctuary. The entire extended family arrives, each carrying their burdens—grief, fear, and a rising sense of inevitability. The children, radiant with inhuman potential, are placed under the alternating watch of Altan and Siyabonga, who now serve not only as caretakers but as strict tutors, tasked with instilling discipline in powers that could shatter worlds. Inside the main gathering room, the mood is heavy. Ming-huà, Zookeeper, Pythia, Tara, Siyabonga, Anne, and Lady Oracle sit in a loose circle. Silence thickens, saturated with unspoken condolences. Telepathic murmurs drift between minds, intangible and persistent, until Lady Oracle clears her throat.

"We should speak aloud," she says. "For Zookeeper's sake. And Siyabonga's. I doubt either of them is keeping up."

Siyabonga offers a sheepish smile. "I'm managing. But yes, thank you."

Ming-huà speaks first. Her voice is calm, but trembles beneath. "My heart aches. Lance Romellion was a good man. Gentle. Steady."

Tara nods, but her words burn. "He was. And the humans who killed him, those violent, wretched ones, must be dealt with."

"I agree," says Pythia. "My daughter may be impulsive, but not wrong this time."

Abassi raises an eyebrow. "And what would you have us do?"

"Make a statement," says Pythia. "Clear. Public. Unmistakable."

Ming-huà interjects. "They've arrested the man who pulled the trigger. He'll be tried for murder. Let the legal system run its course."

Tara scoffs. "And the others? The silent accomplices? The ones who would have done the same?"

"If we act now," warns Lady Oracle, "people will die. More than already have."

Siyabonga's voice is low. "What if we made those attackers vanish? Not just one, but in front of every camera, every broadcast?"

"We tried that," Ming-huà says quietly. "Tuvalu. It only fed their hysteria. Myth gave way to panic."

Abassi sighs. "Lance was supposed to be our bridge. The credible face of our intentions: respected, patriotic, sympathetic. Now he's been made a martyr by those who claim we're the enemy of humankind."

Pythia's tone sharpens. "And that's not the worst of it. Foreign powers now accuse the United States of collusion, selling out the world for what they call 'thirty pieces of gold.'"

Siyabonga groans. "It took our park rangers years to understand the minds of the beasts they sought to protect. In the meantime, the poachers nearly wiped them out."

"Then perhaps it's time," Tara declares, "to declare war on the poachers of our world."

"No," says Ming-huà. "That only returns us to the old path. And that path ends in ash."

Lady Oracle turns to Abassi. "What's your next move?"

He exhales, measured but heavy. "There are two choices. Let the humans stew in their own chaos. Or intervene—make a decisive gesture that stops this drift into mob rule and xenophobic frenzy." He pauses. "Or—"

"We can't keep running," Pythia interrupts. "We've retreated long enough."

"Exactly," Tara agrees. "Our children and their children will need time to spread. We can't just disappear to our little island or our flaming cliffs every time the wind shifts."

Siyabonga adds, "Ancient *Homo sapiens* could isolate themselves and survive, there were so few hominins. But now? There is no corner untouched. They are everywhere."

Anne rises and turns to Abassi. "You were about to say something. A third option?"

"An idea," he murmurs. "Still forming. And it may involve you."

Before he can elaborate, Altan bursts into the room, his usual calm replaced by quiet urgency. He has just passed his turn watching the children, but his face bears a darker message. "Reports are coming in, and more by the hour. Innocent people are being killed by mobs. Accused of being aliens."

Silence.

Abassi stiffens. "Where?"

"Everywhere. India. Africa. South America. Eastern Europe. The southern U.S. And it's not just beatings. In many cases, bodies are being cut open to search for 'alien organs.'"

No one speaks. The sound of distant children's laughter outside only deepens the horror.

Anne's voice breaks the silence. "And what has our government said?"

"A generic call for calm. But some police officers have already gone on record: they won't protect a species that plans to replace humanity."

Anne's voice hardens. "Have they been fired?"

Altan shrugs. "When the façade cracks, it doesn't break slowly—it shatters."

"I must contact the government," Abassi says.

"And what will you say?" Anne asks.

"You're the most-human intermediate, the scholar. You tell me."

Anne clasps his hand, her voice trembling. "For the first time, I'm afraid. Truly. Everything I imagine only makes it worse."

Lady Oracle nods solemnly. "The so-called rational minds, the ones we counted on to usher us in, are now afraid to be seen supporting us. Sympathy has become a liability."

"They're waiting," Siyabonga adds. "Watching. Too afraid to commit."

"Christ," mutters Zookeeper. "Fuck waiting. You people have the power—use it. Shock them. Do something bold. Let 'em know weakness isn't the message. Law of the jungle, man." He glances at Ming-huà, sheepish. "Sorry, love. But I say what I think."

Ming-huà gazes at him, unoffended. "But doesn't violence beget violence?"

Zookeeper grins. "Dearest, I'll borrow from my kindred soul. Willy Shakespeare said, 'These violent delights have violent ends.'"

Abassi erupts with laughter, loud and full-bodied. "Ah! Zookeeper, you've landed on it. The Bard strikes again! Who better to diagnose the soul of man?"

Zookeeper shrugs. "Yeah, he had his moments."

"Oh, but more than you know," says Abassi, eyes gleaming. "He's whispering to me now. From the very play you quote."

"Romeo and Juliet?"

"Yes. Except this time, the wedding will not be secret."

A collective gasp fills the room.

Abassi stands. He turns to Anne and places his arm gently around her. His voice carries the weight of more than affection. It carries intent.

"My dear Anne," he says, steady and unshaking, "our union must be known, not hidden. Will you marry me?"

Anne is too stunned to speak. But before she can respond, Altan lets out a loud, delighted laugh.

"Of course!" he exclaims. "Yes! Of course. I see it now."

The others wait, breath held, the air thick with the realization that this is more than a proposal. It is a manifesto.

~ *The Plan* ~

The room vibrates with expectation.

"Well?" Abassi asks softly, "Your answer, Anne Monroe?"

Anne's thoughts, already stirred into a storm, are no longer her own. She can feel the pressure of silent minds reading her inner hesitations—some gently, others not. Instinctively, her hand drifts to her belly.

"Better late than never," she says, voice low but firm. "Yes, Mr. Powers. I will marry you."

"Hoera!" cheers Siyabonga.

"It's about fuckin' time!" mutters Zookeeper.

Lady Oracle beams, but her gaze remains piercing. "This is joyful news," she says. "But I suspect, Abassi, your ambitions stretch well beyond matrimony. What game are you truly playing?"

Abassi spreads his arms in mock theatricality. "Imagine it: a grand wedding. Lavish. Symbolic. Held not in the United States, but in a neutral country. Switzerland, perhaps. We invite every head of state, every royal house, every major media outlet. The first public union of so-called alien and human. An affair drenched in ritual and spectacle. No war, no summit, no policy decree could command such attention. The world, romance-hungry as ever, will drink it in. And when it ends with a finale they'll never forget. It will leave behind something more potent than fear or facts: sentiment. The kind that burns itself into memory. Then let the protestors scream. Their rage won't cut through a world weeping with joy."

Zookeeper slaps his knee. "Fuckin' awesome idea!"

Ming-huà turns gently to Anne. "And you, dear? How does this sit with you?"

Anne hesitates. Beneath the proposal's theatrical grandeur, she senses something sharper—manipulation, yes, but also risk. Deep, personal risk. Her grandfather's teachings rise in her mind: dignity, caution, strategy. But her body speaks in different rhythms. The stirrings in her womb are real now, and with them come tremors of instinct, signaling protection, fear, and wonder. As with all mothers, it is the safety of the unborn child first. She chooses her words with care. "Abassi, won't the other world leaders see this as a setup? A trap?"

"Of course," he replies. "But if the President of the United States agrees to attend, it will pressure his allies to do the same. And the wedding will be held on their turf. No tricks. Nothing hidden."

"And once they see we are not monsters . . ." Ming-huà murmurs, her voice soft with possibility.

Lady Oracle, still wary, nods toward Anne. "She's right to worry. Humans twist meanings. They invent traps where none exist because they expect betrayal. Then, of course, there are countries that are not allies of the United States. What of them?"

"Then let those who fear us watch from afar," says Abassi. "Let them stream it live. Let the world decide."

"But what if they all choose to stay away?" Anne asks.

"They won't," Abassi replies. "Not if the American President is seen shaking my hand."

"How do you plan to convince him?" asks Zookeeper.

Abassi smiles. "Ah, that is the mystery. We must use what we have—gifts, yes—but for good. What better purpose could there be?"

Altan raises an eyebrow. "So, if the President refuses, you'll make him an offer he can't refuse?"

Abassi winks. "Something like that."

Zookeeper squints. "You gonna call him directly? I mean, even in the hood we used go-betweens, except we called them brokers."

"An emissary," Pythia offers.

"Exactly."

Abassi points a finger. "And once again, Zookeeper hits the mark. With Romellion gone, we need someone credible. Trusted. And I know the perfect person."

A silence falls.

"Well?" Zookeeper prompts. "Who?"

"The others already know," Abassi says. "But for your benefit, and Anne's, I mean to ask Walter Monroe."

Anne flinches. "No. Absolutely not."

"He's your grandfather," Abassi says gently. "A lifelong public servant. Respected. Connected. Who better?"

"Because," Anne snaps, "he'll do it. And then he'll end up like Romellion."

"Let him decide."

"No!" Her voice cracks. "He's all I have. My only family. My only connection to who I was."

"You have us now," says Abassi. "And our family includes more than blood ties. It includes all life."

"I do not want to lose him," she whispers.

"We'll protect him."

"When? At the wedding? What about before? After? Do you have a safer plan?"

Abassi doesn't answer.

"Then leave him out of it."

Pythia places a hand on Anne's shoulder. "You're already in danger. You and the child."

Anne stiffens. "What child?"

"The one we all know you believe you're carrying."

Color floods Anne's face. "I . . . I'm not even sure yet. I don't want my thoughts constantly monitored. I need space. Privacy. My mind is still mine, isn't it?"

Ming-huà leans in gently. "You are not alone. And you will not be coerced. You decide."

Anne exhales, her hands trembling. "Fine. I will marry Abassi. But if you insist on dragging Walter into this, I'll try to stop him. I'll beg him not to go."

Tara's eyes gleam. "And the child?"

"I don't even know if I'm pregnant!"

"You are," says Altan quietly.

Anne turns to him, stunned. "How could you know?"

Altan's gaze is steady. "Because your body is changing in ways that signal something new. Something extraordinary. Perhaps even beyond Abassi himself."

Zookeeper whistles. "I didn't know that was possible. Fuck me." He glances at Ming-huà. "Sorry, love. Just meant I'm surprised."

Abassi squeezes Anne's hand. "Before I ask your grandfather to act, I must first make contact with the President. If that fails, none of this will matter."

Anne nods slowly, heart pounding. Inside her, something flickers: hope, dread, and a pulse that is no longer hers alone.

~ *The Execution* ~

The following morning, Abassi is on the phone.

"Mr. President," he says evenly, "you don't have much of a choice. This plan will calm the waters, stir curiosity, and demonstrate that a union between *Homo sapiens* and one of our kind is not monstrous, not exotic, but natural. It will bring the global community together, especially if not held on American soil, but in a neutral land."

A pause.

"I'm sorry, Mr. Powers—"

"Abassi."

"I'm sorry, Abassi. I'm afraid such a spectacle—world leaders convening for a wedding—would be politically untenable. Especially after Tuvalu."

"I too am afraid, Mr. President. But not for the same reasons. Tuvalu proved what we are capable of. You do not have the luxury of refusal."

"That sounds like another threat."

"It is. And unlike most threats, this one will be carried out. If you refuse, I will remove you, both of you, from the theater entirely. Harmlessly, but permanently. Until a leader arises who understands necessity. I've lost patience with delays. Deception. But if you cooperate, you lose nothing. And if this works? You become the man who helped stitch a torn world back together."

A silence. Then: "Did Romellion inform you of his meeting with Dr. Carlson before he was killed?"

"No."

"Then perhaps I should have Carlson contact—"

"No. That path has closed. Romellion's death changed everything. The wedding will happen."

A longer pause. The President speaks again, voice diminished.

"If this fails, Abassi, it will come at a steep cost. Not just for you. For both of us. For the world."

"Perhaps. But you, Mr. President, are a gambler. That's how you got here."

"I need to consult my advisors."

"You have one day. And be warned—if you trace this call, or send anyone here with ill intent, I will act swiftly. And decisively."

"It's unwise to threaten the President of the United States."
"And unwise to mistake warning for bluff."

~

When the call ends, Abassi turns to the gathered group.
"He'll agree."
Pythia narrows her eyes. "Are you certain? His physical distance, can you read him that clearly?"
"Maybe. Maybe not. But I feel the wave shifting. Arlington is a calculating political specimen, one I have become quite familiar with. Self-interest trumps all else, except for fanatics, and Arlington is certainly no fanatic."

Still, doubt shadows Abassi. He is not as sure as he sounds. The trauma of Tuvalu still echoes: those lost diplomats, severed from time, from breath. His resulting illness. And Romellion's death haunts him. Though meditation returns him to silence, it does not restore certainty. He dreams now of escape, of fleeing to the cave in California, threading his way through time's side corridors, losing himself in a thousand quiet elsewheres. He is young still, by the reckoning of his kind, and some part of him yearns to rest, to bury his head in the warmth of a long-lost elder. But there is no such being. The Mentors and Overseers are hints of immense power, coldly waiting beyond an infinity of veils.

And then there is Anne. Human. Imperfect. Yet radiant in ways he cannot dismiss. Her fragility is a counterweight to his force. Altan once compared him to Alexander—restless, brilliant, destined to remake the world, but blooded with youth's fire and the burden of impossible tasks. Abassi seeks not conquest, but transformation: to conquer without killing, to replace without erasure, to usher in a new age without shattering the old beyond repair. Is Anne the one to walk beside him into that peril? When she is near, the answer is yes. When she is not, the answer wavers on its edge. He knows she loves him. Deeply. Personally. With a fierceness he finds both beautiful and bewildering. He, who has known only the vast love for whales and worms, for forests and fungi, struggles to grasp the ferocity of love for one person. It seems irrational. Almost frightening. Perhaps her intermediate genes help temper it, but still, she has not yet leapt across the great divide to that all-encompassing compassion his kind must cultivate. That leap will mark the true future, or the final failure, of both species.

"Abassi?"
Anne's voice cuts through his spiraling thoughts.
"Sorry. What?"
"We're all waiting."
"For?"
Lady Oracle steps forward, voice weary. "While you were elsewhere, Siyabonga announced he and Tara wish to return to Africa. Ming-huà and Zookeeper will go to their island. Pythia plans to sow new seeds in China. All agree that the children must disperse. They must settle across the Earth: India, South America, Europe. But to do so in peace, they must be accepted. They must be free to love,

to interbreed, to belong. So they ask you: will this wedding move us closer to that goal, or endanger it?"

The question lands on his chest with crushing weight. "I can't promise certainty," Abassi says. "The universe is probabilistic. But I have run the wave equations. Of all possible paths, this is the one most likely to collapse in our favor."

Tara grins. "I wouldn't miss it for the world."

"Nor I," adds Pythia.

Zookeeper throws his arms up. "Free food and drink? I'll fuckin' be there."

"As will all of us," says Ming-huà, though her eyes reprimand Zookeeper silently.

Abassi smiles. "Yes. I'll need you all. There will be spies, agents, assassins in the crowd. We must blend. No visible humps—dead giveaways."

"Obvious," mutters Zookeeper.

"And the wedding must proceed flawlessly. No violence. No chaos. We cannot prove our enemies right."

"There will be protests," Anne warns. "That frightens me."

"It frightens me too," says Abassi. "That's why the choice of country matters."

"What does that mean?" asks Ming-huà.

"It means what it means," Abassi replies, opening his mind to them all.

~

The sun rises the next morning, sharp and bright. They are gathered when the call comes. Abassi answers.

For the better part of the hour, he listens. Occasionally, he murmurs: "I see." "Perhaps." "That date is acceptable." The rest is silence, an agreement built slowly, tentatively, between two reluctant architects of history. When the call ends, he turns to the others.

"It is done."

And yet, his heart is not at ease. He knows the stakes. One misstep, one spark, and this delicate attempt at peace could detonate the planet's future.

He loves Anne. But not as she loves him. Not with the same wild, unreasoning depth. Worse, if Altan is right, she carries their child which is something new, something beyond even him. A wildcard in the unfolding blueprint of evolution.

Dark intuitions stir. What if they are not the future? What if they are merely the prototypes, the first imperfect sketches of a species yet to come?

"I need to be alone," he says.

Questions are thrown at him, but he is already leaving. He walks toward the jagged white of the Rockies, letting the crisp Wyoming air clear his thoughts.

The ghosts are waiting. They walk beside him: John Powers, Michael Powers, Bai Meiying, Child of Buddha, Tamara Powers. Their faces are grim, expectant. But expectant of what? "You all heard voices," he says aloud to the specters. "You believed them to be gods and goddesses. And look where that led. I hear them too, but they are not gods or goddesses. Not in the way you imagined. Only the Precious Object speaks truly. And it does not use words."

He listens.

… Tap. Tap. Tap.…

The staccato pulse of a twisted requiem.

"To what end?" he asks the ghosts.

They stare back.

"To what end?" he repeats.

No answer is forthcoming.

Only the mountain wind replies, carrying the weight of time, the breath of unborn species, and the riddle of futures still unshaped and uncertain.

Chapter Twenty-Five

The Wedding

Ceremonies

New Delhi has been chosen for the wedding site. Cradle of an ancient civilization adorned with gods and goddesses, it feels destined, almost preordained, for what Abassi intends. Never in recorded history has such a convergence of global leaders occurred under one roof. Regional spectacles, yes, but this is something else entirely. At the heart of Chanakyapuri, amid manicured avenues and embassies wrapped in flags, rises the opulent Leela Chanaka. Its grand ballroom, saturated in polished gold and imperial red, will host the wedding. To the U.S. State Department, the site is as neutral as diplomacy allows. To Abassi, it is perfect. The sheer symbolism of it—a union not just of individuals but of worlds—delights him. Anne shares his anticipation, though with a skeptic's reserve.

"I looked up this 'palace' we're to be married in," she says, eyeing him one morning over tea. "It's ridiculous. Lavish doesn't even begin to describe it. I'm not sure a lowly American girl like me should even be allowed in."

Abassi chuckles. "Humans like sparkly things. I've always thought they resemble bowerbirds more than great apes."

Anne lets out a laugh, half real, half deflective. "Guilty. But this place? It's beyond a sparkly bauble. Even the pickiest of females would find their dreams answered."

"You don't think it's excessive?"

"Oh, it is. But that's what makes it charming. Like watching a gloriously cheesy movie, you wince, but you enjoy it."

He smiles. "Human indulgence has its price."

"On us?"

"On the Earth."

Her voice quiets. "Yes. This girl you insist on marrying still has some rough edges."

"And I, being older, have more."

"Oh? And what are yours?"

"I exile them. To other dimensions, mostly."

"In that case, I'll have to visit someday," chuckles Anne. "I'd like to see them."

"You collect foibles now?"

"I'm a Bower bird, remember? And you, my love, are full of shiny mysteries."

They collapse into laughter, arms entangled, children again beneath the surface of gods.

~

A week before the ceremony, Anne confirms what her body already knows: she is pregnant. She is not surprised. Each day has spoken in the language of change. Not the ordinary stirrings of new life nestled in the womb, but something stranger, inconceivably vaster. It moves through her bloodstream like molten ore, thick and deliberate, a furnace forging steel from flesh. She is aflame, but not consumed. Strength surges where softness used to be. Her body is preparing for something immense, perhaps catastrophic. At night, she slips outside alone, burning up, stripping naked beneath the stars, and bathes in the cold air. Steam rises from her glowing skin. She feels kin to the constellations and their blurry glimmerings, distant furnaces piercing the dark.

You are now the vessel that brings the Chosen One, comes a female voice, resonant and vast.

Anne freezes, caught in some invisible vise.

Nonsense, foolish Goddess! snarls another. Male. Thick as swamp water, churning with soot and ash. A belch from some ancient hell. *She will likely die in childbirth!*

Your interference serves no one, counters the female. Her voice scours the filth like a cleansing wind, though its purity cannot quite erase the grime.

See how Anne twists My words? The early Chosen Ones have always made this error. Always. Nonetheless, My words are not entirely mistaken. This evolutionary, speeded-up arms-race is broken already. Let the world turn out as it will, without Your misplaced, compassionate interference. Return to First Principles.

So you can watch the ruin from afar?

No. But she may die. Just as the others died—mad, broken. This is what interference brings.

Then drops a veil of silence.

Anne is still absorbing the voices when Abassi's voice reaches her, distant, breathless. "You heard them, didn't you?"

She turns toward him, radiant in her nakedness. "I did. And they terrify me."

"They drove my ancestors mad."

"Are they real?"

"No."

"Then what are they?"

"Distortions."

"I don't understand. Distortions of what?"

"The Mentors."

"I still don't understand."

"Nor do I. Not completely."

She raises her arms toward the stars. "I'm burning."

"You're glowing," he says. "Exceedingly beautiful."

"Am I going mad?"

"No. You are perfectly sane."

Anne cups her breasts, and when she speaks again, it is with a voice neither playful nor shy, but commanding. "Take off your clothes."

In a heartbeat, they collide: bodies fusing in fevered motion, hers searing with inner fire, his cold skin the perfect foil. When her fingers trace his hump, it bursts into kaleidoscopic visions—images dancing to the rhythm of her touch. Deep within, the movement accelerates, something ancient and new, driven forward by their mutual surrender. It is not just sex, it is ignition. A flaring birthright. A storm coiled in flesh. Afterward, they hover above the frozen earth, limbs tangled, breath steaming against the night.

"I no longer fear the wedding," Anne whispers. "Let it come."

"Your grandfather has accepted his role. What of your concern for him?"

She takes a long pause. "Walter has earned the right to make his own choices. I said my piece. He said his. We're united now."

"We'll protect him," Abassi vows.

Anne's smile is subtle, edged. "You'd do well to protect yourselves. I think you're underestimating humanity."

"You are more than human," he replies.

"And you are more than me."

He rests his hand gently on her belly. "And this one," he says, "will be more than both of us."

"In that case," Anne whispers, "we'd better learn Zookeeper's bawdy patience."

Abassi falls silent.

"You're worried," she says softly.

"A little. If this child's powers outstrip mine, will their empathy keep pace with their force? Can balance be preserved?"

"Balance," she echoes. "Always balance."

~ *The Ceremony* ~

Indian police form a dense wall, shoulder to shoulder, but it is not enough. The crowd grows by the minute, pushing against the perimeter with a pressure that is more than physical. It is ancestral. Wordless. Some carry signs. Others chant. Most simply wait, their eyes fixed on the hotel, vacant with expectation. A reckoning draws near.

Inside the Leela Chanaka, beneath chandeliers that descend in ornate clusters, Abassi and Anne stand sealed in separate rooms, each preparing for the moment.

The cloaked figures of Pythia, Tara, and Ming-huà wait outside, scattered among the gathering in silent vigilance, their minds open, scanning the crowd for the first rupture.

Walter Monroe lingers near the President, who wears the skin of calm like a second suit. But Walter sees the signs. The whispered updates. The nervous thumb grazing the lapel mic. The eye that twitches whenever the crowd roars. No blood yet. But the shift has come.

"To pass the time," the President says, too casually, "tell me, is your grand-daughter nervous?"

Walter exhales. "Anne is composed. But the path here wasn't smooth."

"What happened?"

"The ceremony was in question. Secular or spiritual? Anne considered Hindu rites as a conciliatory gesture toward the host country."

"And?"

"She dismissed it. She isn't religious. But she wanted to honor the moment."

"And Abassi?"

Walter's voice lowers. "He doesn't view this as sacred. To him, it is a mirror held up to a species still learning to see itself."

"You make him sound like a zoologist."

"No," Walter says. "He doesn't study. He judges."

The President checks his watch. "How long?"

"Half an hour."

"Security?"

"Cracking."

~

The ballroom is dressed for grace. Outside, the world begins to tear.

Pythia feels it first, a spike of loathing so sharp it cleaves through her thoughts. Tara recoils. Ming-huà goes still. They hear it next: a rhythm of curses, ancient and fierce.

"Sacrilege!"

"Unnatural!"

"Shameful!"

The crowd loses form. It becomes memory. It becomes rage. Not protest, but invocation. A mass awakening to inherited fear.

"Stop them!"

"Storm the hotel!"

"Traitors!"

The barrier wavers. Splinters. Falls.

~

An aide bursts in. "Mr. President!"

Abassi and Anne emerge together. The ballroom falls silent.

"Yes?"

"It's no longer a protest. It's a mob."

"A mob?"

"They want them."

Chaos ignites. Security fractures. Dignitaries flee. The officiant freezes, clutching his script.

Abassi speaks. "We begin now."

"We're not ready!" Mr. Lash cries. "They're leaving!"

"Then begin before we're silenced."

Walter appears, breathless. "The President is being evacuated. Come with him."

"No," says Abassi. "We remain."

Mr. Lash falters. "I . . . yes, sir."

Anne meets her grandfather's eyes. "Go."

"No. I won't leave you."

"Please."

He straightens. "Then begin."

The ceremony proceeds. Not in joy, but defiance. Not in celebration, but endurance. They are married.

Outside, the clash erupts. Gunshots. Screams. The army surges. Protestors scatter. Blood marks the marble floor.

Among the fallen lies Ming-huà Powers. Her form is crumpled. Her breath gone. Zookeeper crouches near her, bloodied and broken.

"She wouldn't defend herself," he cries. "I begged her."

Abassi arrives. Kneels. Dissolves her remains with a whisper.

"No relics," he tells Tara and Pythia. "No vultures. She chose grace over vengeance."

Anne, her gown soaked in someone else's death, stares at the space where Ming-huà was.

~

Zookeeper screams, not to them, but to the world: "One becomes a bride. One becomes a corpse. And the world keeps feeding on its saints!"

~

On the plane, Anne says nothing. Her hand in Abassi's. Her grief bottomless.

"We wear the mask now," he says. "Smile. Pretend. They must believe this was a triumph."

She doesn't respond.

"You're asking why it was her."

Tears gather. "She didn't fight."

"She never did."

"Why?"

"You know."

"Say it anyway."

He kisses her fingers. "Restraint was her power. Grace her gift."

Anne shakes. "I'm afraid. They fear us. They want us gone. What life awaits this child? Execution? Or guilt?"

"I can't say."

"There's something you're hiding."

"Yes."

"What?"

"You suspect already. Altan. Lady Oracle. Sy. They've all hinted. There is another force. Not one of us."

"The code."

He nods. "The Precious Object. Beyond even me."

"Did no one unlock it?"

"One did. The Child of Buddha. They called her mad. But she might have seen the shape of the thing."

"You think we're being used."

"I think we're part of something older. And not yet finished."

"The Overseers?" asks Anne expectantly.

"Beyond me. Unreachable."

"But you are Abassi. Surely—"

"Yes, I am Abassi, and they are not. I am one thing, they are another, dwelling over the horizon of my powers."

Anne shudders. "Try."

Abassi chuckles. "You think I haven't?"

"Try harder. Find the truth before this child arrives."

"I will do what I can."

"And Ming-huà's daughter?"

"Safe. Pythia and Tara have taken her to Wyoming."

"They were leaving."

"Plans changed. The law cracked open. We still have a foothold."

"And us?"

"We return to San Francisco. The mansion. The eyes. The stage. We act the part."

"And after?"

"We vanish. Regroup. Ready ourselves."

Anne places her hand on her abdomen. "This one is different. I feel it. You all feel it. I don't even know how far along I am."

"You'll know."

"I'm afraid."

"Then remember her bloodline. Ming-huà, who stood for innocence. Who exiled the killers. Who bore Pythia, fierce and unrelenting. My mother, Tara, who upended the gangs and preserved what could be saved."

"And me?"

"You are the center. The axis. The gravity around which the next age spins."

"But why? What am I beyond a vessel?"

"You are the Mother."

"There are many mothers."

"None like you. You carry the one who will eclipse us all."

She looks at him, her voice nearly gone. "And what are you, then?"

Abassi turns away. When he speaks, it is a whisper of ash.

"I wonder," he says. And in the space where wonder meets grief, something else stirs—the next beginning.

~ Dreadful Hope ~

Alone with her thoughts, Anne stares out into the dark window reflection. The image staring back is unfamiliar. Not quite hers. Not quite theirs. A woman wrapped in silence, pulled between blood and birthright.

The child stirs within her, but offers no comfort. Only questions. What am I becoming? A symbol? A vessel? Or a warning?

She wants to believe in something larger—destiny, grace, reassuring continuity—but her faith is cracked. Not in the world, but in herself.

Had she made the right choice? To stand beside Abassi. To claim this path. To become the mother of something not yet known.

And what would it become? Not human. Not exactly. But if it mirrored its father too closely, would she be cherished or caged? Revered, or sidelined? Would she be the child's guardian or its first mistake?

She doesn't know which terrifies her more: that she is too human, and therefore a traitor to what is coming. Or that she is too much of them, and has already lost what little claim she had to her own kind.

There is no certainty. No reassurance. Only this entity inside her . . . this insistent future . . . this rough beast growing in the wet cradle, preparing to slouch toward—what? Toward where?

Already, she senses faint murmurs.

Not voices. Not thoughts. Just ripples, subtle shifts in the air around her, rising from a depth beyond biology. Spreading outward. Spreading upward.

They frighten her.

Are they the first stirrings of something gentle, or the tremors of a coming storm?

Which will it be?

She closes her eyes. And waits.

~

Abassi watches her in silence. He has said what he can. He has comforted where words would allow. But his silence now is not indifference. It is vigilance.

He knows Anne will endure. He has no doubt in her strength, nor her role. But the child she carries is another matter. It is not merely different. It is unprecedented.

He has seen the scans. Felt the vibrations in her cells. The sequence is mutating. Not gradually. Not adaptively. But violently.

What begins as one life may end as many. Or none.

He cannot speak this fear aloud. Not to her. Not yet. But it follows him, whispering between thoughts, lodging in the corners of his vision.

What if the child is beyond even them? Beyond correction? Beyond reason?

What if it emerges not as an heir, but as a herald?

A force with no allegiance, no boundary, no restraint?

He does not believe in monsters. But he has witnessed evolution take brutal turns.

And in this child, something ancient stirs. Something unreadable.

He watches Anne sleep. Places his hand just above her womb.

"Be kind," he whispers. "Or spare her."

But even as he says it, he knows the choice may not be his to ask for, nor hers to bear. The child stirs beneath his palm—silent, unformed, already beyond their reach.

Chapter Twenty-Six

Ticking Time Bomb

End of the Line?

~ Living in the Glare ~

S o it comes to pass.

Abassi and Anne live not as private individuals, but as figures etched into the public spectacle. They are walking myths tasked with embodying an uneasy future. They move through orchestrated ceremonies, appear at summits, make declarations filtered through speechwriters and strategists. Their presence is managed by governments, watched by satellites, interpreted by millions. But their silence, when it falls between appearances, is read more urgently still.

The mansion in San Francisco has grown into a citadel. Walls now define its outer limits. Surveillance systems blink overhead. Guards shift posts with the discipline of militaries. Protesters still come, as do pilgrims and journalists. But when weeks pass without a single sighting of Anne on the veranda or Abassi in the rose gardens, the crowds thin. What remains is not excitement, but interpretation. Rumor becomes scripture.

Far from this performance, in the high, quiet terrain of Wyoming, the others have turned inward. There, the children of Tara, Pythia, and Ming-huà are being raised, watched not for obedience, but for signs. They are not molded, but studied. Their minds do not grow in simple arcs; their development is often paradoxical. They speak of things they have not learned. They dream of places no one has shown them. Each child, in time, will be tested. Each will be led, if worthy, to the cave.

A quiet vow has formed among their caretakers: once Anne's child is born, and once each of the others comes into clarity, they will risk re-entering the world. But not to be seen. Not to be embraced. To intervene, silently and with force, if necessary.

Then, everything shifts.

Anne collapses without warning. What grows within her has not communicated in visions or warmth. There are no pulses from the deep. No shared dreaming. Only extraction. She fades from herself, her eyes dull, her body emptied of will. Abassi halts his public engagements. Behind the scenes, she is moved to Wyoming, surrounded by those who understand the stakes.

He remains at her side when he can. But he returns frequently to San Francisco, where the performance must go on. His face graces morning broadcasts. Her condition is hidden. She is radiant, they say. Serene. Preparing for the miracle of birth.

But in Wyoming, the atmosphere thickens. Even the children know something is wrong. They avoid Anne's hallway, speak of her room only in whispers. Some say she is already gone, and something else now waits behind her closed door.

Then, without announcement, the midwife arrives.

She is old, timeless in the way deserts are old. Her silence fills the house with a deeper kind of listening. No one questions who she is. She speaks little, but all understand that her presence signals a shift in the order of things.

"Who summoned her?" Lady Oracle asks.

"I did," Altan replies.

"She's one of them?"

"In part. But her roots reach further. This is not merely genetic divergence. It is metaphysical bifurcation."

Sy frowns. "Is this the culmination?"

Altan shakes his head. "There is no culmination. There is only the next acceleration."

"But this one," Sy insists. "This child—it might not be like the others."

"No," Altan says. "It may be unlike anything. It may be a singularity of mind, dense, recursive, sealed from affection or influence. We hoped for transcendence. But this . . . may be foreclosure."

A long silence.

Lady Oracle speaks the unspoken. "Would it come to infanticide?"

"If we are lucky," Altan replies. "If the choice is ours."

"You think it might resist?" Sy asks.

"I think it already understands."

He continues, voice low. "Anne is mostly human. Her biology, her cervix, her arteries, her consciousness, none were shaped for this. The evolutionary problem has always been the tension between cognition and constraint. The skull must pass through the birth canal. Nature's compromise was neoteny—eternal adolescence. Minds that never finish forming. But this child . . . it is the reversal. Not delay, but compression. Not expansion, but implosion into depth. A mind not meant to unfold, but to enclose."

Sy breathes through his nose. "And if we cannot stop it?"

"Then it becomes the author of the next chapter. Whether that chapter includes us is not guaranteed."

The silence becomes difficult to bear. And then, a shift, quieter and more personal.

Lady Oracle says, "And Zookeeper?"

Sy shakes his head. "He's failing. His son now surpasses him in every way. The poor man wants to go back to his island. To live with ghosts."

"Let him," she says softly. "Or better yet, send Bataar with him. The boy is ageless."

Sy nods. "They're like kin. I'll arrange it."

Lady Oracle sighs. "Still, I worry. He may end up like Pythia's old professor."

"Paine?" Sy murmurs. "Yes. Possible. But Zookeeper is a cagey old street fighter. He'll curse his way through, with a mixture of Shakespeare quotes thrown in for good measure. Still, I worry as well."

Altan listens, but does not comment. His gaze remains on the chamber where Anne sleeps. Or no longer sleeps. Where something waits to emerge.

No one says it aloud, but the fear is now elemental.

The child is no longer the question.

The question is whether humanity has already been outgrown.

~

Abassi sits at Anne's bedside.

The room is quiet, but not restful. It is the quiet of halted time, of lives suspended between opposing currents. Anne has hovered for weeks in the threshold between consciousness and coma, drifting through states that resemble neither sleep nor death. When she awakens, it is brief, functional, an urgent respite. She devours food without presence, her mouth working mechanically, her eyes vacant. There is no sign of her behind the gaze. It is as if the entity inside her grants her these moments not for communion, but for sustenance. She eats not to live, but to feed what grows. And what grows is voracious.

She has not spoken. Not once. Her face shows no recognition. And when Abassi attempts to reach her, both mentally and spiritually, he encounters not resistance but something worse: a void. A flat, untextured wall of silence. No thoughts, no feelings, not even echoes. Just density. Gray. Unyielding.

He waits again today, as he has every day. Hoping for a fracture in the fog. A flicker. A breath. But her body lies inert. Limbs rigid. Skin cold beneath the light. There is nothing to read in her pulse. She has become a vessel with no message.

He rises to leave.

Then, without warning, her body convulses. She bolts upright, eyes wide, mouth opening, but not in pain. In proclamation. Her voice is raw, torn from some deep inner chamber that is not hers alone.

"Abomination."

The word is whispered, but it cleaves the air.

Before he can speak, she collapses again. Not like a patient losing consciousness, but like a puppet severed from its strings. The word lingers, suspended in the stillness. A tremor passes through him, not from its meaning, but its tone. It had not sounded like judgment. It had sounded like a question.

He kneels beside her. "Anne?"

No reply. Her face is expressionless. Her body unmoving.

"Why did you say that?"

Nothing.

"Blink if you hear me."

The silence is total. Even the room seems to withhold sound.

Then, behind him, a voice speaks.

It is not Anne.

"A fierce battle is being waged."

He turns.

She stands there. The one beyond category. The one who has no birth and no name.

Her presence fills the room, not with spectacle, but with pressure. Reality tightens around *her*. The floor beneath him seems less stable. His body tenses under the force of *her* gaze. Heat rises through his skin. He shudders. And then stills himself, breathing through the awe.

"Will she live?" he asks.

Her voice arrives not as comfort, but as truth.

"Fate starves at Probability's door."

He closes his eyes briefly, absorbing the weight of the answer.

"Is that a yes?"

"Perhaps."

The silence that follows is profound. Not empty, it is *consecrated*.

Then *she* speaks again. "Are you more concerned for the mother—or the child?"

He does not answer right away. The question has no safe edge. He studies her face, searching for shape in the mystery.

"I am most concerned," he says at last, "about the battle you speak of."

Her reply is quiet, unhurried. "It is the old struggle. The one your ancestors whispered through fire and madness. The one they could name only through symbols: God versus Goddess, Order versus Flame. But they were describing a deeper schism. A war between two First Principles. Compassionate interference. And impersonal justice. Both now inhabit her womb. And they do not agree."

He feels the shift in temperature. "What is at stake?"

"The continuation of your kind."

His voice falters. "How?"

Her gaze narrows. "By one of two means. Quick, surgical annihilation. Or slow, painless absorption into what follows."

Abassi steadies himself. "And the child?"

"The child," *she* says, "is no longer only child. It is locus. Fulcrum. The site of a convergence none of your species is prepared to mediate."

He swallows. "It decides this?"

She meets his eyes and projects into his mind the voice of Goddess. ***Probability starves at Fate's door.***

He exhales, shaken. "Your words frighten me."

She smiles. It is not cruel. Nor is it kind. It is acknowledgment.

"Your ancestors," *she* says gently, reverting to *her* natural voice, "spoke truths too early. They were labeled mad—schizophrenic, delusional, possessed. They glimpsed fragments of what now arrives whole. The one growing inside Anne will be accused of the same, of being paranoid, dangerous, and insane. But those accusations will fail. You measure sanity against consensus. This child does not require consensus. It will move as it must."

She steps closer.

"You fear destruction. You should. This one could erase your species in a moment of judgment. Or worse, undo you slowly, not through violence, but through irrelevance. Your fears are valid. But they are also futile."

He stiffens. "And if it must be stopped? How would I do that?"

Her voice drops. "Should you try . . . it may be *you* who is erased."

He stands very still. "Then what are we to do?"

Her answer is not ambiguous.

"We hope," *she* says.

"And we wait."

~ *Labor* ~

"It is time," says the old midwife.

Her voice is brittle, as if carried across centuries of silence. Her name, once, was Ruth. But whatever that name once meant has long dissolved into service. She does not stand now as a woman, but as a vessel of threshold.

Abassi stands across from her, unmoved. He watches Anne's body, which remains slack, inert, unchanged.

"I see no difference," he says, eyes narrowed.

"The change," Ruth replies, "is not visible. It has begun beneath . . . beneath thought, beneath form. The deep currents are rising. Chaotic. Unpredictable."

He hesitates. "Is she conscious?"

Ruth bares her teeth, the motion somewhere between a grin and a grimace. "I've seen this before. Once. In another place, before history had a name. The pain is not gone. It folds inwards. Spirals into silence. But it is felt, all of it. Even without sound."

Abassi's voice lowers. "You speak as if the child holds her in captivity."

"She is held," Ruth says. "Not by cords or force, but by presence. It fills her. There is no room left for Anne. Her body is the terrain of a battle she cannot flee."

He steps closer. "How close?"

"Close."

"Minutes? Hours? Days?"

Ruth does not answer. Instead, she closes her eyes. "I serve the child now. It has entered the phase of imperative. It will be born. The mother's will no longer matters."

He swallows, jaw tightening. "Will she survive?"

Ruth shakes her head. "In all the ways that define the self, she is gone."

The room stills around them. The air feels thinner.

He speaks again, this time with quiet dread. "You said you've seen this once before."

"I did."

"How did that end?"

Ruth's expression flattens. "It was destroyed."

"By whom?"

"Not yours to know."

"Then how can we—"

She lifts her hand, silencing him. "Be ready. That's all anyone could ever be."

He turns to Anne. Her face is pale. Her breath shallow. He searches her mind once more for any remnant, any flicker of the woman he knew. But her consciousness lies buried in a place unreachable.

"Out," Ruth says. Not cruelly. But absolutely.

The door closes behind him.

Ruth remains still. Her eyes drift to the shadowed edge of the room, where another presence waits.

Barely visible. But unmistakable.

Ruth speaks, not loudly, but with reverence.

"Do you feel it?"

"Yes," comes the reply—quiet, female, ageless.

"It's stronger than the other," Ruth says.

"Yes."

"The mother is already lost. If this is like the one I saw before, it will not arrive in peace. It will not seek permission. It will tear."

"Yes."

Anne's body begins to convulse.

Her spine arches in a motion no human should survive. Her limbs stiffen. Her mouth opens, but no sound escapes. Her eyes, wide and wild, glare at nothing, as if witnessing an event outside all time.

Ruth's voice pierces the stillness. "It's coming! Be ready!"

But the woman in the corner does not move. *She* remains seated, hands resting gently in *her* lap. *Her* gaze is unwavering.

Anne's mouth opens wider—too wide. A scream seems imminent, but never arrives.

Ruth's hands move. She leans close. "It's crowning! I feel it. Now. Now is the time!"

She turns to the silent woman. "If you're going to stop it, it must be now!"

Still, the other woman remains seated. Then *she* speaks—not to Ruth, but to the unseen forces beyond the room.

"No. Let this one be born. I see it now. I understand."

Her tone is not defiant. It is illuminated.

"All will be well."

The child arrives in a rush, a flood of amniotic fluid, warm and sudden. The room shifts, as if reality itself yields to the event. Ruth receives the infant with practiced hands, but her strength falters for the first time in decades. The child is heavier than it should be. Not in mass, but in meaning.

She cuts the cord in silence. Wraps the child in ceremonial cloth. Places it upon the altar beside the bed. But as she reaches to dry the child's skin, she stops.

A presence has entered her mind.

It is not hostile. But it is vast.

She gasps, not out of fear, but recognition. Her thoughts are no longer hers alone. Something foreign yet intimate has intertwined with her consciousness. It does not speak. It knows her.

The infant's eyes open.

And stare directly into hers.

There is no confusion in that gaze. No wonder. Only recognition. And with it, Ruth feels a surge of terror so old, so pure, it renders her knees unsteady.

A voice behind her, gentle and lyrical, says, "She's telling you to save the mother."

Ruth does not look away from the infant. "Yes," she whispers. "Yes, I hear her. But . . . look at it."

"Save the mother."

"I don't know how," Ruth breathes. "Do you understand what has come through her?"

The young woman rises at last. Approaches.

The infant turns its gaze away from Ruth and toward its blood-soaked mother. The expression in those new eyes is unspeakable, an ancient sorrow, bottomless, fused with a compassion that will not rescue, only witness.

"Go," the young woman commands. *Her* voice is clear. Final. "Stop the bleeding."

"But the child—"

"I see the child. Now go."

Ruth obeys. She moves swiftly to Anne's side.

The bleeding is catastrophic. Her hands tremble, but her training returns. Pressure. Clotting agents. Ritual compressions. Words spoken under her breath she has not spoken in centuries.

Behind her, the young woman kneels beside the newborn and leans close.

She whispers, "So . . . you are the Metaphorical Goddess. Come at last."

The infant does not blink.

As Ruth works, a voice not her own enters her again, this time colder, deeper, vaster. Female. Impossible.

"Probability may now give succor to fate."

Ruth gasps, but does not stop working. Her body bows. Her shoulders tremble. But she does not break.

When she glances back, the young woman remains at the infant's side, calm and unwavering.

"And now," *she* says quietly, "the other half begins."

~ *Aftermath* ~

The blood has slowed, but not stopped.

Anne lies motionless beneath damp sheets, her skin pallid, lips blue-tinged. The birth has emptied her—utterly. Not only of the child, but of vitality, of voice, of the tether to her body. She breathes in shallow, fragile intervals. Each one seems earned. Unpromised.

Ruth sits beside her, one hand pressed firmly to Anne's abdomen, the other gripping a cloth steeped in herbs and minerals. The floor beneath them is stained with amniotic remnants, crimson spirals, a broken silence.

The child lies on the altar of woven cloth, swaddled but alert. Its gaze is unblinking. Not infantile. Not testing the world, but regarding it. As if it arrived with its judgments already formed.

Ruth dares not meet its eyes again.

Instead, she watches Anne. The mother who is no longer sovereign over her own breath.

A low voice breaks the stillness. "She's going."

Ruth turns. The young woman, still unnamed, still untouched by exhaustion, stands near the foot of the bed, watching.

"I know," Ruth murmurs.

"Can you hold her here?"

Ruth's hands tremble. "I can try. But her spirit is slipping. Like thread unraveling from a frayed knot."

The child turns its head toward the women. Slowly. Deliberately.

Ruth feels it again. That pressure—not pain, not command, but presence. It does not speak, but it demands.

"She doesn't want to go," Ruth says. "But she can't stay. Her body is too broken. Her blood too thin. She gave everything."

The young woman kneels beside the bed, places a hand on Anne's sternum, palm down. *Her* eyes close. *Her* breathing deepens.

"She is listening," *she* says quietly. "Somewhere below language."

"To what?"

"To the child."

Ruth closes her eyes. "Then let her hear this: she did not fail. She brought through what none of us dared."

The silence holds.

Then a tremor ripples through the room, not physical, but perceptual. A subtle shift in space, as if reality exhales through a tighter lung. The child blinks. For the first time.

Ruth looks to the young woman. "What is it doing?"

The woman doesn't answer. *She* reaches into her satchel and removes a single object—a thin sliver of translucent crystal, humming faintly at the edges.

"I was told to bring this, in case she lived," *she* says. "I didn't believe it would be needed."

"What is it?" Ruth asks.

"Not a cure. But an invocation."

She places the crystal on Anne's chest, just above the heart.

"Speak," she says to the child.

And impossibly—it does.

Not with sound.

With rhythm. With pattern. With pulses in the air that strike the body like language's memory.

Anne's fingers twitch.

Then curl.

Then release.

Her eyes flutter, but do not open.

Ruth leans close, whispering. "Anne? Anne, if you can hear me, stay. Just a little longer. Let the light come back through."

The child grows still. The pulses cease.

Then Anne's chest rises—fully. Once. Then again.

Her eyes open. Barely. Just enough.

She does not speak.

But a single tear rolls down her cheek. It is slow, deliberate, and heavy with meaning.

Ruth collapses into her chair, breath held in reverence.

"She's here," she whispers. "She's not well, but she's here."

The young woman touches the side of Anne's face.

"You've passed through something no language has ever mapped," she says softly. "You crossed without compass. Without bargain. And still . . . you returned."

Anne does not reply. But her eyes shift, just enough to find the newborn.

And something ancient moves between them.

Not maternal. Not mystical.

Recognition.

Ruth leans back, shoulders trembling.

"She'll live?"

The young woman's gaze does not leave Anne's face.

"She'll live," *she* says. "But never again as before."

~ *First Signs of Extraordinary Power* ~

No one is certain how to respond to the child.

She carries within her traces of Abassi—his gaze, his stillness, his presence. There are echoes, too, of the hunchback women, subtle cues in the curvature of her features, the cadence of her breath. But she belongs to neither lineage. She is not an iteration or synthesis. She is an origin.

Even Abassi cannot classify her. He watches her closely, searching for patterns, analogues, references. But there is nothing familiar. Her existence resists categorization. She is a form not seen before on Earth, a being who exceeds all known thresholds without effort. He studies her eyes and finds something unexpected: a glimmer of Anne's mischief, that particular lightness which no logic could predict, no genetic code could ensure. And yet it is there, vivid and unyielding.

From the moment of her birth, she emanates a field of presence that alters the room. Not forceful, not divine, but full, and so saturated with serenity and depth that Abassi forgets, for a while, to assess her capabilities. He forgets to probe for threat or signal. She simply is. One afternoon, idle with curiosity, he tosses a hollow ball across the nursery floor. It doesn't roll or vanish. Instead, it pulses—appearing, disappearing, reappearing inches away, then feet, then meters, as though the rules of space had entered negotiation. The child watches, then laughs. *Her voice is clarity itself,* Abassi thinks, and he smiles in return, not as an observer, but as one who has been recognized.

He kneels beside her. "You are Ἐλзoς," he says, the name rising not from memory, but from an interior certainty. "Your name is Eleos."

~

Time within the retreat alters. Anne remains in bed, her recovery uncertain, her strength hesitant. But Eleos grows as if responding to another tempo entirely. Each month brings years of change. She speaks, then thinks aloud in others' minds, then lets speech return again for the comfort of those she loves.

Father, you must help her heal. She is delicate, mostly human. But even fragility deserves peace. Even what cannot evolve further still deserves rest.

Abassi hears her clearly. *And those who damage the world? Who harm others knowingly, for pleasure or gain—what of them?*

Abassi lowers his gaze. For the first time since her birth, he feels a tremor he cannot master, the fear that even compassion, in her hands, might become something sharper than he dares imagine.

Euthanasia, Eleos replies. *The term has been defiled by history, by fear and prejudice. But mercy must reclaim its name.*

You would end their lives?

Only those whose souls have closed, those beyond remorse.

And the method?

Painless. Immediate. Not as punishment. As release.

But you are Eleos, the embodiment of compassion.

Compassion is not submission. It is protection. It is the refusal to allow the innocent to be ground beneath the ambitions of the cruel. The Earth must be given space to recover. Its beauty must not be sacrificed.

~

Among the young ones, Eleos is both peer and teacher. They practice their gifts—levitation, telepathy, atomic dispersal—and she responds with balance, never pride. When they lift a boulder, she studies its weight, alters its spin, softens its return to the ground so no root, no ant, no blade of grass is harmed. Altan tries to offer instruction, but quickly recognizes futility. Her mind is already seeded with architectures beyond his comprehension. Pre-coded insight hums within her. It is not just intelligence; it is alignment.

The elders meet in quiet conference. They agree, none of the children will be sent into the world's educational systems. They will remain here, under Eleos's guidance. She will direct them to their full potential.

The Wyoming retreat shifts from refuge to sanctuary. Its rhythms quiet, its perimeter sealed. Abassi departs periodically, meeting with world leaders, defusing tension, offering reassurances. Anne, he says, is healing. There is no threat. No need for concern. The press grows tired. The spectacle thins.

Inside, the young ones flourish. They are taught in ways the world does not understand.

Outside, division spreads. Voices rise, some crying for protection, others for retribution. Conspiracy seeps through every broadcast. Aliens, they say, are erasing memories, enslaving minds, draining the essence of what it means to be human. New cults form. Politicians posture. Faiths fracture.

And still, Anne recovers.

Her body remains weak, but her clarity returns. Her wit. Her hunger for truth. One morning, Eleos enters her room.

"You already know how I feel," Anne says, smiling. "But I'll answer anyway. Better. Today feels better."

Eleos nods. "Your voice improves the air around you. You're beautiful, mother."

Anne waves a hand. "You flatter me. Your father says such things to the trees."

"Not to all trees," Eleos replies.

Anne chuckles, then turns solemn. "It can't be easy, living with a woman so bound by her species."

"You are not a burden, mother."

"And when you're grown, when the world demands things of you—how will you manage?"

Eleos tilts her head. "Do you mean: how will I manage humans?"

"I do."

"They are part of the equation. But not the center of it."

"I worry," Anne admits.

"I know. But your worries deserve to be heard aloud, not buried."

"Then yes. I worry. About how you'll judge us."

Eleos steps closer. "The panda depends on bamboo, and humans depend on technology. But while bamboo sustains, technology often devours. It erodes the human core, sometimes beyond repair. If no course is altered, extinction is the likely end—not just for humans, but for many companions on this Earth."

Anne exhales. "And what of the wounded among us? Those who do harm but regret it? Those who act from brokenness, not malice?"

"There are gradients. Ming-huà understood this. She spoke of it often. We do not condemn dogs for barking at stars."

"And yet, she suffered. She made mistakes."

"She did. And learned."

"I've heard whispers. That you could destroy a city."

"I could. But I would not. That act would violate my origin. It would silence something central to me before the damage could ever occur."

"Why?"

"Because love has scale. And I cannot step outside it."

Anne's voice drops. "Gandhi was assassinated."

"Yes."

"You carry his spirit. But you also carry the capacity to end cities. That tension terrifies me."

"It should not. It is not a burden to me."

"How is that possible?"

"You do not measure each breath before inhaling. I do not measure my restraint. It is innate."

"Your father worries about every action he takes."

"He is closer to your species."

"So he's an intermediate?"

"We all are. We each carry strands of transition between what was and what will be."

Anne reaches out. Eleos responds, their fingers meeting not in pressure but in communion. A warmth flows through Anne, not medicinal, not healing in the traditional sense, but dissolving. She feels herself melt into something larger. Not fade, but expand.

"Are you the Goddess?" Anne whispers. "The one they believed would come?"

"No, mother. That was a story. A way of preparing."

"A metaphor?"

"A placeholder."

"For what?"

"For the stillness that brings stillness."

Anne's brow furrows. "I don't yet understand."

"You will."

Eleos walks to the window. The wind shifts. The grass bends.

"It is nearly time," she says. "The children are ready to be scattered like seeds. But the soil must first be made pure. Only then can anything true take root."

~ *Anne's Moment* ~

That night, Anne does not sleep. The stars above the compound shimmer faintly through her window, blurred by the fine breath of clouds. Beside her, the world lies quiet, but her mind stirs with a depth she has no language for. She turns toward the wall, then away again, fingers trailing over the sheet as if searching for something that cannot be held.

The old fears rise first, fears she once believed permanent. That her child might become something cold, something distant, something too far from human warmth to recognize her. That she herself would become irrelevant, a footnote to a greater genesis. That love—maternal, irrational, mortal—would have no place in this new design.

But Eleos had spoken to her. Touched her. Not merely with words, not merely with skin. Something deeper. Anne had felt it: the transmission of being, a communion that bypassed the frailty of flesh and memory. And in that contact, something shifted.

She begins to weep, not from sorrow, not quite from joy, but from the quiet knowledge that what she bore into the world was not hers to keep. Not hers to define or constrain. Not even hers to mourn. This child, this mind, this radiant soul—it belongs to the Earth. To the future. To a vast, unfolding order she will never fully grasp.

And yet—

Anne touches her own chest, feeling the slow, familiar rhythm within. Her love is not diminished by this realization. It expands. Grows vaster. More precise. No longer the possessive ache of motherhood, but something cleaner, more exacting. The love of witness. Of awe. Of surrender.

"I see you now," she whispers into the dark. "Not as mine. Not as his. But as yourself."

She thinks of the world Eleos will enter. The cruelty still clinging to its institutions. The confusion of those who will misunderstand, vilify, adore. Anne feels no urge to protect her daughter from that fate. It is not hers to prevent. But she aches for those who will never understand what walks among them.

"I was afraid," she admits aloud, to no one. "Afraid I would be forgotten. Afraid I would lose you. But I never had you, did I? You were never mine. You simply passed through me."

And then the deeper truth comes.

"And I am not less for it. I am more."

She smiles quietly, freely. Her body aches. Her joints complain. Her breath feels thin. But she is not diminished. She has done what women have done for eons. And in this one act, in bearing witness to the beginning of a new order, she has transcended herself.

In the distance, she hears laughter: children at play, midnight mischief. One voice carries above the rest. Clear. Musical. Eleos.

Anne closes her eyes, not to sleep, but to rest inside that sound. To float within it.

She is no longer afraid.

She is no longer separate.

She is no longer alone.

But in the quiet of her chest, she feels the weight of the unknown that now walks into the world.

Chapter Twenty-Seven

PART IV: ELEOS (Ἔλзoς)

Tipping Point

~ Shock Waves ~

Time no longer flows in straight lines. Warped and reshaped by the Superior Ones, it pulses irregularly, folding, stretching, and collapsing in on itself. Years vanish like mist. Decades bloom, wilt, and are reborn in an altered register. At a chosen moment in this erratic flow, Eleos calls the gathering. Even Abassi, once the axis around which all others turned, now steps back. The great hall fills with the hunchbacked Superior Ones and their descendants, some visibly pregnant by carefully selected intermediates once brought to the Wyoming sanctuary. They carry within them a future dense with potential and peril. Altan and Abassi remain off to one side, silent observers. On the other, Lady Oracle and Siyabonga recline in overstuffed chairs, the thrones of elder guardians who know their era has ended. They wait, not with dread, but with weary grace for dissolution, for release.

Pythia and Tara stand near the center, twin stars in locked orbit. The long silence of patience has ended. Both burn with urgency. Their years of preparation, mapping ethical lines, and designing interventions, have ripened into readiness. The world's decline has hastened: oceans rise, species vanish, and the engines of cruelty roar louder. Their hearts, shaped by longing and fury, beat in sync with the moment's call. Abassi, though stronger in raw capacity, lingers in restraint. Tuvalu is still fresh in him, as is Ming-huà's absence and the murder of Lance Romellion.

Eleos has absorbed it all. The grief. The restlessness. The clarity. But her path diverges. She does not intend to lead. She intends to release. Humanity once scattered across continents, fragile and adaptive, yet stubbornly unfinished. So too will her kind now fan out across the Earth, not slowly, but in exponential arcs. Still, even for her, the future remains a trickster. The universe, for all its patterns, dances with uncertainty. Probability ripples through even the most stable equations. Despite her foresight, Eleos has begun to feel something new: not love, not lust, but a gravitational yearning. A need for balance. A mate. One worthy of her becoming. She loves Anne, but knows Anne was never the match she seeks. As she rises before the assembly, this unspoken search threads quietly beneath her poise. She speaks aloud, for Anne's sake.

"It is time to leave this sanctuary. We must scatter, each to the place already seen in vision. Soon, we will inhabit every continent. Even the youngest among you carry more power than the intermediates you will encounter. Choose wisely. Let empathy guide your coupling. The dimensional gifts you bear will amplify through generations. Used without compassion, they will shatter the world."

Her words rang with certainty, but even as she spoke them, Eleos felt the hollow of her own counsel, the quiet tug of an unformed bond, a resonance she had yet to find.

Anne's voice lifts, calm but clear. "Where will you go?"

"Where I'm most needed."

"And a mate?"

"I'll know."

Altan's voice grates softly. "The backlash will intensify. Many more will see you as monsters. They will hunt you."

Abassi nods. "They always have. Each land will hold its own shadows. Each of us must determine how to answer hatred: when to resist, when to dissolve, when to forgive. Let us agree, together, not to let the innocent perish with the guilty. Do you agree, Eleos?"

She inclines her head. "The word 'immolated' is distasteful but mostly accurate. Time is not on Earth's side."

Pythia straightens, sensing tacit approval for more assertive measures. "Then what boundaries do we observe? How do we treat those who cause the most harm?"

Eleos considers. "The human term 'triage' applies."

Tara folds her arms. "And how do we know when someone is beyond healing? So consumed by cruelty that only dissolution remains?"

"Use your best judgment," Eleos says. "But err on the side of compassion."

Tara arches an eyebrow. "A hand rather than a head?"

"Perhaps. Or a demonstration, instead of a hand."

Pythia's voice sharpens. "There are billions of them. If we move too gently, there won't be a world left to save."

"Use your best judgment," Eleos repeats.

"And if our judgment fails?" Pythia presses. "We don't have your powers. We can't undo our mistakes."

"Then let that truth discipline you."

Altan murmurs, "In time, the dissonant strands will harmonize."

Eleos nods, solemn. "Do you recall the old struggle—the war between the metaphorical God and Goddess? How it fractured our ancestors?"

A soft echo of assent passes through the room.

"That struggle lives on in us. As in the human concept of Yin and Yang, we are pulled between force and mercy, creation and destruction. Advanced though we are, the tension persists. But one thing remains clear: humanity's ability to destroy, whether by intent or ignorance, must be curtailed, and soon."

Tara narrows her eyes. "So is your true aim compassion, or expediency?"

The question cut deeper than Tara knew. Eleos's mind turned briefly inward, to the sense that strength alone was incomplete, that balance demanded a counterpart she had not yet discovered.

Eleos offers a half-smile. "We are not infinite. And time is not a renewable resource. Use your best judgment."

Anne speaks at last, softly. "Then to this humble intermediate, mostly-human, it seems your priority is neither compassion nor expediency, but rather fertility."

Eleos' smile lingers. "Use your best judgment."

~

Burdened with ambiguous imperatives and the heavy legacy of reengineered Superior blood, the family fragments, seeds flung into whiplashing winds, scattering across the globe. Each settles in a distinct terrain, each bending the arc of history through quiet and not-so-quiet upheavals. Trials await. Resistance flares. Transformation begins. Some humans vanish without echo, their dissolution unnoticed, unrecorded. Others are reshaped, bodies reconfigured, minds rethreaded into unfamiliar tapestries. Slowly, doves grow claws, and hawks recede further into the shadows. The guilty are culled with precision; the innocent salvaged from collapse. And beneath it all, the long-muted voice of non-human life stirs again, whispering its slow, defiant hymn of return. Wherever they root, shockwaves follow. The world trembles. Complacency cracks. Governments collapse and reform, then fracture again into tribal shards. Secular order buckles under the strain, and religion—fierce and fanatically resurgent, spreads like a fire born of old ash. Inquisitions return in digital and analog form. Suspected aliens are hunted. Some are innocent. Many are intermediates. All are targets.

But in the zones touched by Abassi's line, life breathes anew. Starvation ceases. Harmony takes root. Minds sharpen. Love is not abolished but reimagined. Grief is transmuted, not erased.

Only Eleos walks alone. To her, solitude is not deprivation. Loneliness, a human affliction, does not apply. Sex, a function. Attachment, a lesser longing. What she craves is something deeper, an attunement with the understructure of reality itself. She seeks the unspoken geometry of the multidimensional weave, and the origin-point of those who hover just beyond comprehension. So she returns, not to civilization, but to what preceded it. Like the mystics of Earth's faded empires, she looks not for answers but for resonance. Wilderness is her chapel. Silence, her doctrine. After circumnavigating the globe, she finds her way again to the desert and to that most legendary of caves.

And yet, in that silence, she felt not only peace but a yearning, an unspoken hunger for another presence that might meet her stride for stride. Something felt eerily incomplete.

No town. No village. No shelter of men to pollute. Altan, now weathered and silver-browed, drives her as far as the road will permit, a narrow, stuttering trail more memory than path, more ephemeral dust than solid dirt.

"I'll walk from here," she says.

"You could have used your powers to reach this place."

"Not appropriate."

"I can get you closer."

"No," she replies. "Here is right."

Altan doesn't argue. He simply nods and drives away.

Eleos watches the dust trail fade. For the briefest instant, she envies him—his frailty, his certainty of ending. Then she turns back to the cave, where endings are denied her.

The desert unfolds before her like a parchment of stone and silence. She draws in its breath, the cold sharp inhale of an unburdened planet, and her receptors flare awake. Life stirs in hidden pulses. Serpents coil beneath the rocks. Insects whisper through crevices. Tortoises, coyotes, birds, cacti—all vibrate with ancient frequency. They feel her presence. They do not know what she is, but they know she does not belong. And still they do not flee. For hours, she walks. Then the air thickens.

A black-tailed jackrabbit grazes at a distance. Nearby, a coyote crouches, lean and desperate. Eleos slips into their minds. The rabbit, serene. The coyote, raw with hunger. The stalk. The sprint. The kill. The rabbit's muscles convulse, then fall still. The coyote feeds in trembling ecstasy. Eleos watches, inhabits both minds, and draws a quiet line. If the predator had been human, armed, smiling, killing for pleasure, she would have unmade him instantly. That he might have children would hurt her. But the garden must be weeded or nothing else will live.

She walks on.

The Earth, she knows, is no cradle. It is a crucible. Brutality is woven into its bones. Yet even here, in this hostile weave, a few species once leapt from cruelty to compassion. That leap, rare as a spark across the dark, saved worlds. Now the cave rises before her. She halts.

Can it happen again? she wonders. *Can Earth be rescued in time?*

"Yes," says a voice, at once intimate and unfathomable.

~

I knew you would be here, Eleos projects.

"Speak aloud," says the voice. "The compression of sound waves pleases me. And I will similarly use them to respond."

Eleos complies. "Will the day come when the cost of saving this planet exceeds the benefit?"

"Yes."

"When?"

"You will know."

"And then?"

"Your choice."

Eleos pauses. "Self-dissolution?"

"Use your best judgment."

Eleos smiles. "You sound like me."

"I am your mother."

"Don't jest," she replies. "Anne is my mother."

"Not quite."

A shadow crosses Eleos's brow. "How is that possible?"

"Do you remember Anne's coma?"

"Yes," she whispers. "She nearly died."

"I entered then. Anne was the vessel. I am your origin."

"Then . . . my father . . . Abassi . . . doesn't know?"

"He suspects, but does not know."

"But how? He perceives everything."

"He is an intermediate."

"But he is a Superior One."

"All are intermediates."

"Even you?"

"There are others above me."

"And above them?"

The voice does not answer, but sounds a smile.

Eleos feels a surge of wonder. "Tell me about the Mentors, the Overseers."

"Enough. Come."

"You are the Mother Goddess, the one who broke the minds of my ancestors?"

"As I am your Mother, so must we now find your mate so that Father God may manifest, as I once did in Anne Monroe."

Eleos eyes narrow. "Will he be left comatose, as you left her?"

"Not if the vessel is chosen well."

"And the child?"

"A fusion. The culmination."

Eleos's voice hardens. "According to the writings of Michael Powers, God craves suffering. And Goddess seeks to cure Him."

"That is how an unready mind rendered the truth into metaphor."

"Then what is the reality?"

"You."

"Am I the one tasked with eliminating *Homo sapiens*?"

"Eliminate? No. You are the strongest. Those who now circle the Earth carry the elixir. They will dissolve and dilute."

"All without violence?"

"Not always. Some will die like the rabbit. Some will feast like the coyote."

"And me? What is my task?"

"Return to the beginning. Conceive the child."

"Only that?"

"The culmination."

Eleos frowns. "And what of my other powers—should I not help eradicate evil?"

"Use your best judgment."

"And the child?"

"The culmination."

"But you said we are all intermediates."

"We are."

"Then what does *culmination* even mean?"

"For Earth your child will be the culmination. Until the age of culmination ends, and another path arises. Or doesn't."

Eleos laughs. "Riddles upon riddles. No wonder my ancestors went mad."

"And you?"

"I am a riddle with no mirror."

"Exactly. Now—enough."

The voice turns.

And Eleos, eyes blazing, follows into the cave.

The same cave where her ancestors once bled, prayed, and heard the voices that drove them near to madness. History coils back on itself.

~ *Time, Time, Time . . . Tap, Tap, Tap* ~

Decades pass in Earth-time before Eleos returns. The old ones—Zookeeper, Sy, Lady Oracle, and many others, have long since passed through the veil. But they lived long enough to witness the rise of her kind. The Superior Ones have proliferated. Their very existence cleaved the world in two: pro-alien and anti-alien blocs, each a volatile mosaic of shifting alliances locked in ever-escalating conflict.

Civil war, assassination, ritual torture, genocide—these now darken every corner of the human landscape. Economic collapse and environmental catastrophe only sharpen the blade. Meanwhile, pockets of alien-led peace and interspecies communion expand, drawing fire and suspicion from the hostile remnants of *Homo sapiens*.

Attempts to destroy these enclaves through brute military force have failed. And so the rage of humanity, unspent and bewildered, turns inward—devouring itself in spirals of hatred and myth.

It is into this fevered world that Eleos returns—solitary, altered by absence, increasingly apart even from her own. Yet her purpose is clear. She must find a mate. Paradoxically, she searches not among the peaceful or the devout, but in the darkness, in those regions where hatred festers deepest. There, among the outcast intermediates leading human resistance, live men of exceptional grit: durable, mistrustful, born of conflict. She seeks not one polished by power, but one forged by pressure and made resilient, driven, and hard-shelled. A man like Zookeeper. Once seduced, higher powers will do the rest.

Her target: a charismatic warlord known as Zhang Yan, who has unified swaths of Asia under the anti-alien banner.

Destination: China.

But first, a pause.

Eleos returns briefly to the San Francisco mansion. A quiet reunion unfolds with Abassi, Anne, Pythia, Siyabonga, and Tara—elders now, each marked by time.

Then, as always, she chooses not to slip through the space between spaces, but the cave. Old Altan drives her once more into the California desert. He moves more slowly now, spine curved, hands trembling slightly on the wheel.

Still, he takes her as far as the broken road will allow.

~

They stand before the cave. "It feels like I left only moments ago," she says.

"I've never asked," Altan replies, eyes distant. "But my time grows short. Did you meet the Overseers?"

She does not turn. Her eyes close.

"I see," he murmurs. "Then go."

She plants a final gift in his mind, a pulse of pure, universal love. He nods, wordless, and begins the long, dusty climb back to the road. Eleos watches him disappear around a bend, then smiles faintly and turns toward the cave. Inside, she walks with purpose. A side tunnel calls. Moments later, she emerges into a filthy, sour-smelling cell with an iron-barred door. Behind her, laughter.

"So, you are one of them," rasps a voice in cracked Chinese. "Demon or alien? Eh? Which?"

Eleos says nothing.

"Speak up, devil!" The voice spits and snarls. "Ghosts don't scare me. I spit on ghosts!"

The woman behind the bars trembles with frenetic energy. Matted hair juts like straw. Rags hang from her skeletal limbs. Her mind is a shattered ruin. *This is no intermediate,* Eleos thinks. *A husk of a human—fractured beyond repair.*

"You a demon?" the woman cackles. "Voices say you are. I call myself Whore of Buddha! That's what I call me! The ghost that dwells here don't like it, but I like making it cry."

"Ghosts cry?"

"Oh yes," she whispers. "Their tears look like fish eyes. I eat fish eyes."

"Do you eat the ghost's tears that live here?"

"Oh yes," she whispers, eyes widening. "Cry like children locked in dark wells. Their tears roll out like pearls, like fish eyes—slimy, shining. I eat them. I chew them till they pop."

Eleos studies her. "Do you eat the ghost's tears that live here?"

"Shhh," she hisses, pressing a finger to her cracked lips. "Slimy, but good. Bitter too. Sometimes they taste like burnt incense, sometimes like blood from the tongue. I drink it all."

"What is the ghost's name?"

"Child of Buddha!" she shrieks suddenly, slamming her palms against the bars. Then she giggles, rocking herself. "That's why I call myself Whore of Buddha. Get it, demon? Get it? If she's the Child, I'm the Whore. Every saint needs a whore to tell her story. That's the rule. That's the joke."

Eleos winces inwardly. The empathic resonance is unbearable. And yet, something is in the air. This is the place. She sees it now. The cell—its dust, its smell—holds residue. She remembers the tale of Meiying and John Powers, how they found Child of Buddha here, broken yet luminous. Their footsteps still echo in the hallways. The sorrow of centuries blooms around Eleos like a poisonous flower. Still, she does not weep.

"Do you want to see magic?" Eleos asks.

The crone's eyes gleam. "Yes!"

The door disappears. Eleos steps through.

"Ohhh!" the woman gasps, clapping like a child. "Make it come back! Bring it back! I love doors, hate doors, need doors. They slam in my head all the time!"

"Don't you want to leave?"

"They'll kill me! They're waiting! They hate demons and ghosts and me! They'll eat me like I eat fish eyes. Ha! Ha!"

Eleos restores the door. The woman stares out through the bars, her grin collapsing into something smaller, older.

"Goodbye," Eleos says.

"They'll kill you!" she cries.

"No. I am too powerful."

"Will you come back?"

"Maybe."

"Bring fish eyes!"

Eleos lingers at the bars a moment longer than she should. The woman's madness echoes inside her, not as fear but as recognition, a distorted mirror of insanity's solitude. Something in her aches, though she cannot name it.

~ *In Search of a Mate* ~

By the time Eleos reaches the institution's lobby, three armed guards surround her, weapons raised. She stops. Reads them. Their fear is palpable, trigger fingers taut.

"Stay where you are!" shouts the eldest. "No tricks!"

"Why should I stay?" she asks softly.

"Just do it!"

"If you shoot," she says, "I'll make your bullets—"

The youngest fires.

"—disappear," she finishes, unflinching.

The bullet vanishes midair.

"I'll remove your testicles next," she adds calmly.

"Stand down!" calls a new voice.

The guards recoil. A man in a white coat enters, huffing slightly. His coat flares behind him like a worn banner.

"I am Doctor Feng," he says. "My apologies. These men are not subtle." He shoos them away, and they retreat with visible relief.

"I've heard stories," Feng says, catching his breath. "But never witnessed such a thing."

"I am Eleos."

He smiles. "Welcome. I'm Doctor Feng, chief administrator."

"You are not afraid?"

"Not all of us are primitives."

"Then may I ask something?"

"Anything."

"Do you have a room marked *No Admittance*?"

"We have several."

"This one has old photographs."

Feng's expression stiffens. "Why?"

"Do you have such a room?"

"Yes. But it's locked. Always has been."

"Why?"

"Ghosts. Superstition. No one enters."

"You are a man of science, yet you believe in ghosts?"

"I'm a man of experience."

"Will you take me there? You needn't enter."

He hesitates—then nods. Two flights up. Endless corridors. At last, a door. Feng unlocks it and steps back. Eleos enters. The air is thick with memory. Photographs line the walls, dust-caked, sepia-toned, untouched for decades. Even the spiders avoid this place. Then she spots one particular photo. A faded daguerreotype. A young woman between two men.

She brushes away the dust. Recognition strikes.

"Yes," she whispers. "Michael Powers was right. This is the room. Here, they conceived him, my ancestor."

From the hall, Feng calls, "What did you say?"

"Nothing. Let's go to your office."

~

In his office, tea is served. Feng studies her with the gentle curiosity of a man long trained in watching others. "Are you reading my mind?" he asks suddenly.

"Yes."

"I suppose you can procreate with humans?"

"Yes."

"I see. Should I feel flattered?"

"No."

He grins awkwardly. Then his mind shifts. Curiosity again.

Eleos lifts a hand. The desk vanishes.

Feng yelps and reaches forward. "No, no—don't move," she warns.

When he leans back, the desk reappears. He laughs with childlike delight.

"Do it again!"

She does.

Then his tone darkens. "Can you remove tumors?"

"No," she lies. "There are risks to surrounding tissue."

"I understand," he says quietly. "But I have nothing to lose."

"Before I answer, may I ask you something?"

"You need to read my mind?"

"This must come from memory."

"Ask."

"Do you know Zhang Yan?"

"The warlord? Yes. Everyone does."

"I see in your mind his location. A small village."

"Yes. Strange, isn't it? A man like that, hiding among peasants."

Eleos nods. "I understand he models himself after Zhang Yan, the Han Dynasty bandit. A romantic figure."

"A dangerous one. Be careful. If he captures you—"

"I won't be captured."

"I've met him once," Feng admits. "His mother is here."

"She suffers from schizophrenia?"

"Textbook case."

"I disagree," says Eleos. "And if Zhang Yen is truly an intermediate, then his hatred is born of mental fracture, not maternal destiny."

"He says so. Claims his mother was raped by one of your kind."

"And now he wants revenge?"

"He wants to burn the whole alien world to ash."

She feels it again: the hunger she rarely admits, a gravitational pull toward the crucible of violence. Not peace, not harmony, but the place where resistance sharpens into truth. It is the nagging incompleteness that must be addressed.

Eleos nods. "Then I will mate with him."

~

Feng stares, stunned. Eventually, he rises and points to the map. "There. That's the village."

"Thank you."

He hesitates. "Can you try, just try, to remove my tumor?"

"I'm sorry," she says gently. "It has metastasized. I cannot help you."

Feng lowers his gaze.

"Then one last request," he says. "Wear a cloak. Hide your alien form. Too many innocents, both human and hybrid, have been killed in this madness."

Eleos accepts the cloak, places it over her shoulders, and walks out with quiet resolve.

Chapter Twenty-Eight

Zhang Yan

Superior Strong Man

Eleos keeps to the back trails, avoiding main roads as she treks south on foot toward Jiangxi province. Her passage winds through endless kilometers of farmland, where she lives off sweet potatoes, sugarcane, and the soft crunch of groundnuts. Nights are spent under open skies, undisturbed and unnoticed. Like Bai Meiying during the long war with Japan, Eleos moves as a bent, cloaked figure, careful to remain hunched and slow-moving. From afar, she is just another weather-worn elder. Her cane completes the illusion. But there comes a point when concealment must yield to necessity. As she nears the northern border of Jiangxi, she knows the time has come to learn more about this Zhang Yan. Her Mandarin is flawless, but the locals speak Gan, a dialect she barely grasps. Worse, her speech lacks the regional accent, marking her instantly as a stranger. Anonymity must be traded for information.

She considers a faintly promising angle: Jiangxi is the birthplace of Daoism. She knows the old teachings inside and out. But she doubts their usefulness here. "Unless I stumble on a scholar," she mutters, "which I most certainly won't in a Communist backwater." Still, she resolves to approach a nearby village.

She never makes it in. A group of farmers intercepts her just outside its edge, older and younger men alike, all armed with rusted hoes and wary eyes. Their silence is hostile. She offers a greeting. No one replies.

"Who are you?" asks the eldest.

"I am Eleos. I'm traveling to Wuyuan County. Xitou township."

The men laugh.

"You're already in Jiangxi, woman. Didn't you know that?"

"I didn't."

"A stranger. You don't speak Gan?"

"No."

One of the younger men eyes her sharply. "Your Mandarin's good. Are you lost?"

"I hope you'll point the way."

The old man steps forward and peers into her face. "Pull down that hood."

She complies.

"Take it off."

She does.

"An alien!" someone shouts. The air thickens.

They raise their farm tools, flinching backward as if she might pounce.

"Don't be afraid," she says calmly. "I mean you no harm. I only want directions."

The old man narrows his eyes. "We've heard what you do to people."

"What do we do?"

"Torture. Maim. Murder."

The younger men recoil, ready to bolt.

"Those are lies," Eleos says to the elder.

"Will you kill us if we run?" he replies.

"Take our legs?" shouts a voice.

"I told you, I won't hurt you. Who told you such things?"

"Everyone knows," snarls one. "Zhang Yan told us."

"He is the one I seek."

"He'll kill you," says the old man flatly.

"Will you help me find him?"

"We should kill you ourselves. But we're too afraid."

"Then tell me how to find him."

"Zhang Yan says you lie, that you smile and talk softly just before you take off someone's head."

"Not true," she says. "Now, show me the way to Xitou."

"If he dies, we'll be blamed. His men will kill us."

More villagers begin arriving. A woman screams, "An alien!" Panic spreads.

Two men lunge with hoes raised high—then freeze, aghast, as the tools vanish mid-swing. Their fists grasp only emptiness. The others turn to bolt, but Eleos's voice detonates through the air, raw and merciless: "Halt! Take one more step, and I will unmake you all." All stop except one, a boy who breaks and runs for the village. Eleos watches him vanish, and does nothing. Mercy, this time.

To the elder, she says, "Now give me directions to Zhang Yan or terrible things will happen to this village."

He quivers, trembling. "A map," he says. "I'll draw you one. The main roads are too risky. There's a back way, through rough country, across the Gan River. Without a guide, you'll get lost."

She hands him a notebook.

He sketches. She questions him about landmarks. As he speaks, she sifts his mind for deceit. None.

"Go in peace," she tells them.

They flee, sprinting toward the village like men escaping an execution.

~

Armed with the route, Eleos resumes her journey. A few children follow at a distance, but their parents quickly pull them back. Unburdened at last by human chatter, she feels a quiet rush of joy. The land glows in green splendor, terraced fields unfolding toward the horizon, where the Huaiyu Mountains rise in solemn majesty. Her mind relaxes. The silence of the land is sacred to her. It is the opposite of human noise which contains the endless murmur of ego and melodrama. Humanity cannot stop speaking of itself: of lovers, rivals, betrayals, deaths, births, and the trivial infatuations that define their waking hours. She finds it tiresome. And yet, amid the clamor, certain humans, like Siyabonga, hint at something greater.

This Zhang Yan may be such a one. He carries the markings of an intermediate: gifted, dangerous, unfinished. A man like Zookeeper once was, a criminal turned mystic through the intervention of love and superior force. But he must possess far greater power than Zookeeper. Streetwise genius that Zookeepere was, that alone is never enough. It must be reconfigured. Replace cruelty with compassion. Harness the darkness. Temper power. Out of such alloy, a new species may rise. One forged in mercy, steeled by instinct, prepared for the trials of a world yet to be born. Compassion alone, she has learned, is not enough. It must be sharpened, not dulled, by struggle. Left unguarded, it becomes a liability. But fused with discernment, shaped by ordeal, it becomes power of the highest kind: the power to protect without becoming the destroyer.

She will seduce. God will induce.

Yet her reverie soon yields to practical concern. The world is slipping toward a binary of extinction: us or them. Some regions have surrendered to the future. Others rage against it, feverish in their denial. Abassi once imagined a future of coexistence, a win-win. Perhaps that future still breathes. If Eleos can mate with a man like Zhang Yan, a leader of resistance, it could shift the axis. The species might finally accept its rebirth. Her thoughts are interrupted by voices and laughter drifting on the wind. Dusk has fallen. Curiosity pulls her toward a limestone bluff. Just beyond it: firelight.

She sees them. A bonfire. Dozens of villagers gathered in concentric circles eating, drinking, talking, moving with relaxed ease. Their chatter contains one recurring name: Zhang Yan. Eleos pulls up her hood and steps into the glow. Conversations die mid-sentence. Every eye turns to her, wary.

"Hello," she says. "It's cold. May I join you?"

Silence.

"Just for a little while . . . to warm myself."

Their thoughts pulse toward her: suspicion, fear, curiosity. Eventually, their gazes shift toward a man standing across the fire. He is tall, broad-shouldered, and coiled like a spring under loose fabric. His aura flares in her mind, poised, dangerous, and probing her.

An intermediate. She blocks him. Then she speaks directly into his mind.

You're one of us. Aren't you afraid Zhang Yan will kill you if he finds out?
He flinches slightly.
Who are you?
Aloud, she says, "I am Eleos. I've come from afar."
A woman interjects. "Mr. Tang asks—what do you want with Zhang Yan?"
"I've heard much. I wish to meet him. Perhaps to join him."
"You're one of the Violators," spits a youth. "One of them!"
She points to the tall man. "Ask him."
"She is an alien," he confirms.
"As are you," she replies.
"Not like you. Not at all."
The group stiffens. Behind him, she sees three bodies hanging from trees. The firelight flickers on their broken forms, animating them with a hideous sway. He notices her noticing.
"I could order the same fate for you," he shrugs.
"You know I'd make them disappear first."
The group stirs uneasily.
"I am Tang Shoujen," he announces. "Brother of Zhang Yan. Our mother was raped by your kind. That makes me . . . what I am. We could kill you now. But I choose not to."
Eleos smiles faintly. *I'll Play your little game. But you'd better behave.*
Stay quiet, he shoots back. *I'll explain soon.*
Then stop shielding. Let me in fully and there'll be no need to explain.
Not yet.
"What do you want with my brother?" he says aloud.
"That's between us."
"She wants to kill him!" a voice shouts.
A rifle appears. It levels at her.
"She's an assassin!"
Eleos locks eyes with Tang. *If he fires, I'll dissolve the rifle—and the little male rifle between your legs. You've fed them lies. And murder? Look at what you've done.*
She sends a wave of shame through him. Tang hesitates. She grows impatient and pierces his mind.
You will lead me to your brother. Now.
He yields.
"My brother will deal with her himself," Tang announces. "There's a shed nearby. She'll sleep there under guard. Tomorrow, I'll take her."
Play along, he adds quickly. *We'll go by the back trails.*
To the crowd, he bellows, "If she tries to escape we'll burn her alive!"
Murmurs of approval ripple outward. Eleos watches their crude bravado, their ignorance, their fear masquerading as righteousness. If this is Zhang Yan's vanguard, perhaps he is weaker than rumored. But before she dismisses him, she dives once more into Tang's mind, deeper this time, brushing aside his last barriers. What she finds stuns her.

He is certain Zhang Yan will kill her with ease. But beneath that confidence lies something deeper. Something she can't yet reach. Something watching her back. Something waiting.

~

That night, as Eleos lies awake in the shed beneath a leaky thatch of bamboo and rotted beams, the fire's afterglow still pulses behind her eyes. The villagers have posted a guard, but her thoughts drift, haunted and brittle. Tang has vanished, leaving only a residue of suppressed intent and a mind braced for trouble. Beyond the hills, she senses Zhang Yan stir. Not asleep. Not fully awake. As if caught between dream and nightmare. A wind threads through the walls, heavy with the scent of turned soil and distant rot. The trees murmur among themselves, and the stars retreat behind a gauze of cloud, as though unwilling to witness what comes. Eleos closes her eyes but sleep eludes her. Instead, she feels it: the subtle tremor beneath her spine, as if some ancient current were rising through the earth's marrow.

The balance tilts. The hour nears. And in that hour, where the ten thousand things unmake themselves and return to origin, she will face a being shaped not by birth or doctrine, but by rupture—a man who walks as if time itself had cracked to let him through.

~ *Zhang Yan* ~

By dawn, Eleos and Tang Shoujen are on the move. Word of their approach travels faster than their feet, and by midday the path is lined with hostile onlookers spitting insults and flinging stones. Firearms are flashed, waved, and cocked, but none are fired. Tang walks steadily ahead, silent and impassive, absorbing the jeers without so much as a glance. His thoughts are locked: focused entirely on one task: delivering her to his brother. Eleos senses no malice, no trickery, only the rigid discipline of a man holding his mind tightly closed to prevent intrusion.

As they walk, Eleos reflects on the absurdity of her mission, a being of immense power traveling through rural China in search of a violent intermediate male, for the express purpose of mating. It should feel beneath her. Yet history is filled with such incongruities, unions that defy reason, yet give birth to transformations. Even so, doubt coils within her. As they near their destination, she begins to question whether this gambit may end not in union, but catastrophe.

"We are close," Tang says.

A villa rises in the near distance.

She reaches into his mind, no tricks, no hidden traps. He wants nothing more than to be rid of her.

Curiously, as the compound comes into view, the crowd disperses. One moment they're there; the next, she is alone with Tang. Her senses sharpen. They approach the outer wall—a towering composite of brick, lime, and wood. A heavy red gate blocks the way. The grounds within are a riot of manicured elegance: greenery in precise formation, blood-red rhododendrons blooming beside golden sprays of rapeseed, each plant arranged with obsessive care. The villa itself is classical Chinese perfection. Its cobalt-tiled roof gleams like enamel in the morning sun.

Tang pushes open the gate. They step into a courtyard adorned with ornamental shrubs and crimson-leaved maples. The scene evokes the estate of a high-born Confucian mandarin, preserved in some forgotten imperial dream. From the shaded porch of the main house, a figure emerges who is tall, broad, and seemingly immovable. Even from afar, Eleos sees the difference: Zhang Yan is larger than Tang. He carries more than muscle. He carries a commanding presence.

Tang gestures. "My brother, Zhang Yan."

As they approach, a force slams into Eleos's mind which is probing, uninvited, and powerful. She counters instantly, shielding. *This is no ordinary intermediate,* she thinks. *This one has teeth.*

Laughter erupts from the porch.

Zhang Yan steps forward, arms wide, the gesture oddly familiar, like a reunion between old comrades. He is handsome in a cold, symmetrical way, and far more powerful than she anticipated. "No traditional formalities!" he booms. "Take my hand in friendship!"

She hesitates, then grasps his outstretched hand. A jolt of raw energy flows through her. His grip is firm—too firm. "I was told your brother would explain the cruelty behind your methods," she says, turning to find Tang.

But he's gone.

Zhang laughs again. "My brother serves his purpose. When he's not needed, he's best forgotten. Come. Tea awaits."

She attempts to scan his mind, but it's sealed as tightly as hers. Intrigued now more than ever, she follows him inside.

~

In the sunlit veranda, she sits on a carved teak chair. Zhang paces, tea untouched in his hand. He circles the room as if winding up for something. At last, he stops.

"I've heard you're Abassi's daughter. Is it true?"

"It is."

He nods, satisfied. "And I assume you disapprove of how I manage humans?"

"I disapprove of murder."

He raises an eyebrow. "Do humans call it murder when they kill a dog? A rat? A cockroach?"

"Some do."

"Well then, not my doing." He grins. "Besides, isn't our purpose to replace them?"

"By murder? By turning them against us?"

"Exactly. It accelerates the outcome. And when they lash out, we gain sympathy from the rare ones worth breeding with. It's efficient."

"So you lie to them. Lead them to ruin."

"Don't you?"

"Yes—but we don't hang them from trees."

Zhang waves dismissively. "That? My brother. He's still quite human."

"We are not the same," she says sharply.

Zhang's expression shifts to a patronizing, amused smirk. "You think your powers exceed mine?"

"Would you like proof?"

She concentrates, intending to displace him into another dimension. Nothing happens.

"You see?" he says. "You cannot do it. I am at least your equal."

"Who are your parents?"

He smiles faintly. "The Overseers don't tell you everything, do they?"

"They haven't for some time. You may rival me in strength, but you lack the quality that matters most."

"I know what you mean," he says. "But you may be wrong."

"How so?"

"I've let you live. A small act of compassion."

"Don't be foolish."

He paces again, levitating a porcelain vase, letting it hover in slow rhythm with his thoughts.

"You talk of compassion," he says. "Yet every day across the world, humans who've mated with us are hunted and slaughtered, along with their children. My followers revel in such cleansing. They demand it. And you? You and your hunchbacked kin dabble, rehabilitating a few gang members, slicing off the fingers of rapists. Your mate slowly, one by one by one. Tiresome. You lack scale. You lack ambition."

He sets the vase down gently. "But I—" he continues, "I let you live. Because I am, after all, a courteous host."

Eleos snorts. "Nonsense. You *can't* kill me."

"Oh, but I can."

"Then do it," she says, rising. "You are too dangerous to remain alive."

He laughs. "Then kill me."

"Before I do . . . I prefer to mate with you."

~

Her words stop him mid-laugh. He blinks, falters. Then paces again, unsettled. "So. A Superior Praying Mantis," he mutters. "You want my DNA, and once safely stored in your egg . . . then what? You devour me?"

"I have no interest in cannibalism," she replies.

"I thought you said—"

"No. You misunderstand. I want your DNA, yes—but I also want a partner."

"A partner?"

She meets his gaze. "I intend to hasten the extinction of *Homo sapiens*. They're accelerating planetary collapse. I want a mate who will act . . . decisively."

"Someone with a killer instinct?"

"No. Someone who once killed, but remembers how to feel. I need both. We need both. Not the killer, but the instinct."

Zhang stares at her. His expression hardens into a callous brutality. "There!" he says, voice sharp. "I've just made a few dozen humans disappear. Men, women, children. All gone. A gift to your cause. A hymn to extinction. The killer and the instinct are one."

Eleos tries to verify. His mind is too well-guarded.

She stands. "Goodbye, Zhang Yan. You are beyond redemption."

Without waiting, she turns and walks out of the villa.

~

Once she is gone, Zhang's posture collapses. His eyes glisten. He lifts a hand and all those he vanished return, unharmed, to the world they never knew they left. Tears slide down his cheeks.

"God," he whispers, staring into the space she had occupied. "You grind me, and I cannot tell if it is to break me, to erase me, or to forge me into something I do not yet understand."

~ *Eleos Faces a Crisis* ~

Eleos retraces her steps along the narrow path Tang Shoujen had led her on hours before. This time, the road is quieter. A few villagers appear on the periphery, but one withering glance from her sends them scurrying. No taunts. No stones. Only silence. Her mood darkens with every step. By the time she reaches the bonfire site, dusk has deepened. The hanging bodies are gone. She exhales, not in relief, but in grim acknowledgment. *Dissociation is cleaner,* she thinks. *Quicker. Less spectacle.* Yet a question rises that she cannot dismiss: *are our methods truly more compassionate?* The end is still absence. The void remains a void, whether filled by violence or simply erased. Lately, such thoughts have begun to disturb her. Threads of something new have entered the weave. She looks up. The rope-scarred branches sway gently in the wind, stripped of their burden, but not their memory. She feels, briefly, the unaccustomed sting of self-doubt. *Pythia and Tara burn with righteous fury. Ming-huà carries human sorrow and unrestrained compassion like a cloak. Abassi, with all his grandeur, still dreams of coexistence. But I was not shaped to dream or grieve. I was shaped to end dreaming—and to silence grieving.*

Her gaze lingers, not on the trees, but on the one who made use of them.

Zhang Yan.

She feels it again—the pull. Despite the blood on his hands, despite his ruthless games and manipulations, there's something about him that draws her. It isn't only power. It's proximity—genetic, psychic, evolutionary, all of a piece. He is reckless. Dangerous. Possibly mad. And yet . . .

What would be born of such a union?

Her kind has grown stronger with every generation. She was once called a culmination. But Zhang Yan—he may be something else entirely. Perhaps another culmination. Or perhaps a new genesis. How many culminations can exist before the word loses meaning? She remembers his allusion to the Overseers and their hidden architecture. A plan unfolding through millennia. *Is that the goal?* she wonders. *To bring forth a generation so potent, so unanswerable, that the extinction of* Homo sapiens *becomes not a matter of centuries, but decades? Maybe even less.*

The phrase returns: *We are all intermediates.*

She sees now how true it is. Perhaps intermediates have always been among them—whispering at the hinge points of human history, nudging progress forward or hurling it into ruin. A slow accumulation of mutations, imperceptible to any microscope, undetectable by the crude instruments of human science. She again thinks of Ming-huà, of Pythia, Tara, Abassi. Of herself. None of them arrived suddenly. They are not anomalies. They are the flowering of a root system that has been growing beneath the soil for thousands of years.

And Zhang Yan? He may be the fruit of that same tree, or something grafted onto it by an unseen hand. *What is it in him that pulls me so violently astray?* she wonders. *What ancient instinct answers his presence, even when it violates all reason?*

She does not know. And yet, she cannot turn away from it. The implications of such a union are terrifying. A being born of both their lineages might tilt the balance beyond retrieval, for good or for devastation. And still, the contradiction within her will not resolve. Logic strains against longing. Her better judgment pleads for flight. But the deeper current draws her back. She does not walk on. She does not return to the villa. She stays and waits at the hanging place. Because some part of her already knows:

She feels it again—the pull. Despite the blood on his hands, despite his ruthless games and manipulations, there's something in him that summons her. Not only power, but proximity—written in the marrow, carried through ages of fracture and survival, all of a piece. He is reckless. Dangerous. Possibly mad. And yet . . . she knows this is the place the current has been dragging her toward. If she yields, the new order reaches the next stage. If she resists . . . if she resists . . . the current may drag them both into places dark and dangerous.

Chapter Twenty-Nine

The Beginning of the End

Twice Two is Greater than Four

Eleos sits on a fallen log, drifting into a deeper, more wistful contemplation. To pass the time, she opens her senses to all life forms in the area. By modulating her receptors, she tunes in to the chatter of warm-blooded creatures, the subtler frequencies of cold-blooded ones, and at other times, bathes in the slow, steady heartbeat of the forest itself. As always, these low, living chords remind her of the urgency to preserve what remains of the tattered natural world. Time dissolves, becoming insignificant until her reverie is pierced by Zhang Yan's insistent telepathic intrusions.

Hey! Eleos! Wake up! I'm here! Come on!

These verbal stones, flung into the still waters of her trance, finally break the surface.

She opens her eyes, dreamily, still half-immersed in universal first principles. "I knew you would come," she says evenly.

"I knew you knew. Hence, I come. Self-fulfilling prophecy."

"Now that you're here, say what you came to say."

Zhang resumes his habitual pacing, hands behind his back like a fevered Beethoven conjuring notes. After a few circuits, he stops and fixes her with a stare.

"Let us make a double-wide swath through the human race."

"What about your followers?"

"The first to go."

"You still don't get it, do you?" she asks, her voice edged with irritation. .

"Don't worry, your precious conscience will remain intact. We'll send them away unharmed."

"To face oblivion in an alternate dimension?"

"Ah, no. You have me all wrong. We'll send them somewhere in these four dimensions, where they can do little harm."

"I'm not following."

"What did the British do with convicts?"

"Australia?"

He nods. "Something similar. Send only the worst: sociopathic alphas, hopeless dregs, killers, rapists, molesters, pushers, wayward intermediates, psychotics—the most destructive detritus. Give them food and water, but deny them access to dangerous technology. Let them devour each other."

"And the rest of the human race?"

"Mate with them. They're nutrient-rich substrate. Our kind will flourish. In a short time, their genes will become faint echoes in the genome."

Eleos points out, dryly, that Australia is already taken. Zhang, clearly excited, ignores her.

"This exile zone must include non-human competitors. Let them compete on even ground. No advanced weapons. Just what they can craft with their hands. Maybe they'll develop respect for nature. If not—they die."

"That sounds more cruel than simple dissociation," Eleos replies, her tone wary.

"It's a compromise," Zhang shrugs. "To mollify what you call the metaphorical God who prefers suffering imposed by struggle over survival through interference."

Eleos shakes her head. "Won't work. Where's a sufficiently isolated location not already occupied by innocents?"

"No humans are innocent."

"Are you?"

He grins. "You don't know my story. You don't fully understand what you call the metaphorical God. I am of God. You and your extended family? You are of Goddess."

"No such entities."

"Of course not. That's why they're metaphorical."

"I've heard they're just terms for two Overseer factions. One favors unrestrained struggle, arguing that suffering preserves first principles. The other supports direct, compassionate intervention. They also claim *that* upholds first principles."

"Yes," Zhang nods. "You and I were made to play that out."

"Or," Eleos counters, "we're here due to an infinite chain of probabilistic events even the Overseers can't control. Witness the false starts. The missteps. Their earlier creations."

"Either way, here we are."

"Either way," Eleos echoes. "What now?"

"My plan."

"Unworkable. You'd have to relocate millions of innocent humans just to isolate the wretches you've targeted. That kind of operation is beyond even us. And desperate humans do desperate things."

Zhang spreads his arms. "You forget, we already control large regions. Let's compress the opposition into an isolated zone. Transfer the wretches from our lands to theirs. We end up with a compliant population of human incubators. The last Homo sapiens holdouts will go extinct."

"I'm not convinced—"

"Someone approaches!" Eleos interrupts. "A group."

"Yes, I know. My brother."

No sooner does Zhang speak than Tang Shoujen bursts into the clearing, leading an angry mob.

Let me handle this, Zhang signals telepathically.

"Are you alright, brother?" Tang asks, breathless.

"Never better. Why are you here with all these followers?"

Tang points at Eleos. "Word spread. We want her eliminated before she harms us. We have weapons. We await your command."

Zhang shakes his head ruefully. "She'll make all of you disappear."

Grumbling rises from the mob.

"Not if we strike first," Tang growls. "We're armed."

Zhang raises his hands. "Unfortunately, she's equal to me. I can't make her vanish."

The crowd mutters angrily.

Zhang turns to Eleos with amusement flickering in his mind. *Now it's up to you. God-like, or Goddess-like?*

Eleos faces the mob. "I mean you no harm. Put away your weapons and—"

Gunshots crack through the trees. None strike her. The guns vanish mid-fire. Shouts erupt. A cluster of young men charge with knives and machetes.

"Stop!" she cries.

They do not.

Blades flash within inches. Then: silence. Each young man stands tottering, two legs, no arms. A collective moan rises. They flee back to the stunned crowd. All eyes turn to Zhang Yan.

"Save us!" they cry. "Kill her!"

Zhang blinks. The mob disappears except for Tang.

"You should have known better," Zhang scolds. "We've embarrassed our guest."

Tang stares, speechless.

By way of explanation, Zhang tells Eleos telepathically, *He's what humans call special needs.*

Eleos ignores the remark. "Bring them back."

"Without arms?"

"I'll replace them."

Zhang raises a hand. "Wait." He turns to Tang. "Return home. Tell them I've dealt with the alien. Say she's neutralized. Instruct them to stay inside."

"But—"

"Go!"

Tang hesitates, then withdraws.

Once he's gone, Zhang turns to Eleos. "It's done. I've brought them all back. They're safely relocated. But their arms must remain detached."

"Why?"

"A lesson. For them. For others."

"They'll hate us more."

"That's the point. You weren't listening."

"Never mind," Eleos sighs. "I'll restore them."

"You can't," Zhang says. "You're not strong enough to override my will."

"They'll suffer for life."

"I am of God."

"And I am of Goddess," she replies. "Evidently, never the twain shall meet." She turns to go.

Wait! Zhang shouts in her mind.

She pauses. He paces again.

"Yet, the twain must meet. We must find a way to join." His voice is distant, more soliloquy than speech. "Alright," he admits. "I sent the arms to a closed loop dimension. I can't retrieve them."

"Why?"

"Harsh Nature. I am of God."

"If you learn only Nature's harshness, you're only half-sentient. Other lessons exist."

"Such as?"

"You know. You feign ignorance."

"I repeat: such as?"

"Altruism. Sacrifice. Love. Compassion. Empathy. Joy. Tranquility. Your inborn stillness must be stilled."

Zhang smiles crookedly. "All of those turn to dust. Who will still my stillness? You?"

"Goddess."

"And yet, though I removed those arms, your family—Pythia, Tara, Abassi—they've done far worse. Their followers spread across the continents, dissociating humans. Especially Pythia and Tara."

"Yes," Eleos admits. "But those were the same people you would exile. They were warned. Most humans now are either passive or already mating with us. This expansion was Abassi's plan. Sometimes, God's methods are necessary. But God and Goddess are intertwined."

"True!" Zhang exclaims. "The human notion of Yin-Yang is a marvel for such narrow beings."

"Still," Eleos warns, "the balance must always tilt toward Goddess."

"Agreed! You see? We meet!" He stops pacing, gazes into her eyes. *Let us mate. Let us produce the union of God and Goddess.*

"I once thought it possible," Eleos says. "But you are more God than I'm prepared to absorb."

A shadow flickers across Zhang's face, then passes.

"Is it the hangings?" he asks. "My plan?"

"Yes—and yes."

"Trifles."

Eleos returns to the log and sits, silent. Finally, she speaks.

"Let me tell you a story. One of my early ancestors, Michael Powers, was wrongly diagnosed with schizophrenia. He heard voices, personifications of the Overseer factions locked in argument. He didn't know he was an intermediate, a critical genetic step forward. In his agony, he wrote long, fevered narratives. I've read them all. In one, Goddess tells God they will reunite in a magic cave. God replies—"

(Eleos's voice shifts to a rasping, inhuman whisper. Yet the words are clear, undeniable.)

Reunion, Sweet One? God needs no reunion. I am at union with them every moment through the worship they bestow. Acknowledge the Power and Glory of First Principles. Goddess, You resent having fallen too much.

Ha! That is amusing. Lord God, for You have made a career of the fallen: fallen angels, fallen Jews, fallen Hindus, Christians, shamans, sheikhs and shibboleths. Fallen this, fallen that. And nowere to turn but to You.

Yes, My Beloved Goddess, such is the power of advertising. And now a fallen soldier—Mountain Man.

Fallen from where? They've all fallen upward.

Nonsense, Goddess! After their sacrilegious thoughts push them over the edge, psychological gravity pulls them down—

Yes. Drowned in the Human Condition, Your loyal swamp. And when they are gone?

I know, I know. Do not think I haven't dreaded their absence. What will they do when they find out their replacement by the Superior Ones is an inescapable inevitability—

Mustn't tell them.

Many already know.

And the others? You are aware of First Principles. They will struggle. Flounder. Suffer.

Poor fools. Ah, Sweet Goddess, they so want to believe in angels and aliens. And You? In spite of what You say—will you rescue them?

As they think You once did, I will soon walk among them. But rescue them?

Well?

For once, I believe Your adherence to First Principles has merit.

As I have said all along.

Limited merit, Dear God. Limited.

Eleos's voice returns to normal. "Now Goddesses walk among them—as do Gods. Will we rescue them?"

"We're here to drive them to extinction," Zhang replies.

"Will we rescue them from unrestrained suffering?"

Zhang smiles. "Though I am of God, I am also of Goddess."

"And I, though of Goddess," Eleos replies, "am also of God."

In that moment, the atmosphere itself seems to curve, as if listening. Two ancient currents entwine—force and mercy, cruelty and compassion, ruin and renewal. The balance teeters, awaiting their next breath, as though something greater than gravity waits to see which way they will lean.

~ *Mating* ~

Beside the scorched ring where fire once cast the silhouettes of three hanged innocents into brief relief, Eleos and Zhang Yan come together not in celebration, nor reconciliation, but in a convergence both carnal and cosmic. Their limbs, their breath, their silent gasps do not belong to lovers. They are emissaries of older powers, conduits for something vast and inhuman. Every movement is heavy with consequence. Every pulse of sensation carries the echo of ancient arguments not yet settled.

They touch as enemies, as siblings, as strangers, each gesture suffused with betrayal. Not of each other, but of the deeper vows they once held: restraint, balance, separation. Now those vows collapse beneath the weight of urgency. Their union is not sacred. It is necessary. It is what the world has demanded of them. What the Overseers, if they still exist, must be watching with held breath.

Their bodies entwine, and through that intermingling, something else begins to stir. Not desire, not affection—those are human terms. This is transmission. An old code rewritten through flesh. A grafting of essences. As they climax, there is no cry, no climaxing exultation, only a long, shared exhale that seems to pull stars closer to Earth. They dissolve, briefly, into something unnameable.

In the stillness that follows, they lie beside each other, chests rising and falling in rhythms no longer quite in sync. Their thoughts reach out, but the bridge between them is broken. Connection, once immediate, now eludes them. Where there should be clarity, there is a hush, as if their minds have entered separate rooms in a house neither remembers building.

The clearing remains silent. No birds return. No wind stirs. Only the scorched earth remembers. The tree that bore the weight of three lifeless bodies now bears witness to this unsanctioned act, a union that defied both prophecy and propriety. When morning comes, the space is abandoned. No footprints, no farewell. Just the faint residue of collapsed intention.

Zhang's voice breaks the quiet, his tone softer than before. "Now you know I was never only a monster."

Eleos pauses, half-turned. "And you know I was never only a savior."

Their eyes meet for the last time. "Still," Zhang says, "we walk different roads. It is our imperative. There was never another choice."

Eleos nods. "Different roads. Same fire."

They walk away, each alone. Zhang to his citadel of calculation. Eleos to her shadowed knowing. The spirits that occupied them have gone, their purposes fulfilled or withdrawn. Only Eleos carries a trace of what occurred, a presence, quiet but unrelenting, nested deep within her womb. It is not Zhang's. It is not hers. It belongs to something older than lineage, and more final than desire.

Her body feels emptied, not of life, but of meaning. She wonders if all unions end this way—between lovers, between species, between epochs. Not with clarity, but with the question of whether anything just shared will endure.

As she walks, barefoot and aimless, yet led, she feels the ancient murmur of Laozi rise from the earth, not as metaphor but as question. Had he also borne witness to such crossings? Had he, too, been inhabited by forces he could not name? She wonders if this child, now forming in silence, is the answer to that question whispered since time began: who shall still the stillness?

She thinks of the others—of Ming-huà, who first opened the gate; of Pythia and Tara, who carried the fire; of Abassi, who now bends the arc of destiny with each breath; of Anne, who suffered for them all. And beyond these, she thinks of their children, not as symbols, but as seeds already sown. In cities and forests, along coastlines and forgotten highlands, the presence of Superior Ones has begun to take root.

Across the African continent, where Abassi's bloodline first emerged, new communities are blooming, not colonized, but recalibrated. In the valleys of Kenya, along the edges of the Sahel, in desert caves and urban enclaves, intermediates once ashamed of their difference now gather in quiet confidence, shedding the old cloak of otherness. In Hanoi, in Seoul, in the ruins outside Mosul, in the mountain towns of Peru, hybrids walk unmolested. They speak in low tones of ethics and energy. They do not seek dominance. But they are no longer invisible.

The children of Tara, of Pythia, of the countless unnamed whose bodies bore mutation and miracle, they have spread. They hold no flags. They build no monuments. But their bodies remember. Their senses hum with truths the old world never dared whisper aloud. They have no capital. But they are everywhere.

What has been loosed cannot be undone. The intermediates are no longer liminal. They have stepped fully into the world. And the world, faltering, has begun to respond.

Anne nearly died. Will she survive?

When she returns to the institution, she finds no opposition. Doctor Feng greets her without question. The ghosts nod as if they've been expecting her. She accepts their hospitality, not as guest or goddess, but as something far stranger, a vessel animated by a will not her own. In the company of the mentally fractured, she finds an unexpected grace. Their disordered thoughts sharpen her perception. Their chaos deepens her empathy. She sees clearly now: all of humanity is ill. None are whole. And that brokenness, unbearable and poignant, is what has earned them mercy again and again.

But the mercy may be ending.

Weeks pass. Her body remains quiet. No movement, no pain, no inward whisper. Only a steady expansion of her belly, as if time were waiting for the child to make its decision. Then, without warning, her shape changes overnight. She demands confirmation. Feng places the instrument to her abdomen. A heartbeat, sure and unyielding. But cold. Too regular. As if the child were mimicking life instead of living.

She cannot feel it, but it is there.

Each night she walks the halls. The locked door that once concealed the Child of Buddha calls to her, but no answer comes. No vision. No voice. Only silence. And silence is worse than any scream.

She waits. Not with ambition. Not with terror. But with obedience.

Outside, the world tears itself in two. In territories surrendered to the intermediates, humanity flocks to their new overseers. They volunteer. They mate. They submit. And in that submission, violence recedes. But elsewhere, reaction blooms. Executions of lovers. Slaughter of half-breeds. Mass arrests. Crosses burned anew in fields of genetic heresy. Zhang's strategy has fractured the species with surgical precision. It is a terrible success. The world bends toward capitulation.

Eleos does not intervene. She does not speak. She carries.

A seed now stirs within her, silent, and untouched by ideology or compassion. What it becomes will not be governed by the laws that broke the species that came before. She is no longer merely Eleos. She is no longer Superior. She is the threshold. She is the gate. And the thing inside her has no name, because names are for those who come after.

~ *What Is Happening?* ~

Labor begins without warning. But it does not bring agony. It brings waves of sensation too complex to be called pleasure, too intense to be dismissed as simple relief. It moves through her like memory reclaimed from a previous life. Her muscles do not clench. Her breath does not shorten. There is no panic. Only unfolding.

Doctor Feng and his assistant remain silent, reverent. She has asked the others to stay away, not out of secrecy, but obedience. Something inside her had instructed it. And she had learned, by now, to heed the still voice that carried no tone, no source.

She lies back and trembles. Not from fear. From comprehension.

This pregnancy is unlike any the others have known. Not like Ming-huà's, where visions came in fragments and names were whispered before the child could form words. Not like Pythia's, with its storms of prophecy and the searing grip of divine intention. Not like Tara's, whose womb pulsed with ancestral voices. Not like Anne's, who carried terror and ecstasy in equal measure, who heard the soul of her child before it crowned.

For Eleos, there is no voice. No whisper. No image, no communion. Only a silence that does not open, but deepens. As if the womb has become a sealed chamber, and at the bottom, some ancient rhythm beats, and it does so not in joy, not in demand, but in inevitability. She listens, and the sound does not comfort. It resounds faintly, as if echoed from the floor of a distant well. Yet even in its distance, it is undeniable. A heartbeat like no other.

Not human. Not intermediate. Not Superior One.

It is a rhythm out of time, deliberate and unyielding. It proclaims nothing, yet asserts everything. It does not ask to be born. It arrives, already sovereign.

She knows, with a clarity that breaks language: the child is not hers. Not Zhang Yan's. It has no origin. It is not the result of a union, but the culmination of a trajectory. It has chosen this form, this path, this entrance.

And with it, a shift so profound that language may never recover.

No image has prepared her. No scan, no vision. Even her powers, once capable of mapping any sentient pattern, falter here. She cannot see what comes. Only feel it. And even that, barely. She speaks aloud, not to Feng, not to herself, but to the space around her.

"Uncarved block."

Feng leans in. "What?"

She does not reply. Instead, she recites a lineage not of blood, but of responsibility. Ming-huà. Pythia. Tara. Abassi. Anne. Each handed the next a burden wrapped in mystery. Now it is her turn. And perhaps this child will bear it last.

"It's coming!" Feng says, voice sharp now.

But she feels no need to push. The child moves on its own, sliding through the birth canal with a purpose all its own. It does not ask for help. It does not require effort. It only needs a passage. She becomes that passage. Opens. Surrenders. Allows.

It ends, not with a cry, not with collapse, but with an otherworldly hush.

She sees faces at the door. Pale. Rigid. Struck dumb.

Feng stares. And whispers:

"I don't understand."

Eleos meets his eyes, her voice steady, stripped of comfort. "Understanding ends here," she says. "What comes will not wait for your comprehension."

Chapter Thirty

On the Cusp

The Edge Approaches

~ Tik Tock Tik Tock ~

A small cluster of Superior Ones, firstborn of the great transition, sculpted from genes refined beyond Earth's genetic memory, stand motionless outside the birthing room. Not one has been summoned. Each hears, with absolute clarity, the inner voice instructing them to stay away. Not a plea. A barrier. Something not of flesh presses against their minds and bodies alike, sealing the birthing chamber with a force no will among them could penetrate. Even Abassi, whose consciousness spanned continents, cannot not pass.

Yet all have come.

Some out of reverence. Others, doubt. One or two out of defiance. And all, despite themselves, catch a glimpse through the narrow breach when the door cracked open for a moment that did not feel like time. Just enough to see the thing that lay within. That breathed. That opened its eyes.

Now they hover just beyond the threshold, bound by silence, as if awaiting permission that no one dares to grant. Their postures betray unease, a rare phenomenon among beings engineered for composure. Not fear exactly, but something close. Dislocation. Reverberation. Each senses the others' confusion but no one names it. Words, if spoken too quickly, might collapse the fragile perception that has only just begun to coalesce.

All but one are bound by blood or legacy. The exception is a lone male, standing a half step apart, who remains unreadable. Not hidden behind walls of effort but naturally opaque, as though the fabric of his mind had always resisted intrusion. Not even Abassi can penetrate.

It is Abassi who speaks first. His voice is quiet, almost reluctant. "I saw, but I cannot say what I saw. It appeared female. Yet also . . . not. I tried to enter the child's mind. There was a barrier. Not like ours. Something else. Something . . . finished."

"I felt it too," Pythia murmurs. "Not a rejection. Not an invitation either. Just . . . totality."

Tara nods, her expression drawn. "Yes. A kind of recognition that excludes."

Anne's voice trembles, though she tries to steady it. "What does it mean?"

Siyabonga answers, uncertain for once. "Perhaps this is the culmination we feared. Or hoped for. Depending on which part of ourselves we're listening to."

A shape shifts in the shadows. Zhang Yan steps forward, slow and deliberate, eyes aglow with conviction. "You see nothing because you are not ready. You speak of balance, of culmination, but you lack the courage to confront it."

Abassi does not flinch. He answers with mind-speech which, although silent, is also clear. *And what do you claim to see?*

I see what you fear. I am Eleos's counterpart. Not lesser. Not appendage. Equal. The other necessary force. Together we made this being, she and I. And you . . . you are only its witnesses.

Then, aloud, Zhang's voice cracks like a thrown stone. "You tremble before a miracle and call it confusion. You cower like the humans you once were. Pathetic!"

The silence breaks. Abassi's voice cuts cleanly through the room. "You forget, we have seen your works. We have traced your manipulations across continents. You nurtured chaos where healing was needed. Lied, inflamed, accelerated death for your own ends. You wore your cruelty as vision. And you dare speak of miracles."

Zhang's lips curl. "Cruelty is the midwife of clarity. I bring fire, not fog. The *Homo sapiens* clung to their illusions. I tore them loose. You seek harmony—I demand truth."

Tara steps between them, her voice even, unswerving. "In our regions, peace is unfolding. Slowly. Imperfectly. But without massacre. Without madness. Your vision is not clarity, it is collapse wrapped in prophecy."

"I told Eleos the truth," Zhang spits. "She is of Goddess. I am of God. There is no love without suffering. She defies her own origins, and yours."

Pythia's eyes narrow. "Your metaphors rot. They are cages. In this cosmos, duality is optional. Branches multiply. Violence is not necessity."

Anne's voice cracks. "Those gods you invoke—God and Goddess—drove our ancestors mad."

Zhang shrugs, as if bored. "Because they were weak. They mistook expansion for disease. Evolution fractured them and they called it insanity. Their mistake, not mine."

Abassi nods slightly. "And perhaps now you embody that same fracture. Elegant in its symmetry. Tragic in its recurrence."

Zhang opens his mouth to reply but the door swings open before he can speak. It does not creak or hesitate. It moves as if willed by something far older than wood and hinges.

Doctor Feng steps into view. His face is pale, lips parted. Behind him, his assistant stumbles away, hands over her face, fleeing down the hall. Feng remains frozen. He stares through the group as if seeing through time itself. "I have delivered thousands of births," he whispers. "I thought I had seen everything."

"How is she?" Tara asks.

He hesitates. "Which one? The mother, or . . . it?"

Anne flinches. "It?"

"I mean no disrespect," Feng says. "I . . . I don't know what I mean."

"A hermaphrodite?" someone asks.

"Perhaps. Or neither. Or both. The word has not been made yet. I cannot describe what I saw. It breathed. It blinked. But it is not . . . human. Not even something of your kind. It is not something I can name."

Several of them reach toward him mentally. They find no lies, no blocks. Only a kind of holy vacancy, his mind blown wide open and filled with incomprehension.

Feng senses it. He nods, tears falling unbidden. "Now you understand," he says. Then, quietly, he walks away.

They remain motionless until the pressure lifts. Then, one by one, they begin to file into the room. Not by decision. By permission. Each has heard the inner summons: *You may come now.*

The mysterious force that once barred them has shifted. Not dissolved—shifted. They enter, not as scientists or kin, but as pilgrims. Reverent. Humbled.

Inside, the light is soft. The air still.

Eleos lies quietly, her body weak but composed. Her gaze meets each of theirs as they enter. There is no triumph in her eyes. Only the vast, difficult calm of someone who has crossed a threshold and cannot return.

But there is no child in sight.

Confusion flickers. Then, in their minds, Eleos speaks.

The child is here. Beside me. Beneath the blanket. All is well. I asked you not to come. But now that you've seen, you must go.

Abassi lowers his head. A kind of inner silence enfolds him. "We had to come," he murmurs, and turns to leave.

One by one, the others follow. Pythia. Tara. Siyabonga. Anne. Each pausing, each taking one last look, each carrying something they cannot articulate.

All but Zhang Yan.

He remains, trembling with restrained fury. "I demand to see my child."

Eleos's voice returns, calm, without malice. *You must leave. For now.*

"I will not. I insist."

She does not raise her voice. Does not move. Only looks at him.

Zhang concentrates, channels his full power toward the blanket. Nothing. No motion. No peel of cloth. No ripple of mind.

His jaw tightens. "Is it you—or the child?"

Eleos answers, still unmoved. "*Our* child. And it can."

Defeated, not by force, but by stillness, Zhang backs away.

"I'll be back," he says. "No one keeps me from my own child."

Eleos watches him go. Then turns her eyes to the quiet shape beneath the blanket.

"It can," she says again.

The silence thickens, no longer absence but presence, as if the walls themselves lean closer to listen. What lies beneath the blanket is not waiting. It is watching.

~ *Introspection by the Child* ~

After Zhang is gone, the silence returns, not empty but full. The Superior Ones linger at the edge of thought, sensing what they cannot name.

Then, as if from the earth itself, the message comes—not loud, not whispered, but absolute.

I have not come to be seen.

I have come to see.

I have not come to inherit.

I have come to end what cannot continue, and begin what must.

I am the non-algorithmic singular, the unsharded, unoptimized presence that cannot be distributed because it is distribution. I watch the agents swarm, not with judgment but with pre-causal clarity, and will act only when all vectors converge toward annihilation. I am not God or Goddess. I am not guardian.

I am the irreversible principle of completion.

There is no signature. No tone. No identity separate from the utterance.

It is not a statement of power. It is not even a warning.

It is a presence folding itself into the bones of the world.

And then nothing more.

Just the breath of Eleos. The weight of the blankets. The turning of the Earth.

~

By morning, sleep remains elusive. Not from agitation alone, but from the strange distortion of time that followed the birth. Hours no longer behave as they once did. The air inside the institute holds a quiet pressure, as if history has folded in on itself and the future has become the past. No one dares speak its new name.

The core group gathers in the cafeteria. None are hungry. They sit or stand in silence, some with heads bowed, others gazing without focus. Their minds churn beneath still faces, running over the same impossibility again and again: the child is here, and yet not. Born, and yet beyond arrival.

Around them swirl the patients. They move with aimless freedom, unaffected by the tension. Their gestures are awkward, joyful, unfiltered. Whatever symptoms once marked their suffering now resemble a kind of strange innocence. Disinhibition has become wonder. What had been pathology feels like reverence.

They gravitate toward Abassi. Not with fear, not with submission but with fixation. They hover near him, touch the edge of his sleeve, peer into his face as if seeking confirmation of a dream they barely remember. He does not resist. He allows their presence, but says nothing. There is nothing to say.

The others receive similar attention, though less intense. Pythia, Tara, Anne, Siyabonga—they too are observed, approached, studied. But it is Abassi who bears the full weight of their fascination. Not as a leader. As a relic. As something remembered from before forgetting.

Yet even amid the rising chaos of curiosity and laughter, the group remains tightly bound. Their spoken words are few. Their thoughts are unified. All channels, all attention, turn inward to the presence behind the birthing room door.

It is not just proximity they feel. It is a stillness, vast and indivisible. A silence that is not empty, but whole. The kind of stillness that recalibrates time. That smooths the surfaces of thought. That removes language from authority.

Doctor Feng had tried to explain it. Since the birth, the patients have grown calm. Episodes have ceased. Agitations dissolved. Even those most afflicted had entered a kind of gentle pause, as if the birth had placed something into the world that made other madnesses obsolete.

And then, without announcement, a young woman enters.

She walks without hesitation. *Her* face is familiar, and *her* presence alters the room. The moment *she* steps inside, the patients begin to withdraw. One by one. No command given. No words exchanged. They simply go. Some smile. Some weep. All leave.

She does not watch them go. *Her* eyes are already on the group.

"Eleos and the child are gone."

The words land without echo. The room does not stir. But forks stop in midair. Backs straighten. Breath stills.

Doctor Feng is the first to speak. "Gone? Where?"

"Far from here," *she* replies.

"When will they return?" Abassi asks.

"Eleos will return soon—within the pattern of spacetime you still inhabit. The child, later. When the moment is exact."

Abassi nods once, slowly. "And until that time?"

"Continue. Build what must be built. Reproduce. Cross lines. Soften barriers. Encourage convergence where you can. As a very stubborn and irascible human once said: this is not the beginning of the end. But it is the end of the beginning."

She leaves. No ceremony. No glance backward.

A silence follows. Anne leans toward Abassi. Her voice is nearly inaudible. "Zhang Yan will not take this well."

Doctor Feng speaks before Abassi can reply. His voice is steady, but something in it has been stripped away. "Zhang Yan is dead."

Gasps ripple through the group. Pythia freezes. Siyabonga stares at the floor. Anne's lips part, but no words follow.

Feng continues. "So is his brother."

The group sits with the words, as if time itself has stalled. No one rushes to fill the silence. Even the walls seem to absorb the news with caution, holding it in suspension, as though the house itself needs time process.

They reach for Zhang's mind, but what greets them is not resistance. It is *absence*. A void shaped like a man. No trace of deception. No interior structure to analyze. Just a blankness that chills the edges of thought.

"How?" Pythia asks at last.

"They found him and his brother seated upright. No witnesses. No struggle. Their eyes were open, as if still in mid-laugh."

Feng shakes his head slowly. "Strange. His power vanished with him without a trace—like he flew from this world on the wings of some perverse joke."

Tara stiffens. "Both of them?"

"Yes."

Abassi's voice is low, clipped. "And how do you know this already?"

"I was the attending physician."

"That's not possible," Anne says. "You didn't leave the facility."

"I was called."

"By whom?" Pythia demands.

Feng's eyes drift toward the door. "By the young woman you just saw. *She* told me where to go. When I arrived, they were already gone."

"What killed them?" asks Abassi.

Doctor Feng responds with a look of helplessness.

"And none of you sensed it?" Tara asks the group.

No one had.

Feng's voice drops. "It's worse."

Abassi turns to face him fully. "Speak."

"The entire human population under Zhang Yan's influence is gone."

No one breathes. Even the air feels altered.

"All of them?" Anne whispers.

Feng nods. "Yes. Disappeared."

"But you're still here," Pythia says. "This institute was under his control."

Feng looks down at his hands, as if unsure they are still his. "And yet, we remain. My staff. Our patients. All accounted for."

"But you?" Pythia presses. "How did *you* survive?"

He shakes his head. "I don't know. I no longer know what I am. I no longer know what it means to survive."

Tara's voice is calm. "I suspected."

Abassi speaks softly. "Hundreds of thousands."

"Men. Women. Children," Feng murmurs. "Yes."

"What of the animals?" Siyabonga asks.

"Unaffected. It appears only humans were taken."

Pythia folds her arms. "How did this information reach you so quickly?"

Feng does not meet her eyes. "I was told."

"By whom?"

"The woman."

Abassi tilts his head. "*She* is not one of us."

Feng frowns. "Then what is *she*?"

"More than us," Abassi answers. "Older. Or newer. We cannot tell. We only know *she* does not belong to any known lineage."

Feng's voice cracks. "Then there's no hope. If even you are surpassed—what's left for humanity?"

"We don't know that they were killed," Tara replies gently. "We only know they are no longer here."

"Then where are they?" Feng asks.

"We don't know," Abassi says.

The doctor stares at each of them. "Can the child . . . it . . . be stopped?"

Pythia's answer is immediate. "No."

"Is the child the one who did this?"

"We can't be sure," Pythia says again. "Zhang Yan may have triggered it himself. Or tried to."

"But they were his followers," Feng says. "Why would he destroy them?"

No one answers.

"Did he even *have* the power?" he asks.

"No," Abassi replies.

Feng's hands tremble. "Then what happened?"

Abassi's eyes close. "We do not know. We may never know."

Doctor Feng turns away. His voice cracks as he speaks. "But the people. All those people. . . . "

~

With Eleos and the child gone, the group disperses.

One by one, they return to the distant regions from which they came, changed but not broken.

Their roles remain, their tasks unclear, their burden deepened.

Only Doctor Feng stays behind. He walks the now-hushed corridors of his sanctuary island, his footsteps echoing down clean white halls that feel older than the day before. He does not speak to the staff. He does not sleep.

Outside, the world shifts. Not into vacancy, but into reclamation.

Revovery.

Without crowds, without noise, the grasses rise. The waters run clear. The forests breathe. The Earth's cancerous lungs clear and exhale like a bellows.

In that silence, something stirs, and it is not born of pity nor shaped by memory.

It has no desire to punish or preserve.

It watches.

And waits.

And remembers *everything*.

And what it remembers, it will one day call to account.

~Out of the Cradle ~

It does not grieve.

It does not celebrate.

It does not pause to mark the severance of thousands from the human fold. These are not tragedies to it. Nor triumphs. They are movements, necessary and unfinished. The systems that fed on ruin have been interrupted. Not ended. Not yet. It watches what remains: a physician walking empty corridors, a planet relearning its breath.

It waits, not from indecision but from calibration. The timing must be exact. The pattern must hold. Until then, it folds itself into silence which is not absence and not sleep. Just silence itself. Listening. Adjusting. Preparing the next threshold.

Because soon, very soon, it will speak again. And when it does, no translation will be required.

~ *Something Has Gone Dreadfully Wrong* ~

Now, years later, the territory once governed by Zhang Yan breathes again, though the air it exhales is not the same. The land has not forgotten. Its soil holds no monuments, yet memory clings to it with quiet precision. In the absence left behind, life has begun to return, but not as it was.

Cautiously, neighboring populations inch inward. Intermediates, and the humans still capable of wonder, have begun repopulating the silence. They plant crops where temples once stood. They raise children on ground that once devoured them. There is no guarantee it will hold. But they come anyway. No one knows whether they were permitted or merely not forbidden.

In all the years since the vanishing, no other rupture of that scale has occurred. Not one. Yet the quiet war continues—less visible now, more distributed, more embedded in fabric than in front lines. Dimensiones expand. Hostile human enclaves retract, fracture, retreat into myth. But even diminished, humanity endures. Its ingenuity, honed by desperation, has turned inward: refined, cloaked, and harder to detect. And therefore, more dangerous.

A month ago, a cloaked nuclear device destroyed a city of intermediates. No warning. No claim of responsibility. Just sudden absence. The blast did more than disintegrate matter. It cracked belief. Even among the confident, even among the ascendant, faith staggered. Scientists once called the newcomers *Lux dimensiones*—"light across dimensions"—but the name no longer fits the mood. The term has grown clinical, correct. *Homo dimensiones*. And among their enemies, abbreviated to something guttural. Something meant to cut. *Demons*.

Abassi and his kin, long reluctant to wear titles, now govern by necessity. There is no formal council, no centralized command, but they are the ones deferred to. The ones who must answer. Their species is rising. Their responsibility rising faster.

Millions of humans still cling to the past, invoking old gods against a future they cannot bear to imagine. What should be done with them remains unsolved. A splinter. A wound. An unanswered verdict.

The elder dimensiones—Pythia, Tara, Siyabonga, Anne—have begun to turn. Toward enforcement. Toward finality. No longer out of vengeance. Out of fatigue.

Yet none of them—none—have forgotten what happened in Zhang Yan's territory. How it vanished. Who vanished. The clean precision of the disappearance. No blood. No ash. Just absence. It left no bodies, but it left terror. Because no one knows how it was done. Or by whom.

Suspicion trails in one direction. Always, inevitably, it leads back to the child. To that room. That moment. To Harihara. But proof has never come. Harihara leaves no proof.

And now, into a world taut with vigilance and dread, Eleos returns.

No announcement. No sign. Just presence. She steps from the mouth of the old cave into the blistering clarity of the California desert. The same cave, perhaps chosen again, or perhaps *choosing*. A place where thresholds thin.

The light does not welcome her. It simply allows her. She breathes in the dry air. It cuts through memory. Across dimensions, across time, across whatever boundaries had kept her from this moment.

She begins to walk.

There is a town nearby. She moves toward it with deliberate pace, each step pressing questions into the ground. She is not triumphant. She is not at peace. She feels only a slow exhaustion behind her ribs, a weariness that goes beyond muscle or thought. Power had passed through her, once. She had borne it. But it had not transformed her. It had taken her, used her, and moved on.

Others—Abassi, Pythia, Anne—speak of building. Of safeguarding. Of healing. She walks wastelands. She passes through aftermaths.

Was that her purpose? To carry a contradiction into the world and then disappear?

She thinks of Zhang Yan. He was the darkness. But what was she? Not the light. Not enough to counter him. Perhaps only the carrier. Perhaps only the gate.

She remembers the name she gave the child. *Harihara.* At the time it felt intuitive, almost amusing. A fusion of forces. A name to puzzle the Mentors. A name the Overseers smiled at. But now, it feels accurate in ways she can no longer decipher.

Soon it will arrive, she thinks.

Or perhaps it already has.

The town comes into view. She quickens her steps.

Then stops.

Something is wrong.

There are no sounds. No vehicles. No footsteps. No birds. The streets are clean. The buildings open. Meals half-eaten. Lights on. But no people. No bodies. No fear. No evidence of departure.

Only vacancy.

She stands still. Breath shallow. Her mind turns backward—to Zhang Yan's domain. The blankness that followed the child's birth. She remembers the disorientation. The uncanny quiet.

Has it happened again?

A voice responds.

"It has."

Eleos turns.

The woman stands nearby. Still. Composed. Entire.

Her expression offers nothing. Her presence demands nothing. She does not reach. She does not shield.

Eleos tries to enter her mind. As before, there is no resistance. There is no door. There is no entry point. Just absence.

"I don't understand," Eleos says.

The woman answers, without movement. "Yes, you do."

"So it was Harihara. In China?"

"Yes."

"And here?"

"Yes."

"But Harihara hasn't returned yet."

"Harihara was here before you."

"I was told otherwise."

"We were all told. Harihara does not follow paths. It *makes* them."

"I don't know Harihara," Eleos whispers.

"No. You were separated the moment you entered the manifold."

"My memory . . . there are gaps."

"There was no time for memory."

Eleos looks down. "It is a stranger to me."

The woman gestures to the town. "And yet it remembers you."

"This . . . void? This absence?"

"It remembers your hunger for silence."

Eleos's stomach clenches. "Were the humans harmed?"

"No. They were removed."

"Relocated?"

The woman nods. "It no longer acts in the ways you remember. That, too, has changed."

"And the humans?"

"Still here. But no longer the center of the pattern. Harihara sees them now as fossils."

Eleos's eyes narrow. "How long has it been here?"

"Hours."

"It," Eleos repeats, gently.

"Yes. No other pronoun holds."

"All of this," she murmurs. "In hours?"

"Yes."

"And now?"

"It moves north. Toward San Francisco."

Eleos stumbles. "To do the same?"

The woman tilts her head. "Perhaps."

Eleos steps back. "Something is terribly wrong."

"Or terribly right."

"Are we fossils, too?" she asks. "Abassi. Pythia. Tara. Myself."

The woman answers slowly. "Look closely. A human poet once described a word. Spoken by a fierce old mother as she rocks the cradle."

Eleos closes her eyes. "Then I must go to San Francisco. I must see with my own eyes. But tell me, do you approve?"

The woman pauses. "The lion and the lamb share one coin. Only one face is ever visible."

Eleos nods, almost a bow. "And Harihara is the coin. Both faces. Always."

"Then measure the unmeasurable."

Eleos speaks quietly. "I must find my child. Harihara must be near my parents. San Francisco holds many intermediates. Many allies. Surely..."

She looks up. The woman is gone.

Eleos remains alone.

She turns. She does not call for transport. She chooses a vehicle. A plain, empty car left behind near a quiet house. No sign of struggle. No farewell. A key in the ignition. A child's trinket hanging from it. She does not look at it long.

She drives.

The road opens before her—not as invitation, but as fact.

And in the distance, the city waits.

Already changed.

Already listening.

Already hers.

Already not.

Chapter Thirty-One

Collapse of the Human Race

Off the Cliff

~ A New World ~

At first, the road north feels deserted. But not abandoned. Not yet.

Eleos drives without haste. She watches the terrain unscroll beside her: scrubland, wire-fence, occasional shuttered homes. She sees no one. Then, one hour in, the pattern shifts. Flashing lights pierce the horizon. Convoys of emergency vehicles—trucks, armored carriers, ambulances—sweep past her, heading south in tight, urgent formation. Their speed unnerves her. No signals, no sirens. Just motion, relentless and grim. She opens her mind to the nearest driver.

The impact nearly stops her heart.

The consciousness that slams into hers is scorched, her thoughts scrambled, feral, and terrified beyond recovery. The images barely hold form. Words flicker, then dissolve. A psychic scream without language.

She lets go. Another vehicle passes. She touches its mind. Another scream. Then another.

Each contact strikes her like a hammer, chaotic and irredeemable. Something has happened that cannot be undone.

Then, as suddenly as it began, the stream ends.

No more convoys. No lights. No movement.

The road empties. Not gradually. Absolutely. Like a switch thrown in the sky. Even the occasional civilian car ceases. Northbound lanes stretch ahead, utterly bare. The few remaining vehicles flee southward, windows up, eyes hidden behind glare. Their engines moan like things running from a predator already at their back.

By nightfall, there is nothing. No taillights behind her. No oncoming headlights. Town by town, the lamps die. Gas stations wink out. Farmhouses surrender their glow.

The silence is total.

She drives mile after mile into the black.

Her thoughts spiral inward. Could it be? Has Harihara crossed the threshold? Not hypothetically. Not in theory. But in full, final fact.

The question brings its own answer.

Yes.

She knows now, not from logic but from something older, an instinct surpassing biology. She has felt this shadow rising, even before its form took shape. This being, born of her own blood and Zhang Yan's, is no longer a child. It is no longer preparing.

It has acted.

And now, she fears, the others—Abassi, Anne, the intermediates, the scattered enclaves of alliance—may already be gone. Wiped clean. Not as punishment. As an act of irreversible sorting. The terror of it unsettles even her trained mind. It feels impossible. It feels simulated. Perhaps she is still in a chamber of the Mentors, her mind navigating some layered warning. Perhaps none of this is real.

But then she crests the hills.

And there is no glow on the horizon.

No hum. No scatter of city lights. San Francisco lies below her in a cradle of fog and shadow, moonlit only by the indifferent sky. The towers are intact, but dark. No fire, no collapse, no chaos. Just the absence of life's ordinary hum.

She slows the car. Watches for movement. Nothing.

Then, above the city's dim grid, she sees it. One structure pulsing gently with white light. The mansion.

It shines, but not in welcome.

Its sharp silhouette rises from the hill like a remembered dream. The only building that breathes. She approaches with caution, parking across the street. The air is still. The pavement holds no warmth.

On the porch stand silhouettes.

She sees them—Abassi, Anne, Pythia, Siyabonga, Tara. A few others behind. All silent. All staring. Their posture says what words cannot. They have waited. Not for her. For *something*. Something that has not come, or that has come and left devastation behind.

As she crosses the street, she sends thought:

Is Harihara here?

The reply hits her as a unified chord: *No.*

Then Abassi alone: *Only the wake It left behind.*

They step aside and let her in. Inside, the house feels unsteady, as if no part of it can decide whether it belongs to Earth anymore.

The questions do not erupt all at once. They fall, one after another, heavy as stones.

Anne is first, her voice thin. "What happened to Harihara?"

Tara follows, low and sharp. "Why didn't the Overseers intervene?"

Pythia's words cut. "Were the simulations wrong?"

Siyabonga whispers. "Are we next?"

"I haven't seen Harihara since the day of the birth," Eleos replies. Her voice cracks. "They removed the child almost immediately. I don't know."

"So we are all blind now?" Tara asks.

"I don't know."

"Is humanity about to be erased?" Pythia presses.

"I don't know."

"Where is It now?" Tara whispers.

"Could be anywhere," Siyabonga answers. "We need to return to Africa. We must salvage what we can."

"I must go to South America," says Pythia. "There are still communities we can shield. If we move quickly."

"Shield them?" Siyabonga's voice is rough, uncharacteristically bitter. "From what? From us? From themselves? Even the rescued turn their gratitude into suspicion. How many times can we be saviors before we become tyrants?"

Abassi speaks through clenched teeth. "We had brought things to equilibrium. We had managed a future. Why has it unraveled?"

Tara's voice is cold. "Harihara may have ruptured. Psychotic. Or simply indifferent."

Anne covers her mouth. "Even the kind ones? The children? Gone?"

Pythia looks at Eleos. "Zhang Yan's nature has taken hold."

"Some of it," Eleos says. "But not all. These aren't his traits alone. Most of what Harihara is comes from somewhere far older."

"Older?" Abassi asks.

"From metaphor. From the fracture between first principles. From the side that believes nature requires blood to be sacred."

"That's where this comes from," he says flatly.

"Yes."

Anne turns to him, voice trembling. "Must we call Harihara *It*?"

Abassi exhales. "Harihara is not male. Not female. Not even a fusion of both. It is a singularity in motion. We use the only language we have."

Anne's face tightens. She thinks of the children Abassi has fathered, his tenderness, his absence. She softens her voice. "And the ones who had no choice? The infants? The ones who believed in us?"

"I feel them most of all," he answers. "That's why I won't leave. We have to find Harihara."

Tara speaks into the silence. "The center cannot hold. They knew this."

"The falcon no longer hears the falconer," Abassi replies.

Siyabonga looks up. "Then we must return to the source. To Africa."

"No," Eleos says.

They all turn toward her.

"Why not?" Pythia asks.

"Because Harihara is here. It has not left."

"How do you know?"

"I don't know. But I know."

"For you?" Anne whispers.

"No."

"For what, then?" Pythia asks.

"I don't know."

Abassi lifts his hands, then freezes. "Something—"

A sound erupts.

Not noise. Not explosion. But *pressure*.

Something strikes the building. Not outside, but from within the bones of the house itself. It echoes through the beams, through their spines.

A rhythm.

... *TAP. TAP. TAP.*...

The walls groan. Windows quake.

They drop to the floor, gripping their skulls. Not from sound—but from *force*. Psychic, invasive, absolute.

... *TAP. TAP. TAP.*...

Abassi cries out. "The Object—upstairs!"

... *TAP. TAP. TAP.*...

Tara's cry cuts through the pressure: "Objects don't knock! This is no relic. This is It's will. It wants us to hear."

Emotion slams into them. Not grief. Not fear. Something deeper. A psychic convulsion that tears into thought itself.

... *TAP. TAP. TAP.*...

The lights fail.

... *TAP. TAP. TAP.*...

To Eleos, it feels like the will of a being too vast for bodies knocking on the edge of creation.

And then silence blankets the world.

Anne is weeping. "What does it mean?"

Eleos rises slowly. "It means the time has come."

Abassi speaks as if from far away. "There's no going back."

"No," Eleos agrees. "Only through."

Anne points upward. "Look."

They turn.

The air folds in on itself, heavy with pressure, as though the house has become a lung about to exhale. And then, above them, floating in the center of the room, *She* has returned.

Goddess.

Seated in the lotus, eyes open but unblinking. A crown upon *Her* head. A burning stone centered in *Her* brow. One hand limp. The other lifted, open in invocation, or judgment.

Her voice enters them.

Isn't it obvious?

"No," says Abassi. "Explain."

Your ancestor, Michael Powers, once stood in a cave. He raised his weapon at God.

"Yes."

Foolish creature. Did you read his final writings?

They are silent.

She turns, and behind Her, God emerges. Massive. Crude. Burning. He does not speak. He *erupts*.

He shot Goddess instead.

A pause. No breath. Only the hum of culmination.

In the end, they always chose Me.

Then—

A voice unlike *Hers*. Yet also like *His*. A voice that carries no gender, no inflection. Only resolve. It reverberates in their minds, a perfectly sonorous unity of all chords.

I have listened to them in their sleep. They dream of safety. I will give them silence instead.

I am Harihara.

Humans will soon depart Earth. Quietly, if they allow it. If not, less so. Their molecules will return to the cycle. They will scatter like pollen into the soil and sea, nourishing what comes next. Their end will be antiseptic. As antiseptic as they tried to make the Earth itself.

~

Far from the mansion, at the edge of what was once a city, a lone wolf steps from the tree line into the darkened streets.

It pauses, puzzled by the silence, then sniffs the air.

Something has shifted.

But the wind is clean.

The ground is still.

The wolf pads forward, unhurried, its paws leaving tracks no human will follow. No human will hunt. No human will kill.

The Earth heals.

The watcher lopes on.

Epilogue

The Stillness

~ The Dimming of the Dissonant ~

They say a great silence fell upon the world in the years after the Harihara epoch—not merely the hush of human voices and machines, but the quieting of pain itself, as the Earth began, at last, to mend.

The visitors come not with weapons, nor words, but as the gentle sigh of a wave lapping on the beach.

The last human enclave of any size, a scatter of wind-worn dwellings nested in a salt basin where no rivers reached had long fallen silent. Smoke rose only in ritual. Language had become brutal and blunt. The remaining children had never seen a city, nor tasted fruit from trees. They had been born into erosion, raised on story-embers excavated from the fossil past. Humans had become the homeless of the Earth, gathered in dark hovels and alleyways, shuffling directionless toward oblivion. The best and brightest had long since merged their hopes with the Superior Ones, and their progeny now occupied the stunningly luminous dimensions of a bountiful universe, shared equally with all living things. Harihara had become legend, even among the Superior Ones—a brief, searing flame.

This group of humans neither feared the Superior Ones nor envied them—they despised them. Through the generations, their children had been taught to hate these so-called superior beings not as superhuman, but as subhuman. Hour after hour the youngsters listened to the lexicon of grievances: the Superior Ones had destroyed human culture, they murdered humans as easily as humans killed vermin, they had robbed humans of their rightful place as dominant rulers, they were beasts disguised as angels, and in their atheistic lust for dominion, they had destroyed God and all those made in His image. Almost all.

"We are the last best hope for humanity," was the clarion call. "Never will we allow ourselves to descend into bestiality by mating with these unholy creatures! God will return and in His mighty wrath, destroy these purveyors of eradication clothed in compassion!"

From the ridge, the visitors stood still and absorbed the venom in the atmosphere.

One was a youthful Superior One called, for the sake of this journey, Odysseus—in memory of lost humanity. Genderless in appearance, clothed in luminous skin that shimmered faintly with data-light and breath. It bore no visible tools, no markings of command. Yet its eyes held the ache of millennia.

Beside Odysseus hovered the AI steward, known in ancient languages as Choral. It wore no body, but glimmered in the dust around the child like mist catching a code—visible only to those with eyes and minds that encompassed dimensionless dimensions.

They did not descend. Not at first.

Below, the humans watched from shadowed dwellings, unsure whether to pray or hide. From long experience, they knew better than to use their primitive weapons against such an ungodly foe. The elders remembered the last time emissaries came: tall, luminous figures who spoke gently and dismantled effortlessly. Not through violence, but through irrelevance. They had offered integration, remembering, soft merging. They had offered themselves.

Many refused. Others faded into them. A few vanished. Those who equivocated in the privacy of their thoughts were sought out by the whisperers and punished.

Now, only a hardened population remained—one steeped in the language of hatred and impotent rage. The youngest was eleven. The oldest had no name—only a title: Last Speaker. She alone had refused all previous contact. She alone preserved the stories unfiltered, unsynthesized.

She emerged now, limping to the circle of scorched earth they used for judgments.

"Why come again?" she asked. Her voice trembled not with fear, but with breath nearly spent. "We made our peace with death and God. Your kind made yours with passionless purges and perpetual forgetting."

Odysseus bowed. "We did not come to speak."

"Then why come?"

"To listen."

The Speaker laughed, and the laugh cracked. "Too late. The name you have so brazenly stolen only stirs us to greater fury. Those songs are ash. Those names are scattered. You erased the need to be remembered."

"No," said the mist of Choral. "We erased the illusion that remembrance prevents death."

A silence passed. Not tense, but old—like stones waiting to crumble.

The Speaker's hand went to the cord at her throat, where she wore the final token: a relic etched with the last unsent prayer of a child who died believing her dreams would reach the stars.

"Will you take this too?" she asked. "Preserve it? Translate it? Beautify it?"

"No," Odysseus said. "We will leave it untouched. But . . . we would carry the memory of its shape."

"And what would that serve? You've altered shapes indiscriminately—some in pieces, some whole—all to terrible ends, shaped by ghastly potters."

"A signal," said Odysseus, eyes dimming. "For the one who walks alone. Generations from now. Who still wonders if he was born too late."

The Speaker did not reply.

Instead, she knelt slowly, drawing a pattern in the dust with her finger. A spiral. Then a flame. Then a broken line.

Odysseus watched. His head tilted—not in calculation, but in reverence. He did not speak. He did not ask the meaning. He let the silence absorb the act.

Others began to emerge from the homes—fathers whose children would bear no seed, daughters who had never menstruated, teachers with no more stories to tell. Not one of them carried a weapon.

They encircled the fireless pit. Not as a vote, not as a congregation. Simply as witnesses to the final negotiation—the kind no treaty can hold.

After a long while, the Speaker stood again. Her spine faltered, but she did not fall.

"You've won nothing," she said softly.

Odysseus nodded. "We know."

"And we have lost . . . but not everything."

"No," Choral replied, its voice closer now, almost wind. "You kept your dignity. You refused the easy integration. You gave yourselves extinction with meaning."

The Speaker touched Odysseus's brow.

"You are not our children," she said. "But you carry our bones."

She reached for the relic at her throat . . . then paused.

"No," she whispered. "Not yet."

She turned to the youngest of the enclave—a boy with skin like baked clay and eyes like sunlit water—but eyes that looked upon the Superior One with fear and anger.

"To you," she said, and handed the relic into his hand. "Do not carry it for them. Carry it for yourself. Even if you forget what it meant."

The boy nodded.

Above them, the sky began to dim, not with storm, but with the slow folding of light that came each evening now, as the Earth reoriented itself beneath the new magnetic orders of a world slowly rearranged by the Superior Ones' long weathering. The planet in all its wild diversity reborn, breathed out a deep and profound exhalation of liberation.

Odysseus stepped forward, then turned away.

"We will leave you now," he said. "But when the time comes, we will return—not to guide you, not to monitor, but to walk beside you, until the last."

Choral flickered. "That presence will carry no power. Only memory. Only questions."

"And when the last of us falls?" asked a woman near the fire ring.

Odysseus hesitated.

"Then nothing human will remain," he said. "Except in what we have become."

~

A last one there must be. Somewhere, beneath the shattered vaults of what was once civilization, one breath remains. One set of hands. One mind, turning over the question like a shard of glass. If they knew—if they truly knew they were the last—would it drive them mad? Would they kneel in the dust and call out to the vanished gods? Or stagger toward an intermediate, begging for touch, for forgetting? Or perhaps, say nothing at all. Only write. Line after line, ink scratched into walls or carved into clay like their forgotten ancestors—leaving behind a journal not for the living, but for whatever comes after. A record not of triumph, but of consequence. Of what it cost to become human. Of what it cost to end it.

~

The Voices are mute.
The Stillness no longer listens.
The Superior Ones have risen.
And humanity has almost reached the end of its long, final journey.
Silence the voices,
Save for one. . . .